15 A8

MAGUS OF STONEWYLDE

MAGUS
of
STONEWYLDE

The First Book of Stonewylde

KIT BERRY

First published in Great Britain in 2011 by Gollancz
An imprint of the Orion Publishing Group
Orion House, 5 Upper St Martin's Lane, London WC2H 9EA
An Hachette UK Company

A CIP catalogue record for this book is available
from the British Library

ISBN 978 0 575 09882 4

1 3 5 7 9 10 8 6 4 2

Typeset by Input Data Services Ltd, Bridgwater, Somerset

Printed in Great Britain by Clays Ltd, St Ives plc

The Orion Publishing Group's policy is to use papers that
are natural, renewable and recyclable products and
made from wood grown in sustainable forests. The logging
and manufacturing processes are expected to conform to
the environmental regulations of the country of origin.

www.stonewylde.com
www.orionbooks.co.uk

The Stonewylde Series
is dedicated to the memories of
Jean Guy, my best owl aunt
and
Debbie Gilbrook, my dearest friend.

Slowly, silently, the moon rose over the tower blocks. Patterned with bright squares of light, the great steel and concrete structures thrust up into the city sky like modern megaliths. Inside these teeming hives of activity, people sat mesmerised before flickering screens, busying themselves with electronic devices and gadgets.

The rising of the full moon in the night sky passed unnoticed, except by one girl. Trapped up high in her block, she stood at the window and cried for release. Like a delicate moth, she beat against the cold glass of her cell again and again, desperate for escape. As the moon grew smaller overhead, the wildness in her heart slowly withered and died.

Silent and still at last, she gazed out into the night. No stars were visible; in the city they were outshone by artificial light. Her eyes scanned the skies hoping for one bright jewel of starlight, but found only the winking of satellites and aeroplanes. She looked down. On the swarming streets far below, long white and red snakes of car lights crawled home. The slick pavements reflected a kaleidoscope of yellow, blue and green neon light; the air was heavy with relentless, droning noise. She turned from the bright window in despair, as another month of her life seeped away.

An owl hooted long and low from the dark woods. The boy climbed the hill to the standing stone at its summit, his boots glittering with frost and his breath in icy clouds about him. He hunkered down, his back against the tall monolith, and looked out towards the distant sea. The silver moon danced over the landscape and glinted in the

1

boy's eyes. He gazed up at the dusty white rainbow arched across the black velvet sky; millions upon millions of sparkling stars, bright diamonds flung over the cloak of night.

He sensed the movement of hares further down the hill. Creatures of the full moon, they gathered at this special stone every month and seemed to welcome his silent presence. He took a shuddering breath and touched his cheek. The cut had begun to heal, closing over into a thin scar that would mark him for life. The boy shut his eyes and hugged his knees, shivering and alone in the moonlight. Up here, by the stone on the hill, no one could touch him. Up here no one could hear him cry.

1

Sylvie gazed through the barred window at the white bird of prey circling high overhead. Round and round it flew, just clearing the grimy tower blocks as it marked its territory, waiting for the moment when she became too weak to struggle. Would it then swoop low and carry her away into the dirty sky, a streak of vapour trail proclaiming its kill? She swallowed, her throat parched, and reached towards the water jug. But the coils of tubes prevented her movement. Snaking around her thin arm, they held her fast to a machine that beeped and flashed. Reality flickered in and out of focus. She closed her eyes; everything was just too much effort, even a sip of water.

Sylvie groaned as the pack of white coats approached her bed and surrounded her. A circle of curious faces – snouts, open mouths, bright eyes – watched hungrily as she lay defenceless among them. The alpha male frowned from beneath tufted eyebrows. He scanned her with a practised eye as he picked up her notes. Sylvie's hunted gaze sought out the one kindly face in the group: a young intern who'd befriended her in this terrifying labyrinth of wards, disinfectant and needles. Hazel, fair-haired and rosy-cheeked, gave Sylvie a quick smile.

'Comments?' barked the consultant.

'She's responding quite well to hospitalisation, sir. She's put on some weight.'

'There's evidence of intolerance to wheat and dairy foods; hence the eczema.'

'But it hasn't even started to clear, despite the diet. And she's under-developed for her age. She's what – fourteen coming up to fifteen? I think—'

'Those who've read the case notes,' growled the leader, 'will know her mother was concerned about possible anorexia. She's failing to thrive, though this could be due to acute food intolerances rather than an eating disorder. Whatever the cause, she's clearly wasted away quite dramatically.'

'What about ME, sir? It would account for the listlessness and inability to engage with any stimulus.'

'Mmn, possible but not conclusive. The blood tests show no viral anomalies although she does react to all the usual allergens – house dust, pollen, exhaust particles, propellants. We've now concluded our battery of tests and there's little more we can do for her at the moment.'

'It's as if she's given up on life.'

All eyes turned to Hazel.

'That's your professional diagnosis, Doctor?'

'No, but without the will to thrive, the body starts to shut down. It seems to me that Sylvie's rejected everything around her. She can't cope with the stresses of city life and now she's become allergic to everything, even the air she breathes.'

The consultant wrinkled his nose at this. He picked up one of Sylvie's wrists and felt her pulse, ignoring the tubes and bruising.

'So you propose the symptoms are purely psychosomatic? The self-inflicted result of a refusal to engage with life?'

Hazel shot Sylvie a glance of apology.

'No, not self-inflicted exactly. Rather a physical rejection of the twenty-first century and the artificial and unnatural environment we've created. Sylvie's body can't deal with it any longer.'

'What a fascinating theory. But in the meantime, medication will continue and her diet will be strictly controlled. We'll discharge her at the end of the week and see what happens. An interesting case, I'm sure you'll all agree, but we need the bed.'

Later Hazel came back alone and sat down, taking Sylvie's hand.

'I'm sorry, Sylvie, discussing you this morning as if you weren't there. How are you feeling now?'

Sylvie shrugged. Her ravaged face and pale hair against the pillowcase gave her a look of transparency, as if she were slowly dissolving into nothing. Hazel tried not to stare at the strange girl who'd fascinated her since her admission to hospital a couple of weeks ago. She knew that Sylvie had been ill for some time, and that her mother was frantic and the doctors baffled. What had started as headaches, stomach pains and depression had, over the months, developed into blinding migraines, acute vomiting and chronic tiredness. The food intolerances had become so severe that Sylvie now found it impossible to keep anything down. She was pathetically thin and fragile, her skin sore and cracked with eczema. Her allergies had reached the point where she could often barely breathe, and these frightening symptoms were exacerbated by the constant scans, blood tests and prescribed medication. Hazel knew that Sylvie was only being discharged for expediency, not because she'd been cured or even properly diagnosed.

'I meant what I said, Sylvie, though the other doctors didn't understand. You've rejected this world, haven't you?'

Sylvie's unusual silver-grey eyes met Hazel's kind ones. She knew that Hazel was almost fully qualified now and would make a compassionate doctor.

'I expect you're right,' she croaked.

'But Sylvie, you can't just give up on everything! What about school? Don't you miss your friends?'

Sylvie closed her eyes; school was the dark place of her nightmares. The very thought of those endless corridors and classrooms made her shudder. She recalled the smell of the place, the dirty hugeness of it like the lair of a hydra. No sooner had one hideous head been dealt with than two more reared to take its place, snarling and voracious for blood.

'I didn't have any friends,' she whispered, her tongue dry. 'I missed a lot of school and when I did manage to turn up, everyone seemed to hate me. They said some horrible things, though I guess they were right. I do look weird and ugly and I'm stupid too. I could never catch up on what I'd missed and I was always so tired ...'

'Oh, Sylvie, that's not—'

'It's okay, they weren't the sort of people I'd ever choose for friends. I'm better off away from that school.'

What she didn't add was just how bad it had become. She was the misfit in a teenage society that prized conformity. The more time she spent off school, the harder it was to go back and face the relentless bullying. It had reached the stage where she simply couldn't do it. Her illness had slowly become her whole life. And if she continued to deteriorate, her doctor had implied, it would also be the cause of her death.

Hazel looked at her with sympathy. She knew a little of Sylvie's background from the case study. The girl lived with her single mother in a tower block flat in a run-down part of the city. Hazel had seen her poor mother at visiting times, exhausted from teaching all day and wracked with fear for her ailing daughter.

'Couldn't your mum get a teaching job somewhere in the country? Maybe fresh air and a bit of healthy outdoor living would help you get better.'

Sylvie shook her head listlessly.

'We've talked about it but it's much too expensive to move and everyone's trying to leave the inner city schools. Mum's had so much time off in the past couple of years looking after me she'd never get a good reference. We're stuck here.' She was silent for a moment, gazing at the grey clouds that blotted out the sky. 'I'd love to go to the countryside though. I feel so stifled in the city, like it's a prison closing in on me, crushing me. Even the trees are dirty and grim.'

'I wish I could take you with me to Stonewylde,' said Hazel, squeezing her hand. 'It'd be perfect for you.'

'Stonewylde? Is that your next hospital when you leave here?'

'No, it's a country estate in Dorset,' laughed Hazel. 'My father was born there and I visit every year. It's a really huge place and so beautiful.'

'It sounds romantic – Stonewylde.'

'It is! Everything's done in the old-fashioned way, the food's organic and the religion is . . . different. There are woods, hills, a beach, cliffs – oh, it's impossible to describe just how special Stonewylde is. When I go back every summer I always feel whole again, at peace with Mother Earth.'

'How wonderful,' said Sylvie wistfully. 'A place of healing.'

'Exactly! Healing for the soul as well as the body. You'd love it, Sylvie. It's strange – when I first saw you in here I thought maybe you were Hallfolk.'

'Hallfolk?'

'The people who live in the Hall at Stonewylde. You look so similar. Your silvery hair . . . lots of us Hallfolk have very blond hair, and there's something about your face. I don't know . . . it made me wonder. I've seen your mum's red hair. Do you get your blondeness from your father?'

'I don't know anything about my father. Mum refuses to discuss him. She had me very young and there's some dark secret she won't talk about. My grandparents chucked her out before I was born so I can't even ask them.'

'That's terrible! Well, whatever your parentage you do look remarkably like one of us. I wonder if it would be possible to arrange a stay for you . . .'

When she saw Sylvie's face light up, Hazel knew she shouldn't have mentioned the idea.

'Hold on, Sylvie. I can't promise anything. Outsiders are never allowed into Stonewylde. But Magus is in town and I'll speak to him. Please don't get too excited about it though. He'll most likely say no.'

'Is Magus the owner?'

'Actually no, the estate belongs to his half-brother. But Magus is . . . well, the kind of lord of the manor, the master. He's the most amazing man.'

Sylvie noticed the sparkle in her eyes.

'Are you in love with him, Hazel?' she teased.

Hazel smiled dreamily and patted her hand.

'If you met him you'd understand. Everyone loves Magus and I'm no exception. I'm so excited about the summer.'

'For your next visit?'

'It's more than that. I'll be qualified then. I'm to be the doctor at Stonewylde for a year.'

'That's wonderful! Oh please, Hazel, please try to persuade him to let me visit, even if it's only for a weekend. I'd love to go there and escape from all this dirt and noise. Stonewylde sounds like heaven on earth.'

Miranda, Sylvie's mother, was not impressed when her daughter related this conversation at visiting time. She was exhausted. She'd travelled halfway across London from school, and now faced another long, cold journey back home to the empty flat after this visit. Although she was pleased to see an improvement in Sylvie, she surveyed the girl's excited face with dismay.

'You mustn't get your hopes up, Sylvie. It'll probably come to nothing. And I doubt I could even manage the cost of train tickets all the way to Dorset. I don't think the doctor should've been talking to you like this anyway. It's very un-professional.'

'She's not unprofessional! She's the only nice person here. I'm not raising my hopes, Mum, but wouldn't it be wonderful to visit a country estate? I'd love to be out in the fresh air, with the sea and the hills all around. Maybe we could go in the Easter holidays?'

'We'll see. Let's wait till the doctor has spoken to this man – Magus was it? Such a strange name. It all feels a little odd to me, Sylvie. We don't want to get involved in some sort of cult thing, do we? Cut off from society in darkest Dorset, old farming methods, a weird religion too, you said? I don't like the sound of it at all.'

'Oh Mum! You've always told me to keep an open mind. And Hazel asked about my father. She said ...'

'That's none of her business!' snapped Miranda, her cheeks flaming. 'How dare she?'

'No, not like that, Mum. Why are you always so defensive about it? It's my blond hair. She thought I might come from this place, Stonewylde. She just wondered if—'

'It's not her place to speculate on your background. That's put me off the whole idea, if people there are going to start asking questions about your father.'

'Why are you always so prickly about it?'

'It's a closed subject, Sylvie. You know that.'

'But why? Surely I have a right to know who my father is. I'm old enough now, aren't I?'

'I don't talk about it because it's sordid and unpleasant. It's all in the past which is where I want it to stay. And as to having a right to know who he was – I'd like to know that myself. I never did catch his name.'

Yul leant his forehead against the softness of the stallion's coat, breathing in the sweet smell. He was almost asleep on his feet. Nightwing snickered and turned his head to pluck at the boy with gentle lips. Yul wearily opened his eyes and resumed grooming. This was the one highlight of his punishment; nobody got this close to Magus' horse unless they were an experienced stable hand.

'Come on, lad. You've done enough for tonight. Go on home to your bed now.'

Tom, the head ostler, stood outside the half door. He shook his head.

'Never seen anything like it afore. That horse is usually evil but he's taken a real shine to you.'

Yul nodded, proud of his affinity with the stallion. It was wonderful to groom such a beautiful horse, but he wished he could ride Nightwing too. Tom watched as the boy put away the grooming brushes and newly polished tack. He was strong and willing despite having done a full day's work in the woods, and Tom would be sorry to see the back of him now that the week was up. He still didn't understand why Yul had been sent here every evening. When he'd asked the boy what misdemeanour he'd committed, Yul had merely shrugged and mumbled something about not showing enough respect.

Tom knew the boy's reputation – surly and rebellious. He'd seen the cut on Yul's cheek, which was Magus' style. The master could be a little free with his riding whip and had marked the boy quite severely. But Tom also knew the boy's father. The bruise on Yul's other cheek and the way he winced as he moved – that was surely Alwyn's doing.

'You've worked hard here, lad, and I'll make sure Magus hears about it. I don't know how you got yourself into this trouble but mind you don't do it again.'

Yul gazed at the older man through his dark curls and nodded, too exhausted to speak. He didn't know how he got into such trouble either. He seemed to have a death wish at times.

'Well, mind my words, Yul. And come up to the stables again to see us. But keep out of the master's way, eh? And your father's too.'

Yul grinned at him, raised a dirty hand in farewell and trudged off into the night, melting into the darkness. The ostler shook his head and began to shut the horses up for the night. He was surprised to see the gleam of blond hair in the lantern light as Magus appeared in the stable courtyard.

'Has the boy gone already?'

'Aye, sir. He was asleep on his feet.'

'A pity you let him go. I wanted a final word with him.'

'The lad was worn out, sir.'

'Hard work never hurt anyone, Tom, as we both know. I hope he's learnt his lesson. Can you believe I found the boy lying about in the fields watching hares? He was supposed to be clearing undergrowth in the woods!'

'Yul worked well whilst he was here, sir. He has a way with the horses, right enough.'

'Yes, too much of a way. While I was reprimanding him, he actually had the cheek to stroke Nightwing! Nobody touches my horse – everyone knows that. The boy's lucky I let him off so lightly.'

Tom thought it best not to mention that he'd allowed Yul to groom Nightwing.

'Aye, sir. I'm sure he's been put in his place now. I reckon his father's had a go at him too.'

'Good! There's something in that boy that needs taming – a look in his eye I don't like. He'd better not overstep the mark again.'

Yul flung himself onto his narrow bed, too tired to wash or even undress. He kicked off his boots as he lay on the worn bedcovers, the sharp slope of the ceiling preventing him from sitting upright. The tiny attic room was unlit as his mother didn't like having lanterns right under the thatch. He breathed deeply of the night air that poured in through the small window by his head, listening to the owls calling across the darkness.

The pub down the lane began to disgorge men. Their voices seemed loud in the silent, starry night as they went home to their cottages. He heard his father whistling as he stomped up the lane. Yul shuddered, his body instinctively curling up. The front door opened and closed and he heard his mother's soft voice. His father's voice was only a low murmur so she must have persuaded him to sit down for a bit of bread and cheese.

Yul imagined his father stretched out in his armchair, feet warming by the fire. The cider could make him magnanimous but more often he became irritable and even aggressive. Alwyn very rarely hit his wife or the other children; their fear usually mollified him. But it had always been a different matter with his eldest son, and lately had become worse. Yul longed for the day when he could stand up to his father. He fell asleep thinking about it, and dreamed that he and Nightwing were flying through the black sky, the moonlight on their faces and the wind in their hair.

Miranda's relief at Sylvie's slight improvement during her stay in hospital was marred by a new worry. Sylvie talked incessantly of Hazel's country home and how she longed to escape the city to

11

walk in the hills and woods of Stonewylde. Miranda wished that the proposed visit to Dorset had never been mentioned. The last thing she needed was an expensive trip, which, in her weakened state, might only make her daughter worse. But her hopes that it would all come to nothing were dashed when she collected Sylvie from hospital a few days later.

'Thank goodness I caught you before you left,' cried the young doctor, approaching breathlessly. 'Good news! Magus is in London, I've talked to him, and he wants to meet you both!'

Sylvie, clinging on to her mother's arm for support, beamed at this.

'Can we come to Stonewylde for a visit then? Is it okay?'

'I don't know, Sylvie, but it sounds promising. I thought he'd reject the idea out of hand.' Hazel turned to Miranda, her face glowing with excitement. 'I'm sorry, I know this must seem terribly unorthodox but I honestly believe that a stay at Stonewylde could help Sylvie. We've run all the tests. We've tried all the drugs and creams, the medicines and treatments. Nothing seems to cure her because I think the illness goes deeper than simple physical allergies. Sylvie needs spiritual healing more than anything else. Please give this a try – I'm sure you won't regret it.'

The look on Miranda's face was almost comical. Spiritual healing! But she shrugged in resignation, not wanting to be the one to wipe the animation from Sylvie's thin face.

'Thank you, Doctor. We'll meet him at least, and take it from there. Maybe, as you say, a nice weekend of fresh country air would help Sylvie.'

The meeting was not at all how Miranda imagined. Hazel picked them up a few days later and drove them to Magus' offices in the heart of the City. The building was very grand and they were ushered in by an immaculately groomed woman. Behind a mask of professional welcome, she hid any curiosity the bedraggled pair may have aroused. Magus' office was luxurious and the man himself was a complete shock to both of them.

Instead of the crusty old landed-gentry type in tweeds and brogues whom Sylvie had envisaged, or the bearded weirdo in ethnic clothing, crystals and sandals of Miranda's imaginings, Magus was the most attractive man either of them had ever seen. In his late thirties, with ash-blond hair and velvety dark eyes, he was tall and long-limbed and wore an expensive business suit with effortless style. His face was strong and chiselled; his manner charming and quietly powerful. Miranda rapidly changed her opinion of the whole venture and wished she'd worn lipstick. This was no sinister cult leader bent on brain-washing them for his evil ends, but a cultured and successful man. Maybe Stonewylde would be a similarly attractive proposition.

He put Miranda and Sylvie at ease, for both were flustered and shy. Like Hazel, whom he thanked and dismissed once she'd introduced them, he was fascinated by Sylvie's likeness to the residents of Stonewylde. He couldn't take his eyes off her and apologised for his curiosity with a smile. He was concerned to hear of Sylvie's illness and allergies and questioned her sensitively. His dark eyes glowed with sympathy when she hesitatingly explained her awful medical problems. She felt genuine warmth in his smile and liked the way he listened so carefully, his eyes kind and voice gentle. There was an aura of strength and security about him that she found very comforting, and she loved the smell of his rather exotic cologne.

Magus also wanted to know about Miranda's teaching career and her hopes for the future. When he learned that they didn't extend beyond finding a cure for Sylvie, he nodded.

'Your ideals would fit in well with our philosophy at Stonewylde,' he said in his deep voice. 'We too put health and well-being before material gain. Forgive me for asking, but what about Sylvie's father? I assume he's not part of your lives?'

Miranda refused to be drawn and Sylvie felt embarrassed by her curtness on the subject.

'I only ask because of the striking resemblance between Sylvie and members of my family,' he said gently. 'We're an extended tribe and many of us don't live at Stonewylde. I wondered whether Sylvie's father could be a relation. I didn't mean to intrude.'

He then told them about Stonewylde, and showed them photos of the great country estate. As Sylvie gazed at the slide-show of images she felt a deep longing begin to take root. She was sure she'd regain her health if she could stay in such a beautiful place, even if only for a few days. More than anything in the world, she wanted to go to Stonewylde. She found herself trembling and tried to calm down as her breathing became jagged. Then Magus rang for tea and said he had a proposition to make.

He told them he was impressed with Miranda's values and sorry to see Sylvie's suffering. She was clearly a bright and sensitive girl, unable to cope with her difficult life in London. By luck there was currently a position available in the boarding school at the Hall, teaching English. He offered Miranda the post, with a free place at the school for Sylvie too. Accommodation, food and essentials would be included in the package. The position would initially be for a year, and he'd negotiate with Miranda's school to waive her notice. They could move down to Dorset in the middle of March. He needed to find a new teacher soon, but would give them a week to consider the proposal.

Magus sat back on the sofa and watched them, his dark eyes gleaming. Sylvie appeared to have stopped breathing and stared at him with enormous eyes, her face white. Miranda was flushed and dumbfounded, her mouth opening and closing as the impli-cations of his offer sunk in. She looked across at Sylvie and knew what her answer must be. Their present lifestyle was killing her daughter. They had nothing to lose. She smiled reassuringly at Sylvie, knowing they shared the same bubbling exhilaration and sense of unreality.

'I don't need a week, Magus. I can give you our answer now. We'd both love to come to Stonewylde.'

Sylvie burst into tears and Magus handed her a white linen handkerchief, patting her arm kindly.

'I was hoping you'd say that, Miranda,' he said softly. 'You won't regret it, I promise.'

The next days passed in a blur of frantic activity. There was much to do before leaving behind their old life with its worry and complications of outstanding bills and rent. Even though she was exhausted, the night before their departure Sylvie found it difficult to sleep. She lay on her familiar bed for the last time, listening to the roar of the city and howls of sirens. She gazed through her dirty window at the sodium-lit night sky, where the red and green lights of aircraft flew overhead to unknown destinations. But nowhere could be more exciting than her destination. Stonewylde! At last she was to escape this prison and find the peace and beauty she craved.

Miranda too found it impossible to fall asleep despite the gruelling day she'd spent packing up the last of their things. She hoped desperately that she'd made the right decision and was now besieged by last minute doubts. But then she remembered Magus' kindness that day in his office. He knew they were penniless and alone in the world, and how seriously ill Sylvie was. A man of his means and background would never let them down – he'd take care of them. Feeling comforted by that thought, Miranda finally slept. But her sleep was haunted by the ghost of her past. The memory replayed itself for the thousandth time, buried firmly during the day but using the dark night, as she slept, to rise from the grave.

A great red harvest moon was rising in the clear night. The autumn air was crisp and fragrant as she dared to follow the man through the woods leading away from the house. The party was in full swing behind her but she welcomed the cool darkness ahead. She thrilled with excitement. She was just sixteen and immature for her age, dressed in a sparkling white fairy costume. Her parents had insisted she accompany them to this grand charity fancy-dress ball hosted by her father's business associate. She should've been demurely sipping lemonade at her mother's side. Instead she was creeping off into the woods with a tall stranger, tipsy on a glass of forbidden punch and not caring what happened next.

In a clearing amongst the trees, the man with the pale hair and feathered bird mask stopped. He gazed up through the branches at the red moon in the sky, enormous and unreal. Then he gently pulled her down onto the carpet of fallen leaves and damp grass, her wings crushed beneath her. He spread her long red hair about her head, creating a fiery halo on the earth. She started to protest as his hands touched her and he murmured deeply, hushing her first with his voice and then with a hand over her mouth. His masked eyes bored into hers, but as he entered her, he flung back his head and stared long and hard at the blood-red moon. The sound that escaped his lips was as primitive as a wolf's howl.

2

Yul climbed to the very peak of the bonfire in the Stone Circle and looked around. Groups of people were preparing for the imminent celebrations and today the huge arena felt busy. The great standing stones had been scrubbed of the faded Imbolc decorations left from the beginning of February, and a group of artists now painted the Spring Equinox symbols onto the freshly cleaned stones using beautiful colours prepared from natural pigments and dyes. A pattern of spring flowers decorated the tops of the ancient stones: celandine and violet, wood anemone and primrose. The spring fertility goddess Eostre was represented holding an egg in each hand and wearing a great headdress of flowers and stars.

But the dominant image was that of the hare. All around the Circle, hares were painted onto the stones in every possible stance – boxing, crouching, washing and leaping. Amber eyes and long black-tipped ears formed a great carousel of hares. The hare was the symbol of the festival, totem animal of the ancient spring goddess. The artists were now finishing the finer details, hoping the sudden showers would hold off until the paint and glaze were dry.

Yul was watching one girl in particular. Her pale Hallfolk hair was cut in a bob and she had a pretty cat-like face. Holly was a Winter Solstice child like him, and he wondered, as he had before, if they'd be partners at their Rite of Adulthood later in the year. She'd seemed keen on him at the Imbolc celebrations. They'd known each other for years as all Hallfolk children attended the Village school until they were eight. Since then the segregation had deepened and although in the same community, they were now worlds apart. But differences were forgotten at the festivals and the Rite in particular was a great leveller.

Today, however, Holly ignored him. She hung around the artists offering cloths and paint pots, ostensibly helping but in fact just getting in the way. Merewen, in charge of the decorations, growled at her a couple of times. But Holly was cheeky and a law unto herself, which was one of the reasons Yul liked her. He wondered how to attract her attention without getting into trouble. He was supposed to be packing the gaps in the huge bonfire with smaller branches, carried in a bag on his back, and stuffing in different mosses and lichens to burn with strange colours and effects.

The woodsmen were all around, constructing the great pyramid of wood. They always built the bonfires and took pride in the job; as an apprentice, Yul was learning from experts. The Spring Equinox was one of the four fire festivals of the year, the time when the community celebrated the balance of light and darkness, the returning warmth of the sun and the start of the growing season. The customs dated back far beyond any recorded memory, passed on through the centuries by tradition and folk-lore. Yul particularly liked this festival because of the hares, and looking around the Stone Circle, it gladdened his heart to see the way Merewen and her group of artists had captured the spirit of the hare so perfectly.

He was annoyed to see Holly showing off in front of a young man from the Hall, but amused by his inability to balance on the ladder propped against a stone. Fennel was working on the image of Eostre painted on the largest monolith right behind the Altar Stone, adding silver stars to the halo of flowers around the figure's head. Merewen watched closely from the ground, directing him in her gruff manner. Several times Fennel wobbled precariously and Yul wondered what mischief he could get away with. But he knew he couldn't afford to invite any more attention from Magus.

From his vantage point at the pinnacle of the bonfire he looked over the stones and across the woodlands that clustered around the clearing on the flat hilltop. He saw the blue smoothness of the sea to the south and the soft folds of the hills to the north. He gulped in the fresh air as the salty wind stirred his hair and caressed his face. Merewen glanced across the Circle and her artist's eye was drawn to the striking picture he made, perched so high and looking as if he grew from the bonfire itself.

Holly followed the woman's gaze and wandered away from the artists, bored now with helping. She stood staring up at Yul, impressed by his agility and the way his black curls moved in the wind. He grinned down at her, white teeth flashing in his dark face, and she smiled back. He slithered down the pyramid of great branches but, when only halfway down, he turned outwards to face her. Then he leapt. As he flew through the air he caught a glimpse of her face, open-mouthed at his dare-devil antics. He yelled out in delight, landing gracefully in a crouched position on the earth at her feet. He shook the hair from his eyes and laughed up at her.

'You're mad, Yul,' she giggled, her pretty little face dimpling.

'As a March hare,' he agreed.

'You could've broken your neck.'

'But I didn't, and just as well. Or we wouldn't be able to dance together at the celebrations.'

'Oh I see, you've got it all planned, have you?' She tossed her blond hair so the well-cut bob fell into perfect place. 'And I thought I'd be dancing with Fennel. Or even Buzz.'

Yul snorted at this.

'Why on earth would you do that when you could have me?'

He'd stood up and was pleased to see he'd now grown much taller than her. She was still quite small but curvier, her slim boyishness transformed into something more enticing. Yul puffed out his chest with satisfaction and surveyed the Stone Circle, his gaze sweeping all the people hard at work, busy making the sacred space ready for the Equinox.

Then he noticed Magus. The tall man leant against a stone on the opposite side, watching him. Magus raised a hand and beckoned slowly.

'See you, Holly,' he muttered.

'Maybe,' she said lightly. As he walked away she noted how his shoulders had become broader and his legs longer. She smiled to herself; Yul was shaping up nicely.

Yul lowered his eyes carefully as he approached. He wasn't so much worried about upsetting Magus as scared of what his father would do, should he get into any more trouble. The slash that Magus had given him across his cheek was now a pink weal, but other than that he was at present uninjured and wanted to say that way, with the festival so close. He stopped at a respectful distance and stood with his head bowed.

'I see your manners have improved since our last encounter,' said Magus softly, still leaning against the towering standing stone.

'Yes, sir.'

'And Tom tells me you worked hard in my stables every night.'

'Yes, sir.'

'So let's hope you've learned your lesson.'

'Yes, sir.'

'Mmn.'

Magus surveyed the lowered head before him, not in the least taken in by this apparent show of deference. He could also see the set of the boy's shoulders and the flare of his nostrils.

'So what was the meaning of the acrobatics just now? This is a sacred place.'

'I'm sorry, sir.'

'You were showing off.'

'Yes, sir. I'm sorry.'

'Maybe I need to speak to your father.'

The boy's head shot up and Magus saw the fear in his deep

grey eyes, quickly masked. He gave a small smile.

'Would your father approve of you showing off? If I were to mention it to him?'

'No sir. It won't happen again, sir.'

'It certainly won't. The Stone Circle is the sacred heart of Stonewylde, not a place where dirty young boys swagger around trying to impress girls. Watch your step carefully, Yul. I'm keeping a close eye on you.'

'Yes, sir.'

Magus twitched himself upright and strode off across the Circle. Yul scowled and left quickly. He hurried down the Long Walk where Villagers were placing lanterns among the avenue of stones to light the way for the ceremony. He must keep out of Magus' way for the foreseeable future, and cursed himself for that betraying flash of fear. He'd seen Magus' flicker of a smile and understood exactly what it meant.

The silver Rolls Royce slowed as they approached the boundary walls. Very old and as high as three men, the walls were topped with broken glass and razor wire. The great wrought-iron gates opened slowly at a touch of Magus' remote control. The Gate-house, although old like the walls, was manned by two burly men with radios, and there were security cameras trained on the entrance. Seeing Miranda's startled face in the seat next to him, Magus smiled and explained that the security was to keep out nosy tourists.

'The only way a community such as ours has survived is by shutting out the Outside World. Nobody enters Stonewylde unless they belong here.'

Miranda nodded, smiling slightly at the guards as the great car purred slowly through the entrance. She wasn't quite sure of the protocol with gatekeepers, but noticed how hard they stared inside the car.

'Your arrival is exceptional,' explained Magus. 'We never invite Outsiders into our midst. We have to keep ourselves separate. Of course the Hallfolk liaise with the Outside World and I have a company to run in London, but the Villagers never leave Stonewylde.'

'But surely people want to get away sometimes? Don't they want to go shopping or visit family?'

Magus smiled again at this.

'The whole concept of shopping is alien to Stonewylde folk. We're virtually self-sufficient, and the Villagers' families are all within the community. Why should we want to leave?'

'It'll take us a while to adjust to this,' said Miranda, her earlier confidence crumbling at the reality of just how cut off Stonewylde actually was. 'We can go out if we want to, can't we?'

'Of course you can! You're not prisoners here! And neither, for that matter, are any members of the community. But after a while the Outside World loses all relevance. Stonewylde is a world in itself. Eventually you may feel the same way.'

His eyes flicked to the rear-view mirror and he saw Sylvie nestle deeper into the soft leather of the back seat, a small smile on her face as she surveyed the high walls and tight security. This was the place of her dreams and now she felt safe. Here she'd find sanctuary.

It had been grey and raining as they left London, but the sky was now blue and scattered with feathery clouds that raced across the brightness. Tiny lambs skipped amongst the sheep, dotted throughout the hills. She saw acres and acres of woodlands stretching away, still brown in winter guise. The hedgerows were starry-white with blackthorn blossom and the banks smothered in early primroses and celandine. Over a field a pair of great golden-brown buzzards circled and drifted on the air currents, the pin feathers of their wings splayed open like fingers.

Magus pressed a button and Sylvie's window slid open. A burst of pure country air poured in and engulfed her. Her face broke into a smile of delight as she exhaled the last of her city breath and drank deeply of Stonewylde. She caught Magus' dark eyes watching her in the mirror and they shared a moment of understanding.

'Welcome home, Sylvie,' he murmured.

Miranda and Sylvie were to live in a tiny cottage tucked away beyond the Hall and secluded by woods. The cherry tree in their front garden was in full blossom and they walked to the front door under a shower of white-petal confetti. Sylvie laughed as it settled all over her mother's glossy red hair, teasing her that she looked like a bride.

Inside the cottage they stared around in wonder. The furniture was crafted from natural materials and the polished floorboards scattered with rag rugs. There was no central heating, no boiler, no fitted kitchen or bathroom and no electricity. It could have been a home from the Victorian age or even earlier.

'You'll find it strange at first,' said Magus as he showed them around. 'When you've integrated into the community you may like to move up to the Hall and I'll arrange a suite of rooms for you. We have all the mod cons there. But I thought at first you'd prefer some privacy while you settle in, and while Sylvie regains her health.'

'It's amazing!' said Miranda, gazing at the simple whitewashed walls and old beams. 'About as far away as you could get from our grotty flat in London.'

Sylvie wandered around in a dream, opening the back door wide and gazing out at the woods beyond.

'Normally you'll join us in the Dining Hall for your meals, but keep some food here as well, and for the settling-in period, Cherry my housekeeper will call daily to look after you.'

'Thank you. I feel a bit ... overwhelmed, to be honest,' gulped Miranda.

He smiled at her.

'Understandable. Living here will require quite some adjustment for you both. If there's anything you need, anything at all, don't be afraid to ask. As part of our community you share whatever we have. And as Hallfolk you have access to many things. There are computers, televisions, a library and stables up at the Hall.'

'Stables? Wow – we've never ridden horses before,' said Miranda. 'I hope it's not compulsory!'

Magus laughed, towering over her in the small sitting room. Sylvie had sunk onto a chair, her face pale and eyes drawn. She pulled out her inhaler and took a quick puff.

'Of course not! And Sylvie, as your health improves I'm sure you'll make friends with the other young people there. You'll find we have a thriving social life at Stonewylde, but it'll seem odd to you at first, I warn you. In fact we have a big event tomorrow, but I think you need a little time before you start joining in our celebrations, don't you?'

'Oh absolutely,' agreed Miranda. 'We'd feel awkward not knowing anyone and Sylvie's not strong enough yet. Magus, you haven't said when you want me to start teaching. I could—'

'Not yet. Our priority is to get Sylvie healthy again. I want you to treat these first few weeks as an extended holiday, one that you both need very much. Enjoy the countryside and spring weather and reconnect with nature. Many of the students you'll be teaching are away in Europe anyway. They won't be back until Beltane, so there's plenty of time to really settle in.'

'Beltane?'

'Sorry,' he smiled, 'I forget how different it is here. We celebrate Beltane at the beginning of May. Lots of rural places do, though some call it May Day.'

'Maypole dancing, with a May Queen and Morris dancers you mean?' asked Sylvie in delight, perking up again. 'I've heard of that. I hope I'll be well enough by then to come and watch.'

'I'm sure you will, and it'll be a lovely introduction to our customs. Beltane is my favourite festival of the year. Now I'll leave you to unpack and I'll send Cherry over shortly. Just relax and enjoy the peace and quiet. Stay in the gardens of the Hall until I get a chance to show you around properly.'

'We will, Magus. And may I say,' said Miranda a little shyly, 'just how grateful we are. You've been so very kind to us . . .'

Magus smiled down at her as she faltered; his eyes were dark and deep and seemed to look inside her soul.

'Not at all. We have so much here and we're happy to share it with you. You're both very welcome.'

Cherry bustled in later like a broody chicken and soon took control. They were unpacked and settled in before they knew it. She examined the painful eczema on Sylvie's skin and held up one of her thin arms in bemusement, jowls quivering in disbelief. Miranda's explanation as to why Sylvie had become so ill in the first place confirmed all her suspicions about the Outside World.

'Aye, I been told of what they do out there. The poison they add to food and how they cook things in strange ways, spinning it around so 'tis done in a wink of the eye. Whoever heard of such nonsense! I thank the stars we don't have none of that here. We cook on a range and we eat wholesome food the way nature intended. We'll soon get some flesh on your poor bones, little maid. And have that sore skin cleared up in no time.'

On the Equinox Eve Cherry excused herself, leaving them food and firewood for the following day, and careful instructions about cooking on the range. She explained that she'd be joining in the celebrations and wouldn't be able to come over, sorry though she was to leave them alone so soon after their arrival.

'But Cherry, what do you actually do at the celebrations? Is it like a party? Where do you go?' asked Sylvie.

'Magus said you'd come to it in your own good time,' she replied evasively. 'He said you don't do things as we do, not in the Outside World. 'Tis not my place to go prattling about it, he told me. But you'll see soon enough. I'll be back the day after tomorrow. Just mind you don't let the range go out, my dears.'

That evening they heard some of the ceremony, as the drumming carried through the twilight. When the community raised their voices in unison it could be heard clearly in the cottage. The hair on Sylvie's arms stood on end, for the sound was primeval and quite compelling. She longed to join in. All her life she'd lived in isolation, on the periphery and never belonging. She'd always been different; one of those children who don't fit in. Her strange colouring made her stand out, and her quietness formed a barrier around her. Sylvie had led a lonely life, and as she heard the people of Stonewylde chanting together, she wanted more than anything to join the circle of belonging.

'Mum, can't we just go out and have a peep? See what they're up to?'

'No, darling, we can't. You heard what Magus said. And it would be very rude to turn up unannounced. It sounds like some sort of religious ceremony, doesn't it? Although not exactly what you hear in church on a Sunday!'

'It sounds wonderful, almost unearthly. I can't wait until the May Day events that Magus told us about.'

In the flickering light Sylvie's eyes shone brightly and Miranda smiled. Life had returned to her daughter. Miranda had spent the whole of Sylvie's life feeling guilty for failing her. Guilty for getting pregnant and not telling anyone until people noticed the tell-tale bump. For going to university and not being a full-time mother, and then for teaching but never earning enough money. She felt constantly guilty about Sylvie's illnesses and unhappiness which she was sure were her fault for not caring for her daughter in the way she needed. Miranda had spent the years since she was raped in a wood suffering from endless guilt. Even that, as her parents had constantly reminded her, was her own wicked fault because she'd willingly followed the stranger and hadn't put up a fight. The burden of blame she'd carried was heavy and had often come close to breaking her altogether. Now, as she saw the light in her daughter's silvery eyes, she felt a glimmer of hope. Maybe now, at last, she might be absolved.

Yul's heart beat slow and hard as he watched Buzz strutting about by the cider table surrounded by his gang. Only minutes earlier Yul had been dancing with Holly, admiring her bright eyes and animated face as they tore around the Great Barn together. And now he stood alone, his fists clenching with a strong urge to punch Buzz's smug face.

He'd had a good feeling about this evening and up until the moment when the adults joined them, everything had been going well. The Barn was decorated with spring flowers and greenery in honour of Eostre, the tables were laden with food and the musicians on the dais were playing their hearts out. The effects of the ceremony cakes and mead still tingled through their bodies as Yul and Holly danced, their feet skimming the flagstone floor. But as soon as the adults had arrived, their additional ceremonies and rituals in the Stone Circle completed, everything had changed.

A group of young Hallfolk, several of whom had just undergone their Rite of Adulthood, had swaggered into the Great Barn showing off their new robes and necklets and boasting of their initiation. Holly's head had swivelled round and then she'd dragged Yul off the dance floor.

'Thanks for the dance,' she said breathlessly, her cheeks flushed. 'Got to go now. My friends are here.'

'But ... is that it? I thought we were going to spend the evening together.'

'No!' she laughed. 'Whatever made you think that? I'm joining them.'

She nodded towards Buzz and his group, who'd already attracted a gaggle of girls. Yul glared at her, his grey eyes smouldering.

'Why do you want to be with them? They're all idiots. Especially Buzz.'

'I wouldn't speak about Buzz like that if I were you,' she said sharply. 'And they're not idiots. They're all very clever, unlike you, Yul.'

His face tightened at this and he released her hands.

'It's your choice, Holly. You'd have much more fun with me. But go and join the herd if that's what you want. If you're lucky Buzz might just notice you, although you've a lot of competition by the look of it.'

'You really should watch your tongue! For a Villager you've a very high opinion of yourself. How could I possibly have more fun with you? You're nothing but a dumb peasant, Yul, and you'd do well to remember that before you start insulting Hallfolk.'

Holly had turned and threaded her way through the noisy crowd. Yul's hands shook as he watched her go. He'd lost sight of her for a minute and when he saw her again she was near the cider table and surrounded by the group. She threw her head back and tossed her hair. The Hallfolk boys closed round her, all vying for her attention. She was obviously very popular with the boys, and she stood on tiptoe and spoke into Buzz's ear, holding onto the collar of his new robes. Yul saw Buzz, the leader of the group, look across at him and then laugh loudly.

Now Yul's heart thumped in his chest as the anger rose. He turned and pushed his way through the throng of people towards the open doors. He was sure the whole crowd around Buzz and Holly were watching him and laughing, and all he wanted was to be outside, away from the lot of them. He passed his sister Rosie near the door and she tried to stop him, but he shook her off angrily.

Once outside in the cool night he took gulps of air, trying to steady his heartbeat. He hated Holly, stuck up little cow. He'd never dance with her again. And as for his Rite of Adulthood ... she was the last person he'd want to partner. He hated Buzz and his gang of friends more than anything. In fact he hated all the Hallfolk, he decided, with their pale hair and stupid way of talking. They were useless. As far as he could see they provided nothing for the community and leeched off the hard-working Villagers. He hated every one of them. If he had his way there'd be no Hallfolk at Stonewylde.

Yul stomped off down the lane, his Spring Equinox celebration completely ruined. He'd go home to bed. He'd been working hard all week, unlike the fools panting over Holly like a pack of dogs sniffing at a bitch on heat. He kicked viciously at stones as he marched furiously along the track– until he heard tuneless whistling ahead. He instantly jumped off the lane, crouching behind a bush. It was his father! He must have gone home to change out of his robes.

Luckily Alwyn hadn't seen him. That was all he needed tonight; another beating. Not that he'd done anything wrong, but Alwyn didn't need an excuse. Yul stayed crouched behind the bush waiting as his father passed by. He was a beefy man with arms like hams and fists the size of overgrown swedes. The only good thing about his size was that it made him slow. Yul could sometimes get away or dodge the blows. But often that just made it worse, and Alwyn worked himself up into a spitting, scarlet rage that wouldn't be quenched until he'd given the boy a good thrashing. Yul thanked the stars that he'd heard his father coming. He waited until Alwyn was well past before emerging again. The shock of the near-miss calmed him down and his previous anger evaporated. Buzz and Holly and all the others could go and stuff themselves for all he cared.

But then he heard a shout from behind. He swung round and saw a group of figures outlined against the light streaming from the Great Barn.

'Hey! Stop right there, Village boy!'

He recognised Buzz's arrogant voice.

'Piss off!' he shouted back.

'I said stop! I order you as an adult!'

It was one of the pivotal laws of the community that children respected and obeyed adults; not only their own parents but any adult. Yul felt the rage start to pound inside again. If Buzz was an adult it was by a matter of an hour or so; he'd only just had his Rite. But as he hesitated, the group approached and he knew he must face them.

'Don't bother, Buzz,' said Holly. 'Just leave him and let's get back to the dance.'

'No, I want to sort this little runt out. You told me what he said and he's not getting away with it. You stop right there, Yul!'

He caught up and grabbed hold of Yul's arm. Buzz was taller and far more heavily built, and Yul felt the familiar helplessness descend. It was a while since Buzz had had a go at him, but all the incidents from the past came flooding back.

'I've got a bone to pick with you, boy.'

'Oh really?'

'Yeah, really! First, stay away from Holly. She's way out of your league. Next, don't you—'

'What do you mean, out of my league? She wasn't complaining when I danced with her earlier.'

'Well she is now!'

Holly smiled, enjoying being argued over.

'Are you complaining, Holly?' Yul asked, his voice slow and cold.

'I—'

'Don't you dare start questioning her! Or questioning my authority! You—'

'You've only just become an adult. Why should I do what you say?'

'Because I'll beat the crap out of you if you don't! Just like I used to.'

Yul laughed tauntingly at this, darts of anger shooting about inside his chest.

'I don't think so. Not any more.'

Buzz yanked at Yul's arm, raising his other hand into a fist. But Buzz was small fry compared to Alwyn. With a sudden twist Yul wrenched himself free and started to run. The others followed, yelling taunts and threats. As he ran, Yul realised he couldn't go back home. None of the cottages in Stonewylde had locks and they'd just follow him inside. So he raced on past his home and headed out of the Village. He heard Holly and the other girls shouting from some way back, calling for the boys to stop and come back to the Great Barn.

Yul guessed that all five of the Hallfolk boys were chasing him, for there was a lot of gasping for breath and shouting. They were young and reasonably fit but Yul was fitter. Unlike them, his life was spent doing physical work. He soon gained a lead and slipped through a gap in the hedge into a field. He flew across the damp grass, his feet hardly touching the ground, thankful now that he wasn't wearing long robes. The boys, further behind now, yelled insults and commanded him to stop.

Yul had no intention of stopping. He'd have fought one of

them, or maybe even two. But five was impossible and he didn't want to get beaten up, especially not in front of Holly. He crossed the field and turned back into the lane further up the hill, heading for the woods he knew so well. But one of the boys must've stayed in the lane for he felt an arm shoot out of nowhere to grab him. He pulled away and sped on, finally turning into the shelter of the woods.

'Quick! He's just out of the lane! I nearly had him!'

It was Fennel. Yul turned to yell an insult and failed to see the tree stump ahead. He went flying and his knee slammed hard into the ground. He cried out in pain but struggled up and started to run again, dragging his leg. Buzz threw himself at Yul, knocking him face-down onto the ground. All the breath was forced out of his body and Buzz sprawled across him, pinning him to the earth. Yul's chest heaved but with Buzz's weight full on him he could hardly breathe.

'Got you, you bastard!'

The other four crowded round the prone figures, gasping for air and laughing at the same time.

'Nice one, Buzz! Great tackle!'

'Let's really teach him a lesson!'

Buzz pushed himself upright, the heel of his hand forcing Yul into the ground as he knelt up. He straddled the boy, sitting astride his back. Yul couldn't fill his lungs under the weight of the heavy youth and started to panic, wriggling and kicking frantically.

'Bloody hell, he's still fighting!'

Buzz put his hand on the back of Yul's neck and shoved his face down hard, into the wet earth.

'Keep still or you'll suffocate. You won't get me off.'

Yul stopped struggling, trying to get a proper breath. Buzz shifted his weight so it settled more firmly onto the boy's back. Yul grunted as the air was forced out again.

'Just like old times, isn't it, Yul? I'd forgotten how good it feels to put you in your place.'

The other boys laughed and jeered.

'Not so cocky now, is he?'

'Pity the girls aren't here to see him get his come-uppance. Holly would kill herself laughing.'

'Ah yes ... Holly.'

Buzz had recovered from the exertion of the chase and was enjoying himself.

'I was in the middle of advising you to stay away from Holly. What have you got to say to that now, boy?'

Yul tried to answer but his face was pushed into the ground and he got a mouthful of earth.

'Hah! He's eating dirt!'

'Very fitting,' crowed Buzz. Yul's face was thrust harder into the ground and he spluttered and choked, still unable to breathe under the dead weight.

'Tempting though it is, I'm not going to beat you tonight, Yul,' laughed Buzz. 'It'd be too easy and I don't want your blood on my new robes. And you wouldn't be fit for work if I smashed you to pulp. We can't have you unfit for work, can we?'

Yul spluttered again and Buzz brayed with laughter.

'Sorry, didn't quite catch that. Never mind, probably drivel anyway. Just remember, Yul, that I chose to let you off tonight. Stay away from Holly and any other Hallfolk girl in future. They're way too good for a dirty Villager like you. And next time I give an order, make sure you jump to obey me.'

With a final shove of Yul's face into the earth, Buzz got up, jabbing his knee viciously into the boy's back as he did so. Yul groaned loudly despite himself. Still cracking jokes, the Hallfolk boys turned and left. Yul remained where he was on the ground, the tears welling up. Before he knew it, his body was racked with harsh sobs. He spat out the soil and tried to sit up. His back and ribs were agony and his knee throbbed badly. But he had to get back before the celebrations ended and his father returned home. He started to hobble back the way he'd come. Angry tears streamed down his grimy face forming rivulets in the dirt.

As he let himself into the shadowy cottage, a figure stood up from one of the armchairs. Yul jumped but then realised it was only his sister Rosie.

'What's happened, Yul?' she gasped, peering at him in the soft light from the single lamp.

'Nothing. Never mind.'

He tried to push past her to go upstairs.

'Oh Yul, stop! You're hurt and you're covered in dirt. Was it Buzz and his gang? I saw them leave just after you.'

He nodded, hanging his head. His thin cheeks were streaked and his mouth was caked with bits of earth. He felt so ashamed, even in front of Rosie.

'I don't want to talk about it, Rosie. I must get to bed before Father comes back and sees me like this.'

They both eyed the leather strap hanging from its hook on the door, but Rosie shook her head.

'Don't worry, he won't be home for ages. I only came back because Geoffrey and Gregory were so tired. They're in bed now and the little ones are sleeping down in the Nursery. But Mother was still enjoying herself and Father was going strong at the bar when I left. Sit down, Yul. You can't go to bed like that. I'll clean you up.'

He sat on one of the hard chairs at the table while she brought a cloth and bowl of warm water from the kettle. Very gently she washed his face and hands. She noticed his swollen, grazed knee and bathed that as well.

'You need to go to the bath house tomorrow, Yul. You're filthy. What did they do?'

'Not much really. It could've been a lot worse.'

'Why? Because of Holly? She's not worth it!' spat Rosie.

'I know that now.' He stood up stiffly and ruffled her hair. 'Thank you, Rosie.'

She smiled and stood on tiptoe to kiss his cheek. He followed her into the kitchen and watched as she made them both a mug of tea.

'You seem greedy for trouble, Yul,' she said. 'Why do you do it?'

He shrugged and took the mug from her.

'I don't mean to. Everyone's on my back all the time.'

'It's the way you look at folk, as if you're challenging them.' She traced the pink slash on his cheek. 'You must be careful, Yul. Swallow your pride and keep your eyes down. If you do as you're told and look humble, they'll leave you alone.'

'I can't, Rosie. I've tried but I just can't do it. There's something in me that gets so angry and I can't back down, even if it means taking a beating.'

She shook her head sadly, her eyes full of love.

'Mother and I worry about you, Yul. All these people crying for your blood. The way you're going, we wonder if you'll even make it to your sixteenth birthday at the Winter Solstice.'

3

The morning after the Equinox, Miranda and Sylvie had just finished breakfast when there was a knock at their front door. Magus' body filled the door frame and the sun gleamed on his ash-blond hair.

'Bright blessings, Sylvie! Put your shoes on. I'm taking you out for a walk.'

'Okay. I'll get Mum.'

'No, just you and me. That's alright with you, isn't it Miranda?'

She'd followed Sylvie out of the kitchen and looked a little surprised at this.

'Er, yes, of course it is. Get your coat, Sylvie, and make sure—'

'No fussing now. It's a beautiful warm morning. Remember, Miranda, this is the beginning of a new way of life. Sylvie needs fresh air and exercise.'

They walked under the cherry blossom to the front gate and Magus led her in the opposite direction to the Hall, along the little path which wound into the woods. Early morning sunlight streamed through the branches in golden shafts. The buds were tight with green promise and sweet birdsong filled the air. They walked slowly in silence for some time and Sylvie became increasingly aware of the man by her side. He was subtly different today. He glowed with a strange radiance that she sensed rather than saw. An aura of energy pulsed around him and she felt drawn to him, as a pin to a magnet. She found it a very odd sensation.

They stopped in a small clearing just as she was beginning to tire. The dappled sunlight played upon the ground, still littered with dark leaves from last year but bristling with spiky green shoots that would later flower into bluebells. Birds flitted around in the branches and the woodland was alive with light, movement and the music of nature.

Sylvie fished in her pocket and drew out her inhaler, but Magus shook his head and smiled.

'Just breathe deeply, Sylvie,' he said softly, aware of her fatigue. 'Slow deep breaths. Can you feel how pure and fresh that is?'

She nodded, but still felt the tightness in her chest.

'You really don't need that artificial stuff, Sylvie. Feel the air going down, deep into your lungs, then flowing into every part of your body.'

She stood motionless, the light filtering onto her upturned face. She closed her eyes and drank the air.

'That's better – good girl. What does it feel like?'

'It feels like I'm tasting heaven,' she whispered.

Opening her eyes, she found him watching her intently. He spoke gently.

'Then that's just what it is. You must draw that heaven deep into your body; dissolve all the chemicals and toxins, the drugs and the poisons they've pumped into you. You need to get Stonewylde into your veins. Can you breathe easier now?'

'Yes, I can. You're right, I don't need this.' She put the inhaler away and he smiled at her, his eyes dancing and bright.

'I want you to go walking every day, Sylvie, whatever the weather. Drink in the fresh air and get your limbs moving. You're very weak and you've wasted away to nothing. Walk a bit further each day and work up a good appetite.'

'Yes I will – I know it's what I need. But what about school? Will I have to start soon?'

'We need to get you well first. We have different priorities here, remember. Plenty of time for school once you're fit and healthy.'

She felt relieved at this, not ready yet to face a whole new regime of schoolwork, teachers and students. She smiled at Magus; he instinctively seemed to understand her fears and needs.

'Yes,' he murmured. 'School can wait. I want you to be cured. I want to help you.'

He gazed down at her, the dark fire burning in his eyes, mesmerising her. She couldn't look away and he reached and took her hands. She flinched as their skin touched, feeling a tingle in her fingertips which spread throughout her body. She gasped and almost stopped breathing, for the sensation was so strange. She was scared but he smiled, his face shimmering before her in the sunlight.

'Don't be frightened,' he said softly. 'I can help you. Take what I'm giving you, Sylvie. Take the energy and use it to heal yourself. Let it flow into you and don't fight it. Trust me, Sylvie. Trust me and open yourself up to me.'

She stood absolutely still, trying to be calm, trying not to wheeze. Then suddenly she felt it; a flood of power that washed through her into every cell, every pore. Magus' deep brown eyes gleamed, holding her in their thrall, piercing her soul with their intensity. Her thin body vibrated with the rush of energy surging out of him and into her. He released her hands and brushed her face with his fingertips, tracing the eczema that crusted her skin. His fingers lingered gently on her eyelids, cheekbones and jaw. Her skin prickled beneath his feathery touch.

'You will be beautiful again, Sylvie. The Earth Magic of Stonewylde is in your soul now and your body will be healed and whole.'

He stepped back and she opened her eyes. She gazed up at him in bewilderment. Then to her embarrassment, she started to cry.

Further up the path Yul was tucked away behind a smooth beech trunk, sitting amongst the green dog's mercury and white wood anemones. He was wolfing down a hunk of bread, grabbed as he left the cottage very early on his way to work. Birds darted around him gathering material for their nests, oblivious to his camouflaged presence for his clothes were rough-spun and brown, his hair and skin dark.

He heard voices in the clearing below. He knew Magus' voice of course, and realised the girl must be one of the Outsiders. The whole community knew that two people had come to Stonewylde and moved into Woodland Cottage near the Hall. Everyone was curious about them but so far only Cherry had seen them.

Yul shrank against the beech trunk keeping very still, his hands clutching the remains of his bread. His legs were tucked up out of sight, knees under his chin. His dark curls rested against the lichen-covered bark and he closed his eyes, praying that Magus wouldn't discover him. Greenbough had sent him over to this part of the woods to look at some hazel coppicing, and he'd taken the opportunity to eat his breakfast. Magus would be furious if he knew Yul was there.

It went quiet and he risked a peep. He saw Magus, tall and motionless as a tree, radiating the strange power that always came to him during the festivals. His hands reached out and held the girl's. She was like an elfchild, white skinned and almost white haired, thin and delicate. Maybe more of a fairy than an elf, he thought. In profile she was beautiful but so frail. Yul could see her glowing slightly too, and it had nothing to do with the sunlight falling on her. He knew of the magic that danced in the master but he'd never seen it shared before.

Magus touched her face as she looked up at him and Yul felt a flicker of shock at the sight. The powerful man was so very gentle, touching her as if she might break under his fingers. Then Yul saw her crumple and Magus take her in his arms and hold her against his chest. He stroked her hair soothingly as she clung to him, her body shaking with sobs. Yul pulled back behind the tree; he felt he was intruding on something private.

After a while he heard them talking again and peered round. They were walking out of the clearing up the path towards him. He stared at the lovely girl and was struck by two things; the strangeness of her silver-grey eyes and the scaliness of her skin. It looked sore and rough, and his sense of awe at such beauty was punctured with disappointment. He shrank further into his hiding place as their voices became clearer.

'You're very special, Sylvie. I knew it when I first saw you in London. You'll get better, I promise you. Earth energy is the strongest force there is and it'll heal you completely. I'll take you up to the Stone Circle soon and then maybe you'll understand.'

'Is that what you did to me just now?' she whispered. 'Was that Earth energy?'

'It was. And now it's alive in your body and soul, working its magic. Now remember, you're to walk every day in these woods. Everywhere in Stonewylde is safe. It's not like the Outside World so don't worry, nobody here would hurt you.'

'I feel so peaceful in these woods. I'll enjoy walking here,' she said softly and her voice sounded strange to Yul.

'I'm sure you've been ill because your spirit has starved. You're a magical girl, Sylvie, and you need to be in touch with the magic of the earth and all living things. Stonewylde will nurture and nourish you and it won't be long before you're healed.'

Sylvie sighed, feeling secure in the cocoon of his warmth and care.

'You're such a kind man.'

'I'm the magus,' he said simply. 'I'm the guardian. I look after Stonewylde and everyone who lives here.'

As they disappeared out of sight Yul touched the cut on his cheek and smiled bitterly.

Back at the cottage Sylvie joined her mother and Magus for a cup of tea while they discussed her diet. Miranda was worried about reintroducing wheat and dairy foods so quickly but Magus dismissed her concerns. He told her to let Sylvie eat whatever she fancied, but in moderation at first.

'I believe, and so does Hazel, that Sylvie's been needlessly drugged up to the eyeballs. All these food intolerances are a symptom, not the cause, of her illness. What she needs is fresh air, exercise and wholesome organic food with no chemical additives. The sooner she flushes the poison out of her system the better. We've made a start today with the healing process, haven't we Sylvie?'

They smiled at each other and she nodded happily.

'Is there actually a doctor here?' asked Miranda, a little anxious that they'd get caught up in some alternative medicine that might do more harm than good.

'Oh yes. Tomorrow you can come and meet him and he'll give Sylvie a thorough check-up. He'll be here until Hazel arrives in the summer. We always have at least one doctor at Stonewylde. Hallfolk come and go all the time and nobody usually stays for ever.'

'I didn't realise that. Why don't they stay?'

'There are a great many Hallfolk, everyone loosely related, and there's simply not enough room for them all to live here at once.'

'But the Villagers you've spoken about ... they stay, don't they? You said they never leave Stonewylde.'

'That's right. The Villagers work the land and sustain the whole community with their labour. They're rooted here, and they enable us to be self-sufficient. But the Hallfolk are different; they go into the Outside World to study and earn a living. They bring skills back into the community, sometimes just for a period of time and occasionally by moving here for longer.'

'So that's why Hazel's coming here this summer?' asked Sylvie. 'I'm really looking forward to that.'

'Yes, Hazel's will be a very welcome return to Stonewylde. She's young and full of new ideas. We try to combine modern medical practice with the more traditional healing remedies of Stonewylde. So Miranda, don't worry about Sylvie not receiving proper medical care. She'll get the best here, believe me. She's already feeling a great deal better, aren't you Sylvie?'

She nodded again, her eyes sparkling with a new light. Miranda was struck by the change in her daughter that seemed to have happened so quickly. Magus stood up and stretched his long legs.

'I'll give you a tour of the Hall when you come up later this afternoon. Oh, one more thing before I go. I'm sending a Village boy here daily to provide you with water and firewood, and also to dig over the back garden. It's been lying fallow for a while and it's very overgrown. Everyone grows fruit and vegetables in their cottage gardens. The boy will do the heavy digging and other manual work, and then if you choose to stay in the cottage, you can learn about growing food once the soil's prepared.'

'That's very kind,' said Miranda. 'But maybe we should do the digging ourselves if—'

'No, you're Hallfolk. And this is a punishment for the boy. He's been a little wild lately and needs his wings clipped.'

'Is he aggressive or anything?'

Magus smiled at this and shook his head.

'No, but he's been getting above himself and I need to knock him back down with a little extra work to tire him out. You'll learn the protocol about Hallfolk and Villagers – just keep your distance and don't encourage him to be your friend. Don't bring him into the cottage except to carry in the firewood and water. His name's Yul.'

Yul received his summons later that day, just when he was beginning to think the previous night's trouble may have gone unreported. Greenbough had commented on his limp but Yul said he'd overdone the dancing in the Great Barn, and he worked extra hard so as not to draw attention to it. But his heart sank when he saw Harold, a young servant from the Hall, making his way up the path towards the woodsmen's hut. Harold talked to the head woodsman, who then beckoned Yul over.

41

'You been in trouble again, boy?' he growled.

'No, sir,' said Yul quickly.

'Well you been called up to the Hall to see Magus. It better not be trouble. You're letting us down, Yul, and I won't have it. I know what you're like for getting into scrapes and I ain't having no trouble-makers amongst my men.'

'No really, sir!' protested Yul, very worried. He loved working in the woods but was only an apprentice woodsman; to lose his position would be terrible.

'Well, be off with you then. And keep your nose out of mischief.'

As they walked down to the Hall, Yul plied Harold with questions. They were of a similar age and Harold was bright and hard-working like Yul, although he too had never made it to the Hall School. But he knew nothing of why Yul had now been summoned.

'Am I in trouble? Did Magus seem angry?'

'I told you, Yul, I don't know.'

'Has that bastard Buzz been in with him today telling tales?'

'How should I know? You don't realise what it's like up there. There's loads of extra Hallfolk staying at the moment because of the Equinox. I don't know who's been talking to who, do I? I've been busy cleaning out bloody fireplaces all morning, not listening to Hallfolk talk.'

By the time they reached the Hall, Yul was quaking inside. He'd done nothing wrong last night yet he knew that he'd get the blame. He was scared that Magus would punish him, scared his father would find out and half kill him, and scared that Greenbough would stop his apprenticeship. Magus was the only higher authority at Stonewylde and renowned for being just, but Yul had no faith in him. He recalled Magus' flicker of pleasure up in the Stone Circle. Magus disliked him for some reason, and as they walked round to the back of the vast building, he felt like a mouse at the mercy of a large cat.

The Hall looked especially beautiful today. Thousands of tiny diamond Tudor window panes twinkled in the afternoon sun.

The mellow grey building with its many wings and forest of chimneys seemed to breathe and bask like a living entity in its green setting. Villagers came here regularly for a variety of reasons, but Yul couldn't recall a time when he'd felt so nervous. Harold led him through the back corridors down endless passages until they arrived in the Galleried Hall.

It was a very large double-height area, with a panelled gallery running along two sides. Tapestries and banners hung from the walls, and the ancient flagstones on the floor predated even the mediaeval building. Light flooded in through many stained-glass windows set up high near the roof. The ceiling was a great arched curve of age-blackened rafters, and countless carved bosses studded the panelling and beams. A huge fireplace took up most of one wall and antique oak settles lined the others. There were many pointed stone archways leading in from different corridors.

The Galleried Hall was the heart of the great labyrinthine building, and the place where Magus meted out justice. Anyone with a grievance or problem could bring it here to the master. Retribution was swift and relevant; perhaps whipping for the most serious misdemeanours, but more often forced labour and atonement to injured parties. The system was feudal but it worked. Magus was fair and the punishments not excessive, and there was little crime at Stonewylde because of it.

'Magus said you're to wait here,' said Harold, eyeing the dark-haired boy with sympathy. He knew Yul of old, always getting into trouble, and didn't envy him now. 'And good luck to you, mate,' he muttered under his breath, disappearing through an arched side door.

Yul stood alone in the centre of the Galleried Hall, not sure whether to sit on one of the settles or stay where he was. He looked up at the ceiling and saw many carved Green Men staring down at him. Their gaping mouths sprouted foliage as if in horror at his predicament. Magus kept him waiting for nearly an hour, during which time Yul became more and more distressed. His hands and face were dirty and his scruffy work clothes caked with mud. He was thirsty from his labour and fear now parched his throat.

Finally he heard firm footsteps clipping along a stone corridor. He stood awkwardly, trying to stop his hands from trembling. Scared as he was, he was damned if he'd let Magus see it. He turned towards the approaching sound and raised his chin, shaking the curls from his eyes. Magus wore riding clothes; the high, polished boots and well-cut jodhpurs accentuating his height and almost regal bearing. He appeared under an archway and strode across the flagstones, flinging himself into a throne-like chair set on a dais against a wall. The chair arms were carved in the shape of wild boar, the wood dark with a patina of age. He sat back, crossed his long legs, and surveyed the tousled lad who came to stand before him, head slightly bowed.

'Right then, boy. You know why you're here.'

Yul looked up and met his eye squarely.

'I don't, sir.'

'I'm not in the mood for any nonsense from you, Yul. I'm referring to the incident last night at the celebrations.'

'Yes, sir.'

'I wasn't happy when Buzzard told me what happened.'

'I'm sorry, sir.'

'Good. You're not denying any of it, then?'

'No, sir. But I'm not sure what I've done wrong.'

They looked at each other. Magus wondered if the boy was being deliberately insolent. Yul tried to match this hard-faced frightening man, who exuded such authority and power, with the one he'd watched just that morning in the woods comforting the young girl.

'I'm referring to your behaviour with Holly, the disrespectful remarks you made to her about Buzzard and the way you insulted a group of Hallfolk adults and disobeyed their orders. You also acted irresponsibly by running off into the woods in the dark and attempting to start a fight. Do you deny any of this?'

Yul tried to swallow but his mouth was too dry. His heart had started its angry pounding.

'Well?'

'No, not exactly, but—'

'No buts. If those things are true then you're guilty and will be punished.'

'I did run into the woods, and—'

'So you directly disobeyed Buzz and ran away when he told you to stop?'

'Yes, but only because he said he'd beat me.'

Magus frowned down at the boy, irritated by the blaze of boldness in his grey eyes.

'Hallfolk are not in the habit of brawling with Villagers,' he said curtly. 'I think you misunderstood.'

'But—'

'Did Buzzard actually strike you?'

'No, but he knocked me down and sat on me. I couldn't breathe.'

'He told me he tackled you to stop you from running further into the woods. And as for sitting on you – that's hardly violent behaviour, is it?'

Yul remembered the dead weight deliberately crushing his ribcage and the vicious thrust of a knee hard into his back.

'It was meant to hurt.'

'Oh come on, boy. Nobody ever got hurt by being sat on.'

'And he forced me to eat dirt. I thought I was going to choke.'

Magus surveyed him coldly.

'Hallfolk don't make people eat dirt, Yul, as you well know. I think you're twisting the facts to make yourself sound like the victim. You've broken several rules for which you'll be punished.'

'Yes, sir.'

Yul knew then that there'd be no justice. Magus had judged him guilty before even summoning him to the Hall. He should take Rosie's advice of the night before and accept whatever punishment Magus chose. But he wanted to scream at the injustice

45

and felt humiliatingly close to crying. Magus watched the boy and felt a surge of power deep in his abdomen, similar to the primeval pleasure of reining in and subduing a spirited horse.

'So, my boy, do you admit that you're in the wrong and deserve to be punished accordingly?'

'Yes, sir,' whispered Yul, his tongue cleaving to the roof of his mouth.

'Very wise. In that case, your punishment is as follows.'

He paused, noting how the boy was trying to mask his fear. He smiled slightly, prolonging the moment until Yul's eyes locked into his in supplication.

'In addition to your normal duties in the woods, you'll report to Woodland Cottage every evening and all day Saturday and Sunday, where you'll work until sunset. The new occupants are to be supplied with firewood and fresh water from the pump in the kitchen gardens. You're also to clear and dig over their back garden ready for planting up. Do you understand?'

Yul nodded, unable even to croak an answer. As punishments went it wasn't too bad. He wasn't to lose his job or be whipped. Unless Magus made a point of telling him, his father needn't know that he was helping the newcomers as a punishment. It would be heavy work and gruelling after a day's labour, but it wasn't unpleasant. The real sting came from the fact that he'd have no free time during daylight. Yul would lose his freedom just when spring was coaxing the beauty from the land. Magus' dark eyes examined the dirty boy before him, noticing his struggle to keep his anger and tears under control.

'I've chosen this particular punishment as a reminder. You'll be serving two Hallfolk and that is the role of the Villager, a fact you seem to have forgotten. Never insult a member of the Hallfolk again, and never disobey an adult. Those are two of our most fundamental laws and you've broken them both. You will also, of course, apologise to Buzzard and his friends for your rudeness and disobedience. I'll call them in now. You're very lucky I'm not having you whipped as well, so bear that in mind in the future. Do I make myself clear?'

'Yes, sir.'

Magus smiled.

'Good. It had better be a contrite and heart-felt apology, Yul, or else I may change my mind about the whipping.'

4

Sylvie took Magus' advice and walked in the woods every morning after breakfast. She loved the jubilation of birdsong, the profusion of pale yellow primroses and the tiny violets with their dark heart-shaped leaves. She felt so much better already; she was eating well, her breathing was easier and the eczema was healing miraculously fast. Every day as she reached the little clearing amongst the trees she stopped, remembering how Magus had laid hands on her and filled her with his healing energy. He had a true gift and she knew she'd always be indebted to him. She hadn't told Miranda about the strange experience; her mother wouldn't approve and probably wouldn't believe it either.

Miranda had other things on her mind anyway, Sylvie thought wryly. She was convinced her mother fancied Magus. She'd noticed all the signs – the giggling, fussing over her appearance, the breathless comments. She found it hilarious to see her serious mother behaving like a teenager. When she'd asked Miranda outright she'd been firmly ticked off and told to stop being ridiculous, which only confirmed her suspicions. Sylvie could understand it though. Magus was very attractive and he'd appeared like a knight in shining armour at Miranda's darkest hour. She just hoped her mother wouldn't make a fool of herself.

Sylvie had visited the Hall now on a couple of occasions and had been overwhelmed by its grandeur and beauty. She particularly loved the mediaeval and Tudor parts with their stone-flagged floors and dark panelling. There was a strange, magical atmosphere in these oldest wings of the Hall and Sylvie felt the history of the place seeping into her bones.

She also loved the massive Edwardian wing, which was used as the school. It had polished floors and large, well-proportioned rooms with French windows over-looking a long stone terrace and rolling lawns. It was a world away from the shabby comprehensive in London where she'd learnt to hate the education system. Sylvie had already been given her own computer with access to the network. The girls whom Magus had introduced to her were an attractive lot, many of them sharing the blond Hallfolk hair, although none as silvery as hers. She'd felt their curiosity but it wasn't hostile, and they were full of vitality and exuberance. When she started coming up for lessons she hoped to make some friends. In the meantime she'd collected books from the library to keep herself busy during the long peaceful days spent in the cottage.

The Village boy had started work in their garden and was different to the Hallfolk boys she'd seen in the school wing. She knew he was being punished and that she mustn't speak to him, but that made her more curious. On the first evening he'd arrived unannounced. They'd heard a noise outside and had seen him by the chopping block near the back door with an axe in his hand. She'd been fascinated by the long, almost black hair hanging in his eyes and the surly look on his hollowed face. There was an air of darkness and secrets about him which Sylvie found intriguing. He hadn't smiled or looked them in the eye when Miranda opened the door to acknowledge his presence, but muttered something in a rather outlandish Dorset accent. He'd chopped a pile of logs efficiently and stacked them in a little shelter built onto the cottage. Then he'd started digging the garden, continuing until it grew dark. Sylvie had watched him surreptitiously from her bedroom window and felt a little sorry for him. There was something almost tragic about him, as if he carried a deep wound inside.

She wondered what he'd done to deserve the punishment.

He came again the next night and started digging straight away. His hands were filthy and Sylvie couldn't understand how he got so dirty at school. His hair was wild; uncombed and curly and full of bits of twig and dead leaves. When he looked up she saw his eyes and was surprised at how attractive they were – a clear, deep grey and slightly slanted at the corners. He was handsome in a rough, dirty way she decided, and then felt annoyed with herself for even thinking such a thing. She was as bad as her mother.

Yul worked very hard that evening; it started to rain but he carried on. He had no coat, just a thin shirt, old trousers and the strange brown leather boots that Sylvie had seen other Villagers wear. When the rain grew heavier, Miranda opened the window and called out to him to go home if he liked. He didn't even answer but shook his head, becoming soaked to the bone as the shirt clung to his lean frame. Sylvie hated to see anyone looking so wet and exhausted. She asked Miranda if they could give him something to drink but her mother was anxious not to go against Magus' wishes.

Magus called in at Woodland Cottage one morning not long after, while Sylvie was out on her morning walk. It was Sunday, the day of leisure at Stonewylde. There was skittles in the pub, games for the children in the Great Barn and archery practice on the Village Green. Boys went up to the warrens armed with catapults and heavy sticks, for rabbits were plentiful and formed a staple part of the Villagers' diet. On the playing fields by the river youngsters played the Stonewylde versions of hockey and rugby. In the Village School there was country dancing, with many practising the intricate Maypole dance for the next festival, whilst in the Nursery, musicians taught interested youngsters how to play a variety of instruments. Yul, however, turned up at Woodland Cottage.

Earlier he'd noticed Sylvie leave by the front gate heading for the woods. He'd seen her out walking on several occasions, usually around the same time, and found reasons to be there himself. He always remained hidden, perfectly camouflaged in his rough clothes, but he liked to watch her as she wandered along the path. She gazed around and stopped frequently to examine flowers and plants, and often closed her eyes and just stood still, smiling slightly. Yul thought her beautiful, especially now her skin had lost most of its sore patches. Her silky hair was like a waterfall around her delicate face; her silvery eyes seemed far away and dreamy. When he saw her like this, alone in the woods, he felt a strange and almost painful sensation inside. He wanted to protect her, although from what he didn't know. But he didn't dare even show himself, let alone talk to her.

Yul was digging when he heard the front gate creak open. He looked up, thinking it was Sylvie returning, but saw through the windows of the sitting room that it was Magus. Luckily he was here and hard at work. He glanced again and saw the silhouette of Magus inside the sitting room. The great man came to stand by the window and watched for a moment. Yul nodded respectfully and put his back into the digging. Inside the cottage Magus sat down in one of the comfortable armchairs whilst Miranda made coffee.

'I came to invite you and Sylvie down to the Village this evening. We have these wonderful storytelling events every so often and they're great fun. I know you'll both enjoy it tonight, even though it's not really a Hallfolk thing.'

'Storytelling? That does sound fun, and very traditional too,' said Miranda warmly.

'Well, the Villagers don't have television or film, so this is something special for them. Everyone needs the power and magic of story in their lives. It's a very basic human need.'

'Oh yes, absolutely! But I hadn't realised the Villagers don't have television. Isn't there an uproar?'

'Not at all. You don't miss what you've never had and, believe me, their lives are the better for it.'

'But isn't that terribly elitist? You have television at the Hall, after all. Is it fair to deny the Villagers something which is such a crucial part of our culture? Shouldn't they at least have the choice?'

Magus smiled as he sipped the coffee, his eyes appraising her in a way that made her feel like a schoolgirl again. She remembered that they were alone in the cottage, and found the coffee cup trembling slightly in her hand.

'You're very refreshing, Miranda,' he said. 'I'm not used to being challenged by anyone at Stonewylde. The point is that television may be crucial to your culture, or indeed, Outside World culture, but it's irrelevant at Stonewylde. I explained the day you arrived that we've had to cut ourselves off in order to preserve our community. Television, radio, film, newspapers – they're all modern media that have no place here. It would be an invasion, a threat, to bring such things into the Village. Can you imagine what it would do to our way of life?'

'No, of course I can see that modern media wouldn't fit in here,' she said. 'I can honestly say I haven't missed any of it since we arrived. But I just thought the people in the Village should have a choice.'

'It wouldn't work. Simply by giving them access to the contemporary world with its rampant consumerism, we'd shatter the simplicity and harmony of their lives irrevocably.'

'I suppose . . .'

'You don't know how our society works here, Miranda. The Villagers live the lives of their mediaeval ancestors, but without the negative aspects like disease, hunger and exploitation. They're in touch with the natural world in a way that's virtually unheard of nowadays in western civilization. They're productive and creative, and not materialistic or avaricious in any sense. Television – and all the other stuff – would destroy that.'

'Yes, I can see what you mean, but what about the Hallfolk? It doesn't really seem fair. They visit the Outside World you said, and there's television and the Internet at the Hall. They have a choice.'

'Yes, they do, and many of them choose to leave Stonewylde

for good. They hanker for the modern world and find it stifling and slow here. Likewise, many leave, then become disillusioned and want to come back again. And most of them flit between the two worlds, spending time in both. But they're educated differently to the Villagers. They're taught to analyse and make informed decisions.'

'But is that right? Surely the Villagers should also be taught to analyse and make decisions.'

'It's a matter of intelligence. We're a closed community and our gene pool is relatively small. The Villagers are practical, hardworking and physical, and they're the lifeblood of the community. But they're not generally intelligent in the cerebral sense. They accept their position in Stonewylde society because they don't question anything and don't want the responsibilities they know the Hallfolk's lifestyles bring.'

'But surely there must be some intelligent Villagers? You make them sound like a bunch of half-witted peasants!'

Magus threw back his head and roared with laughter at this. He rose from the armchair and stretched, smiling down at her, his dark eyes dancing with amusement.

'I'm so pleased you've come to Stonewylde, Miranda. I'm looking forward to getting to know you better. I think your arrival will shake us all up a bit.'

She felt herself going pink at this, watching him covertly as he moved over to the window to observe the boy in the back garden.

'How's Yul been doing? Turned up every evening, I trust? Working hard?'

'Yes, very hard indeed. He even carried on when it was pouring with rain.'

'And so he should. Rain never hurt anyone. And neither did hard labour.'

'May we offer him a drink or something to eat? He's quite thin and Sylvie and I feel a little sorry for him.'

Magus turned to her, his eyes hard, and Miranda felt a prickle of shock.

'Absolutely not! He's not thin, just fit and wiry. And he's here as a punishment, not to be fed and watered. If I think you're molly-coddling him then I'll find him something far more unpleasant to do. As it is I'm beginning to think I've let him off too lightly.'

Miranda stood up and joined Magus at the window, peering out at the boy in the garden. Sweat ran down his grimy face as he put all his energy into digging the heavy soil. He straightened, his back obviously aching, and pushed the damp hair from his eyes leaving a great streak of mud across his face. Then he glanced across at the window and saw the two adults watching him. With almost ludicrous alacrity he took up the spade and set to again. Magus smiled and sat down, accepting another cup of coffee.

'It's all a question of multiple intelligences, to return to your question. Many of the Villagers are very creative and have great physical and motor intelligence. Not so many are academically gifted. That's why we gear their Village School and curriculum to their needs. But we regularly screen every child. If any Villager shows real potential they're moved up to the Hall School, and eventually will live there and become one of the Hallfolk.'

'Well that sounds a little fairer,' said Miranda. 'I'm not criticising but I really hate to see anyone kept down because of a social thing. I saw too much of that in London – kids never standing a chance in life because they were born in the wrong place. Stonewylde does seem very feudal. You know: the lord of the manor and his privileged family living in luxury while the unwashed villeins do all the hard labour. But I can see perhaps it's not quite as simple as that.'

Magus sighed impatiently.

'No it's not, and as you settle in you'll see the logic and fairness of life in the community. Believe me, Miranda, the Villagers lead very full and happy lives. They're certainly not exploited, which is what you're implying.'

'No, I'm—'

'You're mistakenly equating hard physical work with a poor, unfulfilled life. But it's not like that! I sometimes wish my life was as rich and uncomplicated as the Villagers'.'

He stood up again, brimming with a restless energy that prevented him from relaxing for any length of time. Miranda could almost feel the crackle in the air around him.

'I'm sorry if I've offended you,' she said hastily. 'I realise it's not my place to start questioning the social structure here.'

'You haven't offended me,' he said. 'You just don't understand yet. I realise that to an Outsider, Stonewylde must seem archaic and maybe even cruel. In time you'll see just what a perfect society we have here.'

She nodded, hoping he wasn't irritated. She didn't wish to antagonise him with misplaced criticism. His warmth and approval were like sunshine and she wanted to bask in it without any dark clouds of displeasure threatening to overshadow her.

'So what time should we come to the Village tonight, for the storytelling?'

'Come at dusk, and don't eat beforehand because there'll be food and drink in the Great Barn.'

'Do we need to bring any money?'

He chuckled at this.

'Miranda, haven't you realised yet? We don't use money at Stonewylde.'

'Really? No I hadn't realised! How extraordinary!'

'You have so much to learn about our lifestyle. You must remember that before you pass any judgements. But we've all the time in the world for you to get to know our ways and become one of us. And I really must go now. Come to the Village at sunset. You're in for a treat tonight, I promise.'

'Who's the storyteller? Someone famous?'

'He is, actually. He's a bit of a nomad, our Clip, and he's just got back from Australia. You can meet him properly tomorrow up at the Hall if you wish.'

'So he's one of the Hallfolk?'

'Oh yes, I should say so. He's my half-brother!'

The late March afternoon wore on slowly, showers and sunshine chasing each other in the cool breeze as Yul continued clearing the overgrown garden. He'd stopped at mid-day to eat his bread and cheese, but now felt quite faint with hunger. The light was fading and soon he'd be able to stop. He was desperate to leave and get back to the Village for the Story Web in the Great Barn tonight.

As he arrived in the Village he realised how late it was. The main cobbled street and Village Green were deserted which meant everyone must be in the Barn already. Picking up clean clothes from his cottage, he hurried to the bath house. The doors were shut and the place empty. Yul lit a lantern and looked around. All the bath cubicles were vacant, as was the communal shower room. Piles of rough, clean towels were stacked neatly by the entrance. Yul heard the boilers heating the water, partly fuelled by the solar panels on the roof and partly by the wood-burning stoves. With nobody else around, the water would be piping hot for once.

Half an hour later a very different boy emerged, scrubbed and glowing, hair glossy and fingernails clean. He left his muddy work-clothes bundled up outside the doors to collect later and hurried along to the Great Barn. He could hear nothing for the doors were shut, but guessed that Clip would be in the middle of his preamble to the first story. He slipped in one of the small side doors and was hit by a wall of warm air and the smell of many people gathered together. The Great Barn was transformed into a theatre in the round, with tiers of wooden benches encircling a central stage. The entire Village community was seated on the benches, all focused on the man who stood in the centre.

Clip was dressed in sky-blue robes decorated with silver stars and strange symbols. His hair was pale blond like Magus', but he wore it much longer, hanging to his shoulders in wispy strands. He was tall too, but not so powerfully built. His eyes were deep and penetrating and his face lined, from hard living rather than old age. He shared Magus' magnetism and the audience was spellbound. He was in the middle of a story, his soft voice filling the Barn, long arms moving gracefully to emphasise a point. A small fire flickered on the stage, the smoke rising to find an opening concealed in the roof. The firelight etched lines and hollows in his face, for the Barn was only dimly lit. The air was aromatic and tense with anticipation.

Yul wriggled down a narrow aisle between two tiers of benches and crept onto a seat at the front. The firelight lit him too, making his loose white shirt and the clear whites of his eyes gleam in the shadowy light. His glowing skin and hair were burnished by the flickering of the flames, and Sylvie stared hard at this person who'd just appeared. She and Miranda were sitting opposite him, near the front with a small group of Hallfolk. Sylvie couldn't decide if this attractive boy was actually Yul, whom she'd left filthy and exhausted in her back garden amongst the weeds and mud only an hour ago. It looked like him and yet the transformation was astounding.

Clip wove the story in and out, around and around, encircling the audience and catching them in his threads until he had them trapped and waiting for the finale. The fire suddenly flared into brilliant blue flames as he ended with a flourish. People roared their appreciation and the applause was thunderous. They were invited to have a break for food and drink. Yul slipped away as soon as the story finished and ravenously helped himself to food. He saw his mother and waved; she smiled her approval at his clean and presentable appearance. He also noticed Alwyn over by the bar swallowing down a tankard of cider as fast as he could, dribbles of the liquid running off his chin into his collar. He finished the drink and immediately held out the tankard to be refilled from one of the barrels. He looked up and caught Yul watching him; his face darkened instantly. Yul quickly broke eye contact and melted away into the shadows. He thought it best to go outside for a while to avoid his father.

It was cool and fresh and the stars glittered above. A fat,

gibbous moon hung over the trees. Yul felt content; clean and full of food at last, with the prospect of another story to come. He leant against the stone wall of the Barn and breathed deeply, his tired muscles relaxing.

'Don't you agree, Clip, the likeness is uncanny? It could almost be her.'

Yul jumped at the sound of Magus' voice coming from the other side of a stone buttress.

'You're right. Just like that photo in the archive room, the one in the silver frame. She's almost identical.'

'I tell you, the day she walked into my office in London I went cold. Hazel had said she looked like Hallfolk but I'd no idea ... The face, the hair, the eyes – everything's exactly the same. I'm only going from the photo, of course, but you remember her better.'

'Not that much. I was very young myself when she died and we didn't see her often even when she was here, did we? Where did you find this girl?'

'Living in some wretched tower block in London. She's been seriously ill but the Earth Magic has started to heal her and she's a great deal better already. Hazel came across her by pure chance at the hospital where she's working.'

'But we know nothing ever happens by pure chance, don't we? There's obviously a purpose, a reason for her coming here. It's just too much of a coincidence, that extraordinary likeness. Doubtless all will be revealed when the time is right. How old is she?'

'Fourteen, coming up to fifteen at the Summer Solstice, would you believe? Definitely one of us! And there's something else about her ... I can't quite put my finger on it. She's got a certain quality ... Anyway, we need to get back inside. Are you ready?'

'Give me a moment to finish this divine cake. Nothing else compares with Violet's special cakes. Make sure you keep me supplied with regular batches next time I'm away.'

'Clip, if I knew where you were, I would. But you disappear off the face of the Earth.'

'Alright, I'm ready now. You'll like the next story; it's an Aborigine myth. Watch the staff carefully.'

'Oh no,' chuckled Magus. 'I know when to look away. You won't catch me out with your tricks. I know you far too well for that.'

Yul wove his way through the crowds to get back to his seat for the second half, still puzzling over the strange conversation he'd overheard. Suddenly he found himself face to face with Sylvie and Miranda, also trying to get to their seats.

'It *is* you!' gasped Sylvie, touching his sleeve.

He looked down at her upturned face. For the first time, Yul stared into her eyes, so beautiful and strange. She smiled and he felt blessed by her warmth. He smiled back, unable to tear his gaze from hers, his heart hammering unexpectedly.

'Sylvie!' hissed Miranda. 'Come on!'

She yanked her daughter away and Yul stood perfectly still amongst the jostling crowd, shocked at the intensity of his emotions.

People were finding their seats; some, including Alwyn, still lingered by the bar and food tables. Clip stepped onto the central stage and there was instant hush. Those still standing quickly found their seats and everyone was still. He had exchanged his robes for a strange garment made from strips of every colour, iridescent and vivid and swirling about his spare frame. In his hand he held a long wooden staff. He began to move around the stage slowly, circling the fire, walking a spiral pattern that turned in and out of itself. He spun as he moved so the rainbow strips shimmered and fluttered about him. He started to hum, then softly chant. The people picked up the chant and joined him until the great building was filled with the sound. He began to move faster and the rainbow blurred. He was difficult to look at. Something strange was happening on the stage.

The chanting rose to a crescendo and there was a mighty green flash. A black bird appeared in the circle of the stage, wings flapping. It settled onto Clip's shoulder and pecked at his hair.

'Long, long ago there was … a raven!' he intoned in his

musical voice. Many people gasped at this and there was a fidgeting and rustling along the benches. Yul noticed Magus frown, shaking his head slightly. Clip smiled and winked at him.

The story continued, weaving and weaving its strands; a tale of magical animals and birds, of the world being born and the power of the rainbow over the people. The story was told as darkness fell, and Clip held everyone spellbound as he danced around the stage, staff in hand, with the black bird – a jackdaw, not a raven – on his shoulder. Yul sensed that the story was heading towards its climax and felt a drowsy dreaminess creep over him. The air was sweet with the smell of herbs and spices burnt on the fire. The storyteller's voice had dropped to a soft chant, almost an incantation. Yul dragged his eyes away from the swirling rainbow colours of Clip's robes and looked at the firelit faces of the audience around the circle. All shared the same faraway, mesmerised look.

The hum started again and grew louder and louder. The story-teller's voice told of the magical Rainbow Snake which wriggled and writhed into the world. As he whispered, every person in the Great Barn was completely silent, all leaning forward enraptured. Clip held his great staff horizontally across the palms of his hands. He circled the stage again, leaning out towards the audience as if offering the staff to them. Yul watched with fixed eyes and saw the staff begin to change colour. The bleached wood took on the hues of the rainbow, subtly at first, then deeper and brighter. When the staff came close to him, Yul's eyes widened in amazement. He could've sworn it wriggled slightly.

'See the snake! See the Rainbow Snake!' chanted Clip, pacing the circumference of the stage, a sea of faces gaping at him open-mouthed. Yul felt his hand twitch involuntarily, reaching towards the rainbow-coloured stick which was now definitely moving. Clip noticed the boy's movement. But rather than with-drawing the staff from reach so his sleight of hand would go unchallenged, he smiled. His deep eyes burned into the boy's.

'This boy sees! This boy sees the snake! Come, boy. Come and touch her.'

He beckoned to Yul, his eyes gleaming and mesmeric, his smile saturnine. Without thinking, Yul rose from the bench and stepped onto the stage, his hand still outstretched. Clip offered the snake to him and Yul touched it. His sharp gasp was audible throughout the Barn.

'It's real!' he whispered.

'Behold, the Rainbow Snake! Do you feel her scales?'

'Yes!'

'Do you feel her move?'

'Yes!'

'Now take the snake, boy. Take her in your hands.'

Yul held out his hands, palms outstretched, and Clip placed the writhing snake there. Yul felt the cool roughness of the scales, the pulsating life in the lithe body.

'Hold her up to the skies! Raise her above your head!'

Yul lifted his arms high, the snake slightly drooping between his hands. Clip continued the story but Yul found he couldn't concentrate; all his energy was focused on holding the great snake up to the roof. He heard Clip shout. With a cry the bird flew from his shoulder in a mad flapping. There was an enormous bang and a flash, this time a spectrum of colours, and the sharp smell of gunpowder. He felt the snake's body go rigid. He looked up and realised he was holding a bleached wooden staff once again.

The crowd went wild, clapping, shouting and stamping feet. Yul slowly lowered his arms and passed the staff to Clip, who took it with a bow and smiled conspiratorially.

'And a cheer for the boy who believed, and whose belief made the magic more powerful!'

Everyone clapped with renewed vigour and Yul returned to his seat, burning with embarrassment but also pride. He knew he'd been part of the enchantment that night.

The following night Sylvie lay in her bed listening to the eerie cries of an owl in the woods. She couldn't stop thinking about the Story Web of the night before. She was convinced she'd witnessed real magic. How else could the change have happened? There was no way the snake or the staff could have been concealed and switched – it just wasn't possible. This had been a genuine transformation, true magic, rather than trickery. Yul's amazement as he held the snake had clearly been genuine.

As she thought of Yul she felt a little thrill of excitement. He'd looked so handsome standing up on the stage and she sighed, remembering the dark curls falling into his eyes, his high cheekbones and chiselled jaw accentuated by the firelight. The moment when she'd bumped into him had been a revelation. Those slanting grey eyes had held hers for a long heartbeat. When he'd smiled at her it was like the sun blazing suddenly from behind a dark cloud. She'd only ever seen him sullen and miserable; this was a different boy. Her heart had leapt at the sheer energy and vitality behind that smile. Sylvie had admired his slim, straight body as he held the heavy snake above his head, and decided that he was far more interesting than any of the Hallfolk boys she'd seen.

But then she recalled sadly how he'd been this evening in the garden. She'd looked forward to his arrival all day. But he'd reverted to his old self, ignoring her as she stood in the window and keeping his head down as he thrust the spade into the earth with almost vicious dedication. It wasn't until Sylvie had tapped on the window to wave, and he'd looked up like a startled rabbit, that she'd noticed the black eye. He looked away instantly but in the second before he hid behind his hair, she'd clearly seen it. His eyebrow was swollen and cut, the skin dark around his puffy eye. Sylvie had felt so disappointed. He'd probably been brawling in the street after the storytelling, which just confirmed what Magus had told them about him being a trouble-maker. It was difficult to equate the beautiful smiling boy of last night with the sullen wretch of this evening.

Putting her silly feelings of disenchantment aside, Sylvie closed her eyes and breathed in the night smells of the woods flowing in through her open window. The owl was still calling outside, joined now by another. She smiled in the darkness, remembering the smells and sounds of night time in London. Traffic, sirens, shouting and screams, and the sour, filthy smell of the streets. But this was paradise. She'd never before felt so calm and at peace with her environment. Everything about Stonewylde was perfect.

Sylvie knew she was becoming more confident and today, at Magus' invitation, she and Miranda had visited the Hall to meet the storyteller Clip. He was as bizarre in the daylight as he'd been the night before. Today he'd worn a purple robe and had smelt of incense, his pale hair falling to his shoulders, light grey eyes startling in such a tanned and lean face. He'd been very charming, fussing over them both and ushering them up to the strange round tower attached to the Hall where he lived when he was home.

They'd sat on old leather sofas while Clip made some exotic tea. His tower was like a magpie's nest of treasures, and Sylvie and her mother stared around in bemusement at the curious objects that crowded every surface of the circular room. Clip explained that he travelled extensively and collected things wherever he went; stones, pieces of wood, native artefacts. He told them how he loved to roam the world, living simply off the land with the indigenous people and gathering stories and magic. He said if he stayed too long at Stonewylde, much as he loved it, he began to feel claustrophobic. He preferred the spartan life of the nomad to the luxuries of living at the Hall.

Sylvie had enjoyed talking to him and listening to some of his tales. He was other-worldly and eccentric, and she liked that. His grey eyes twinkled and he moved about the huge circular room restlessly, his long, thin limbs almost dancing with nervous energy as he showed them precious things and fed them snippets of information. Sylvie had felt at ease with him. He seemed kind; less overpowering than Magus whose presence could sometimes be almost too intense.

Miranda, however, had been less enthralled, suspicious of his strangeness and uncomfortable in his company. So Sylvie had

had to do the talking, asking him questions and telling him of their life in London before Magus had transported them to this place of her dreams. He'd smiled at her enthusiasm.

'You do belong here, Sylvie,' he'd said. 'It's in your voice, the way you speak of Stonewylde. Sol's told me just how ill you were when you first came here barely two weeks ago. The magic of Stonewylde is healing you.'

'Sol? Do you mean Magus?'

'Yes of course. Magus is only his title. His name's Sol, short for Solstice.'

'And Clip? Short for . . . ?'

'Eclipse. I was born on the night of a full lunar eclipse. And Sol at the Summer Solstice.'

'And you're half-brothers?'

'That's right. Same mother but different fathers. When my father died, Sol's father became my guardian and took over the running of Stonewylde as I was only a child.'

'But then he passed it on to his son? Why not you? I don't understand . . .'

'Leading the community is something I've never wanted to do. Sol and I grew up as brothers but we're very different. He can't understand why I need to travel and roam. I can't understand how he can be so rooted. Even though he regularly visits the Outside World to run his company, he can't bear to be away from Stonewylde for long.'

'I see. So you're happy for Magus to be in charge?'

'Yes – he's a good leader and I'm certainly not! Strange how things work out.'

Sylvie noticed the great staff from the Story Web propped against the wall and rose to take a closer look. Her fingers traced the smooth wood in wonder.

'How did you do it?' she asked in awe. 'I'd never have believed such magic could happen right in front of me.'

Clip smiled, his eyes bright, and shook his head.

'Magic cannot be explained,' he said softly.

'And no conjuror divulges his tricks,' said Miranda stiffly.

'It wasn't a trick, Mum!' said Sylvie. She felt embarrassed at her mother's coolness towards this fascinating man who was, after all, the owner of Stonewylde and as such deserving of her civility. 'You saw Yul and his reaction when he touched the snake. That was genuine, I'm sure.'

'Ah yes, the boy. He was very good.'

'Yul's been working in our garden every evening,' said Sylvie. 'As a punishment.'

'Really? Well, the boy was a help to me last night.'

'So just how did it happen?' said Sylvie, still stroking the staff. 'I've been racking my brains to think how you made a piece of wood change into a live snake.'

But Clip had merely smiled enigmatically, staring deep into her eyes until she felt almost uncomfortable.

'Seeing is believing,' he'd replied, as if that explained everything.

Sylvie now opened her eyes in the darkness, restless and still unable to fall asleep. She knew why; the cause peered through the branches at her. The moon was now almost full. She thought of her mother sitting downstairs, reading some of the texts she'd soon be teaching. She hadn't told Miranda of her fears, which grew nightly as the moon waxed fuller. She knew how worried her mother had been in London at her apparent madness every month, even though they never discussed it. The lunacy had become a taboo subject, for Miranda couldn't believe that Sylvie had no control over her actions as the full moon rose. Sylvie had never been able to talk about it openly and explain her feelings.

How could Miranda understand what the full moon did to Sylvie when she didn't understand it herself? She'd hoped that coming to Stonewylde would cure her of it, just as it was curing her other ailments. But inside she knew that nothing had changed. In another night or so the moon would be full, and she felt it calling to her. In fact it was even stronger here at Stonewylde than in London. Nor did it help that the moon shone in through her bedroom window, bathing her in silver all night long. Maybe she should ask Magus for advice. But she decided to wait until she knew him a little better, and anyway, he probably wouldn't understand. Nobody understood what happened to her at the rising of the full moon.

5

It was late afternoon and Sylvie paced the sitting room restlessly. The tension and frustration were building as sunset drew closer. She looked out into the garden where Yul was again hard at work thrusting his spade savagely into the heavy clods, his pent-up anger releasing itself into the earth. Miranda came over and watched him for a moment, fascinated by the dark energy of the boy. She'd seen the same anger and aggression in teenage boys she'd taught in London; there it spilled out into violence and vandalism. At least, she thought, at Stonewylde it was put to good use and channelled into hard physical labour.

'Sylvie, will you be alright if I go up to the Hall for a while? Or do you want to come with me?' asked Miranda, turning from the window. 'I need to use the Internet and get some more books.'

'Of course I'll be alright,' Sylvie replied. 'You go on up.'

'I thought I may stay there and go straight into dinner rather than come home first.'

'Good idea.'

'Will you be alright coming up on your own to the Dining Hall? You won't be scared in the dark?'

'For goodness sake, Mum, I'm not a baby!'

'There's no need to snap, Sylvie!'

'Well honestly, you fuss over me all the time and I'm sick to death of it!'

Miranda frowned in bewilderment, at a loss to understand where this was coming from.

67

'Oh Mum, I'm sorry!' groaned Sylvie. 'Please don't look like that. You know I don't really mean it.'

'Maybe it's your hormones, Sylvie. Perhaps you're starting all the awful moody adolescent stuff?'

'I don't think so, Mum. Look at me! It's ridiculous. I'll be fifteen in a few months' time but I still look about ten years old.'

'Actually, you don't. I was only thinking today that you've started changing recently. I've heard that sometimes if development has been delayed, as yours has, when it does happen it's really fast.'

'About time too! Anyway, I'll be fine on my own here. In fact, I'll stay here for the evening and have a sandwich. I don't really fancy coming up to the Hall.'

Miranda looked doubtfully at her daughter.

'Alright. I'll be back around nine. Just make sure . . .'

'Don't say it! I'll be fine. And please don't hurry back.'

'Sylvie! That's very hurtful.'

'I just meant don't worry and rush back to check up on me. Please, Mum. I can't stand the fussing. I'm not sick now, and I'm not a little kid anymore.'

'Alright. But don't talk to that boy out there. Remember what Magus said about him.'

'Yeah, yeah.'

'Sylvie! I mean it. There's something wild about him, something almost dangerous. He looks so angry. Even without Magus' warnings I don't like the thought of you having anything to do with him.'

'Okay, Mum. He's not exactly friendly anyway.'

Miranda finally left and Sylvie threw herself into an armchair with a groan. Her mother was driving her up the wall. How come she'd never noticed before just how irritating she was? The sooner she could start school the better. She looked out of the window again. It was a lovely clear evening and the garden was bathed in golden light. Yul's cheeks were hollow and shadowy and the hair fell over his eyes as he attacked the clods of earth. Her mother was right – there was something wild about him. His

68

powerful arms thrust the spade viciously into the earth and she saw the muscles in his back rippling as his thin shirt pulled taut with every swing of the spade.

Sylvie felt a rush of something she'd never felt before, a visceral somersault of longing deep down inside. Her fingertips trembled and there was a strange feeling in her chest as she gazed at him. Then she remembered; tonight was the full moon and the sun was nearly setting. Of course her bizarre feelings had nothing to do with Yul at all – this was her moon madness starting.

Feeling a little reckless, she opened the back door and walked into the garden, stopping at the sea of mud.

'Would you like a drink?'

Yul looked up in surprise. He hesitated and then nodded. She returned with a glass of water, which he gulped down in one.

'I'll get you another.'

She returned with more water and a piece of Cherry's fruit cake. He took both with muddy hands and drank the water first, before biting hungrily into the cake. She watched in fascination. Then she noticed the black eye again, as he shook his hair back from his sweaty face. It was nasty – the skin around the eye dark and swollen.

'How did you get the black eye?'

He shrugged, still wolfing down the cake.

'Did you have a fight with someone?'

His face darkened.

'Yeah, something like that.'

He brushed the crumbs from his hands, picked up the spade and turned his back on her.

'Thanks for that,' he mumbled.

'It's okay. Can't you stop and talk for a while?'

She was amazed at herself. Maybe it was the moon madness making her more assertive. He shook his head.

'I daren't. If Magus sees I'll be in even more trouble.'

'Why? What have you done?'

'Please, miss, I can't talk to you. Leave me alone and let me get on with my work.'

'Fine! If that's how you feel. I was only trying to be friendly.'

With a flounce she turned around and stamped back into the house, slamming the back door. Then she felt stupid and childish and wished she hadn't. She wanted to scream. Nothing went right for her. First her silly mother annoyed her and now this boy wouldn't talk to her. What to do, what to do? She marched around the room, touching things, kicking the armchair, wanting to yell, full of twitchy energy.

Yul continued to dig, cursing himself for a fool. She'd come out specially and had been kind to him but he'd been surly and unfriendly. She'd probably never bother speaking to him again. That possibility twisted his heart.

But ... she'd asked about his black eye, the humiliating evidence that he was a pathetic victim and at his father's mercy. Once again, Alwyn had branded him for all the community to pity. He simply couldn't bear the thought of that beautiful girl feeling sorry for him. Molten anger welled up inside him and he yelled out loud into the still garden. Yul hated his father more than anyone had ever hated anybody before. He carried this hatred like a great black serpent inside him. He'd done nothing wrong, nothing to deserve the beating he'd suffered.

Yul remembered how happy he'd been on the night of the Story Web. He'd felt honoured to have been part of the magic, and proud that Clip had chosen him to go up on the stage. When he'd arrived home that night, his mother and Rosie had just got back themselves and were making tea. The younger ones were sleeping in the Village School with all the other children. His mother and sister had made a fuss of him and Yul had just started explaining how the snake had felt when the door crashed open and Alwyn stomped in. Yul seethed at the memory.

Alwyn was spoiling for a fight, his jaw jutting aggressively and his small eyes alight with belligerence. He picked first on Rosie and then Maizie, both of whom jumped to obey him. Then he turned on Yul. He berated the boy for showing off, for making a fool of himself on the stage and thinking he was better than everyone else. Yul kept his head down and did nothing to antagonise his father in any way. His very lack of response seemed to enrage Alwyn even further. Maizie could see what was coming and tried to get Yul and Rosie up to bed. But Alwyn needed to vent his brutality and of course it was Yul who bore the brunt of it.

Alwyn had knocked him about the cottage until the boy was a cowering heap on the floor. Then he'd taken the strap from its hook. Rosie ran and shut herself in her room, trying to block the sounds that carried up the stairs. Maizie stood in the kitchen trembling, tears running down her face, her hands over her ears. She longed to protect her son, to beg Alwyn to stop the beating. But she knew from experience that any intervention on her part only made him worse. So she stood huddled up in the kitchen whilst Alwyn laid into Yul.

At last his anger was assuaged. The beefy man stood panting with exertion, his face scarlet and the room reeking of his sweat. He grimly surveyed the boy lying at his feet. Then grabbing hold of his damaged shirt, he hauled him upright.

'Hang up the strap,' he growled, and Yul staggered across to the door to obey. He was shaking so badly he could barely hook the piece of leather onto its nail.

'Let that be a lesson to you. You're not special. You're the bottom of the pile and don't you forget it. I don't want to see you showing off again. Next time I'll use the whip and then you'll be sorry. Now get up to bed, you little shit!'

With a grunt he aimed a kick but Yul was already halfway up the stairs, trying to control the urge to retch. He was alive with pain. But the worst of it was the searing rage in his heart. Another beating in a long line of punishments stretching back as far as he could remember. He wouldn't forget this night. The memory of it now was enough to make Yul's fists clench with overwhelming, white-hot desire for revenge.

Sylvie looked out of the front window. The shadows were growing longer. Soon the sun would set. The daylight would start to fade and then the hush would come, the expectant hush as the moon's rim cleared the horizon. A strange tingling like fiery

71

ice shot through her. She had to get out of this confinement and into the open. She banged out of the front door, tripped up the garden path and turned towards the woods.

Yul saw her leave and wondered. Surely she should be going to the Hall for dinner? The thought of food made his stomach tighten. As the sun was now almost set he decided he could at last go home. His mother would have kept him some supper and he was starving hungry. He put the spade away and trudged to the back gate leading into the fields and the muddy short-cut down to the Village.

He paused. Why had she taken the path into the woods? He'd seen her mother leave a while ago for the Hall. Sylvie obviously wasn't going to join her. It would be dark fairly soon. Suppose she got lost, or fell and hurt herself? He knew the woods well but she certainly didn't. He felt again that urge to protect her, and retraced his steps. He went round the cottage and out through the front gate, turning towards the trees as she'd done.

Now I can breathe and feel the earth under my feet. The moon will bless me! She calls to me and tonight, at last, I can come to her.

Yul saw her shoes lying abandoned on the path and frowned. What was going on? He caught a glimpse of her pale blue dress up ahead and quickened his pace. Why had she taken her shoes off? He heard her voice rising above the soft call of the wood-pigeons. She was humming; a strange, high sound that carried in the still evening air. He saw her hair gleaming almost white in the dusky woods. The sun had gone down and the sky was soft with fading light. The trees thickened around the path, which now wound deeper into the heart of the woodland.

Lovely trees reach for the sky, reach to touch the silver moon. I shall sing her a song of reverence and honour. She is rising!

The music she sang made Yul's skin prickle. It was like no other song he'd ever heard, with words that were not words but reminded him of birdsong. He narrowed the gap between them and wondered whether he should call out and let her know he was there. He knew her name was Sylvie. Sylvie with the silver hair. Should he call her name?

She walked fast, speeding through the woods, pale hair rippling over her shoulders and down her back. Her feet and legs were bare beneath the blue dress and she skipped in her haste. Then suddenly she stopped dead. Yul almost ran into her. Slowly she started to raise both arms into the air as if unfolding her wings. Yul felt the hair on the back of his neck rise. Was she mad? What on earth was she up to?

She turned to face him and he blinked in shock. This deep in the woods the light was fading fast. But he could see enough to recognise that she was in some kind of a trance. Her beautiful silver-grey eyes were wide open and fixed. Her lips were moving and the strange noises still poured from her. She stared upwards through the branches, her arms stretched to the heavens. And then the truth dawned on him.

She is rising! She brings bright blessings to all. I sing to your beauty and magic, my silver lady. At last I am here to honour you.

He'd seen moongazy hares like this. He knew about moon magic. She was in the thrall of the rising moon and was glorying in it. He'd known she was special from the first moment he'd seen her walking in the woods with Magus. She was moongazy. Now he understood. And he knew how to help her too.

'Come with me, Sylvie,' he said gently, moving up close to her. She turned sightless eyes to him, listening. 'I'll take you to a special place where you can gaze at her in all her beauty. Come with me, Sylvie.'

She allowed him to bring her arms down and put a hand on her elbow, guiding her along the path.

'Just a little way along here and then we can cut out of the side of the woods and climb to the hill-top. Just a little further, Sylvie.'

She walked silently with him and he felt a great joy in his heart to be so close to her. Within a few minutes they were off the main path and heading to the edge of the woods. Here the sky was a much lighter shade of blue than amongst the dark trees. They left the trees behind and stepped onto the grass. Sheep were scattered around grazing quietly in the slight mist

73

that rose from the warm earth. Yul and Sylvie made their way up the hill towards the top, skirting around the boulders. It was quite steep but Sylvie climbed with light feet, humming again under her breath. Yul felt the silken brush of her hair on his hand. He longed to feel it between his fingers and stroke down the flaxen length of it, but he couldn't take advantage of her entranced state.

It was violet twilight when they reached the summit of the hill. A single standing stone rose from the ground, ancient and sacred. The grass here was cropped short by the nibbling of many teeth. It was the place of the hares. Yul led Sylvie towards the stone and when they reached it, he gently turned her around. They looked together across the purple folds of land stretching away towards the sea.

On the horizon floated the moon, pink and misty. A strange keening rose from Sylvie's throat, a cry of mingled joy and longing. Yul still held her elbow and felt her body shudder. Her arms rose up again as if she spread her wings and he let her go. She needed to dance, to fly. She raised herself onto tiptoes, poised, and then she was off.

Yul slid down to the ground in his usual spot, his back against the tall standing stone, and watched her dance. She seemed to fly over the grass, skipping, leaping, arms reaching out in joy. She was as graceful and light as thistledown in a summer breeze. She danced around the stone in a great spiral, sometimes singing her strange song, sometimes silent. Her silver hair flew out and her white limbs flowed. Yul had never witnessed anything like it. She was joined by a trio of hares, speeding long-limbed around the magical circle. Yul had seen hares do this before but he'd never dreamt they'd dance with a girl, even one so moongazy.

The moon rose from her violet bed up and across the sky, turning first pink-gold, then gold, and finally buttermilk silver. Shy stars prickled through the darkening sky to take their place in the dance. Still Sylvie danced with the hares, more gently now. The silver of the moon gleamed on her hair and in her eyes; her skin glowed like pearl in the moonlight.

At last, her energy spent, she sank to the ground near the stone. She knelt with her head thrown back, gazing up at the moon. Yul watched her in wonder. The hares too had stopped and sat a little distance away, their long ears laid down against their backs as they moongazed. He hugged his knees as he watched Sylvie, his black serpent sleeping. The pain he'd felt all over his body since the brutal beating seemed to disappear as the silver magic of the night caressed him. Something deep within him started to awaken, to stir for the very first time. Yul closed his eyes and sighed, feeling tears peppery and hot behind his eyelids.

How long they sat Yul didn't know, but after a time when the moon had sailed up high and become a small silver disc, he decided that Sylvie should get home. It was cold and she wore only a thin dress. He got up stiffly, feeling beyond hunger, and moved softly to where she knelt.

'Sylvie,' he murmured.

He touched her shoulder with light fingertips. Slowly she lowered her eyes from the moon and looked at him. Her eyes were far, far away, but he watched as she gradually brought them back into focus.

'Yes?' she whispered.

'We must go back now. Your dance is over. You must go home.'

Obediently she rose and followed him as he led the way down the hill, then cut into the dark woods. The blackness was thick, but through the branches they saw the star-spangled sky and the bright silver moon. Sylvie stumbled, and remembering her bare feet, Yul took her arm. He knew every tree root and obstacle on this path, even in the dark. His hand tingled where it touched her skin and he trembled at her quicksilver. Her body was alive with it, almost glowing.

She was silent as they walked through the wood but seemed at peace now, her earlier strangeness and agitation vanished. Yul wondered if her mother was back yet and quickened their pace. The last thing he needed was a search-party of Hallfolk finding him alone in the woods with Sylvie. All was silent as they reached the point where the path left the woods. Yul found her shoes and watched as she slipped them onto her bare feet, longing to take her in his arms and hug her goodbye. He shivered at the thought of holding her close to him.

'Are you alright now?'

'Yes! I feel wonderful. Thank you, Yul. I …'

'There's no time to talk. You must get home quickly, before your mother does. And if she's back, you must think of something to tell her about where you've been. Please, I beg you, don't mention me at all. I'm in enough trouble as it is.'

'I understand. Thank you again.'

She gave his arm a little squeeze and slipped away, going ahead of him. The cottage was still in darkness. He breathed a sigh of relief and headed for home, hoping that his supper would be waiting and his father out.

6

The land had now truly awakened from its winter sleep. As the warmth of April settled over Stonewylde, the trees became smudged with a green hue. Sheep and well-grown lambs were taken up into the far hills for grazing, and cows were led to the water meadows now that the winter floods were drying out. Cartloads of beehives were driven up to the heath for the early blooming gorse and spring flowers, whilst the Village pond bobbed with ducklings and squirming slicks of tadpoles.

Villagers put away their thick winter clothes and woollens and shook out their lighter flax garments from storage. Cottages were spring cleaned, rugs thoroughly beaten, thatched roofs repaired after winter damage. Vegetables in the cottage gardens began to sprout in profusion. The dry compost privies at the end of each long garden were given a complete clean out, and the compost containers that caught the waste were exchanged for empty ones.

Senior students revised for their imminent exams, confident that they'd do well, as standards in the Hall School were high. Cherry was busy supervising the spring-cleaning of the great stately home; a massive job done by an army of regular servants and extra recruits brought in from the Village. She'd stopped visiting Woodland Cottage as Miranda and Sylvie took their meals in the Dining Hall with the other Hallfolk, and were happy to look after themselves.

Every day Magus left the stables at dawn, where Nightwing was saddled up ready for him, and rarely returned before dusk.

He rode far and wide all over the vast estate, visiting every field, every wood, every hill-top. He rode along the cliffs, the beach and even the caves. He rode up to the great boundary wall that kept the Outside World at bay and personally inspected its entire length, miles and miles of it. This month was his time to check all the land at Stonewylde and take stock.

Once this was done, he began to meet with each group of Villagers to put together his reports. He visited the dairies, looking at production of milk, cream, butter, yoghurt and cheeses. He visited the tannery, the slaughterhouse, the mill, the bakery, the butchers, the meadery and the cider press. He checked on the bee-hives, orchards, chicken-houses, cowsheds and pig-pens. He looked at the buildings where cloth was woven and wool produced, where fabric was dyed and cut, where clothes and boots were made. He visited the potters and coopers, the furniture makers and fence builders, the woodsmen and charcoal-burners. He checked on the blacksmiths, builders, brick-makers, flint-knappers, stone-carvers, carpenters, thatchers and tilers. He called on the sewage workers who managed the recycled waste, the plumbers and the wind farm engineers, and every single farmer, labourer and herdsman.

In April, Magus visited every household for his annual survey and census. This was prior to the busy summer months ahead when so much of the work and production was done. He needed to ensure that everything was managed and run properly. He gathered information about the whole community from every member. He must look ahead and see where young Villagers could be trained, where more labour was required, and where inefficient methods were wasting valuable resources. He was an absolutely determined and dedicated master and nothing escaped his eye.

Clip also spent his days roaming Stonewylde, but on foot. He too would set off at dawn with his staff and a small bag of food and water. His robed figure could be spotted sitting deep in the woods amongst the trees, or striding along the skyline on the Dragon's Back ridgeway. Sometimes he'd sleep out, finding shelter where he could. Clip fed his soul with Stonewylde, immersing himself in the essence of growth all around him, and felt his own spirit growing too. He spent much time in solitary meditation, visiting and exploring other realms in his role as shaman of the community.

As the month progressed, the garden at Woodland Cottage was completely cleared and dug. Yul was then released from his daily punishment as Greenbough needed his apprentice in the woods from dawn to dusk at this busy time of year. The punishment had been beneficial in one way, for Yul was now stronger and more muscular. His boy's frame was changing; he was taller and had far more stamina and resilience than before. This was what he desired above all else.

He saw little of Sylvie after their visit to the Hare Stone on the night of the April full moon. He no longer watched her walking in the woods every morning, for she'd started at the Hall School. She found that despite the large gaps in her education, the system at the school enabled her to join in at her own level. Sylvie did her best to mix, although the Hallfolk youngsters seemed to have a bond which she didn't share. They were so steeped in the ways and philosophy of Stonewylde that she felt on the periphery, but she hoped this would change in time.

Miranda had started work and found the teaching style at Stonewylde very different to working in inner-city classrooms, where she'd been obliged to adopt military tactics in order to survive. She was happy, not least due to her increasing attraction to Magus. During April when he was out all day every day, she looked forward to the evenings and seeing him at dinner. He always appeared just before the gong, immaculately groomed and glowing after a hot bath, striding into the great Dining Hall to take his place at the top table. Several times he'd invited Miranda to sit by him and she found herself falling under his spell.

Magus was well educated, amusing and extremely good company. When he was in a room everyone was aware of him. He gave out an aura of energy even when exhausted from so many hours spent out on the estate. After dinner he usually retired to his office as his April stock-taking created a great deal of paperwork. Occasionally he'd join some of the Hallfolk in the elegant drawing room where they sat chatting, reading or watching television or a film. When he arrived, the atmosphere changed subtly as people vied for his attention. Everyone was brighter and more energised, feeding off his compelling presence. Miranda was no exception.

One evening towards the end of the month, Miranda had taken her after-dinner coffee into the library. It was in a different wing to the drawing room, and very quiet and shadowy. She sat alone in a window seat of the vast room reading a book. The door swung open silently but she sensed someone approaching. She glanced up to see Magus smiling down at her. He sat further along the window seat, watching her as he sipped his coffee. He then placed the empty cup deliberately on a nearby table. Her heart raced at his proximity and their isolation.

'Well, Miranda, at last I've found you alone. I wanted to speak with you, if you're not busy?'

She put the book to one side and smiled back, her hands trembling slightly.

'I was just re-reading a text to use tomorrow with the students.'

His mouth twitched at this.

'Very admirable. But don't work too hard, make sure you leave time for pleasure and relaxation in the evenings.'

His eyes gleamed and she wondered if he meant what she thought he did.

'Teaching here isn't hard work after what I've been used to,' she replied a little stiffly.

'I'm delighted to hear it. Sylvie isn't the only one who's blooming at Stonewylde. I've noticed how different you are too – how much calmer and happier. And how very attractive you are.'

She blushed under his gaze, feeling ridiculously tongue-tied and unable to think of anything clever to say. She held her breath, her heartbeat loud in her ears.

'Do I make you feel uncomfortable, Miranda?' he asked softly.

'Yes you do! I'm sorry; it's not your fault. You're just so ... so ...'

She glanced at him in desperation, floundering out of her depth. He laughed quietly and moved closer to her on the long cushion, taking the rattling cup and saucer from her hands. She caught a waft of his scent and all her senses tingled. He was so assured, so much in control. She dreaded what may come next and yet longed for it too.

'Oh dear! I've no wish to cause you discomfort, believe me. I wouldn't dream of abusing my position here. I'd like to get to know you better but only when you're ready. You must learn to relax with me and be yourself; the woman I met in London who impressed me so much with her strength and determination. The woman who gave me a grilling about the feudal system and half-witted peasants being deprived of television. I like your independence and your spikiness, Miranda. It's rare here, where everyone else tries to please. Don't lose it, will you?'

She shook her head and swallowed, feeling his dark gaze on her. She took a deep breath and turned to smile brightly at him. He looked amused at her effort to be herself.

'I'd never lose my independence,' she said. 'It was the only thing that kept me going all those years. But you're quite over-powering – I feel like a comet being drawn into the sun's gravitational field.'

He laughed again and reached across to stroke her hair in an affectionate gesture. His fingers brushed her shoulder as he felt the texture of the silky auburn swathe that flowed halfway down her back. She closed her eyes at his touch, his scent filling her nostrils. He seemed so big sitting this close, his body powerful and radiating energy.

'Your hair is exquisite,' he murmured. 'I'm so pleased you came to Stonewylde, Miranda. It's clearly been an excellent move for both you and Sylvie. I hope you intend to stay. I'd like that very much.'

'Oh yes! Me too!' she whispered. 'I can't imagine ever leaving here.'

'Wonderful! In that case, I'd like to mark your joining our community with a public ceremony, if you don't object. I thought Beltane may be a good time.'

'That would be lovely! A public ceremony.'

"It's a major festival for us and a very joyous occasion,' he continued, taking one of her hands and tracing the bones with gentle fingers. 'It would be the perfect time to initiate both of you into our ways and customs. I think Sylvie's ready for it too. She doesn't have any doubts about staying here, does she? I haven't spoken to her alone for a while.'

'She absolutely loves it here,' Miranda assured him. 'She's thriving in a way I'd never have dreamed possible, and certainly not as quickly as this. I'm so grateful to you for saving her life.'

'It wasn't me – it's the Earth Magic,' he said, still stroking her hand. 'The healing energy of Stonewylde. I'll give her more at Beltane.'

Miranda looked at him a little sceptically and he laughed, patting her hand and releasing it.

'You've seen nothing yet, Miranda,' he said genially. 'You wait. You'll have no doubt in your mind about the veracity of that magic when the Beltane holiday's over, I promise you. Now, I must get on with those never-ending reports.'

'You work so hard,' said Miranda. 'I take back what I said when I first came here. You work harder than any labourer I've seen.'

'Well, April is my busiest month, I must say. I couldn't keep up this pace throughout the year. Can you speak to Cherry about Beltane? You'll need the proper costumes and she'll arrange for a dress-maker to fit you both for white dresses. Can I leave that with you?'

'Of course,' she nodded. 'White dresses? It sounds bridal!'

'And so it is, in a way. Brides for the Green Man. I should warn you, I'll be very busy at Beltane itself as I have to stay with the May Queen. But after May Day, I'd like us to spend an evening together, just you and me. Would you like that?'

She nodded in delighted acceptance, an arrow of excitement shooting through her at the very thought.

*

While Miranda spent as much time as possible at the Hall in the hope of running into Magus, Sylvie passed her free time out on the estate, roaming first in the beautifully landscaped and manicured Hall gardens, and then farther afield into the wilder parts of Stonewylde. She still loved the woods next to the cottage, and spent many evenings after school meandering up the path that led deep into their heart.

During April, more and more greenery had appeared and now everything was opening into leaf and bursting into blossom. The early bluebells in the woods were exquisite, blueness on blueness appearing in a mist of fragrance on the woodland carpet. The liquid music of birdsong soothed the senses despite its jubilant volume. The sun was warm as the days increased in length, and soft pink dawns and golden dusks promised a balmy summer to come.

Hares and leverets were everywhere, leaping and racing in the fields, nibbling voraciously at young green shoots now their mad March boxing was over. Sylvie watched them at length one evening up on the hills and marvelled at them. She'd never seen hares before coming to Stonewylde and loved them for their wildness and freedom. She had a hazy recollection of silver hares leaping with her on the night of her moon dance but wasn't sure if she'd just imagined it.

It wasn't until she found herself wandering one evening along the track leading to the Village that Sylvie realised she was looking for Yul. She stopped and considered – was this what she really wanted? She'd missed him since he'd stopped coming to dig the garden, and she'd never had the chance to thank him for looking after her that night. She felt embarrassed that he'd seen her acting so strangely, yet delighted that she'd finally found the answer to her mysterious behaviour. Never again would she suffer on the night of the full moon. Thanks to Yul, she now understood how she must honour the rising moon.

Now she stood on the track, the hawthorn blossom snowy on the hedgerows, and debated the wisdom of searching out Yul.

She could picture him perfectly: sullen and angry in the garden, rapt and glowing on the stage at the Story Web, gentle and knowing in the night woods. Dark curls falling into his deep grey eyes – his face haunted her. With a sigh she continued along the track until she came to the Village.

It was like walking onto a film set, she decided, or going back in time. Smoke curled from the thatched cottages, people dressed in roughly woven clothes and boots went about their business, ducks waddled around the muddy edges of the pond. It was a beautiful evening, the sun still golden in the sky, and everything looked slightly smudged as if in soft focus. Men sat on benches outside the pub, drinking from tankards, and from within there came the sound of many male voices. A group of older children played tag on the Village Green, chasing and calling out in their strange accent, unique to Stonewylde. Laughter and splashing could be heard from the bath house, with mothers scolding and chivvying their children. Sylvie wondered where Yul would be at this time of evening. Hearing music and voices coming from the Barn, she approached the open double doors and looked inside.

The place was full of youngsters of about her age. Several groups sat around tables, playing cards and board games. Others played instruments and some danced. There was a skittle alley set up at one end where a throng had gathered, making a great deal of noise. At one table an old man had a group around him all whittling away at pieces of wood, whilst at another table several girls were sewing with a couple of women. Many just sat or stood around talking and laughing. Sylvie gazed in wistfully. They all belonged, they all knew each other and were part of a society she knew little about.

She scanned the faces, looking for Yul's dark hair and secretive hollow face but couldn't see him anywhere. The group nearest the doors noticed her standing there and they stared. Sylvie smiled diffidently, feeling very awkward. It suddenly struck her that there wasn't one blond Hallfolk teenager in the building. They were all Villagers.

'Blessings, miss!' one of them called. 'Are you lost?'

Reluctantly she edged towards them, feeling out of place. Several more groups now saw her and the noise seemed to suddenly die down. She felt herself blushing.

'No, I'm not lost. I just ... I'm sorry, I didn't realise this was for Villagers. I didn't mean to intrude.'

'You're welcome, miss,' said another girl. 'Magus said you didn't know our ways. Hallfolk usually stay up at the Hall in the evenings.'

'I'm sorry,' Sylvie repeated. 'I'll go now.'

'Farewell then, miss. Be seeing you at Beltane no doubt.'

Sylvie nodded and gave an embarrassed wave, hastily retreating from the Barn and into the welcome fresh air outside. She stood for a while looking over the Village Green where a half moon glowed dimly in the pale blue sky. A squabbling flock of sparrows flew across her vision and she watched them disappear into a tree. She noticed how the great trees encircling the Village Green were now in bud, some of them already green and others tinged with the promise of leaves.

It was a beautiful setting and she almost wished that Magus had placed her and her mother in the Village, to live as Villagers instead of Hallfolk. Magnificent though the Hall was, there was a feeling of peace and antiquity here that struck a chord in her soul. She'd love to dress in the simple homespun clothes and leather boots the Village girls wore, with a bright shawl around her shoulders and a wicker basket on her arm. But then she remembered her hair. She could never be a Villager with silver-blond hair like hers. It set her apart immediately. She was Hallfolk whether she liked it or not.

She walked through the Village looking at the buildings, smiling at the solar panels on some of the larger roofs. They seemed out of place, yet she was pleased that Magus had decided on modern technology rather than keeping the place totally in the Middle Ages. There was no sign of Yul at all, and she wondered what he did with himself in the evenings. Why didn't he mix with others of his age in the Great Barn? Surely he wasn't old enough to be with the men drinking in the pub?

Slowly she followed a path that led down to the river, and stood gazing at the rushing water still swollen with winter rain. Willows edged its muddy banks, the long yellow-green shoots feathered with new pale leaves hanging down like a girl's hair. The water was pure and sparkling and caught the golden glint of the evening sunlight. Sylvie took a deep breath and felt an almost overwhelming love of the place well up inside her. She never wanted to leave Stonewylde. The Outside World held no attraction for her whatsoever and she'd stay here for the rest of her life. As she explored this sudden certainty she noticed Yul.

He sat on a small stone bridge that spanned the river slightly downstream, his head bowed. He had his back to her, his legs hanging over the edge, and was absolutely still. Her heart had skipped at the sight of him, but now she wondered if she should speak to him or not. What would she say? He was cloaked in solitude, in a closed world of his own with a web of stillness protecting him.

Sylvie stood undecided, wanting to quietly retrace her steps and leave him undisturbed, but also wanting to speak to him. Was he really the beautiful boy she kept thinking about, or was that dark thundercloud the true Yul? The decision was taken from her as he suddenly swivelled around. She smiled uncertainly. He glared at her and the smile faltered on her lips. She began to turn, realising she'd made a mistake, but then his face lit up with pleasure and he raised a hand in greeting.

Her feet moved towards him and he gazed up at her as she stood before him on the bridge.

'I thought I was imagining you,' he said quietly. 'I was thinking of you and there you were. I thought you were a dream.'

'I'm real,' she replied. 'Can I join you?'

He nodded and she sat down next to him on the stone parapet of the bridge, careful not to sit too close. Her legs dangled over the edge beside his and she looked downstream where he'd been staring. Although the sun had almost set, the river was gilded with hazy brightness. She saw the great wheel of a mill around a bend, and the reed beds becoming broader as the river widened, approaching the sea. The air was patterned with the choral music of birdsong, different voices weaving in and out of each other in glorious harmony. She felt good to be alive and so pleased she'd found him.

The boy next to her sat in silence. There was a stillness about him tonight that she found comforting. Then he touched her sleeve gently and nodded at the far riverbank.

'See the kingfisher?' he whispered. 'Over there by that clump of reeds.'

She saw it and smiled in wonder at the brilliance of its plumage, its pertness as it perched on the reed. Then it darted off in a streak of pure blue, and Yul turned to her.

'Do they have kingfishers in the Outside World?' he asked.

'Yes but I've never seen one. I didn't live in the country. I came from a big, dirty city.'

'But now you're home,' he said simply.

They sat in silence again for a while.

'I was looking for you,' said Sylvie, turning to him. He glanced at her in surprise. She noticed that the black eye was fading, the cut on his eyebrow just a scab now. 'I wanted to thank you for looking after me that night.'

He smiled and shook his head.

'I was worried you'd get lost in the woods.'

'I would've done. You were very kind to me. Thank you.'

''Twas nothing, miss. Forget it.'

'Sylvie,' she said. 'Not "miss".'

'Sylvie,' he repeated.

'Were you really thinking of me just now?' she asked.

He looked away quickly and shrugged. She stared at his profile. He was so dark and quiet, wrapped in his solitude, alone behind the walls of his seclusion. She gazed at his shadowed face and then suddenly, without warning, it hit her. A great wave of pain and hatred that made her gasp out loud. A black and bleak despair that writhed so hard within him it hurt. This was Yul; this was what he carried inside; this was what he lived with. She felt tears choking her throat and blinked hard, staring down at the water below to quell the rush of emotion. She'd never had such a sensation before. It was as if a window to his soul had opened momentarily, allowing her to glimpse inside. His spirit was shrouded in utter darkness. The poor boy, she cried to herself. The poor boy, living in such fear and misery.

As he'd done a little earlier, she reached across and touched his sleeve. His eyes found hers and she gazed into them, wanting desperately to comfort him.

'Yul, I ...'

She faltered, locked in the depths of his deep grey eyes. Words were inadequate. Instead she poured out her silent sympathy and hoped he understood. But he stood up abruptly.

'I must be getting back,' he said gruffly. 'Farewell, miss.'

Beltane was fast approaching and the entire community was in uproar preparing for this major festival. Costumes were sewn, dances and songs rehearsed, food organised and prepared. The Great Barn was decorated with the hawthorn blossom that had turned every hedgerow pure white, whilst papier-mâché Green Man masks, decorated with real leaves, were hung from the rafters and pinned to the walls. Magus had chosen his May Queen and informed the lucky girl of her good fortune, dashing the hopes of countless others in the process. Everywhere the preparations were in full swing, people becoming ever more frantic and busy as the date approached.

Miranda and Sylvie, now in possession of the plain white dresses they must wear for the occasion, were bemused by all the fuss. Magus took time one morning after breakfast to reassure them about the festival. He explained that the Beltane celebrations were held in two stages, the first part on May Eve, the night before May Day. At the fire-lit ceremony in the Stone Circle, the spirit of the Green Man was invoked. He was always represented by Magus, who led the festival with the May Queen. The rituals continued late into the night, and there was a vigil in the Stone Circle for the May Day sunrise. During May Day the festivities involved the whole community down on the Village

Green. The day was spent in celebration, with a party in the evening in the Great Barn. The formal invitation for them to join the community would take place during May Eve.

'Clip will run through the words with you,' said Magus. 'It'll be very straightforward so don't worry about it.'

'I can't wait to see the Stone Circle,' said Sylvie. 'It sounds so exciting.'

'It's the heart of Stonewylde, the place where the earth energy is strongest. Not because the Stone Circle's there, of course. The magic came first. The circle was built by our ancestors to mark the place where the Earth Magic could be channelled. And don't look at me like that, Miranda. I know you find this difficult to believe. But that doesn't mean it's not real. I think Sylvie understands.'

She nodded, remembering the day after the Spring Equinox when Magus had taken her into the woods and filled her with his healing energy.

'It is real, Mum. It's what's made me better.'

Miranda still looked doubtful. She reluctantly excused herself from the library where the three of them sat, as she had a lesson to teach.

'And you've got a class too, I believe,' she said to her daughter.

'She can skip that,' said Magus. 'I want a word with her.'

Miranda frowned but left the library, and Magus took Sylvie outside onto the long stone terrace overlooking the lawns.

They stood together by the stone balustrade gazing across the gardens. Sunlight had transformed the dew on the grass into a carpet of sparkling crystals. A group of great horse chestnuts were already in full leaf, the fat sticky buds now burst and the palmate leaves unfurled. These trees were home to a community of rooks; they boasted noisily of their splendid nests and fussed with extra twigs to add to their messy creations. Sylvie watched them with amusement.

'They're like a group of gossiping old women,' she laughed. 'Look! Every time one of them flies away, another one steals a twig from its nest. And they're so loud. What have they got to make so much noise about?'

Magus smiled at her.

'You're really happy here, aren't you? I asked your mother the other evening if she was certain about making this commitment at Beltane, and I'd like to ask you the same thing, Sylvie. You'll be making sacred vows in the Circle and I want you to be sure.'

She turned to him, her strange grey eyes shining.

'I'm sure.'

'We originally said there'd be a year's trial. But I think you belong here.'

'I do. I've come home.'

She realised she was echoing Yul's words.

'I'm so pleased, Sylvie. I really believe it's the right decision.'

She smiled and took a deep breath of the fragrant morning air. Her body tingled with vitality. Since the moon dancing she'd felt better than ever before. Magus' dark gaze scanned her glowing face, the ravages of eczema almost banished, her eyes no longer sunken and dull and her frailty finally receding.

'I want to share the Earth Magic with you again at Beltane,' he said, 'to complete the healing we started last month.'

She nodded and remembered her outburst of tears after Magus had filled her with his gift of energy. It was embarrassing, for he'd seen her at her most vulnerable.

'You were very ill,' he said gently, as if reading her mind, 'and it's not surprising you felt so emotional. But this time you'll feel strong and powerful. Beltane energy is the best and without it I'd never be able to run Stonewylde as I do.'

'Really? So it's not just for healing then?'

'No, it's green energy from the Earth and it can be used for healing of course, but also just to give extra strength and vitality. Leading Stonewylde is the most gruelling job and almost too much for one person. The magic comes to me and I use it, but as the magus it's also my privilege to share it if I so choose. So during Beltane I want you to stand with me in the Circle and take your fill. After that you'll be whole.'

'You're very good to me,' she said in a small voice. 'You make me feel cared for and special.'

'You are special, Sylvie. That's why you're here. Outsiders are never normally invited into the community, as you now understand. But I knew when I first saw you that day in London that you belonged at Stonewylde. I can't wait for Hazel to see you in the summer. She'll be amazed at your transformation.'

'I'll always be grateful to her,' said Sylvie. 'I dread to think how I'd be now if she hadn't rescued me.'

'Don't think of it,' said Magus firmly. 'It's behind you. You'll never be weak again, Sylvie. I shall make sure of it.'

They watched the rooks for a while longer. A young gardener wheeling a barrow appeared from around the corner of the building. He bowed his head respectfully to Magus and Sylvie and headed off towards the formal gardens.

'So – no doubts then? You'd like to officially join our community in a couple of days' time?'

'Yes please! I've no doubts at all.'

Magus smiled and gave her a little hug as they stood side by side.

'Good. And now I really must go to my office. I've completed my annual tour of the estate and there are so many reports to write up. I've got plans to—'

They were interrupted by Martin, a tall, sombre man who shared the blond Hallfolk hair but was a servant.

'Sorry to intrude, sir, but there's a call for you from London.'

'Thanks, Martin. You'd better get back to your lessons, Sylvie. Tell your teacher I needed to talk with you. And Sylvie . . . I can't wait till you become of one of us.'

Yul was busy once again adding the final touches to the bonfire in the Circle. He'd watched the Spring Equinox hare decorations on the great stones being washed off and repainted with images of the Green Man. Fennel once more climbed up and down a ladder, adding glints of gold to the faces sprouting oak leaves. Yul had another strong urge to knock him off the ladder, especially as

Fennel had been one of those involved in the incident at the Equinox, but he was learning to curb his temper and bide his time.

Buzz had just appeared in the vicinity, supposedly supervising some Village youngsters laying lanterns, but in reality throwing his weight around and showing off. Yul watched him from beneath lowered eyelids, trying not to attract any attention. He knew only too well that no Villager would ever dare defend him from Hallfolk victimisation. Buzz could bully him with impunity, as he'd always done.

It was while he was perched near the top of the massive bonfire that Buzz noticed him. Yul was stuffing a certain type of lichen-covered bark into gaps where it would burn with a blue-green flame when the fire was lit.

'Look what we've got here – a monkey up a tree!' cried Buzz, abandoning the lanterns and swaggering over to the bonfire. He'd put on some weight lately as well as growing taller, and was becoming quite bulky. Several of his cronies from the Hall turned around to look, and Fennel laughed.

'Yeah, but with only half the brains of a monkey!' he sneered, and promptly wobbled precariously on his ladder.

Even though the consequences were inevitable, Yul couldn't ignore them.

'Do take care, young master!' he called. 'You don't look too safe up on that high ladder. Any minute now you'll wobble too far and fall flat on your precious arse.'

Buzz growled at this, advancing closer to the bonfire. Yul was perfectly placed at the top, one leg wound around a thick supporting branch, his strong body braced and balanced. He gazed down at Buzz from his lofty height and then across at Fennel, trying to get down the ladder with some dignity. Yul made a show of rolling up his sleeves just to prove that he didn't need to hold on at all.

'Shut your ignorant mouth, boy!' Buzz grunted, reaching the foot of the bonfire.

'Or what?'

'Or you'll suffer. Worse than last time.'

'I didn't suffer at all last time. Chasing me into the woods – that's hardly making me suffer, is it?'

'Yeah, and Magus punished you. He told me.'

'Punished me? Oh, you mean the bit of gardening at Woodland Cottage? That was no punishment. I enjoy gardening.'

Yul knew he was pushing his luck. Buzz was right; he'd suffer for this. He could never win; the odds were stacked too heavily against him. As Buzz glared up at him forming his reply, he noticed the residue of bruising around Yul's eye.

'Hah, a black eye! So someone else taught you a lesson.'

'The bastard who gave me this could no more teach anyone a lesson than you could!' retorted Yul sharply.

'You come down here and say that!'

'I know, why don't you come up here and then I will! Though a great lump of lard like you couldn't climb an anthill!' Yul replied, an insolent grin on his face.

Enraged, Buzz started to climb the enormous bonfire. Very soon he was completely defeated, his legs trapped inside, his arms pulling wildly at the tangle of wood. Branches and brushwood fell out everywhere around him. Yul was still perched on the top laughing at Buzz's humiliation, though the damage to the bonfire dismayed him. The other Hallfolk boys gathered around and yelled insults at Yul, throwing the dislodged sticks up at him to stop his mocking laughter.

One of the woodsmen ran to fetch Greenbough, working nearby. He came puffing up the Long Walk and when he saw the scene, nearly exploded with rage. He may only have been a Villager and they Hallfolk, but his precious bonfire came above such considerations. As the head of the woodsmen, his responsibility for the bonfire superseded any natural obedience towards Hallfolk. He burst into the Circle and roared at the youths.

'Stop it! Get off that fire, you fools. 'Tis the sacred bonfire for Beltane! Get off!'

He grabbed hold of Buzz, roughly pulling him free from the snarl of branches that held him fast. Greenbough was old but had worked in the woods his entire life and was very strong indeed. He wasn't worried about putting a pup like Buzz in his place, Hallfolk or not. Buzz was yanked off balance and fell heavily onto the ground.

'Stupid bloody idiot!' he shouted, his face scarlet.

'You show some respect for your elders,' growled Greenbough. 'Now bugger off away from this here fire or I'll kick your arse all the way back to the Hall.'

Trying to muster any remaining shreds of dignity, the large blond youth picked himself up and stalked off. But not before he'd pointed up at Yul and spoken slowly and distinctly.

'You wait, Yul! You're *dead*.'

7

Sylvie lay in the white marble bath at the Hall soaking in sumptuous bluebell bath oil. Steam from the enormous tub rose in fragrant clouds around her head, misting up the gilt mirrors. This was the best bathroom of all and she was lucky to have got it; usually she used one of the ordinary bathrooms down the corridor.

She sighed and closed her eyes. Tonight was May Eve. Her heart raced with excitement at the thought of the ceremony at the Stone Circle, and she was looking forward to May Day tomorrow too. Then the day after that was another full moon. Sylvie couldn't believe it was four weeks already since the last one. She sat up in the bath, steam eddying around her, hair hanging like pieces of string about her flushed face. Time to get ready now. Her white dress hung in a room in the girls' dormitory wing. Tonight she'd be making her vows and she couldn't wait.

Yul too was getting ready for the ceremony. The bonfire had been repaired and he'd received a wallop from Greenbough when he'd leapt down to the ground after Buzz's departure. The old man knew it wasn't Yul's fault, but was furious that the sacred fire had been put in jeopardy. Yul accepted this tough discipline, knowing he'd deliberately goaded Buzz. He now lay in a chipped enamel tub in a small cubicle in the Village bath house, a world away from Sylvie's white marble opulence. No clouds of fragrant bluebell steam for Yul – his water was tepid and he washed with plain rosemary soap. But he enjoyed the comparative luxury of it and was looking forward to the night ahead. Like everyone at Stonewylde, the festivals were the cornerstones of his existence and he loved them.

Yul sat up and began to wash vigorously. As always, he was very dirty, and knew he'd see Sylvie tonight. This would be the first time since the evening on the bridge when she'd sought him out and then made him feel so wretched. The memory of her strange silver-grey eyes and their flood of pity still upset him. The last thing he wanted was her pity. The thought of her churned up his insides and he almost dreaded their next encounter, despite longing to see her again. She made him feel confused and unsure of himself.

Glowing from her bath, Sylvie padded along the corridor and climbed a half-flight of stairs into another corridor. The Hall was a labyrinth and she was only just beginning to find her way around, especially upstairs. It didn't help that the building had grown over the centuries, each era adding extra wings on different levels. She opened a heavy oak door that led into another part and heard the sound of many girls' voices coming through open doorways. There was giggling and shrieking, and the palpable energy that mushrooms when a group of girls get ready together for a night out. She hesitated, suddenly feeling shy. When Dawn, an older girl who'd recently befriended her, had suggested that Sylvie join them in the girls' wing to get ready for Beltane Eve, it had seemed like a good idea. But now she wished she'd gone back to Woodland Cottage to get ready with her mother. She couldn't change her mind though, for her clothes hung in the communal room. She steeled herself and walked in.

Many faces turned at her arrival and she felt her cheeks burn. But there were smiles of welcome and Dawn, sitting on a sofa in her dressing gown, stood up and greeted her. She was given a plate of cold food and a glass of milk, and a space was found for her on a cushion on the floor. The big room was packed full of girls of around her age, most of them blond haired. They were all eating supper and excitedly discussing the night ahead. Being part of a group like this was strange for Sylvie. She sat quietly, savouring the experience as her hair slowly dried down her back.

'How long have we got now?'

'Less than an hour. We need to get a move on soon and start getting dressed.'

'Can I still borrow your old cloak? I'll be getting my new one next Solstice at my Rite, and I hate the old one.'

'Yeah, I said you could. I don't need it now I've got robes.'

'Will you do my hair?'

'Only if you'll do mine. Lots of little plaits.'

'I still can't believe he chose that stupid Rowan.'

'Did you see her yesterday? I saw her walking back down to the Village after she'd finished work. She was smiling so hard I thought she'd split her bloody face open.'

'It makes me sick. Why didn't he choose a Hallfolk girl?'

As the conversation progressed Sylvie realised that she wasn't part of the group at all, for she'd no idea what they were on about. Dawn noticed her puzzled look.

'We're talking about the girl Magus chose as May Queen.'

'Is she a Villager?'

'Yes she bloody well is!' said July bitterly. 'She works in the laundry here.'

'How could he pick a laundry maid? Maya's sixteen this festival, and there's Linden and Tulip. They had their Rite at the Spring Equinox. Not to mention Megan and Saffy at Imbolc. What's wrong with them? It makes me sick!'

'He has to be fair,' said Dawn in a conciliatory tone. 'It was a Hallfolk girl last year and the Lammas Queen too. The Villagers would get upset if he never chose one of them.'

'So? Let them get upset. What are they going to do about it?'

'How's Eleanor? I bet she's nervous.'

'It's Eleanor's Rite of Adulthood tonight,' Dawn explained to Sylvie who nodded, none the wiser.

'She's okay. Her parents are here and she's in their rooms with them. Her new robes are beautiful.'

'What's her totem?'

'A hedgehog, would you believe? I thought she was joking when she told me!'

'Eleanor's always loved hedgehogs.'

'Yeah, but not all over her robes and on her necklet, surely? Let's hope she's not as prickly tonight!'

'So who's partnering her? Fennel?'

'Buzz. But I don't mind,' said Holly. 'He spoke to me about it and it's okay. He's mine at the Winter Solstice. Unless I get lucky, of course!'

They all laughed at this and Sylvie tried to join in.

After a while they put their plates to one side and started to get dressed for the evening, the under sixteens in tunics and the older ones in their robes.

'You don't wear that until tomorrow,' said Holly, noticing Sylvie taking her white dress off the hanger.

'Magus said I had to wear it tonight,' said Sylvie. 'And my mum's wearing hers too.'

'They're having a special ceremony,' said Dawn. 'Magus is welcoming them into the community.'

'Really? How odd. What's he going to do?'

The pretty girl stood unselfconsciously in the middle of the room wearing only her underwear. She stared hard at Sylvie, who clutched her white dress and coloured slightly at being singled out like this.

'I'm not really sure,' she replied. 'We'll be making a vow to uphold the laws and customs of Stonewylde, I think. That's what Clip said.'

'My parents couldn't believe Magus had brought Outsiders here. They arrived yesterday for Beltane and they were stunned when they heard,' said Holly, pulling the tunic over her head and shaking out her blond bobbed hair. 'Mother said it's never been done before.'

Sylvie was silent at this. She hoped people weren't going to resent them.

'Don't worry, Sylvie,' said Dawn. 'You know you're welcome here.'

'Yeah, but it does seem a little unfair that real Hallfolk aren't allowed to live here permanently even though they'd love to, and then Magus goes and brings in Outsiders.'

'Why aren't they allowed to live here?' asked Sylvie, worried now about upsetting people.

'Magus says there isn't enough room for all the Hallfolk,' said Holly. 'Most of them are only allowed back for one or two of the festivals a year. That's why my parents are here now. But they'll have to leave after a week. It's the same for all the visitors who've come for Beltane.'

'Not all of them want to stay here permanently though,' said Wren. 'My parents don't. Dad's an Outsider anyway and he'd hate Stonewylde. Mother always comes on her own and she says a week's enough for her.'

'Well, I just hope the visitors don't mind,' said Holly. 'Two complete strangers taking up valuable Hallfolk spaces.'

Her dark eyes watched Sylvie closely; she was trying to pluck up the courage to take off her bathrobe and change into her dress.

'Of course they won't!' said Dawn, putting an arm round Sylvie's shoulders. 'Do you want to get dressed in my room, Sylvie?'

She nodded thankfully and followed the older girl down the corridor to a bedroom. Her breathing felt tight and she wished she'd brought her inhaler. She hadn't used it for ages but maybe she'd need it tonight after all. But it sat uselessly in a drawer in Woodland Cottage, and Sylvie realised she'd just have to manage without it. Dawn pushed her bedroom door open and ushered Sylvie inside, smiling kindly at the younger girl.

'There, it's more private here. Don't take any notice of Holly. She's just a bit jealous of you, that's all.'

'Jealous? What on earth for?'

'You're new and you're getting a lot of attention. She likes to be queen bee. She overheard the boys talking about you and she didn't like it. But don't worry, she's always bitching about someone or something. It's nothing personal. I'll leave you in peace to get changed. Use any of my stuff. We need to leave in about twenty minutes though, so don't take too long.'

When Sylvie returned to the communal room the noisy chattering died. The room fell silent as everyone turned to stare. Sylvie stood just inside the doorway unaware of how beautiful she looked. The white dress was of the finest linen and very simple, emphasising her slim body and delicate features. Her hair had dried into a shining silver cloud that brushed her bare arms and fell almost to her waist. She looked shyly at the sea of faces. Everyone was dressed in their tunics and robes which made Sylvie, in white, stand out even more. Abruptly Holly pulled on her cloak and broke the silence, chivvying the others.

'Come on! We'll be late if we don't hurry up!'

They trooped along the corridors and down the stairs, a great gaggle of girls, meeting others also on their way downstairs. The huge entrance hall was full of Hallfolk gathering to leave for the Stone Circle.

'Have you got a cloak to wear?' asked Dawn. 'It can get chilly, especially on the walk back.'

'Mum's bringing our cloaks I think,' replied Sylvie. There was an atmosphere of tense excitement amongst the milling people and Sylvie's heart beat faster. She saw Miranda talking to a small group and went over to collect her new cloak.

'Are you alright, darling?' her mother asked, looking stunning herself in the white dress. Sylvie nodded, her eyes bright.

'A bit nervous. I do hope it goes alright. I can't believe this is happening to us!'

Miranda smiled and gave her a hug.

'Neither can I!'

Sylvie stayed with Dawn and the girls as they walked down the gravel drive and along the track, turning off for the Long Walk which led to the Stone Circle. It was still daylight but not for much longer.

'Where's Magus now?' asked Sylvie.

'He'll be up there already,' said Dawn. 'And so will Rowan. She must be so scared. It's a great, great honour to be chosen as May Queen. Don't listen to any nastiness about her from the girls. It's only envy. Magus always makes sure the Villagers get their chance at the festivals and their Rites. He's very fair.'

'So she's a good choice then?'

'She's lovely. Very pretty and curvy, just as the May Queen should be. She represents the fertility of the Earth Mother and Rowan's just right for it. There's a sort of earthiness about her. I can understand why Magus chose her.'

As they walked, Sylvie heard the girls in front discussing Buzz. She recalled Dawn's words and wondered what Holly had overheard the boys saying about her. She wasn't used to being an object of interest to boys and found it flattering, if a little alarming. And she certainly didn't want to upset Holly. Then she heard Yul's name mentioned and listened more closely to the conversation.

'Buzz is livid,' said Holly. 'He's out to get Yul.'

'Oh Goddess, I hope there isn't going to be any trouble this Beltane.'

'You know they had a fight at the Equinox? Over me?'

'Yes, Holly, you told us.'

'I think they're still at each other's throats about it. Buzz said today he'll kill him.'

'Even Buzz wouldn't go that far.'

'No, but you know how he gets when he's angry. Still, I'm sure Yul will survive. He's used to it after all.'

They laughed and Sylvie asked Dawn what they meant.

'It's a bit of a joke, Yul's battle-scars.'

'Oh, you mean his black eye?'

'He's always got some injury or other, that boy. It's not funny though.'

'Does he fight a lot then? He seemed quite gentle to me. Not that I've had much to do with him, of course.'

'No, it's his father. He's an absolute brute. I remember when I was much younger at the Village School. You know the Hallfolk

101

children go there until they're eight? Poor Yul was always battered and bruised even then, as a little boy.'

'That's horrible! And that was his father's doing?'

'Yes, and it doesn't seem to have got any better now he's older. I do feel sorry for him. Although he's a sulky lad most of the time and maybe he brings it on himself. Buzz has always had it in for him, right from when they were much younger.'

Sylvie was silent, remembering the awful darkness she'd sensed inside Yul. She thought that now she understood why, and her sympathy for him grew. She hoped to see him tonight and wondered if she could warn him about Buzz. She'd noticed the great crowd of Hallfolk boys up ahead and felt even more nervous of them. What had they said about her?

They'd been making a lot of noise, but now in the Long Walk everyone became quiet. The trees overhead formed a tunnel, their leaves half unfurled, and the way was shadowy. Waist-high stones marked the wide path, candlelight from the lanterns twinkling amongst them. As Sylvie followed the crowd making their way to the Stone Circle she felt a sudden rush of spirit and understood why everyone was silent. She sensed that she was approaching a sacred place. She heard the soft throbbing of drums from up ahead and her heart quickened to match their beat.

The entire community, Villager and Hallfolk, poured from the Long Walk into the great arena, completely filling it. The huge standing stones loomed around the body of people, jutting tall against the pale sky. The atmosphere crackled with anticipation. They'd been blessed with perfect weather – a clear, balmy evening of soft pink skies and a sunset edged with pure gold. The Stone Circle thronged with adults and children dressed in their cere-monial robes and tunics. As the sun went down the bonfire was lit, flaring blue-green in great shooting flames. The Beltane Eve ceremony commenced, to the sound of drumming and many voices singing.

Miranda and Sylvie were awestruck. They'd never witnessed anything like this before and were overwhelmed by the power generated within the Circle. There was movement and dancing, chanting and singing. The drum rhythms entered the bodies of everyone present; there was no escape from the beat. This wasn't simply an auditory experience but a corporeal one. The Circle itself magnified and enclosed the sound which entered every torso as if each were another drum. Sylvie could feel the beats reverberating in her chest and skull. She was unaware of the real power of drumming, when the body itself becomes a skin that amplifies and vibrates with the sound.

The massed voices of the community in the Stone Circle, the stars peppering the sky above, the waxing gibbous moon shining through the trees; Sylvie gazed around in silent wonder. She felt the energy – whether from the community or Mother Earth, or maybe both – throbbing within the Circle, and within herself too. She glanced at her mother. Miranda stood swaying, her eyes closed, as she finally abandoned her scepticism and began to understand.

The Green Man and the May Queen were spectacular. Magus wore a green costume sewn with leaves of every kind, and his face and body were painted green. He was unrecognisable as the handsome master of the community. His crown was a wreath of woven foliage and even his silvery hair was green and full of leaves. He'd become the embodiment of the male spirit of growth, the potent force to impregnate the fertile earth.

The girl chosen to be May Queen was as lovely as Dawn had said. She had glossy brown hair hanging down in rich waves, held in place by a wreath of hawthorn blossom interlaced with bluebells. Her face glowed with excitement, cheeks rosy and eyes bright. There really was a look of wholesome earthiness about her, a ripeness waiting to be tasted. She wore a gauzy white dress, the tight bodice emphasising her young, full curves and a swirling skirt revealing bare calves and feet.

Sylvie loved the feel of the soil under her own bare feet. She felt in tune with the earth and all the people who'd danced on this sacred ground before. The stones were so very ancient; she tried to imagine the countless people who must have celebrated here over the centuries. Magus led the chanting and the people echoed him, their voices weaving around the flutes and drums. His deep voice filled the arena as he sang. He invoked the spirit of the Green Man, calling on him to bless the folk of Stonewylde with his virility and spirit of growth, and to enter the Circle tonight.

Sylvie felt something change, her subconscious picking up a difference in the drumming and a collective ripple of excitement. She watched as the children approached the Green Man and May Queen for the communion of mead and cakes. She saw Yul move towards the Altar Stone, his dark curls gleaming in the firelight. Magus had told Miranda and Sylvie to wait and not go forward at this point; their turn would come later. So they stood, moving to the rhythm, watching as everyone else shuffled along to receive their ladle of mead and saffron cake.

They sensed the transformation in the atmosphere after the sharing of cake and wine. The energy was raised even further until it seemed that the whole Circle vibrated and pulsated with it. The firelight and blazing torches created a flickering light, making the images of the Green Man painted on the stones appear to move and grin. Sylvie felt his spirit really had entered the place and was now present amongst the community.

When everyone had taken communion, two thrones decorated with greenery and flowers were brought forward. The Green Man and the May Queen were seated and the drumming slowed and quietened until only the soft sweet music of the pipes and flutes could be heard. There was an expectant hush and everyone became still.

'Tonight we have two newcomers in our midst,' came the powerful voice of Magus. 'Two people from the Outside World.'

There was a collective sigh; Sylvie's body thrilled sharply.

'Miranda and Sylvie, come forward.'

Miranda took Sylvie's hand and gave it a little squeeze, then together they stepped into the centre of the circle and approached the Green Man and May Queen. Sylvie felt she was in another world. This experience was far beyond anything she'd ever heard of or read about. Magus had become the Green Man in a way she'd never have thought possible, seeming to have lost his own identity to transform into the spirit of Beltane. He was huge, masculine and very green, his face unrecognisable behind the pigment, his eyes gleaming. The beautiful May Queen embodied young, fresh femininity and was his perfect counterfoil, glowing whitely next to him like the blossom in the greenery all around Stonewylde. Neither of them seemed real any more.

Firelight danced on the primeval pair as it had done throughout the ages on other Beltane partnerships; this was religion at its most elemental and rooted. All around them the throng of people waited in silence, eyes bright with reflected flames and the communion they'd just shared, faces sheened by the heat generated in the Circle. Then another figure stepped forward, staff in hand. Clip was dressed in ceremonial robes too, brilliant green embroidered with gold thread, depicting faces of the Green Man encircled with emblems of the radiant sun. He stood between the thrones and addressed the mother and daughter, twinkling grey eyes belying the solemnity of his words.

'Miranda and Sylvie, you have lived in Stonewylde for a short while. Do you now want to make the commitment to join our community and become part of our way of life?'

'We do,' they chorused.

'Will you uphold our laws, will you live by our values, and will you take Magus to be your lord and master, obeying him in all things, and accepting that in the community of Stonewylde, his word is the law?'

'We will.'

'Will you enter into the spirit of our community, celebrating the joy of the life force of this earth, taking part in all our ceremonies and rituals? Will you honour the Earth Mother and the Solar Father, the mystical union of the two great spirits of female and male, who together hold the life of the planet in balance and continuous regeneration? Will you celebrate with us the Eight Ceremonies in the Wheel of the Year, the Solstices, Equinoxes and Cross Quarter Festivals, handed down to us by our ancestors? Will you take as your own the symbol of the Sacred Pentangle, representing the five elements which govern the planet and all who live on it – Earth, Air, Fire, Water and Spirit?'

'We will.'

'And will you join us in celebrating the magical power represented by the Moon Goddess? She who governs our souls, who waxes and wanes to the rhythm of the earth and the seasons, who ensures our regeneration and our fertility and fecundity, and who ripens every month just as our women ripen?'

'We will.'

'And finally, newcomers, will you enter into the spirit of our sacred landscape at Stonewylde? Will you serve the land and the forces of nature with your lives and your hearts? Will you contribute to our community the gifts you have been given, dedicating your souls to Stonewylde?'

'We will.'

Clip bowed. Magus stood up from his throne, a massive figure of green virility, and took a couple of steps towards them. He too bowed.

'Miranda and Sylvie,' he said. 'You have made sacred promises tonight to become as us, part of the community of Stonewylde. You have made these promises in the Stone Circle, a place of ancient power, and in front of our people. You are now bound by these promises. As the Magus, I offer you lives of joy and fulfilment. You will never want for food, for shelter, for companionship. You are part of our community and in return for your hard work, loyalty and obedience, I promise you will lack for nothing. You are also free to leave if you so wish, but you must swear never to speak in the Outside World of our community or our ways. By the magic which we are able to invoke and to cast, I warn you that should you ever speak of us Outside, you will be cursed and suffer accordingly. Do you accept this condition?'

'We do.'

Magus stepped forward again. He bent and kissed Miranda and then Sylvie, his green lips brushing their mouths. He turned them around, one on either side and took their hands. They faced the roaring fire and the mass of faces glimmering in the flickering light. He raised their hands with his and cried out.

'Folk of Stonewylde, we welcome Miranda and Sylvie into our family! They are now members of our community!'

A great roar of approval reverberated around the Stone Circle, so powerful it made Sylvie quake. She was close to tears and guessed her mother felt the same. They were part of something magical and ancient.

'And now they will eat, drink and dance to the Spirit of the Green Man and the May Queen, to the magic of Beltane.'

Clip bought forward a round wooden tray of ancient wood, upon which sat two small pottery goblets and two speckled cakes. He bowed and offered them to Magus, who took the green-glazed goblets and handed them to Miranda and Sylvie.

'Drink of the mead, elixir of Stonewylde, and become one with us.'

They tipped back the goblets and swallowed the sweet liquid. Sylvie felt its fire course down her throat and into her stomach. A glow expanded inside her.

'Eat of the fruits of Stonewylde, and join us in sharing the Earth.'

They each took a cake and bit into it. Sylvie felt a strange sensation take hold. She swallowed the rest, and within seconds the world began to change. Her lips tingled and tongue felt numb. Her head had become separate, almost, everything inside it colourful and blossoming. Her body was on fire with passion; prickling, twitching, superhuman. She looked up at the great Green Man next to her and it seemed that everything was in slow motion. She smiled at him, a blissful smile, and he smiled back, teeth white in his green face. He squeezed her hand, his eyes blazing into her soul.

The drums started up again and Sylvie felt herself move involuntarily, all shyness gone. Magus, Clip and the May Queen stepped back and Sylvie was left in the centre of the Stone Circle with her mother. They began to dance, moving to the rhythm of the drumming. The strange floating sensation was still within her and she felt so light, as if she could fly. She laughed at the freedom of spirit as her feet skimmed the earth, following the spiral pattern of energy on the soft floor. The Green Men painted on the stones flickered and grinned, quickened by the magic of the ceremony. Mother and daughter danced under their gaze; the primeval dance of Beltane for the regeneration of the Earth Goddess. She who lay breathing beneath their feet.

After a while the drums changed again, signalling the children, young mothers and the older generation to return down the Long Walk to their beds. The rest of the community stayed in the Stone Circle for the Handfasting and Rites of Adulthood. These rituals continued long into the night; many couples would celebrate the joy of union in the bluebell woods surrounding the ancient Circle. Those leaving formed a procession and began to move down the Long Walk. As a fertile adult, Miranda should have stayed behind to join in the rituals, but Magus had asked her to wait till another time. They were silent with exhilaration as they followed the lantern-lit walk.

Sylvie was unaware of Yul close by in the shadows watching her. The sight of Sylvie dancing in the Stone Circle had inflamed his soul and now he burned for her. She was so ethereally beautiful, so delicate and enchanting. Everything had slid into place and all was laid out before him, clear and bright. Yul no longer felt confused; he now knew exactly what he wanted. He still tingled from the cake and mead and had to force himself to hang back and keep out of her sight. This new-found certainty could not be rushed; Sylvie had now joined the community and would be staying at Stonewylde. The future was his but must be entered slowly.

At least he was safe tonight from Buzz and his gang; as adults they'd remain in the Stone Circle for the further rituals and then stay out all night in the woods. Yul knew what went on at Beltane Eve in the Stone Circle and amongst the bluebells in the ancient oak woods. He was relieved that Sylvie was too young to join them. The thought of her larking around in the woods all night, with Buzz on the loose, made his blood run cold.

The Hallfolk turned off from the Long Walk onto the track leading to the Hall, and the Villagers carried on towards the Village. Everyone wished each other a joyful Beltane and Yul managed to catch Sylvie's eye in the lantern light. She smiled at him and raised her hand in a little wave. He nodded, feeling suddenly shy, and trudged off towards the Village to his waiting bed. Before the final bend he glanced back and saw her blond hair and white dress glimmering as she disappeared into the darkness with the other Hallfolk. He recalled the last festival when he'd followed Holly down to the Barn. He smiled to himself. He'd known nothing then, understood nothing. That attraction was just a pale and false imitation of his feelings now. He wondered for a moment how it would be at the next festival – the Summer Solstice. He thought of the magical girl who danced like an angel for the Moon Goddess, and felt a sudden prickle of premonition snake down his spine. His whole world would have changed by then. Everything would be different.

8

The Stone Circle was very different the following morning in the grey, pre-dawn chill. The great stones rose from a wispy mist that swirled above the beaten earth inside the Circle. There were many people present, though nothing compared to the previous night when the whole community had filled the arena. The great bonfire had died down to a smouldering white-hot pile of ash. People lay curled up and sound asleep in their cloaks, as close to the heat as they dared. Sylvie glanced around. Of Magus and Rowan there was no sign, but Clip was there and directed others to awaken the sleepers. Sylvie shivered in the cold half-light and edged closer to the bonfire, spreading her hands to the radiant heat.

'Blessings, Sylvie,' said Clip, spotting her as he prodded curled-up bodies with his staff. 'A Bright Beltane to you.'

'And to you,' she smiled. 'Isn't it freezing?'

'You'll get used to it,' he said. 'Just wait till the Winter Solstice sunrise – now that is cold! Is Miranda not with you?'

'No, I left her fast asleep in her warm bed. Magus said she didn't need to come to this ceremony.'

'It's good then that you came. Brave of you.'

'Magus wanted me here for the sunrise. He's going to give me more Earth energy.'

'Is he now?' mused Clip. 'That is a surprise. And tell me, did you enjoy your welcoming ceremony last night?'

'Oh yes!' exclaimed Sylvie. 'It was wonderful! The most

magical, incredible ... Thank you so much, Clip, for making it special. And for allowing us to join your community and be part of Stonewylde. I can't tell you what this all means to me ...'

He smiled and patted her shoulder.

'It's a pleasure. I'm as delighted as Sol that you've decided to join us permanently. And now I must make sure the mead's ready.'

'Where's Magus?'

'He should be coming out of the woods any time now. Sunrise is about ten minutes off. Look – here they come.'

The Green Man and May Queen had appeared through a gap in the stones, somewhat dishevelled after their night in the woods. Rowan's head-dress had gone. There were smears of green paint on her face and she huddled inside a long green cloak. Magus put his arm around her and helped her over to the Altar Stone. She looked exhausted and leaned into him, resting her tousled head against his chest. He sat her down gently on one of the thrones from the night before and nodded across to Clip, standing by the May Sister. On top of this special aligned stone, decorated with a radiant sun, was a brazier. This was where the Bel Fire would be lit. Clip gave a wave of affirmation and Magus climbed up onto the Altar Stone, magnificent as the Green Man and not seeming tired at all. He turned to face the May Sister and stood silent and still whilst the drums started to beat a rhythm, soft but insistent as the sky became lighter.

Yul stood with the group of woodsmen clustered under the Bel Fire next to Clip. It was always the woodsmen's job not only to build the fires, but also to light them. They'd stacked enough chopped wood around the back of the stone to keep the brazier burning all day through to sunset. Greenbough had divided them into shifts to tend the fire, and Yul had been given first shift, which was why he was now present. He was pleased because now he'd be free for the rest of the day to join in the sports and games.

He'd seen Sylvie's arrival with a leap of the heart, not having expected her to attend this early ceremony. The whole event now took on a deeper significance and he glowed with pleasure at her presence. She looked pinched and cold in the grey light. Her cloak was wrapped tightly around her with the hood pulled forward, almost hiding her face. Only a long skein of hair, spilling like silver silk down the front of her cloak, gave away her identity. No other girl had hair quite like it.

She stood slightly apart from everyone as her mother wasn't there, he noted, and neither were any Hallfolk girls of her own age. But then Buzz appeared from the other side of the smouldering bonfire where he must have been asleep, and made his way over to Sylvie. Yul watched as the big youth stood beside her, making some comment which caused her to smile up at him and allowed the hood to fall back from her face. Yul felt resentment boiling inside him. *He* couldn't stand next to her to chat, but that bastard Buzz could. Where was the girl he'd been with all night? Surely he should still be with her and not Sylvie?

The drums picked up the pace and Greenbough mounted the ladder leaning against the far side of the May Sister. He was getting old but still liked to light the Bel Fire himself; after so many years' service it was his privilege. Magus had begun to chant, his deep voice echoing in the misty Circle and bouncing off the tall stones. Sylvie shivered at the sheer poetry of it, and then Clip gave a cry. Just as the first beam of sunlight blazed around the edge of the stone, Greenbough flicked the lighter and there was a fizz of green flame in the brazier.

The small kindling caught and flickered with orange tongues. The golden light streaming around the stone fell onto the Green Man on the Altar Stone, and Sylvie gasped. She saw him grow; his head-dress and costume shimmer. His green face glowed, the brilliant shaft of sunlight etching the shadows in his eye sockets and under his cheekbones. He looked inhuman in that instant; not Magus at all but the Spirit of Beltane. He raised his arms out wide, chanting powerfully, and then the sun blasted him as it cleared the stone altogether, mingling with the crackling flames in the brazier but rendering them invisible in its magnificence.

The Green Man closed his eyes as the dazzling light washed his face, his body shuddering slightly. Sylvie blinked. He was so

112

radiant it was impossible to stare at him. Yet she could've sworn he was actually giving out light himself, a strange green brightness that glimmered around him. It must surely be a trick of the light, she thought; a reflection of the rising sun on the green pigment. The drumming had reached a crescendo and now began to slow and quieten. A choir of men took up the Green Man's chant and he fell silent, standing perfectly still with his arms outstretched as the sunlight poured over him. Sylvie swallowed and found her mouth was dry. Buzz, still by her side, glanced at her and whispered something, but she couldn't hear and didn't want to turn her attention to him. She moved away slightly, transfixed by the glorious green figure on the Altar Stone.

Yul too watched in wonder. He'd never seen the Beltane sunrise from the Stone Circle before, as no children were usually present for this ceremony. Much as he resented Magus, Yul found himself moved by the sheer splendour. He was awestruck by the power swirling around the Green Man, visible to his eyes if not Sylvie's. He felt the spirals within the Circle and how they coiled by the Altar Stone. He saw the green energy emanating from the Earth and fusing with the sun's pure spectrum of light. As this new force pierced the figure on the stone, his heart lifted with elation at the magic of such natural alchemy. Magus was truly blessed. He glanced across at Sylvie and saw rapture on her face too as she gazed up at the shimmering Green Man.

Once the whole Circle was bathed in golden light, Magus bowed and stepped down from the stone. Goblets of mead were passed around and when everyone had one, the Green Man took the hand of his May Queen. He toasted the Bel Fire blazing on top of the May Sister.

'Bright blessings at Beltane!' he said. 'May the magic of the Green Man be with you all, at this festival and throughout the year.'

'Bright blessings at Beltane!' everyone chorused and drank the golden mead. It wasn't the fiery brew used in the communion, but nevertheless Sylvie felt its strength as it hit her empty stomach. She noticed Buzz manoeuvring himself towards her once more and edged away to stand next to Clip. Then she spotted Yul on the outer edge of the throng, his eyes fixed on her. She felt her cheeks flush, wondering how long he'd been watching her. She hadn't realised he was here. He raised his empty goblet to her in a silent toast and she nodded back with a small smile. Then he turned and next minute she saw him climbing the ladder to the brazier and feeding more small branches into its maw. He was so agile; she couldn't imagine Buzz climbing up there with such speed and fluidity.

An old-fashioned carriage arrived in the Circle, decorated with boughs of greenery and white blossom and pulled by a beautiful horse of purest white. Sylvie watched as Magus led his stumbling Queen over towards it, his arm around her shoulders supporting her. She said something to him and he stroked her cheek tenderly, smoothing the tangled hair as he answered her. He bent to kiss her forehead and then helped her into the carriage, tucking her cloak in around her and shutting the door. Her pale face peered out from the shadowy interior as the carriage pulled away and Magus turned to face the people.

'Down to the Great Barn for a hearty breakfast, folks!' he said with a smile. 'I'll be joining you in a while.'

People began to move towards the Long Walk, talking together companionably. Buzz came over to Sylvie and beamed at her.

'Will you walk down with me, Sylvie?' he asked.

'I think . . .'

'She's staying up here with me, Buzz,' said Magus, clapping the young man on the back. 'She'll be down later.'

The Circle was almost empty now with just a few Villagers staying behind to tidy up. A couple of woodsmen poked at the remnants of the bonfire, pushing half-burnt branches towards the centre where they'd be consumed. Yul helped them as his Bel Fire was stoked for a while. An old woman cleared the flat stones of the remains of cake from the night before, sweeping the crumbs into a flaxen bag and picking up any larger pieces from the ground. Two men loaded the nearly empty barrels of mead and chest of goblets onto a waiting cart. Sylvie watched all this activity in trepidation, unexpectedly fearful now that the moment had come.

Magus turned to her and smiled.

'Don't be scared,' he said softly. 'It won't hurt, you know. But I must be careful not to give you too much. Take care you don't touch me as I release it.'

She nodded and stared up at him nervously, her eyes enormous in her face. She trusted him completely. And yet it was strange to be standing in a stone circle with a bright green man covered in leaves, about to be doused with magic. She grinned suddenly at the incongruity of the situation and Magus smiled back, white teeth flashing in his green face.

'I do like your sense of humour, Sylvie,' he said. 'This is a really serious and solemn occasion but you're right, it does have some bizarre aspects.'

'How do you always seem to know what I'm thinking?' she asked.

'I don't. But I'm very in tune with you and sometimes I pick up on it. Just a vague impression of your feelings, not specific thoughts. Come over here behind the Altar Stone, away from all these Villagers. I could send them away but they'd only have to come back later, so just ignore them. They won't be aware of anything.'

He was wrong there. Yul watched them covertly but intently, wondering what on earth was going on. He edged away from the bonfire and discreetly climbed the ladder propped against the May Sister. Peering over the top through the dancing flames of the Bel Fire he could see them perfectly but knew they wouldn't notice him. He watched as Magus led Sylvie around the flat stone and stood facing her. She seemed so tiny compared to him. He spoke and she nodded, raising her arms out before her, palms down, fingers outstretched. Magus too raised his arms to form an arch with hers, their fingertips not quite touching. They stood for a second like this.

'Do you feel the Earth Magic?' murmured Magus. 'Keep very still and just feel.'

115

There was nothing for a moment, and then she sensed a crackling around him. She concentrated hard and saw the air all about him quivering, like summer heat on a tarmac road. Her eyes widened and he smiled.

'Good, you've found it. I'm alive with it, Sylvie. It's very, very powerful right now so be careful. I'm opening up and loosening it a little. Normally I keep it locked tight within me. I want you to gently feel it with your fingertips. Don't touch me, remember. Just let your fingertips sense the energy.'

She felt a burning itch in her fingers, an effervescence of sensation as she picked up the aura around him. She nodded and stared up at him, recoiling slightly from the black fire that blazed in his dark eyes.

'Now draw a little of the energy into yourself. Just a little or it will overwhelm you. Take it, Sylvie. Take what I give you now and be whole, healthy and healed.'

Holding his gaze she gingerly pulled at the force-field around him and felt her fingertips begin to throb. He heard her sharp intake of breath and saw something in her eyes flinch as his power entered her. He felt her tentatively drawing energy from him, her soul sipping at his magic. He smiled radiantly, his eyes dazzling black.

Yul gasped as he realised what was happening. The same thing he'd witnessed in the woods back in March! Only this time Magus was almost exploding with Earth Magic. Beltane is a powerful festival and he'd only minutes before received the energy himself. Watching them through the crackling flames of the Bel Fire, Yul couldn't be sure exactly, but it seemed as if the green magic was flowing from Magus' fingertips and into Sylvie's. The aura around the great man shimmered like a bubble blown into the wind, its edges and definitions ever-changing. Sylvie now glowed slightly, the green radiance strange around her. She's quicksilver, not Earth Magic, Yul thought to himself. She doesn't need this. It's too much, with the full moon tomorrow.

But then the green began to fade and as Yul watched, the aura drew itself back into the Green Man's body. They both lowered their arms and Sylvie nodded as Magus said something to her. She looked fine – brimming with joy, it seemed. To his surprise, Yul discovered a knot of resentment inside him. He didn't like the idea of Magus healing her. He didn't want her to share the man's magic when she had so much of her own. He watched as they walked together out of the Stone Circle and into the Long Walk. Angrily he jammed a log into the brazier and leapt off the ladder onto the soft earth. Maybe after this Sylvie wouldn't be moondancing tomorrow night at all. And then she wouldn't need him to take care of her.

Magus and Sylvie walked in comfortable silence for a while. She stared up at the overhead tunnel of new beech leaves interlacing above them, the bright blue sky visible and vivid against the brilliant green. She felt more alive than ever before in her life. The Green Man smiled down at her.

'Thank you,' she said.

'You're welcome. All the Outside World has gone from you now. You belong to Stonewylde.'

'Good.'

She grinned up at him, almost skipping beside his long strides.

'You have the most amazing gift.'

'It's not mine. It's the gift of the Earth Goddess and she's chosen to bestow it upon me. I realise how honoured I am.'

'Do you heal many people?'

'None at all. I don't believe that's why the Earth Magic is given to me. I keep it for myself because without it I couldn't run Stonewylde effectively. It gives me the energy I need to lead the community.'

'So why did you heal me then?'

'Because you're very special and I didn't like to see you suffering. You've been ravaged by all the poisons and toxins they've forced into you. Your body's been damaged, and I don't like to see beauty violated. You'd have recovered anyway living here. I simply speeded up the process.'

'I feel as if I could fly!'

'Maybe you could! Sometimes I feel like that myself. I've learnt how to control the energy now, but I remember as a young man when it first came to me how I wasted it. I let it flood out of me at every opportunity. But not now. I'm careful now, like a dragon guarding its hoard.'

'You certainly don't look tired, even though you've been awake all night. Poor Rowan looked so exhausted.'

'She'll be asleep now,' he said. 'I'll give her another hour or so, then she must come down to the Village for the festival.'

'Did you have a nice time last night?'

He shot her a quick glance and his lips twitched with amusement.

'Very nice, thank you.'

'It must be fun staying up in the woods all night. A bit creepy though, I'd have thought.'

'Creepy? No, not at all! The woods are beautiful at night-time, especially at Beltane.'

'Rowan looked such a mess! What happened to her head-dress?'

'It's left under a tree as a sort of shrine.'

'Oh, I see. Has she gone home now?'

'No, she's at the Hall. Actually, she was a little upset that I didn't stay with her. It's the custom for me to ride in the carriage with the May Queen and look after her at the Hall, especially if she's a Villager. Rowan couldn't understand why I needed to stay behind here this morning. But Cherry's looking after her, running the bath and putting her to bed, so she'll be fine.'

'I hope so. I wouldn't want to have spoiled it for her.'

'Don't worry, I'll make it up to her. She's probably better off enjoying the luxury on her own.'

'Oh yes! She'd be so embarrassed if you were around. That's okay then.'

He shook his head and chuckled.

'Sylvie, you are so sweet. You and I must have a talk at some point about the reality of Stonewylde and all that we do here. But not yet. And here's your turning for the cottage. See you later on down in the Village. Wish Miranda a Bright Beltane from me.'

'I hope I can take part in this next year,' said Sylvie, as she and Miranda sat watching the Maypole Dance on the Village Green later that morning. She longed to join the girls who skipped and weaved around the great decorated pole, long hair and white dresses flying, smiles on their faces.

'It looks incredibly complicated,' replied her mother. 'See how the ribbons and all the creepers and leaves not only get plaited, but how the plaits are then woven together?'

'I'd really like to learn,' said Sylvie. 'It's a beautiful dance.'

May Day was clear and sunny and the Green was full of people, Villagers and Hallfolk together. Everyone had breakfasted in the Great Barn and was now dressed in white or green. Magus still wore his Green Man costume and wreath of leaves. Although the pigment had been washed off his skin, traces of it lingered, giving him a leafy green tinge. Rowan the May Queen was beautiful in a fresh white dress and newly-made wreath of hawthorn blossom and bluebells. But she was somehow different today, if anyone had looked closely. Her sparkle had gone and her eyes were tired.

Sylvie should've felt tired too as she'd been up since first light, but instead she bubbled with new energy. She felt more alive now than at any point she could ever remember. The drips and doctors seemed like a distant nightmare today. She lay back on the grass next to her mother and gazed up at the forget-me-not blue sky. She felt the warm earth beneath her back and stretched out her hands, caressing the grass under her palms. She smiled with perfect contentment. Miranda glanced down at her daughter affectionately, happy to see her looking so healthy and joyful.

'Look, darling, it's the boys' turn now. This must be the Morris dancing you asked Magus about when we first arrived here. Do you remember? Oh don't they all look lovely! It's like stepping back in time.'

Sylvie sat up on the grass as a large group of young men trooped into the centre of the Village Green, replacing the young women who'd now finished their dance. Dressed in green trousers and jerkins, with white ribbons tied in fluttering bunches around their wrists and knees, the boys milled about in readiness for the next event. Sylvie noticed Yul immediately, his thin dark face serious as he tightened the ribbons and accepted his wooden staff from the leader. Buzz was also there, laughing and joking with his group of Hallfolk friends as they waited around for everyone to get into place.

'Oh – look, Mum, there's someone with a black face!' said Sylvie.

They both stared at the young man, a Villager dressed in a strange, tattered costume, whose face had been blackened. He wore a tall hat spiked with pheasant tail-feathers and his ragged outfit was decorated with many brightly coloured ribbons. He stood inside a woven hoop of wicker that had been placed flat on the grass, in the centre of the group of men. They all now took up position around him, forming a huge spoked circle.

'How strange,' said Miranda. She turned to a plump woman sitting close by, surrounded by a clutch of young children, and asked her about the man. The woman laughed, delighted to talk with the Newcomers.

'Why, 'tis our Jack in the Green!' she said. 'You watch, my dears. See how he gets caught up as the dance goes on.'

'But why's his face been painted black?' asked Sylvie.

'He's in guise!' said the woman. ''Tis all part o' the dance and the mumming. 'Tis only soot and grease. We have 'un at Yule too, with the Bone Horse. But at Beltane 'tis Jack in the Green – you'll see how he's trapped in the branches.'

The musicians sat together and re-tuned their instruments as a large crowd gathered to watch. The music began and the men were off, leaping over the staffs, banging wood with other young men and kicking high in the air. The dance was intricate, with potential for injury as the thick staffs cracked together up high and down low. Yul was supple and graceful and Sylvie enjoyed watching him dance. He caught her eye and flushed with pleasure at her attention. Being heavier and larger, Buzz wasn't so light on his feet, and the previous night's antics had taken their toll.

Several times he stumbled and cursed, and Yul had to bite his tongue every time he came close. Buzz noticed his mocking glance and his face flooded scarlet.

'You wait, you little bastard! I'm going to get you today.'

The dance moved round and Yul was unable to reply to this, so contented himself by making a flicking sign instead. At Stonewylde this dismissive gesture was the ultimate insult, a contemptuous flick of the open hand towards the earth implying 'Go to the Otherworld!'. The music increased in tempo and the lone figure in the centre, so incongruous in his jaunty hat and tattered clothes, began to skip and hop on the spot. Then he lifted the woven ring of wicker from the ground and held it around himself at chest height.

The dancers crashed their staffs hard together and uttered cries of 'Hey!' as they leapt about. Sylvie noticed that the Jack figure now stood still within his wicker hoop. One by one the dancers stepped forward and propped their staffs upright on the ground against this circle, gradually forming a kind of pointed pyre of wood around him. More and more branches followed, the empty-handed dancers leaping around the figure now rapidly disappearing inside his cage of wood.

Finally every dancer had placed his staff to form the central cone. They circled fast with many kicks and skips, and the wild music reached a crescendo. The Jack could no longer be seen at all behind his framework, and suddenly the music stopped and all the dancers leapt high in the air and shouted, 'Jack – ho!' Sylvie jumped, quite shocked at the suddenness of the noise and the way the man in the centre had apparently vanished.

'There, see what I mean? 'Tis powerful stuff, our Jack in the Green dance,' said the woman, a baby now suckling contentedly at her great breast. 'They do say, some of the old 'uns, that back in the past, they'd set the Jack afire now.'

'Really?' exclaimed Miranda. 'How extraordinary!'

'Aye, burn him as he stood there trapped in his cage. And afore that, they'd poke him through the branches with knives, so as he couldn't run.'

121

'Ooh – but not nowadays?' said Sylvie, horrified.

'No, maid!' chuckled the woman. 'Not nowadays! Not at Stonewylde!'

The dancers turned to the audience sitting all around and bowed. Everyone cheered and clapped, and then they all took their staffs and revealed the hidden man still standing holding his wicker ring. The audience cheered again and the Jack made a great bow as everyone started to disperse. Yul grinned across at Sylvie, pleased that she was still watching him. Miranda caught the look and glared at him.

'Don't encourage him, Sylvie,' she warned. 'You know what Magus said about him.'

'I'm not!' retorted Sylvie indignantly. 'He only smiled. There's no law against that.'

'You know what I mean. That boy's trouble, I can tell.'

'I don't see how you can say that, Mum. You don't even know him.'

'No and neither do you, so let's keep it that way. If you're starting to take an interest in boys, there are plenty of nice Hallfolk ones. Look over there – one's smiling at you now.'

She nodded towards Buzz, hot and sweaty from the dance, and Sylvie grimaced.

'No thanks!'

The Naming of the Babies, held later in the morning, was a lovely ceremony. Sylvie and Miranda were amazed at how many little bundles there were, from newborns to babies almost a year old – all the children born during the year since the previous Beltane. The babies were carried in turn up to the dais where the Green Man and the May Queen sat together on their thrones. One by one, mothers handed their babies to Magus. Holding the baby aloft, he announced its name, kissed it and blessed it with Bright Beltane Blessings. Rowan then presented the mother with a small silver charm on a ribbon for the child to wear. The charm represented the festival nearest the baby's birthday, the same symbol that would be embossed on the silver disc presented at the Rite of Adulthood ceremony in years to come.

The babies were well behaved and the ceremony went smoothly. Clip, standing nearby and smiling indulgently, chatted as they watched the procession of mothers and babies circling the Green.

'Don't they look sweet!' exclaimed Sylvie. 'They're all adorable and none of them are crying.'

'The Villagers have such enormous families,' said Miranda. 'There are a few Hallfolk babies and mums, but it seems most of them are Villagers.'

'Since Sol became the magus he has great plans for expansion. There's plenty of fertile land to grow enough food, but we'll need a lot more labour.'

'That sounds a little cold-blooded and calculating,' said Miranda, watching Magus's smiling face as he kissed each baby in turn, with a word and a hug for every proud mother too. 'I can't believe that's the only reason behind this incredible ... brood of babies.'

'Well, Sol's actively encouraged all Village women to have more children and he tells everyone they're the future of Stone-wylde. He's made it desirable and praiseworthy for a couple to have a huge brood, to the point where it's now become the norm. Seven or eight children in a family isn't uncommon, and there are a couple of families, I believe, with more than ten.'

'Ten? That's crazy!'

'Regardless of Sol's motives, it's lovely to have a big family knowing the children will grow up in a happy community and want for nothing. Plenty of good food, clothes and shoes, a warm cottage and lots of space to roam free. And we have a wonderful Nursery here in the Village, so every mother gets all the support and assistance she needs.'

'Yes, I suppose so,' agreed Miranda, looking at the rosy-cheeked babies dressed in delicately embroidered white clothes and decorated with garlands of flowers. 'It makes me feel quite broody.'

Clip smiled a little slyly.

'Well, doubtless it'll be your turn soon.'

Miranda went pink.

'No chance of that,' she retorted.

'Don't say that, Mum! You never know ... you're still young enough and I'd love a little brother or sister.'

'You're being ridiculous, Sylvie,' said Miranda sharply.

'Do you have any children, Clip?' asked Sylvie. 'I don't even know if you're married or not.'

'No, I've never been blessed in that way.'

'Maybe one day,' said Sylvie.

'No, there's no chance of that,' echoed Clip. 'I'm the shaman and must live a life of solitude and aestheticism. I tread a lonely path and leave the riotous living to my brother.' He glanced at Miranda's expression and smiled. 'Only joking, of course.'

The final event of the morning was lunch, served out in the open on the Green at long trestle tables. The older women responsible for the food had prepared a feast. Everyone sat around on the grass eating and drinking, and afterwards many wandered off home for a rest as the next events weren't to take place for a couple of hours or so. Yul knew it was times like these that were the danger spots of his day. He could see his father over by the food tables and bar, his plate laden, swilling down cider. At least he'd be incapacitated by so much food and drink. Magus was eating lunch with the May Queen and would be mixing with the Villagers until the games started. Yul located Buzz lying on the grass near the edge of the Green teasing Holly, who pushed him away irritably.

He decided to go up to the Stone Circle where it would be peaceful and quiet. The Bel Fire would be burning and one of the woodsmen would be there tending it. Without a word to anyone, for nobody would question his absence, Yul slipped away. A young blond boy who'd been playing near the edge of the Green raced across the grass to where Buzz was flicking and pinching Holly.

'Buzz, Buzz, he's gone!'

'Okay, ssh now! Come over here.'

Buzz stood up and pulled the child away from the group of Hallfolk.

'He went up towards the Long Walk! Just a couple of minutes ago.'

'Alone?'

'Yes.'

Buzz smiled at this and signalled to his gang. They heaved themselves off the grass and came over to join him.

'But Buzz, you said there'd be a reward if anyone noticed him going off on his own.'

'What? Oh yeah, remind me later on at the Hall and I'll give you something.'

The little boy frowned as he watched Buzz lumbering off with four of his mates in tow. He wasn't sure he'd done the right thing after all.

It was warm and drowsy at the Stone Circle. The sky was brilliant blue, the air hummed with bee-song and the sun beat down surprisingly hard for so early in the year. The Green Men painted on the stones looked down sleepily at the bonfire embers still smouldering at one end of the Circle. The Bel Fire in its brazier up on the stone burnt brightly. Yul saw that it had been recently built up again for the iron basket was full of unburnt logs. One of the older woodsmen was propped up against the stone, cider jug by his side, snoring loudly.

Yul smiled and walked around the great Circle touching each of the huge stones reverently. He thought of all the ceremonies he'd enjoyed in this place. The Stone Circle was a place where magic could be invoked and cast. He'd seen it done at many ceremonies. Yul tried to imagine what it must be like to be the magus and have such power at your disposal. Once he'd seen Magus shoot blue flames from his finger tips, and at sunrise one solstice had seen him levitate just off the Altar Stone as the first rays touched him. He shivered at the thought of it. The Stone Circle was a truly sacred place.

Yul felt sleepy, having been up since long before dawn, and

decided to have a nap. He spread himself on the Altar Stone like a sand-lizard. Heat emanated from the ancient rock and the sun was a bright yellow disc on his closed red eyelids as he stretched out, relaxed and at peace. He sighed with contentment and began to drift off to sleep. Suddenly it went dark. He opened his eyes just as a large hand covered his mouth. A pair of light blue eyes only centimetres away gazed into his startled grey ones.

'Gotcha!'

Buzz clambered up on the stone and sat down hard astride Yul, pinning the boy's arms onto the stone with his large knees. Yul grunted as the breath was forced from his lungs. The hand remained over his mouth and Buzz grinned gleefully. Yul felt a strange sense of detachment.

'Beltane Blessings!' crowed Buzz. 'And what are we going to do with you, Village boy? Any ideas?'

Yul gazed at the blue sky, ignoring the dead weight on his stomach and chest and the pain in his arms. There was a feeling of inevitability about the situation. He'd spent his childhood at Buzz's mercy, but today he sensed would be more serious than the usual bullying and tormenting. Buzz's next words confirmed his fear.

'We've decided, Yul, to make this a proper punishment. You said that you enjoyed the last one Magus gave you. Gardening, I believe. But there's no danger you'll enjoy this, is there, lads?'

They all chuckled.

'Now, we've got to get you out of the Circle without any fuss. It'll just make it worse if you struggle, so don't bother.'

Buzz lugged himself off Yul, who took a gulp of air. A piece of material was quickly tied around his mouth in a rough gag. Hands dragged him off the stone and hoisted him upright. His arms were pinned behind his back and tied at the wrists. He gazed ahead unfocused, trying to disassociate himself from the situation.

'Now we're taking you off to the woods and out of earshot. But there's something I've got to do first. It's been so long since I gave you a good going over.'

Buzz pulled back his fist and punched Yul in the stomach as hard as he could. The pain was excruciating and Yul jack-knifed forward, only to be yanked upright from behind. He choked, nearly vomiting as the pain rolled around inside his stomach. The blow had winded him and he couldn't catch his breath around the gag.

'Just a little taste of things to come. Off we go then.'

The gang frog-marched him into the oak woods behind the Circle, well away from the snoring woodsman beneath the Bel Fire. They found a suitable tree and untied Yul's arms. Then they pulled the green jerkin off over his head to reveal his back.

'Shall we get his trousers and boots off too?'

'No, we'll do it just like the proper whippings in the Village Green. Tie him up against the tree. That's right, stretch his arms around the trunk, so his back's nice and open. Tie the wrists tight. I don't want him falling down halfway through it.'

Yul's cheek and bare chest and stomach were jammed against the rough bark of the oak tree. The rope bit into his wrists as they bound him with swift, vicious tugs. The gag was still in place and he couldn't move at all; he was completely at their mercy. The gang stood back and surveyed him.

'Look – someone's had a go at him already,' said Fennel, frowning at the criss-cross of old stripes on his back and arms, and the fresher weals and patchwork of ugly bruises from the beating after the Story Web.

'That'll be his father,' said Buzz. 'But Yul still hasn't learnt his lesson, has he?'

'So that's where we come in,' said Fennel. 'This little shit is going to be sorted out once and for all.'

They laughed excitedly at this.

'Okay, you've all got your knives?' asked Buzz. 'Let's cut the switches now, and make sure they're young shoots, nice and whippy.'

They wandered off amongst the trees, slicing off young branches whilst Yul remained silent and still, wrapped around the oak tree. His heart thudded against the serrated bark and he imagined the tree's heart reciprocating in sympathy.

'Right, let's get on with it. We don't want to miss the games or the tug o' war. Before we start, Yul, I should tell you something.'

Buzz walked around to the side of the tree so Yul could see him. Yul tried to look beyond him but Buzz jammed his face up close.

'In case you get any ideas about running to Magus and telling tales, you need to understand that there'll be consequences if you do. This morning during the Maypole Dance I noticed a little dark-haired Village girl who quite took my fancy. I'm lining 'em up, you see. One of the joys of being an adult at last. And then I realised that this pretty young girl is your little sister Rosie, all grown up.'

At this, Yul jerked against the tree and Buzz laughed.

'Obviously she's still too young, but it won't be that long till her Rite of Adulthood, will it? She's thirteen, I was told, nearly fourteen, so just a couple of years. By the look of her she's going to be a real juicy little plum. So you see, Yul, if you go blabbing to anybody about today, I shall make absolutely sure that it's me that Rosie gets for her Rite. I'd come back especially, even if I was away at university. I'd enjoy showing your little sister what it's all about. Do you understand? Nod your head.'

Yul nodded violently.

'And are you going to tell anyone about this beating? Shake your head.'

Yul shook as much as he was able against the tree. Buzz smiled.

'Good. I'm pleased we've got that one cleared up. Now, I'm going to start, lads, and we'll take it in turns.'

'How many shall we give him?'

'No idea! As much as he can take. I've never done this before so I don't know how long you can keep going. But it's got to be a bloody good thrashing, no half measures.'

'So we don't have to be careful about marking him after all?'

'No. Looking at the state of him, this won't be the first time, so nobody's going to be too bothered if he gets another beating, are they? His father will probably thank us.'

'How hard shall we slice him, Buzz?'

'As hard as you can. Watch me, boys. Like this!'

9

Sylvie sat bolt upright on the grass.

'Mum, I want to go up to the Stone Circle!'

Miranda was almost asleep, dozing in the heat after lunch. She was feeling happy as Magus had chatted to them earlier and said how beautiful she looked in her white May dress with flowers in her hair. She smiled dreamily at the thought of him. Even with slightly green skin he was still divine.

'Now, Mum! I've got to go right now!'

Sylvie jumped up.

'What's the rush, darling? We're meant to be resting, ready for this afternoon.'

'I'm going, Mum. Don't worry, I'll be fine on my own.'

'No, I'll come too. I could do with a walk after all that food. You go on ahead if you're so desperate to see the stones and I'll follow. See you up there.'

Buzz was panting slightly, perspiration beading his upper lip and brow even in the shade of the woods.

'That's no good, it's completely split! Here, use mine instead for the next one. Birch is definitely the best.'

He felt exhilarated, pulsing with power. The woods were very quiet in the hot afternoon sun, silent but for the insistent clear call of a cuckoo. Yul was acutely aware of the roughness of the oak bark against his cheek and front, focusing on that small hurt rather than the searing pain that raged across his back.

Sylvie ran up the Long Walk under the shade of the over-hanging beeches, the lime-green soft-haired leaves unnoticed in her haste. She reached the top and entered the Stone Circle. It was peaceful up here, the heat quite overpowering as it shimmered off the stones. But something wasn't right. She noticed the old man sprawled against a stone and raced over to him; his deep snoring told her he was breathing and only asleep. She darted around the stones, listening and looking, all senses alert. She knew something was very wrong.

Then she heard it – faint laughter and an exultant shout. She ran into the wood towards the sound and saw movement. Green figures crowded around a tree, capering with glee. She saw the largest of them step back, take a run up, and slice viciously at the tree with a long stick. She heard a swishing crack and a howl of triumph from the group. Then she saw what was tied to the tree.

'Stop! Stop, STOP!'

It came out as a scream as she crashed through the bluebells and hart's tongues to reach the dreadful scene.

'Sylvie! What are you doing here?'

'What are *you* doing? How could you? Oh no!'

She gaped in horror at the exposed back and the dark weals slashed across it. She recognised the tousled mop of curls even though Yul's face was hidden by hair and the gag.

'Now, Sylvie, it's not quite what it seems . . .' began Buzz.

'No,' Fennel continued quickly, 'you wouldn't understand as an Outsider, but this is a Beltane custom. It's part of the rituals for the festival.'

'I don't believe you!' cried Sylvie. The five youths frowned down at her, all of them red in the face. She glared fiercely back at them. 'I'm going to ask Magus if this is a Beltane custom. And you can all come with me.'

'You're joking! Look, little miss nosey, if you think . . .'

'Untie him now!' shouted Sylvie, anger overcoming her natural timidity. 'Right now! And the gag! Yul, are you alright?'

'Ah, she knows his name,' mocked Buzz, recovering his com-posure quickly.

'Of course I know his name. He's been digging my garden all month as a punishment,' Sylvie replied icily. 'Come on, untie him and we're going to see Magus. I can't believe he'd allow this. You're all sick!'

The gag had come off and Yul swallowed hard, trying to moisten his throat. The rope binding his wrists was eventually unknotted and he uncurled his stiff arms from around the trunk, trying to straighten up. He staggered, as much from shock as from the pain that lacerated his back, but managed to stand upright.

'I'm fine,' he said, shakily. 'No problem.'

His legs were trembling so much that he sat down quickly and made a great show of rubbing his badly chafed wrists. His hands were white from lack of circulation and he tried to flex them, wincing as the blood started to flow again.

'Sylvie, I think you'll find that Yul won't want you to tell Magus. Isn't that right, Yul?' said Buzz, prodding him hard in the ribs with his boot. Yul looked up at them all through his dark hair, his mouth bitter. He nodded silently.

'Yul?' Sylvie asked incredulously.

'Yes. It's a private matter and I don't want him to know. You mustn't tell him.'

'So if you don't mind, Sylvie, we'll go back to the Village now. We don't want to miss the tug o' war. Do we, lads?'

They chorused their agreement and trooped off, laughing loudly.

'See you at the games, Yul, old mate,' Buzz called over his shoulder. 'If you're still up to it!'

Sylvie sat down beside Yul. She waited silently, remembering the emotional aftermath following a session at the hands of a gang. The feelings of frustration, anger and helplessness, and the apparent futility of trying to get an adult to intervene.

'We'd best be getting back to the Village for the games,' Yul said at last, his voice almost normal.

'Do you feel up to it? I don't think you—'

'That bastard's not going to stop me! He'll love it if I don't go.

I'm going to take part if it's the last thing I do,' Yul replied fiercely.

'But you're injured!'

'It's okay, really. I've had worse than that.'

'Let me see. Turn around a minute.'

He swivelled about and she winced at the sight of the thick red weals that slashed across his brown back. She felt a strange urge to lean forward and kiss the soft skin at the base of his neck between his shoulder blades. Instead she traced one of the purple-red ridges with a gentle finger.

'The skin's not broken,' she said.

'Makes a change,' he muttered.

'So who's done this to you before?'

'My father.'

'Does Magus know?'

He laughed sharply at this.

'What difference would that make? It's not against the laws to beat your son. He's never seen fit to stop my father. In fact, Magus has it in for me as well. See this scar?' He pointed to the pale pink line across his dark cheek. 'That's from him.'

'*From Magus?*'

She stared at him in disbelief and he sighed bitterly.

'It doesn't matter, Sylvie, if you believe me or not. It's the truth. You don't know the half of it.'

'But Magus isn't cruel! He'd never hurt you, surely? Or let your father beat you. Magus is a kind man, a gentle man.'

'You don't know him at all. You've only seen one side of him. There's another side, a darker side.'

Sylvie gazed at him in consternation, wanting to believe him but finding it impossible to reconcile the gentleness she'd experienced at Magus' hands with what Yul told her now. She felt Yul trembling, his arms hugging his knees, trying to hide the tell-tale signs of trauma as the reaction set in. His distress was genuine, but this was Buzz's doing, not Magus'.

'I've only seen Magus being kind. I just can't believe he'd treat one of his people so badly. He seems such a wonderful man. He rescued me from the most awful life, and he's healed me with the Earth Magic.'

'I know. I saw him do it.'

'Did you? Oh . . .'

'I'm sorry – I didn't mean to. I know he's been very kind and gentle with you. He's not cruel to everyone, I admit. But he really hates me.'

'But why? What have you done to deserve this?'

'I don't know! I can't . . .'

His voice cracked and he took a shuddering breath, struggling to control himself. He would not cry in front of Sylvie. She longed to hug him but knew that would be the worst thing possible right now.

'Come on then,' she said briskly, jumping to her feet. She picked up his green jerkin and tossed it to him. 'Better put this on or they'll all see what's happened. I still think you should tell Magus what Buzz did, but . . .'

He pulled the jerkin over his head, flinching with pain. He stopped as she spoke, his face half out of the neck hole.

'Sylvie, promise me you won't tell Magus. Please!'

'Well okay, if you really—'

'Seriously. Don't think you'll let him know anyway because it's the right thing to do. I can't tell you what would happen if you did, but it's not me who'll suffer, it's someone else. And I would kill Buzz rather than allow that. Promise me!'

She looked into his smoky grey eyes, so full of distress. Her heart cried out to him but she kept her face impassive.

'I promise.'

'Thank you. And thank you for stopping them. You were very brave to stand up to them. They'd have done a lot worse if you hadn't arrived. They were still only getting started and Buzz was really enjoying himself.'

They made their way out of the woods towards the Circle and the bright sunlight.

'Why was Buzz having a go at you anyway? Was it because of

134

Holly? She said yesterday that you and Buzz had been fighting over her.'

She was surprised to find that the words stuck in her throat. But Yul laughed harshly at this.

'I'd never fight anyone over Holly! She just likes to imagine everyone's interested in her, and it's certainly not the reason that Buzz has it in for me.'

'So why did he do this today?"

'It's been going on for years, for as long as I can remember. He's a bully and he sees me as his punch-bag. He's just using Holly as an excuse to pick a fight with me. I told her back at the Equinox what I thought of Buzz and I expect she's been stirring it up again.'

Sylvie nodded, recognising that perhaps Holly liked to place herself at the centre of things.

'How come you were up here?' he asked. 'Everyone else is in the Village having fun.'

She shook her head.

'I really don't know. I felt—'

'Sylvie!! There you are! Where on earth have you been?'

Miranda came marching towards them, red-cheeked. She glared at her daughter and glared even harder at Yul, who looked down guiltily.

'What's been going on? If you've even touched my daughter—'

'No, Mum! For goodness' sake! I found Yul in the woods.'

Sylvie was horribly embarrassed at her mother's intimations. How could she be so stupid and insensitive?

'Beltane Blessings, Ma'am,' mumbled Yul. 'I'll be off to the games now.'

He loped off down the Long Walk and Sylvie turned furiously on her mother.

'How *could* you, Mum? I'll never forgive you for embarrassing me like that!'

'Hold on a minute, miss! You dragged me up here and then you disappeared. I couldn't find you and I was worried sick. The

135

old man over there hadn't seen you at all. Then you come wandering out of the woods with that boy, who we both know is a trouble-maker and a nasty piece of work—'

'No he isn't!' Sylvie almost screamed at her. 'How dare you say such things! You don't know anything!'

'Sylvie, calm down and listen! You know what Magus told us about him. You know—'

'I know Magus has told us a load of rubbish and lies! Magus has it in for poor Yul, and he—'

'Sylvie! That's enough, thank you! I will not have you speaking against Magus. It's thanks to him that we're here and that you're still alive. Have you already forgotten what our lives were like before Stonewylde?'

'No, but—'

'And what about that beautiful ceremony last night? Magus is a wonderful man and that boy has twisted the truth around if he's told you otherwise. I know who I believe and it's not that Village boy.'

'Yes, well I know who I believe, and it *is* that "Village boy"! God, have you heard yourself, Mum? You sound like one of those stuck-up Hallfolk.'

'Well we are Hallfolk now. And not stuck up. It's just the natural order of things here. Magus told me that Yul's a trouble-maker. Magus said he's cunning and sly.'

'Oh, Magus said, Magus said. I'm sick of you parroting what Magus said just because you fancy him!'

Back in Woodland Cottage Sylvie still wasn't talking to Miranda when the evening dance started in the Great Barn. Miranda had abandoned attempts to patch up their argument, and given up expecting an apology. She ignored her daughter whom she wanted very much to slap. Instead Miranda concentrated on making herself lovely for the evening ahead. Her long red hair gleamed in a silky flow down her back; her green-grey eyes sparkled. She was still a young woman and for once was going to put herself first. If Sylvie wanted to sulk and spoil the

136

evening, that was her choice and her problem.

'Are you coming to the dance then? Because I'm leaving now,' said Miranda to Sylvie's back. Sylvie shrugged. She desperately wanted to go but couldn't give in.

'Fine, well have a nice evening at home. See you later.'

Sylvie spun round and glared at her.

'So you're going to leave me here alone?'

'Yes I am. You're always saying you want more space. And if you're old enough to have flouncy little adolescent tantrums then you're also old enough to stay here by yourself.'

'But I want to come!' wailed Sylvie.

'Then for goodness' sake snap out of it!' said Miranda in exasperation. 'Brush your hair, wash your face and let's go!'

'But I haven't got changed!'

'It doesn't matter, Sylvie. Most people will still be wearing their white May clothes I expect. Just come on, please, so we don't miss too much of it.'

The dance was in full swing when they arrived. Everyone was merry and hot from stomping around the Great Barn. People had spilled on to the Green as it was so warm and the food and drink had been set up outside, leaving more space inside for dancing. Sylvie scanned the crowds for a glimpse of Yul but he was nowhere to be seen. She saw Buzz and his gang and breathed a sigh of relief. At least they weren't tormenting Yul in some dark corner. Buzz caught sight of her and waved.

'Hey, Sylvie, come over here and join us!'

She shook her head.

'Come on! Or do you want me to come and get you?'

Reluctantly she went over to join the group clustered around Buzz. Holly was with them, and some older Hallfolk girls too. They looked tired and a little irritable.

'You'll dance with me, won't you Sylvie?' boomed Buzz. He was flushed and excited, his blond hair damp and blue eyes bright. She shook her head again.

'Oh yes you will. Come on!'

He grabbed her arm and pulled her towards the mad scrum of dancers.

'I hope you've seen sense about that business this afternoon.'

'If you mean am I going to tell Magus, the answer's no. But only because Yul doesn't want me to.'

'Good girl. Because if you did it would be ten times worse for him, you know.'

She shook her head in disgust.

'Oh Sylvie, lighten up. You're new here, you don't understand our ways. What you saw today was nothing. It's a tougher world here, people get hurt sometimes but Yul can take it. These Village kids are very resilient, believe me. Yul beats his brothers all the time.'

'I doubt it. He wouldn't do that.'

'Don't go soft on him, I warn you. Hallfolk don't fall for Villagers. It just isn't done. Yeah, you can have a bit of fun with them, but never anything serious. If I find out you're keen on him I'll tell Magus. He doesn't think much of Yul anyway, and if you give him an excuse he'll really lay into him.'

'It's so unfair!'

'Not really. Just the way of the world. Now come and dance with me and look as if you're enjoying it, please. Every other girl here would jump at the chance!'

'I can't see why,' Sylvie muttered to herself, but knew from the jealous looks thrown her way, as he took her hands in his, that he was right.

Much later Sylvie went outside onto the Green to cool down. She stood near the encircling trees gazing up at the starry heavens and plump yellow moon, now almost full. She'd had an enjoyable evening chatting to a few girls who'd befriended her and dancing with different partners, but was still anxious to see Yul. Miranda was dancing with Magus. She'd never seen her mother so animated and excited, and had mixed emotions about this. She didn't want Miranda to get hurt and that seemed inevitable. The community was too small for Miranda to hide herself away if it all went wrong. Sylvie was very wary of the whole thing, especially now she knew Magus wasn't quite what he appeared to be.

She felt a tap on her shoulder and spun round to see Yul standing in the shadowy darkness. She beamed at him.

'I've been looking for you all evening!'

'Well here I am.'

'How are you feeling? Is your back alright?'

'It's fine. As I said, I've had a lot worse.'

'It certainly didn't stop you this afternoon! You were great at the games.'

'Thank you.'

'You're such a fast runner. And the tree climbing event! Wow!'

'Well, I am a woodsman so I should be good at that.'

'And then you beat Fennel at the hurdles and he was so sure he was going to win!'

He smiled at her, the memories of the successful afternoon blotting out the earlier incident.

'Are you coming in to the dance?' she asked hopefully. She imagined Yul would be much lighter on his feet than Buzz. He shook his head.

'No, I'm keeping out of everyone's way. My father's had a bellyful of cider and I don't want to bump into him. And as for Buzz and his gang – they probably see me as unfinished business. So I'm going to disappear now. I just wanted to catch you first to ask you something.'

Her heart skipped a beat and she smiled at him expectantly.

'Do you want to go up to the Hare Stone with me tomorrow night?'

She looked away in embarrassment. Of course – it was the full moon tomorrow. The excitement of Beltane had pushed it to the back of her mind.

'I . . . well, I'm not sure.'

'It's just that I was worried about you wandering in the woods alone. I thought you might like me to guide you up there again. But it's alright if you don't want to.'

'Yes, I mean, no, I do . . . oh, I don't know!'

139

'Listen, Sylvie. Magus is over there and he mustn't see me talking to you. I'll be waiting in the woods tomorrow, just before dusk. If you don't come, that's fine. But I'll be there if you need me. Blessings!'

He melted into the darkness and Sylvie returned to the Barn. But somehow, knowing that Yul had left, the evening lost its magic for her.

In the end she had no choice in the matter. As dusk approached the following evening she felt the familiar rising of tension and pressure within her, the desperate need to get out into the open air and up somewhere high. Her fingertips tingled, her heart palpitated and her mouth was dry. Dimly aware of what she was doing, Sylvie removed her shoes and slipped out of the door. Her mother was conveniently out with Magus this evening, on the closest she'd managed to a date with him, any full moon worries forgotten in her excitement.

Sylvie wandered down the path and out of the gate, turning towards the woods. She stepped from the golden blue dusk into the darker shadows and then a new shadow joined her. A woodland spirit materialised from the trees – Yul! He smiled at her, his teeth white in the gloom, and she smiled vaguely back at him with unfocused eyes. He recognised the signs and this time boldly took her hand. Her slim hand was cool and dry in his and together they walked through the woods. The light was fading fast around them, the birds heralding the approaching dusk with glorious song.

It is time! The Lady approaches in silver splendour. I shall dance with feet of feathers and wings of thistledown. Hurry!

They came out of the wood onto the hill and climbed swiftly up to the standing stone. Sylvie lifted her arms to the heavens, the strange humming rising from her throat. Yul once again felt his arms prickle and his back go cold. It was almost unearthly, as if she were some kind of moon angel unfurling her wings and singing in celestial voice. The moon hadn't quite appeared. There was a pink glint on the horizon across the purple folds which foretold the imminent rising. The sky was a beautiful violet blue and still light, from where the sun had set behind them.

Noiselessly, a great white shape appeared out of the woods, passing by in front of the pink rim of the rising full moon. Yul's heart leapt as he realised it was a barn owl. Silently it glided past, its face turning this way and that as it peered to see the field down below. Sylvie emitted another strange sound. Rather than being scared away, the barn owl flew closer and circled them with soft pale-feathered wings. Still Sylvie called, not imitating the owl but singing her strange moon song. The moon rose steadily, losing its bright pinkness as it cleared the horizon. Then Sylvie was off, her feet skimming the grass.

It was dark now and Yul sensed the hares in the long grass below. The owl drifted about the hill, gliding in and out, calling with its eerie voice. And Sylvie flew around, her silver hair gleaming in the moonlight. Yul sank down against the stone, careful of his back. He felt humbled watching this magical girl and the creatures she'd summoned. The quicksilver moondance wove its web around him and he felt something deep inside start to melt. He knew that Sylvie was very special – a moongazy girl. He felt such a strange tugging at his heart when he looked at her or even thought of her. He'd do anything to protect her, anything at all. He'd die for her if he had to.

Later, when she'd moongazed for long enough, he took her hands and raised her up from her kneeling position. The hares lowered their heads from moongazing too, pricked up their long ears and twitched their whiskers. The owl had gone, but earlier had landed on the stone itself, its heart-shaped moon face staring out at the silvery scene below. Yul had never seen anything like it. As he helped her to stand, Sylvie threw her arms around his neck, embracing him in a fierce hug. He shuddered at the shock of her cold body pressed up against him so tightly. Happiness almost choked him as he returned the hug. Then she released him silently, took his hand in her icy one, and together they walked down the hill. The hares around the stone were left alone to their moon vigil.

*

The next morning Sylvie lay in bed looking at the bright blue sky outside. She could hear birds singing in the woodland trees and cows lowing from nearby pastures. She felt at peace, for she'd honoured the moon last night and was now free and released for the rest of the month. Downstairs, Miranda too was singing. It was very early and she was brimming with joy. She laid the table for breakfast, wanting to chat to Sylvie before they went to the Hall for school. When it came to it, however, she didn't know where to start. She wasn't even sure if she ought to speak to Sylvie about this, but there was no one else to confide in and she was bursting to tell someone.

'You were late back last night, Mum,' said Sylvie, buttering her toast.

'Yes, I was. I was with Magus.'

'Yes, you said.'

'I mean, I was on my own with him.'

'Oh, right.'

'Just the two of us.'

'Mmn.'

'Sylvie, I'm trying to tell you something.'

'What?'

'Well, we were alone together, like on a date really. And we ... well, it was very romantic.'

'Mum! Did you get off with him?'

Miranda blushed schoolgirl scarlet at this.

'Yes, I did.'

Sylvie shrieked with laughter, which wasn't the reaction Miranda had expected at all.

'That's gross!'

'Sylvie, don't be so unkind. For goodness' sake, I'm only thirty, remember. It's quite normal behaviour for a single woman, you know.'

'And how old is he? Getting on for forty?'

'He's in his late thirties and that's not old at all. Just right for me in fact. Stop being so horrible. Do you want to hear what happened or not?'

'Well, yes, up to a point. But no revolting gory details, please.'

Miranda poured some more coffee and settled into her chair.

'Well, we had a picnic supper.'

'How sweet.'

'Yes, it was. First we went for a lovely walk down on the beach and then we climbed up the path onto the cliff-top. It's a really special place. There's a great flat rock up there overlooking the sea. It's enormous, round and white like the moon itself. There was a beautiful woven blanket, all spangled with stars, spread over the rock, with silk cushions and candles in lanterns. And there was a picnic all ready for us, and even champagne in an ice bucket.'

'Laid out by magical elves?'

'Don't be silly. Obviously one of the servants had prepared it all for us beforehand.'

'Ooh, one of the servants. How posh.'

'Stop teasing, Sylvie. Anyway, we ate the picnic together and drank the champagne, and watched the sun setting far out to the west. The sky was beautiful. There were swallows swooping above us and I felt so happy. And then ...'

'Yes?'

'He kissed me.'

'What, just like that?'

'Oh, it was so romantic, Sylvie! The sky was blue and gold, and then the moon started to rise over the sea, all pink and glittering. He was so gentle, so loving. I just melted.' She sighed dreamily, her eyes faraway. 'And one thing led to another, and ... well ...'

'You didn't, did you? *Mum*!!'

Sylvie was really shocked. Miranda looked away in embarrassment, realising too late that she really shouldn't be discussing this with her daughter who, after all, still wasn't quite fifteen.

'I really do care for Magus, Sylvie. It's not a casual thing. I think ... I think I've fallen in love with him.'

'Mum, that's ridiculous! You've only known him a few weeks. Just because he made sweet lurve to you on a cliff-top in the moonlight, you can't honestly believe you're in love with him. You're behaving like a kid.'

Miranda burst into giggles at the incongruity of this. The situation was absurd.

'Seriously, I'm really pleased for you, Mum, and it's lovely to see you so happy. Just don't get hurt, please,' said Sylvie. 'I'm sure Magus likes you very much, but I doubt he feels quite the way you do. I mean, he's the king here, isn't he? I'd have thought he could have any woman he wants.'

'And he said he wants me.'

'Yes, for now. But it probably won't last and I don't want to see you upset. And I really don't want to have to leave Stonewylde because you and he have fallen out.'

'I promise that won't happen. If I see he's not as keen as I am, I'll hold back and I won't make a fool of myself. I've managed all these years on my own. I still can.'

Sylvie gazed at her mother across the table. Miranda was different this morning. She was languid and at ease, softer around the edges. She even moved differently. There was such a change that it worried Sylvie. She thought about Yul's warning.

'I don't want to burst your bubble, Mum, but I should tell you something. About Magus.'

Miranda's eyes shone and a little smile played on her lips.

'Yes? Go on then. We can talk about him all morning as far as I'm concerned. He's such a gorgeous, unique, special, wonderful—'

'No, Mum, please be serious and listen to me. It was when I was with Yul at Beltane up by the Stone Circle. I won't go into all the details, but Yul warned me about Magus. He's not all he seems. He's treated Yul badly. Yul said—'

'No!' Miranda's dreamy expression had vanished and she glared at her daughter. 'I don't want to hear anything that boy's told you! We know he's not to be trusted.'

'But Mum, Magus slashed him across the face with his riding whip. And—'

'Stop it! How can you say anything about Magus after all he's done for you? How can you even repeat such lies, let alone think they might be true? Magus saved your life, Sylvie, I'm sure of it. If we hadn't come here, you'd have been taken back to that hospital sooner or later and I really think it would have killed you. And look at his generosity! This lovely cottage, the welcome he's given us, my job and a first class education for you.'

'I know, Mum, I know. I've thought of all that too. I'm not against Magus. It's just—'

'Then you should remember who deserves your loyalty, and not listen to a pack of lies. You're to keep away from that boy, Sylvie. He's evil.'

10

Miranda needn't have worried about Sylvie seeing Yul; he was busy working in the woods almost every waking hour and had no time to seek her out. One beautiful May afternoon the woodsmen sat in the clearing around their hut finishing their lunch and drinking tea. A couple of men had lit up pipes and some of the older ones were gently snoozing in the warmth, making the most of the last few minutes of their break. Old Greenbough drained his mug and called Yul over.

'You can run an errand for me this afternoon, boy. A nice trip out, as you've worked well this morning.'

Yul smiled at this; he was trying hard to get back into Old Greenbough's good books. Winning the tree-climbing competition at Beltane had helped, and he was really putting in the effort at work.

'I found a lovely little crop o' Beechwood Sickener this morning up along the swallets. I want you to pay a visit to old Mother Heggy and tell her.'

Yul gulped, but was determined to show willing.

'Yes sir, I'll do that. Beechwood Sickener – that's the red mushroom, isn't it? With a sweet smell?'

'Aye, that's the one. Smaller than Fly Agaric, and a shorter stalk. Quite rare here, and I happen to know Mother Heggy used to value those mushrooms very highly for one o' her concoctions, back in the old days. Don't know if she still uses the things, but you tell her we found a good crop today. Tell her if she wants 'em picked we'll do it for her, right enough. But I have a feeling they must be picked in the waxing or maybe even Dark Moon, so you tell her we ain't touched 'em till we gets word from her. You got that, boy?'

'Yes, sir.'

'Good lad. You're a bright boy, Yul, too bright for us really. Don't quite know why you ain't up at the Hall with them clever ones. 'Tis a mystery to me.'

'I failed the tests, sir, that's why.'

Old Greenbough peered at him through bushy grey eyebrows.

'I know you failed the tests, Yul. Question is, why? 'Cause we both know you could've walked them tests. You're brighter than most of them Hallfolk put together. Still, if you choose to be one o' us, I ain't complaining. You're a strong lad and a hard worker, and you've a feel for the trees that I ain't seen in a long time. Just you stay out o' trouble and you'll do well. Now go on with you, boy, and when you've seen Mother Heggy, take the rest o' the afternoon off.'

'Thank you, sir!' Yul grinned.

Yul climbed the path leading out of the Village and up towards the cliffs. He reached a fork in the track, marked by a stunted and grotesquely twisted hawthorn, and knew that this was where he must turn off. He hesitated, nervous about meeting the oldest inhabitant of Stonewylde whom people spoke of with hushed voices. Sitting on a branch of the strange hawthorn, where even the blossom was blighted, was a large black crow.

As Yul approached, the crow shuffled and fussed, flexing out its wings and opening its beak in a silent squawk. He stopped and stared at it, wishing he'd never been sent on this errand. The crow seemed hostile – malignant almost – as if it didn't want him to pass.

'I've come to see Mother Heggy,' said Yul, glad no one was about to hear him addressing a bird. 'I bring a message from Old Greenbough.'

The crow let out a noisy *caw* and, in a messy fashion, launched itself from the branch. It flapped off along the path which Yul must now follow, disappearing from sight around a bend. Yul duly followed it and finally reached the place that he'd been told never to visit. Mother Heggy's home was strictly off limits to every child in the Village and most adults too. Yul swallowed hard.

The tiny cottage was ancient, its thatch green and rotten and the cob walls tumbling apart in places. It spoke of neglect, which was unusual at Stonewylde. A thin wisp of smoke rose from the chimney so Yul knew Mother Heggy was in. He certainly couldn't have told from looking in the windows, which were very small and so thick with grime as to be opaque. He forced himself to knock on the bleached wood of the old door, hoping she wouldn't hear him so he could leave without seeing her.

'Lift the latch and come inside!' called a high, creaky voice.

The cottage smelled musty and strange. It was dark and at first Yul could see nothing other than the dull glimmer of copper pots on the walls and a meagre fire smouldering in an inglenook. He blinked, looking around for her.

Mother Heggy sat hunched in a rocking chair. She wore a shapeless sack of a dress that almost reached her cracked ankle boots, with a ragged grey shawl pulled around her and a battered hat on her head. She was very old and very ugly. She had a broken clay pipe clamped in her shrivelled mouth, from which came a ribbon of foul-smelling smoke. She sat in the corner like a baleful spider waiting in her web, and Yul's skin prickled with apprehension. She gestured with a claw for him to sit in the wooden chair opposite her, where a little light fell from the window.

'Bright blessings, Mother Heggy,' he began politely.

'Blessings to you, Yul of the Winter Solstice.'

'You know who I am?' he asked in surprise.

She cackled and sucked noisily on her pipe.

'I should do! I were the first person on this Earth to set eyes on you, son o' Maizie.'

'What? You know my mother too, Mother Heggy?'

'Aye, I knew Maizie right enough, and a fine young girl she was. A fine woman too, so as I've heard. Too fine for her own good, that one. Especially in the spring time when the hares are leaping and the moon is ripe.'

Yul thought her mind must be wandering.

'Is the little sister growing well?'

'Er, yes, she's fine. She works at the dairy.'

'Not her! The tiny one, born at Imbolc. Little maiden.'

Yul frowned. She must mean Leveret, the youngest in the family.

'She's very well thank you. She's two years old now.'

'Aye, she would be. Two years at Imbolc. And you're coming up to sixteen this Winter Solstice. Who'd o' thought it? Nearly sixteen and I remember the night you were born.'

She spat into the corner and rocked a little, peering at Yul. He felt awkward and decided to deliver his message and get out as quickly as possible.

'Mother Heggy, I've come to—'

She interrupted him with a horrible cackle.

'You don't know why you've come, boy! You have no idea what's truly going on. Only Mother Heggy knows that. Now sit still and let me get an eyeful of you. Waited nigh on sixteen years for this visit, I have.'

She surveyed him carefully, her milky eyes roaming his face and body.

'You're a moon-blessed boy, for all you were solstice-born,' she said at last, her voice as dry and crackly as autumn leaves on the ground. 'You have the moon in your eyes. Red Moon too, I recall. Maizie was surprised. But they come when they're ready, I told her, especially the ones destined for magic.'

Yul swallowed and kept quiet.

'You were the last one I brought into the world. The last babe of so many. I remember it clear. Who could forget that night? Too many now, babies all over the place, and where will it lead? Sol has grand ideas, too grand. 'Twill all fall about him. He's

149

sown the seeds of his own destiny. Told him that years ago, but he didn't thank me for it. Oh no, not him.'

She spat into the corner again, her face grimacing even further into its wrinkles. Yul had no idea what she was on about.

'And how is Maizie? She were a pretty maiden. Brung her into the world too. Dark hair, grey eyes, used to be a lot o' that around but it's died out now. You're like her, young Yul. I can see you're a spirited one too, and you suffer for it, don't you?'

Yul nodded. His strong spirit was always his downfall with practically every person with any authority over him. Mother Heggy cackled again and rose creakily from her rocking chair. She was tiny and almost bent double. She shuffled over to the range and started fiddling with a pot whose contents bubbled gently. She ladled some into a stone mug and added a pinch of something, giving it a good stir. Then she shuffled back and handed it to Yul. He took it reluctantly, for the mug looked filthy.

'Drink, drink,' she said impatiently, settling down again painfully in her rocking chair.

The concoction tasted strange. There was a bitter aftertaste and it burned on the way down like the ceremony mead. Yul felt his body start to relax and knew with sinking certainty that he'd been drugged. His legs felt indescribably heavy; he could no more have stood up than flown to the moon. His head was thick and muzzy and his tongue far too big for his mouth. He grinned weakly at the crone, who rocked slowly and clicked her tongue at him.

'That's better, my boy. Now you're mine for a while. I need to get inside you, Yul. I need to see if I were right. I'm old and worn out, but I been holding on for this time to come round. And after all these years o' waiting, here we are at last.'

She dragged her chair closer and, leaning over, took his lifeless hands in hers. He could smell her, a disgusting smell of old woman and mould. She stared into his dilated pupils and he felt something tugging at him, as if part of him was being dragged out. Her own eyes were rheumy with age, the irises blurred, and he wondered blearily if she could see at all. She reached out a filthy claw to trace his sharp cheekbone and the deep hollow underneath. He couldn't move but had to endure her touching him, all the while locked in her gaze.

Mother Heggy pinched his dark curls, wrapping them around her gnarled fingers. Her hand slid down, feeling the angular jaw bone, over his neck and into the hollow beneath his throat. Everything inside him screamed; he couldn't bear it. Nobody ever touched him. His eyes pleaded for her to stop. Her shrivelled mouth broke into a toothless leer and she raised her hand from his neck to run a clawed forefinger across his lips. Then she let him go and sat back in her chair, rocking gently and surveying him.

'You've no need to be scared o' me, Yul. I ain't against you. Old Mother Heggy's on your side. Always have been, right from the very start. You've enough folk crying for your blood without setting against me. You'll be needing my magic afore this thing is finished, for all that you have so much of your own.'

She picked up the mug from which he'd drunk, swilled it around and threw the remains on the floor. Then she stared into the dregs left behind. All the while Yul sat transfixed, unable to move and barely to blink. She nodded slowly, turning the mug this way and that.

'Everywhere I look the story is foretold. Blue and red, red and blue, just as I told him all those years back. Black and silver too, and the silver is come now. You must beware, Yul. You think 'tis that man Alwyn is the danger. You think 'tis them boys from the Hall are the enemy. Aye, all o' them will hurt you when they can. But the true danger is not from them. Oh no. The one you must heed, the one who has the real power to harm you, is Magus. Beware of him, Yul. Beware of Magus for he is out to destroy you.'

Yul heard her words, although they meant nothing to him. His eyelids were growing heavy. They began to droop and his head fell forward, chin resting on his chest. He slept, oblivious of the crone in the room with him. He slept all afternoon and when he awoke it was even gloomier in the dirty cottage, for the sun had moved right round. He sat up with a start, his heart pounding. How long had he been asleep? What had she done to him whilst he slept? Muzzily he scanned the room. She was over in a corner turned away from him. A great black crow sat on the back of her empty rocking chair fixing him with its jewel-bright eye. It let out a loud *caw* and she turned and shuffled over, clutching another mug. He shook his head but she pressed it into his hand.

'No, drink it. 'Twill clear your head. Trust me, boy. Drink.'

He did, and found the concoction refreshing and delicious.

'Please, Mother Heggy, I must go now,' he mumbled, his tongue still feeling strange.

'Aye, I've learnt all I needed. Forgive me for tricking you, but I had to find the truth. You'll come to see me many a time after the Summer Solstice, but you'll come afore then too. Now you've found old Mother Heggy, you'll seek her help.'

He nodded obediently, still looking into her eyes.

'And I want to meet the girl, the newcomer. Bring her to visit me.'

He nodded again.

'There was a message for me?'

'Yes, there's a fine crop of Beechwood Sickener in the woods. Old Greenbough said we can pick them now if you want, or wait till you say the time is right.'

She scrunched her ancient wrinkled skin into something resembling a smile.

'Aye, good. Beechwood Sickener. 'Tis a long time since I worked with them. Slow and sure they do the job, right enough. This is as it should be, all falling into place as I always foretold. The only one to touch 'em must be you. You will pick them on the night of the next Dark Moon, at sunset. Put them in a flaxen bag and tie it with a string of ivy. Leave them on my doorstep.'

'Yes, I will. Blessings, Mother Heggy'

Walking down the track in the evening sunlight, with gulls from the nearby cliff screaming overhead, Yul thought ruefully of his wasted afternoon. He could've gone up into the hills or down to the beach. Instead he'd sat in a drugged stupor inside the crone's filthy home while she pawed at him and filled his head with strange talk that meant nothing to him. He was annoyed, and didn't relish the prospect of a return visit. He certainly didn't intend to take Sylvie there. Maybe he'd manage to avoid Mother Heggy when he brought her the mushrooms, and could then forget all about her.

He thought of some of the strange things she'd said to him, and couldn't see how he'd ever need her help. She was far too old and immobile to be of any use to anyone. It was she who needed help. He wondered how she'd known straight away who he was. And why was she so interested in Maizie? Strange that his mother never talked about her, when clearly she'd known the crone well in her younger days. Yul entered the Village, greeting people on their way home from work, and visited the bath house for a shower. The griminess of the cottage still clung to him and he wanted to wash away the lingering, fusty smell.

That evening after Alwyn had left for the pub, Maizie and Rosie washed the dishes, tidied up, and then settled down in the parlour with their sewing. Yul was still bringing in logs for the range, and then had water containers to fill from the cart outside. He was helped by one of the younger boys, Geoffrey, while the other, Gregory, fed the slops to the pig. The three youngest children were already asleep upstairs. Maizie called for the two middle boys to put the chickens down for the night and mind the hen-house door was tightly fastened, then go to bed. Eventually, his jobs done, Yul fetched his wood and knife and sat with his mother and sister. He had a fine piece of holly and was carving an owl.

'I went to Mother Heggy's cottage this afternoon,' he began, hoping his mother would explain some of the things the old woman had told him. He hadn't dared mention it earlier when his father was around. When Alwyn was in the house, Yul was silent unless asked a direct question. He didn't speak to his mother or brothers or sisters either, but tried to shrink into himself and not be noticed. He'd learnt how to make himself almost invisible when Alwyn was around. Sometimes it worked.

Maizie looked up from her sewing and stared at him.

'Did you now? And what was that in aid of?'

'Message for her from Old Greenbough. But she said some strange things, Mother, and I didn't understand most of it.'

'Well, she's a strange one herself, Yul. You mustn't set any store by what she says. She's very old and rambling in her mind.'

'The weird thing was, she knew who I was even though I've never seen her before. She called me "son of Maizie" and she spoke like she knew you well, Mother. She asked after you – and Leveret too. Why only Leveret and not the others? I thought that was very odd.'

Maizie glanced at him sharply.

'Like I said, she's rambling in her mind. 'Tis a wonder she's still alive. She were so important here in the old days but now she's almost forgotten. 'Tis what comes of having no family to look after you in your old age.'

'Didn't she have any children then?' asked Rosie, looking up from her embroidery.

'No, Rosie. She was the Wise Woman and they don't have children. Nor husbands. Keep their strength and energy for their magic and nought else.'

'She said she brought me into the world,' Yul added. 'I was the last one.'

'Aye, that's true. After your birth she ... well, she fell from favour. Magus told us all to go to the doctor at the Hall if we were sickly, and the midwife up there must help us with birthing. He said Old Heggy was a menace and a danger. So people stopped visiting her for potions and the like, and over the years she's been forgotten by most. There's only a few who still call on her and keep her in food and firewood.'

'Poor old thing,' said Rosie. 'How sad for her, after caring for folk all her life.'

'No, Rosie, 'tis for the best because she's a little touched. Full of rantings and ravings that are best ignored. Don't you go listening to her, Yul. Keep away from Mother Heggy, like I've always told you. She'll fill your head with nonsense if you let her.'

Maizie got up to make them all a cup of tea, but found Yul and Rosie still discussing the crone when she returned to the sitting room.

'She doesn't think highly of Magus,' said Yul. 'She said his ideas were too grand and it will all fall about him.'

'Pah! What does she know?' said Maizie. 'If it weren't for Magus we wouldn't be here now sitting in this cosy little cottage, warm, dry and well-fed. Mother Heggy would do well to remember just what Magus has done for all of us before she starts on about him. She never did know when to keep that mouth o' hers shut.'

'Do tell us, Mother,' said Rosie eagerly. 'I love hearing about the old days at Stonewylde.'

'What's to tell? You know what it was like here when I grew up as a girl. I've told you that story many a time, Rosie. Folk always hungry, cottages falling down, the fields not farmed properly. Times were very hard. I grew up in hunger and cold, not like you lucky ones today.'

'And Mother Heggy was the Wise Woman then?' asked Rosie.

'Aye, and believe you me, her healing powers were needed, right enough. Children were sickly and under-fed, always ailing. The men fought and hurt each other, for there was no justice, no proper laws. Women died in childbirth, couldn't feed their families, couldn't clothe their children and keep 'em warm. There were accidents on the farms because everything was so run down and broken. Terrible hard times they were. Mother Heggy was certainly needed then and we all went to her for help.'

'Who was the magus then?' asked Rosie.

'When I was born 'twas Basil. A weak man, they say, who lived in a world of dreams and couldn't be bothered with running the estate. Let it all go to disrepair and wildness. His father before him had started the ruin, because they do say in the very old times back before him even, 'twas perfect at Stonewylde. But the old father had been a dirty dog who only lived for his women and his mead. Used every woman on the estate, they say; fathered countless children all over the place. So Basil inherited a mess and he weren't the man to sort it out. There were so many Hallfolk then, all living a life of ease up at the Hall, off the backs of the Villagers. Us poor folk lived in squalor, in damp and cold cottages with no food because the Hallfolk took it all. There was a Village School right enough, and children were taught a bit o' reading back then, but fat lot of good it did them with no food in their bellies.'

'And Basil was Clip's father?' said Yul.

'That's right. He had several children himself but Clip was the special one on account of his mother. Basil had a right old passion for her.'

'I think I've heard about her. Wasn't she a Villager?' asked Rosie.

'Aye, she was. A fey, strange girl called Raven. She grew up in Mother Heggy's cottage, for her own family were all dead and there was no one else to care for her. Old Heggy doted on her – Raven was the child she'd never had. But she was an odd one, they say, feckless as a flea. This was before my time, o' course. She died just before I were born. Basil was mad for her but she didn't want to know him. She was moongazy, folk say. As moongazy as they come, completely wild and free.'

Yul's heart quickened at this. He'd heard something about a moongazy girl in the past, and this must be her. The older folk were always reluctant to speak of these times, so his information was very piecemeal.

'I've heard tell of Raven too,' he said carefully. 'So she was like a daughter to old Mother Heggy?'

'Aye, though maybe more of a granddaughter. She grew up in that old cottage on the cliffs with Heggy, never going to school but spending all her time out in the open, gathering and harvesting ingredients to make the potions. She gave birth to Clip, born at the eclipse of course, and for a while the baby stayed in the cottage. But Raven wanted none of him. She weren't woven to be a mother. So Basil took him up to live at the Hall. They do say Heggy were wild with rage, for she wanted care of the little boy even if Raven didn't.'

Yul thought of the filthy hovel he'd visited that afternoon; it was hard to imagine someone of Clip's standing being born and raised in such a humble place.

'So Basil would've been pleased to have his little boy close with him,' mused Rosie. 'Even though Raven didn't love him.'

'Aye, but then Basil died. By rights little Clip was the new master, for Basil had written it on a piece of paper to make it lawful. All o' Stonewylde to go to the boy. But Clip was much too young of course. So his uncle Elm, Basil's younger brother, he took over. And things went from bad to worse.'

Maizie picked her mending up again and began to sew.

'Well go on, Mother! Don't stop there! What happened next?' said Rosie.

'Elm was another bad 'un, folk tell. Couldn't be bothered with sorting out the estate neither. He roamed around taking what he wanted from whoever he wanted. And he decided he wanted the wild girl Raven too. But whereas old Basil had been a bit daft and dreamy, Elm was a different matter. A hard man he was, hard and cruel. I remember him myself, for he was the magus when I was growing up. How my old mother hated him!'

'I can't imagine what it's like having a bad magus,' said Rosie. 'Poor you, Mother. It must have been horrible.'

''Twas horrible. Life was difficult for every Villager at Stonewylde in them days, when Elm were in charge. And little magic around then, I can tell you. They barely celebrated the festivals, other than to drink and take the girls. The power was fading. The Earth Mother, the Moon Goddess, the Green Man and the elements – nobody honoured them or channelled the Earth Magic. 'Twas seeping away slowly but surely. A few of the older Villagers, they tried to keep the old ways going, and Mother Heggy was one o' them. They celebrated the Eight Festivals of the Wheel, they danced for the moon, honoured the Mother, planted and harvested at the correct times as far as they could. But Elm – he couldn't care less.'

'And little Clip was still living up at the Hall was he? Mother Heggy didn't get him back when Basil died?'

'No, Elm kept him up there, for 'twas Basil's wish. And Clip would one day become the new magus when he were grown.'

'And what happened to Raven?'

'She'd turned even stranger. Dressed in old rags and tatters, bare feet, silver hair in a great tangle. I remember my mother telling me all about her. She were a tiny little thing, all skin and bone, and lived like a wild creature. But Elm had a passion for her just like Basil before him. Goddess knows why, for she sounds completely mad. Maybe 'twas the moongaziness – they do say those girls with the moon in their eyes drive the men crazy with passion. They have some sort o' hold over men. I don't know about that. There's no moongazy girls around nowadays, thank the stars. Anyway, before she knew it, little Raven was carrying again, but this time round it were Elm's child. Who was born at the Summer Solstice.'

'Our Magus!' said Rosie.

Maizie got up out of her chair and trimmed the lamp.

'That's right. Now you two better be off to bed before your father gets back.'

'But what happened to Raven? Please tell us, Mother,' begged Rosie. Yul, already scooping up his wood whittlings at the mention of Alwyn's return, paused to hear the end of the story.

'Well, after the second baby was born, Raven lost her mind completely. She hated Elm even more than she'd hated Basil. I told you Elm was a cruel man. I believe he forced Raven, and of course Mother Heggy despised him for it. There was very ill feeling between her and the Hallfolk, and they say she tried to hex him. He took the baby away from her too, just as Basil had done. The two little boys, Clip and Sol, grew up together as Hallfolk in Elm's care. Clip was as dreamy as his father before him, but Sol was different. He was wild as a boy – fighting, causing mayhem, riding around on a horse too big for him, upsetting everyone. He was very bad and the young Villagers feared him. He could be as cruel and wicked as his father.'

'But he's not like that now, is he, Mother?' asked Rosie.

'No, not any more. Things got so bad that Elm sent both the boys away to a school in the Outside World. A school where they stayed for most of the year and only came back from time to time. It calmed Sol down, made him mend his ways. Gradually he started to take an interest in Stonewylde. He began to visit the folk, talk to them and find out what the problems were. I remember him well. I was only a young girl then.'

She paused, her eyes faraway.

'He was a lovely young man, so full of energy and life. Then the best thing happened a few years later: Elm died and Sol took over. Left his work in the Outside World and came back to Stonewylde for good. And that's when our lives changed.'

'But surely it should've been Clip who took over?'

'It should, but he didn't want it. Didn't want to be magus, didn't want the hard work of sorting out all the problems at Stonewylde. He liked to go off into the Outside World on his travels, as he still does to this day. And they do say the Earth Goddess herself chooses who's to be the magus. There was no doubt about it – the Earth Magic came to Sol. I remember it well, one summer solstice. A great crack and a flash of green and he almost fell off the Altar Stone at the sheer power of it. From that moment on we knew things would be alright.'

'I've seen the Earth Magic come to him on the Altar Stone,' said Yul.

'Aye, the Goddess loves him alright. She fills him to the brim and gives him the strength he needs. And he certainly needed it then, in them early days. Stonewylde was just about as bad as it could be. Magus spent years pulling the estate up to what it is today. He had all the cottages and buildings repaired and new ones built. He organised the fields and livestock so there was enough food for everyone to eat, not just them greedy Hallfolk. Sorted out the woodlands, repaired the school and the Great Barn and, best of all, he started celebrating the festivals again properly, as they should be. The poor man worked himself to the bone, he did. In the saddle from dawn to dusk every day for years, for there was so much to be done. You don't realise, growing up in these good times, just what our magus has done for us all.'

'Didn't he get rid of most of the Hallfolk too?' asked Yul. 'I remember Greenbough talking about that once.'

'Aye, he did. Weeded 'em out, sent most of them packing. There'd been far too many of them lazing about up there. Like rats cast out of the granary, they were. Magus said they could come back once or twice a year for the festivals and that was it. He took their children into the Hall School if they wanted, but even they have to leave when they're grown up, most o' them.'

'Good thing too!' said Yul. 'There are still too many Hallfolk to my mind.'

'You can see why everyone loves Magus so much,' said Rosie. 'He was our saviour. Without him we wouldn't be here now, so happy and content. Outsiders would've taken over. Magus built up the great boundary wall, for that had crumbled in places, and he put guards on the gate. One Samhain, in the Great Barn, he told us all of his dream for Stonewylde. And we've been living that dream ever since.'

'I heard when I was at school, that "magus" means "the wise one" and "the magician",' said Rosie. 'And from what you've told us, he really is.'

'Aye, he is,' said Maizie warmly. 'Goddess bless him!'

'What I don't understand,' said Yul, 'if he's so wise and magical, is why Mother Heggy told me today that I must beware of him.'

Maizie looked at him sharply.

'What did she say exactly?'

Yul was surprised to see the two bright spots burning on her cheeks. They were always a sure sign that she was angry. He shrugged.

'She just said to be careful and not make him angry.'

'Good advice you should heed, my lad. You've upset him a great deal lately and you'd do well to beware of upsetting him any more. The crone spoke right. Was that all she said?'

'I think so.'

'Good. And my advice is to stay away from her. She's an interfering old busy-body and she's caused a lot of harm in her time. Stay well away from her, Yul, I'm warning you. I don't want you visiting her again, and you can tell Greenbough that if he tries to send you there on another errand.'

But she was talking to thin air. Then she too heard the tuneless whistling that heralded her husband's arrival. Rosie's skirt was only just visible at the top of the stairs as the front door banged open. Breathing a sigh of relief at her children's speedy departure, she picked up the empty tea mugs and went into the kitchen to prepare Alwyn one of his late night snacks.

11

Sylvie sat in one of the empty schoolrooms working on her geography project. On the table were several books from the library, and she was engrossed in her research. Outside it was wet and grey, all the bright new greenness dripping damply. A gardener pulled up weeds in a flower bed near the window, but Sylvie, curled up on cushions in the window seat with her computer on her lap, was unaware of anything other than her study. She looked up with a frown as a couple of the older girls entered the room.

'Oh hi, Sylvie. How are you doing?'

'Fine thanks. Just researching this volcanoes project.'

'Oh, yeah, I remember doing that last year. There's a good programme on Pompeii in the library – very interesting.'

'Thanks, I'll look out for it.'

Sylvie smiled, still appreciating the novelty of being treated kindly by the other students. Nobody from her London school would have even thought of offering help.

'Have you seen Buzz?' asked July. 'He promised to revise some history with us. He's really clever and he's going to sail through his exams.'

'No I haven't seen him, but I'll tell him you're looking for him if I do.'

'Thanks. See you later.'

Sylvie settled back again, wriggling into the cushions, the computer cradled on her knees. Outside, the rain pattered against the diamond panes of the mullioned window. She closed her eyes in contentment; this was the way to study, not sitting in rows surrounded by a mob baying for the teacher's blood.

'You won't learn anything like that,' came a voice from the doorway. Sylvie's eyes shot open and she groaned quietly.

'July and Wren are looking for you,' she said. But Buzz came in and closed the door behind him, crossing the polished wooden floor to sit next to her on the window seat. She felt a flicker of irritation. She really didn't like him despite his huge popularity amongst the Hallfolk teenagers, and she'd felt uncomfortable near him ever since the incident with Yul in the woods by the Stone Circle.

'I know they are. I'm trying to avoid them.'

'They're hoping you'll revise some history with them.'

'Yeah, I know. But it's not revision they're interested in, believe me.'

Sylvie raised an eyebrow at this but kept silent. She couldn't understand his popularity. The girls hung around him, flirting and giggling. And the boys were just as bad, always deferring to him, vying for his attention. Surely she couldn't be the only one who found him conceited and over-full of his own importance?

He leaned over and looked at her screen. He was big and masculine, clean smelling but exuding a male scent that made her nose wrinkle. His arms were covered in curly golden hair and he wore a heavy gold chain bracelet.

'Ah, volcanoes. That's an interesting subject. I could help you if you like; I've got my old project on file.'

'No, I'm fine, thanks very much,' she said quickly.

He sat back against his corner of the window seat and studied her.

'You really don't like me, do you Sylvie?'

She felt embarrassed. Was it that obvious? She shook her head quickly.

'No . . . I mean, yes, I—'

163

'You don't have to pretend. It's alright – we just got off on the wrong footing, you and me. But I'd like to get it sorted out before I go away for my exams. I really like you. You're different from the others here and I want us to be friends.'

Her heart sank.

'Of course we're friends, Buzz. It's just that you're much older than me and I don't feel comfortable with someone who's so much more grown up than I am.'

He smiled at her and she realised that he was quite attractive after all, in a large, blond way. His face was smooth and small featured for someone so big, and his eyes were an interesting shade of light blue and very intense. He had a nice smile and white, even teeth, with a masculine dimple in his chin. Then an image of Yul came to her mind – dark tousled hair, thin face and deep grey eyes. There was no competition.

'At Stonewylde we all reach adulthood at sixteen, and I only recently had my sixteenth birthday – at the Spring Equinox. I was told you'll be sixteen next year, at the Summer Solstice? So you're not that far behind me. And surely it's good to have someone a bit older and more experienced to help you through everything?' His pale eyes gleamed and he cracked his knuckles as she searched for a suitable reply. 'I was going to ask you to come for a walk with me, but it's a little wet outside.'

'Yes, much too wet.'

'Pity. But anyway, I was hoping for your help with my Religious Studies revision.'

Sylvie realised she wouldn't get rid of him quickly so she saved her work and put her computer on the table. She tucked her feet back onto the window seat and looked across at him, knowing she must try to be friendly. They lived in the same small community and he was making a big effort to be nice to her. She should really be flattered that he'd singled her out when the other girls were all so keen for his company.

'Okay, if I can, but I'm sure you know much more about it than I do.'

'Your hair is amazing, Sylvie. It's almost white. It's like silk.'

'Thank you. So what did you want to ask me?'

'Oh, about the Christian Church. I know about the rites of passage, like baptism and confirmation. I just wondered if you and Miranda were churchgoers before you came here, and if you could tell me what it's like. Just some general background stuff in case I get a question about it in my exam.'

'I'm afraid I can't really help. We never went to church. My grandparents were apparently very religious and they disowned Mum, and—'

'Really? Why?'

'Because she had me so young and wasn't married.'

'That's awful!'

'Yes, not very caring at all, chucking out a young girl to fend for herself. So my mum's always said the whole idea of religion was a load of hypocrisy and she wouldn't go near a church. But there were some beautiful churches in London. It's strange that there isn't one in the Village, isn't it? An old village like that, there's always a church. It's as traditional as the pub and the village green.'

'Yes, it is, but there's never been a church here. That's how we've managed to keep apart from the Outside World.'

'Aah! I've wondered how Stonewylde has stayed so separate and cut off.'

'It's all very interesting – we learned about it a couple of years ago from this funny little Hallfolk chap who visits every summer. He's an Oxford don, a professor of history I think. Magus got him to give us a special talk about his research into Stonewylde's history. Apparently the separation began when the Normans invaded and conquered England, because up until then there were many small communities like Stonewylde.'

'So why isn't there a church here?'

'I can't remember everything the professor said, but somehow the community at Stonewylde managed to resist the Normans. William the Conqueror ordered his barons to build churches all over the land, alongside their castles and manor houses, and usually on pagan sites. It was how he took control of the country and subdued the Saxons – and also how the Old Religion was officially stamped out. But for some reason – maybe a pay-off of some sort – no Norman baron ever settled at Stonewylde.'

'How fascinating,' said Sylvie. 'I love history.'

'Me too!' beamed Buzz. 'So we do have something in common, Sylvie.'

'Mmn, maybe. And there's never been a church here at all?'

'No, it's always been a pagan community, following the old, indigenous beliefs that were around long before Christianity. That's why you don't find people at Stonewylde with Biblical names, like Matthew and Rachel. The Villagers have never even heard of the Bible. We do have some old names, Celtic and Saxon, but we choose most of our names from things in the natural world – trees and birds and plants.'

'That's why you're Buzzard?'

'That's right. I've always thought one day I'd name my children after birds, like me.'

He smiled at her and Sylvie found herself warming to him a little. He wasn't quite as insensitive and uncouth as she'd thought, and he really seemed to love Stonewylde. She smiled back and he looked ridiculously pleased. Sylvie had always considered herself unattractive and wasn't used to having any kind of effect on the opposite sex. It was really quite fun.

She flicked her hair back so it rippled down her shoulders, enjoying Buzz's gaze of blatant admiration. She was like a child discovering a box of matches but knowing nothing of fire.

'You're leaving soon for your exams, aren't you?' she asked.

'Yes, we're all staying at a public school near Exeter, owned by a Hallfolk relation.'

'I don't see why you can't take your exams here. Why do you all have to go to another school?'

'Because we're not a registered centre at Stonewylde. Magus doesn't want inspectors poking their noses in. The place in Exeter's lovely, although not as grand as Stonewylde.'

'Have all the Hallfolk got houses and jobs in the Outside World?'

'Most of them, yes. We can't all live here, like the Villagers. They support the community and they're happy labouring in menial jobs, but we need to earn money. That's how Hallfolk do their bit to provide for the estate. Most of the Hallfolk live out, and many of them are very successful.'

'I didn't realise that. Do they all come back here to visit?'

'Yes, but not all at once. They come back once or twice a year for a stay, always during one of the festivals and especially Summer Solstice. Magus regulates who comes for which festival so we're not completely swamped. Most of them send their children here to be educated and pay a fortune for it, just like any other public school.'

'And have you always lived here?'

'Full time since I was eight, when I started Hall School. Before that just for long visits.'

'Do your parents live here now? I don't really know who's related to who. It's quite confusing.'

He laughed.

'It's very confusing! And we're all related somehow. Magus has an enormous family tree in his office. Sometimes he has tests done too, to see how closely we're related. We have to be careful about who we partner because of the dangers of inbreeding. My mother lives in the Outside World, but she sent me to live here when I was eight because she wanted me to grow up as Hallfolk and be educated at Stonewylde. I go and stay with her every year. I'm due for a long visit straight after my exams actually.'

'And what about your father? Is he one of the Hallfolk too?'

He looked at Sylvie in surprise.

'My father? Of course he's Hallfolk! Didn't you know? I'm Magus' son!'

Sylvie was taken aback. There was no evidence of a wife, so she'd assumed that Magus was single and childless.

'You look shocked, Sylvie. Hadn't you guessed?'

'I ... no, I hadn't. I didn't realise he had a child. Or a wife.'

Buzz laughed out loud at this.

'Oh Sylvie, he hasn't got a wife! He's the magus. Every girl, Hallfolk and Villager, dreams of having him for her Rite of Adulthood. They all choose him for their initiation. He certainly couldn't perform his role as the magus if he were married. '

Sylvie looked down at her hands. It seemed sordid and disgusting, the thought of Magus with so many different women, all wanting his attention and favours. And then she remembered her mother. Miranda was falling in love with him but she was just one more woman to add to his list. Sylvie felt quite sick. How could she ever tell her?

'But I don't understand. The Rite of Adulthood ... what do you mean? Do people make love then? Up in the Stone Circle?'

'Yes, it's part of the ceremony. After the others have left, you cast off childhood and embrace adulthood. It's a very special and sacred ritual.'

Her throat felt tight and she wanted to cry. It was horrible and repulsive. She'd thought Stonewylde and the magical ceremonies were so perfect, so beautiful. Instead it was all about sex.

Buzz looked concerned and leant across, tipping up her chin.

'Hey, what's wrong? Are you crying? Oh Sylvie, don't be upset!'

He shifted across the seat and put an arm around her, pulling her close into his chest. His gentleness undid her and she burst into tears.

'Hey, hey, stop it, silly girl. There's no need to cry. What on earth's the matter?'

She shook her head, unable to speak. Just then the door opened.

'Oh, there you are Buzz! We—'

The girls stood in the doorway staring at Buzz in the window seat, his arm cradling Sylvie against his chest, her long hair spilling across his lap. Their mouths dropped open.

'Not now, girls. I'm busy at the moment. I'll catch you later.' He frowned and gestured them away with a peremptory wave. 'Come on, Sylvie, we're going to be disturbed here. It's stopped raining now. Let's go out for a walk. You'll feel better out in the fresh air.'

It sounded like a good idea and she didn't want anyone to see her crying. He found a couple of jackets and they left the Hall through a side door. They walked along the side of the wing and into a part of the Hall gardens that was new to Sylvie. Passing through some tall clipped yew hedges, they entered a formal garden where the paths were of fine raked gravel and wooden benches were set into hidden alcoves.

'Holly! Holly, you won't believe what we've just seen!'

July and Wren burst into a music room where they knew Holly had gone earlier. She'd been watching herself in the long mirror as she practised a dance, and her cheeks were flushed. She flicked down the volume of the music and frowned at them.

'What?'

'It's Buzz! He's with Sylvie!'

'What do you mean, "with Sylvie"?'

'We found them alone in one of the schoolrooms!' said July excitedly. 'They were sitting on the window seat together.'

'So?'

'And he was cuddling her,' said Wren. 'She was all nestled up against him and he had his arms round her.'

'The bitch!'

'He told us to go away. He didn't want to be disturbed.'

'I don't believe it! How *could* he? I could kill her!'

July and Wren nodded in sympathy.

'We thought you should know.'

Holly's eyes glittered. She switched off the music and marched out of the room in her leotard and leg-warmers, the older girls in tow.

'Which room? I'm going to have words with him! And her, the little cow! How dare she come here and try it on with Buzz?'

But when they got to the room, they found the window seat empty. Holly had to be content with planning how she was going to deal with this new development.

'Do you like it here?' asked Buzz as they gazed around the formal garden. 'It started as a Tudor knot garden, I believe, and was added to later. Even in Stonewylde, the Age of Civilization left its mark.'

Sylvie smiled weakly. Her tears had stopped but her throat still ached and her heart was heavy. Everything was ruined. They walked slowly around the garden which was larger and more complicated than it seemed at first because of its labyrinthine design.

'You think it's all distasteful and nasty, don't you?' asked Buzz, looking down at her bent silver head. She nodded.

'It's no worse than anywhere else, Sylvie. In the Outside World everything revolves around sex.'

'I know it does and I hate it. I thought it was different here. Everything seemed so beautiful and clean at Stonewylde. So natural.'

'And it is, believe me! Magus explained all this just before my Rite of Adulthood. Sex is so powerful. You can't deny it or pretend it isn't there; it's part of the life force. Everything at Stonewylde is a celebration of the life force, the power of regeneration and renewal. It's a mystical thing, a vital element of our ceremonies.'

'I suppose so. I just don't like the thought of it.'

'That's because you're still a child. You need someone older and more experienced to guide you, and I hope it will be me. I want to look after you, Sylvie. You bring out my gentle side and I like that. I know I can be loud and over the top, but you make me tone it down. I really hope we can be friends.'

He spoke softly and put an arm around her shoulders in a kind, brotherly way. She looked up at him and he smiled down at her gently. Sylvie realised that maybe he was quite a sweet person after all. Perhaps there was something attractive hidden underneath the brash exterior. Something that others could see but she'd missed. She shouldn't have been so quick to judge him. She smiled back.

'That's better. I'm so sorry if I upset you. I must've said things in the wrong way. You're so young and innocent. Please don't tell Magus I made you cry. He'd be furious with me.'

'It's not your fault, Buzz. You've been kind to me. I'm just being naïve and silly.'

He led her into an alcove in a clipped yew hedge where there was a hidden seat. It was still wet from the earlier rain and the wood looked slippery. He took off his jacket and spread it across the seat.

'Come and sit down.'

He patted the seat and she had to sit close so they could both fit on the jacket. She felt very small next to him. His legs were broad and powerful and now his arms were bare again, she could see the thick golden hair on them. He put one of them around her and held her by his side.

'It's alright, Sylvie. I'll take care of you.'

She felt awkward so close to him. She could smell his anti-perspirant. She didn't know what to do, how to act in this situation.

'Have you seen my pendant?' he asked, holding up the silvery disc hanging on a short chain round his neck. She peered at it and reached across for a closer look. The thick disc was just a little bigger than a ten pence coin and embossed on both sides. On one side was a buzzard, wings spread, and on the other a leaping hare.

'It's lovely,' she said. 'So everyone gets one of these when they become an adult?'

He nodded.

'The images vary, of course. On one side you have your own personal totem. Mine's the buzzard, of course. Everyone chooses theirs just before the ceremony and Magus has it made up specially. The other side is for the image of the festival nearest your birthday. So the hare's here because my birthday's near to the Spring Equinox and it's the spring symbol. There's a different symbol for each of the eight festivals.'

'So what would mine be?'

'You're Summer Solstice, aren't you? That's an oak leaf, and Winter Solstice is a sprig of mistletoe. Beltane's a Green Man and Samhain a crow. Spring Equinox a hare and Autumn an acorn. Imbolc's a crescent moon and Lammas a head of corn. What would you choose for your totem? Any ideas?'

'I'm not sure. I love hares. And owls too. I don't know.'

'You don't have to choose yet. Nearer the time, you'll be sure.'

He smiled at her, his arm still round her shoulders, fingers playing on her hair where it cascaded down her back.

'But what about when I'm sixteen and it's my Rite of Adulthood?' she asked, a note of panic in her voice. 'I don't want to do all that– the sex stuff!'

'Of course not,' he said soothingly, stroking her hair. 'Nobody will make you do anything you don't want to, I promise. I'll be here and I'll look after you.'

'But what if Magus says I have to?'

'Sylvie, just before you're sixteen Magus talks to you to see if you're ready for the Rite. Nobody is ever forced into anything. Okay?'

She nodded. Maybe it wasn't all quite as dreadful as she'd thought at first. Although there was still the problem of Miranda falling in love with Magus. A sudden thought struck her.

'At Beltane, when Magus was with the young May Queen. Did they . . . you know, was that her Rite of Adulthood?'

He laughed at this.

'I should say so! And what a night to celebrate it! Rowan was really lucky to be chosen. Some of the Hallfolk girls were less than impressed.'

Sylvie closed her eyes and groaned. How naïve she must have sounded to Magus the following morning. No wonder Rowan had looked tousled and exhausted at the sunrise ceremony. The whole thing was repulsive – how could a young girl want someone so old? And Miranda's romantic picnic at the full moon, coming straight after his night with Rowan, must have meant very little to him. How could he deceive her mother like that? Should she tell her?

Sylvie realised that although she and Miranda thought they'd become part of the Stonewylde community, clearly they had little idea of the true nature of life here. Should they cut their losses and go back to the Outside World? But the very thought of that made her shiver with horror. There was no choice at all; she'd have to accept this underside of Stonewylde.

'Thank you, Buzz. I'm pleased you told me. Shall we go back indoors?'

He was still stroking her hair rhythmically and he held her there, his powerful arm blocking her small movement to stand up.

'Can we just sort out one more thing, please?'

She looked up at him questioningly and was surprised at the expression on his face; a mixture of tenderness and something else, something more animal. She sat still, not wanting to upset him when he was being so kind and unsure how to extricate herself gracefully. She wished now that she'd stayed in the school room.

'It's the business of that Village boy and what you saw at Beltane in the woods.'

Sylvie jerked in his grip but he held on to her, smoothing her hair again to quieten her.

'No, listen. I've got to put this right between us because I don't want him spoiling our friendship. Will you listen and let me explain?'

'Well alright,' she said, 'but I still think—'

'Hold on, Sylvie, and hear me out. First, you must realise that the Villagers lead very different lives to us. More like mediaeval lives. They're tough and Yul's especially tough. He works in the woods all day and he's strong and hard. Okay?'

'Ye-es.'

'Next, he's led a brutal life. You saw the other marks on his back? Yul's father is a tanner, a real brute of a man. Yul's always been a trouble-maker and his father's had to discipline him more than most boys. He doesn't feel pain like we would – he's used to it. I expect he's told you about his tough upbringing. You saw that black eye he had? And the new scar on his face?'

'He said Magus did that.'

'What? I hope you didn't believe him! He's such a liar. You'll very rarely see him without some sort of bruise or cut – he's always got injuries. His whole family are rough and hard and Yul's a bully himself. He's a really nasty piece of work.'

'I can't see that—'

'You just have to trust me, Sylvie. Of course he won't show you his true nature, will he? Whipping may seem barbaric to you, but it's a punishment we use at Stonewylde. We don't have a prison. That's barbaric to us, the idea of taking away somebody's liberty. We don't fine people because we have no money here. We don't have community service because we all do that anyway, perfectly willingly. So there are few deterrents left, and whipping is a quick, painful punishment that's over soon, takes a while to heal which reminds the person of their wrongdoing, but there's no lasting damage.'

'It just seems so cruel.'

'In the Outside World maybe, but not here. Yul had to be punished for something awful he did to a Hallfolk girl. Magus made him dig your garden after work every day in the hope he'd be so worn out it would keep him out of mischief. But it didn't work. I told you: Yul's tough, and he just laughed at the punishment.'

'But—'

'Don't you want to know what he'd done? What he was being punished for?'

'Well, yes, but—'

'His crime, at the Spring Equinox, was to have a go at Holly.'

'What do you mean, "have a go"?'

'I'll leave that for you to work out, Sylvie. But Holly was very upset about it, so the lads and I decided to discipline Yul ourselves

174

at Beltane. I know it looked awful to you, and I can understand your shock, but it really didn't mean that much to Yul. Do you understand now?'

She looked up at him, her pale grey eyes candid and trusting.

'I suppose so, when you explain it like that. But Yul's already told me he isn't interested in Holly, and honestly, she doesn't seem upset to me. In fact she's been boasting that you and Yul had a fight over her. But it upset *me* a lot to see how you treated Yul. He seems nice and I felt sorry for him.'

'I can understand that. There's something of the underdog about him and he'll play on your sympathy. But you must *never* become friends with him. Magus is watching him carefully and he'll be furious. You don't want to see Magus when he's angry, believe me. So you must have nothing more to do with the boy at all. Okay?'

'Okay.'

'So are we friends now?'

She nodded. It seemed easier to just let it go, and maybe Buzz was right – life was tougher at Stonewylde. She'd better learn to accept that and all today's other revelations. He smiled and gave her shoulders a squeeze.

'I'm so pleased. I'll look after you, I promise. And Magus will be pleased too as I know he's keen for us to get on. Let's go indoors now and have some lunch, shall we?'

In the Dining Hall, Sylvie sat next to her mother and was very quiet as she picked at the food on her plate.

'Anything the matter, darling?'

Sylvie shook her head.

'It's alright, Mum. I've just got things on my mind.'

'Anything I can help with?'

Sylvie looked up and saw her mother in a new light. She'd be so disillusioned when the truth about Magus came out. How could she tell her?

'No, it's nothing anyone can help with.'

'Where were you before lunch? I tried to find you.'

'I went for a walk with Buzz in the formal garden.'

'That's good. He's very popular here, isn't he? Does he like you?'

'Yes, but not in that way I hope.'

'Well, you're almost fifteen and you're very beautiful. It's quite natural that boys will be interested in you. Far better someone like Buzz for your first boyfriend than that nasty Village boy.'

Sylvie glared at her, pushing her plate away.

'That's where you're wrong. You're not really a very good judge of character, are you, Mum?'

Holly watched Sylvie across the crowded room.

'I hate her!' she hissed

'Don't be silly,' said Dawn. 'She's done nothing wrong.'

'Just pinched my boyfriend, that's all!'

'No she hasn't. What July and Wren saw was probably nothing. Don't be nasty to her, Holly. It's not fair.'

'She's hardly playing fair either, is she? Don't worry, Dawn, I'll find out exactly what's going on. And then she'd better watch out! I've spent a lot of time and energy hooking Buzz and I won't give him up without a fight.'

Dawn shook her head.

'She's a nice girl and you've got it wrong. It's Buzz you should be annoyed with, not her. You speak to him and find out what's what. Don't blame Sylvie.'

'I blame them both,' muttered Holly. 'But I want him and I don't care what happens to her. She deserves all that's coming to her.'

The Dining Hall was noisy with the clatter of cutlery and chatter of voices. The servants scurried about ensuring that every member of the Hallfolk was fed. Magus sipped his water and scanned the great room, noting Sylvie and Miranda engaged in conversation. He watched them with dark eyes, his face inscrutable. Then he caught Buzz's eye further down the table and raised a questioning eyebrow. Buzz nodded and they smiled at each other before returning their attention to the tender lamb on their plates.

12

On the morning of the Dark Moon, Yul rose even earlier than usual. He needed to find an old flaxen bag and couldn't ask his mother in case there were questions. He'd seen her antagonism towards Mother Heggy and knew he shouldn't get involved in helping the crone. It was unlikely that the Beechwood Sickeners were needed for any healing remedy and she was probably up to no good, but he felt a compulsion to obey. It never occurred to him not to harvest the red mushrooms as instructed.

Yul crept downstairs to look for a bag, as there may be no further opportunity today. He heard his mother moving around upstairs on the creaky floor and knew he had little time. She usually came down just after him and busied herself stoking the range, putting water on to boil and cooking breakfast for the family. Rosie had already left for the dairy as she had the earliest start and was given breakfast there. Yul's father would soon be down too, stomping about with a sore head and demanding his bacon and eggs. He rarely spoke in the mornings but shovelled down his breakfast in morose silence.

Yul always kept out of sight in the back garden, feeding the pig and chickens and chopping firewood. As Alwyn ate his breakfast at the table, Maizie would silently pass Yul his lunch wrapped in a cloth, and some bacon and bread for his breakfast. He'd eat this as he walked to the woods. The five younger children in the family, all still at the Village School or Nursery, waited quietly together upstairs until their father left for work. Everyone kept out of Alwyn's way in the morning. But today was different.

Yul found a flaxen bag in the parlour dresser and stuffed it into his trousers for safekeeping. He heard Maizie coming down the stairs and waited to say good morning, not realising that Alwyn was right behind her. It was too late to open the door to escape and Yul froze, his heart thumping. He looked down at the floor, hoping his father would go straight through into the kitchen and out to the privy in the back garden.

'What are you doing here?' Alwyn grunted.

'Nothing. I was just on my way out.'

'You should be outside already. I don't want to see your ugly face in the morning. Get out of my way, you little shit.'

Yul wasn't in his way but he shrank back against the wall. He held his breath, praying that maybe it would be alright. His father stamped across the room, heavy jaw jutting and piggy eyes alight with belligerence. He was an unattractive man with a huge barrel-belly, gingery hair and a greasy red face. Yul was glad, every time he looked at him, that he'd inherited none of his father's looks whatsoever.

Alwyn drew level with Yul and stopped. The boy had flattened himself against the wall with his head down. Maizie was already in the kitchen clattering the frying pan onto the range, keeping out of the way. She knew not to intervene when Alwyn started on Yul as it only enraged him further. Over the years she'd learnt to act as if nothing untoward was happening, and the children followed her lead. So Yul's beatings took place in front of a silent family who averted their eyes and ignored the terrible scene taking place right under their noses. Nobody ever dared say a word for fear of making it worse for Yul.

'Wipe that look off your face, you little bastard!'

Yul kept his head down.

'Did you hear what I said?'

Yul nodded.

'Answer me when I'm speaking to you!'

Alwyn's hand shot out and hit Yul hard around the side of the face with a loud crack. The boy swayed, his head reeling.

'I said get that look off your face! I'm warning you ...'

As Yul was looking at the floor, expressionless, there was nothing more he could do to obey. With a growl of rage, Alwyn's huge hand shot out again and grabbed Yul by the throat, pushing him hard up against the wall. Yul choked and spluttered, gasping for breath. His father held him there, the boy's feet on tiptoe almost off the floor. Alwyn's face was scarlet, his mouth flecked with spittle. His other hand bunched up into a fist. The heavy blows to Yul's torso were measured and deliberate; the sound of knuckles thudding into flesh and bone was sickening.

Yul clamped his mouth shut, determined that no humiliating cries of pain would escape. Alwyn grunted with the effort of every thump and the strain of pinning the boy to the wall. Finally he let go and Yul crumpled to the floor, curling himself up as small as he could. Alwyn towered above him breathing heavily, his fists clenching and unclenching. Undecided whether to continue with the strap, he looked down at the boy at his feet. Yul shook violently and despite his best efforts, he whimpered with pain. Alwyn nodded in satisfaction.

'Your breakfast's ready, my love!' Maizie called from the kitchen. 'And I cooked you some extra sausages as well.'

The smell of bacon distracted Alwyn, making his mouth water and his stomach rumble with anticipation. The boy could wait – he'd continue the punishment tonight before he went to the pub. With a final grunt he kicked Yul in the side and stomped into the kitchen. Groaning, Yul staggered upright and held onto the wall for support. He managed to open the front door and lurched down the track, until the intense pain in his side slowed him to a limping shuffle.

If Greenbough noticed anything was wrong, he didn't say. He saw the swollen lump on Yul's cheekbone and the boy looked increasingly pale as the morning wore on. But he refused the offer of sharing any of the other men's lunch, and took himself off to sit hunched up in a quiet corner, with his back to everyone as they ate. Yul was silent all day and by the afternoon

Greenbough could see he'd had enough. He winced with every movement and his neck seemed stiff and painful.

Greenbough wondered if he should tell Magus. The tanner was renowned in the Village for his violent temper and readiness to use his fists, and Yul was entirely at his mercy. The boy must live in terror. One day Alwyn may go too far and do some permanent damage; this already went well beyond tough parental discipline.

'You can stop now, Yul,' said Greenbough, seeing the boy struggle to wield his axe.

'It's alright, sir, I can do it.'

'No, you've had enough. Go home.'

Yul looked at him, his grey eyes full of pain.

'Come on, lad. You're no use to anyone like this. Should you go up to the Hall and see the doctor maybe?'

'No!' said Yul quickly. 'I'm fine really. But maybe I'll go for a walk. Thank you, sir.'

Greenbough watched the boy trudge away and shook his head, resolving to speak to Magus. Something must be done to stop Alwyn's cruelty. He decided to do it right now, and told the other men he was going up to the Hall for a while.

Yul decided to go to the Stone Circle. All he wanted was to be alone. He couldn't go home and he had to be in the woods at dusk to harvest the mushrooms at the Dark Moon. He felt hollow as he'd eaten nothing since the evening before. His neck was agony, his throat hurt when he swallowed and he was bruised all over. He was worried he'd cracked yet another rib when his father had kicked him.

Worst of all was his bitter rage and frustration. He wanted to kill Alwyn. He knew Maizie would be better off without him. She didn't love him and the children were all terrified of him. Alwyn had drinking companions but no real friends. His death would be a blessing to everyone. Yul made his way up the track that led to the Long Walk, his head down and his step slow, oblivious to the beauty and fragrance of the white and pink hawthorn blossom lining his route.

At the Hall, Old Greenbough called in the back entrance and spoke to one of the servants in the kitchen. Before long he was taken to the Galleried Hall to wait for the master. His audience with Magus started very differently to that of Yul's, the day he'd been summoned here. Greenbough was a respected member of the community and Magus treated the old man with deference. After they'd chatted about the woodlands at Stonewylde, Greenbough cleared his throat and prepared to broach the purpose of his visit.

'I wanted to talk to you about young Yul, sir.'

'Ah yes, Yul. His name seems to be cropping up a great deal lately. What's he done now? I warned him recently if there was any more trouble he'd face a whipping.'

'Oh no, he's done nothing wrong, sir. No, no, he's a good lad. He's a hard worker and a very bright boy.'

'Really? I had him down as sly, devious and lacking in respect for anyone.'

'No, sir, that's not the boy I know.'

'Oh well, we obviously see him in different lights.'

Magus sat relaxed in his carved chair, long legs stretched out before him. With one elbow on the boar's head armrest and his chin on his hand, he surveyed Greenbough with a cynical expression that told of his disbelief. The old man felt uncomfortable. Magus usually addressed him with pleasing courtesy.

'I'm worried about the way his father treats him.'

'In what respect?'

'Well, Yul is beaten regular. The poor lad's always damaged in some way or another. But now his injuries are getting worse, sir, and I don't like the way 'tis heading.'

Magus smiled coldly and shook his head.

'You surprise me, Greenbough. I'd have put you down as someone who'd approve of a boy being brought up tough.'

'Oh aye, sir, I do, right enough. 'Tis just that Alwyn goes too far. Much too far.'

'But surely, Greenbough, you agree that it's up to a father how he disciplines his son?'

'Aye, but—'

'It certainly isn't your place to interfere in issues between parent and child. Nor mine, for that matter. My involvement would undermine something central to our philosophy at Stonewylde.'

He smiled at Greenbough again, a smile without warmth. The old man looked down at his work boots and cleared his throat. He'd have one more try. Alwyn must be stopped. If he carried on, the boy could be maimed for life – or worse.

'Fair enough, sir, I do take your point. You know me well enough. I wouldn't bother you for no good reason, but I—'

'Of course, Greenbough. You did right to raise your concerns. And now if you don't mind, I have a great deal of business to attend to.'

Magus stood, signalling that the interview was over, and Greenbough hastily stood up too. He was annoyed that he hadn't had the chance to speak plainly.

'Sir, will you please look into it? I'm concerned for the boy's well-being. He's my apprentice and he can't work when he's injured so bad.'

Magus raised his eyebrows and sighed.

'Very well, Greenbough. If it's affecting his ability to do a proper day's labour, I will look into it. I'll come by the woods later on.'

'Thank you, sir. But . . . well, the boy ain't there now.'

'Why not?'

'I gave him the afternoon off.'

Magus frowned at this.

'A foolish decision. You know the laws of the community. Everyone puts in an honest day's work. If Yul thinks he can skip his duties because of a few bruises, he'd take advantage of you in no time. I shall definitely look him out this afternoon, wherever he may be. Good day, Greenbough.'

He strode off, his boots clicking on the stone floor. Greenbough tramped sadly back to the woods. He had a terrible feeling he'd just made it worse for the lad.

When he entered the Stone Circle from the Long Walk, the change in Yul was almost tangible. The sharp pain in his side subsided and every injury hurt less. Yul knew it was wrong to enter a sacred place feeling dejected and angry, so he shook the dark hair out of his eyes and lifted his chin. With a straight back he stepped slowly across the Circle, feeling a sudden thrill of power. As he walked across the beaten earth his feet tingled and he felt stronger, more whole. He stopped in the centre.

Tonight was of course the Dark Moon and maybe that made a difference. At the Dark Moon, the Crone ruled and the power was of dark magic, of destruction. Women would start to bleed, their wombs emptying ready for the following month's fertility. Yul knew it was women who were in tune with the moon's cycle, but he also recalled Mother Heggy's words that he was moon-blessed. Maybe that's why he felt so strange here today.

He moved across to the great horizontal Altar Stone. He swung his legs up as he'd done at Beltane, remembering how Buzz had pinned him to the stone. He sat hugging his knees and closed his eyes. It was late afternoon and the May sunshine was warm, although it was a little windy and the occasional cloud drifted overhead. Gradually Yul loosened the tight grip on all he'd endured and kept locked inside since the beating that morning. He uncurled his body and sat straighter, empty-ing his mind. He let go of the image of Alwyn that he'd been carrying all day.

'Dark Goddess, help me. I can't take any more,' he whispered. At that moment the sun went dark as a cloud passed in front of it and the skin on Yul's arms raised in gooseflesh. He felt dizzy and strangely disconnected.

'Goddess, you decide what's to be done. Please, stop my father before he kills me. I leave him to you.' Then he heard hoof beats;

the sound of a cantering horse. He opened his eyes quickly as Magus, astride Nightwing, approached from the Long Walk.

Magus reined in the great black stallion. Man and horse looked into the Stone Circle and saw a strange sight. Yul sat crossed-legged on the Altar Stone, straight backed with his head raised proudly. The great arena of stone was bathed in bright sunlight except for the Altar Stone: this was in shadow. The effect was uncanny. Magus drew breath sharply at the sight of the boy, still and silent in his pool of darkness. The horse reared slightly and side-stepped in agitation. Then the cloud passed and Yul too was washed with light.

Nightwing trotted across the Circle and came to a halt by the stone. Yul was aware that he should get off and stand respectfully at Magus's feet. This was similar to the incident in March when he'd failed to show proper deference; he now had a scar across his cheek to remind him. But today he'd had enough and really didn't care what Magus did to him. So he sat there cross-legged, staring up through his hair at Magus astride his great horse.

Magus surveyed him with narrowed, dark eyes. As he looked at the boy, tight anger knotted in the pit of his stomach. He felt a desire to strike him; to show him who was the master and crush him completely. He controlled this urge, clenching his thighs around Nightwing who champed at his bit in protest. Yul dipped his head and Nightwing dipped his in response. Then to Magus' amazement, the black stallion took a step forward and nuzzled into Yul's chest. Yul stroked the velvet nose and whispered softly. With an oath Magus jerked the reins viciously, pulling Nightwing away so hard that he reared.

'Touch my horse again and you're dead!' he hissed.

Yul regarded him steadily, his deep grey eyes locked into Magus' dark brown ones. Magus raised his whip, controlling the dancing horse with one hand and his powerful legs.

'I'll cut you to match the other side, boy,' he said, menacingly. 'Stand up when I'm talking to you!'

In a fluid movement Yul obeyed, standing on the stone so he was actually higher than Magus. He looked once more into the man's eyes and felt his own surge of unexpected power. Then he jumped from the stone and landed lightly on the ground. He shook back the tousled hair and gazed up. Magus' face was palely dangerous and contorted with anger. His eyes were black chips of jet, his lips thin and white. In a movement as fluid as Yul's he swung off the horse and landed on his feet, strong and agile as a panther. He let Nightwing go, knowing he wouldn't wander far, and faced the boy. He stifled the urge to slash him with his whip or knock him to the ground. The boy's defiance had fuelled his temper dangerously but he didn't need to indulge in shows of brute strength. He had other methods of subjugation at his disposal.

'Why aren't you at work, young man?' he asked, his temper now reined in.

'Old Greenbough said I should go, sir,' Yul replied.

'And why would he do that? It's not a half day holiday today, is it? No festivals to celebrate. Why did he say you could leave so early?'

Involuntarily Yul touched the livid swelling on his cheekbone.

'I was finding it difficult to work properly, sir. I ... my rib hurt when I chopped wood.'

'And what's wrong with your rib?' asked Magus sternly, whip tapping his riding boot.

'I ... it's just sore, sir. I must've cracked it.'

'Let me see. Take your shirt off.'

Yul gulped at this, but Magus stared at him implacably. He pulled the rough-spun shirt over his head, trying not to wince. Magus' eyes widened at the sight of the boy's torso. Yul was covered in ugly dark bruises, with a nasty swelling on his side. He stood straight, shoulders back and chin up, determined not to show his shame. He looked very thin as he didn't carry any spare flesh and lack of food today had hollowed him further.

'Turn around,' commanded Magus, 'Let me see your back.'

Yul obeyed and Magus saw many long stripes slashed across his skin, the bruising still visible from Buzz's whipping at Beltane.

Magus saw too all the older scarring, evidence of the years of abuse.

'Alright, cover yourself up, boy. You're a dreadful sight.'

Yul pulled the shirt on again and stared at his boots in humiliation.

'I assume this is your father's handiwork?'

'Yes, sir.'

'And what did you do to deserve such punishment?'

Yul had asked himself that question many times.

'I don't know, sir. This morning he didn't like the expression on my face.'

Magus barked with laughter at this.

'I know exactly how he felt – I don't like it either! You have an insolence I've never encountered before at Stonewylde. I know you're not very bright. I seem to remember you failed the school tests quite appallingly. But surely even someone as simple as you must realise the consequences if you stare with defiance and surliness at those in authority over you? It's not difficult to understand, is it?'

'No, sir,' muttered Yul.

His throat ached with unshed tears. How ridiculous, to have imagined the Dark Goddess had answered his prayer. How stupid to have allowed himself, for a fleeting moment, to think that Magus would bring Alwyn to justice.

'In the last couple of months,' continued Magus, 'I've had to bring you to heel on several occasions. Nobody else on the estate causes me to reprimand them more than once. This really is your final warning, Yul. If anything else happens, anything whatsoever, then the next punishment will be severe. Do you understand?'

'Yes, sir.'

'If you continue to defy me, I'll break you. You *will* learn to serve me well. You *will* learn to obey me absolutely. I am the magus. And you – you're nothing. Remember that, boy.'

Magus gave Yul a final dark glare, then whistled. Nightwing trotted into the Circle and Magus took the reins. Grasping the front of the saddle, he put his boot in the stirrup and gracefully swung up onto the great stallion. With the gentlest of pressure he commanded Nightwing to canter out of the Circle and away down the Long Walk. Yul's grey eyes followed him, wishing he were on that horse, wishing he had all that power. He let out a broken sigh. But a glance at the sun brought him back to reality. He must hurry now to get to the woods for dusk. There were mushrooms to be picked.

As he left the protection of the Circle his body started to hurt badly again. He was now so hungry that a dull pain gnawed constantly at his insides. He trudged up the woodland track and gradually the enchantment of the place worked its magic, soothing his soul. The evening sunlight filtered through the leaves and branches, dappling the woodland floor with gold and enhancing the vividness of the bluebells. Yul smelt the exquisite sweetness of lily of the valley and wild honeysuckle. Birds sang joyfully, and in the distance he saw a small herd of deer camouflaged against the trees. Yul felt a flood of his familiar affinity with the ancient and hidden woodland spirits and the foliate Green Man of the forest.

He passed the place where he'd first seen Sylvie walking with Magus, and recalled his joy at discovering someone so beautiful and ethereal. Yul hadn't then foreseen how their paths could ever cross, and yet they had, again and again. She'd somehow become part of his life, a single bright star in the dark void of despair. As he walked through the woods, Yul let his imagination roam into unchartered territory. A flood of excitement washed over him at the thought of being together with Sylvie.

At last he reached Beech Grove and the strange, deep craters in the ground known as swallets. Old Greenbough had told him that they'd sunk down centuries ago, created when the layers of chalk underground were slowly eroded by water until the ground above collapsed. He knew the swallets were old because large beech trees grew inside them as well as all around them. All the trees here were tall and graceful, with smooth, green-grey trunks and a fine feathering of twigs smothered in lime green foliage. This grove was particularly special as it was home to a great colony of bats that nested inside several old hollow trunks.

The place held happy memories for Yul. As children he and Rosie had often played here, rolling down into the deep swallets on a carpet of old beech leaves onto the soft bed of moss at the bottom, before scrambling up the sides for another go. His feet now crunched on the beech mast that littered the ground, the cases discarded by squirrels who feasted on the kernels in autumn and winter. Yul remembered how he and his sister had nibbled at the beech seeds, savouring the nutty taste. He must bring little Leveret here, he thought to himself. She'd love it too.

Yul walked reverently through the green, living cathedral listening to the anthem of birdsong. He savoured the incense of the fragrant evening and the majesty of the great trees, their stately pillars and bright canopy more awe-inspiring than any man-made edifice. High above, squirrels performed their acrobatics in the leafy branches. A jay flew by, pink-brown with a black and white flash to its rump and vivid blue-striped feathers on its wings. The woodland grove was alive with creatures and Yul felt at one with Nature, a tiny part of the whole beautiful creation.

He stopped, closing his eyes, and felt again a flicker of the power he'd experienced earlier at the Stone Circle. As the sun set he felt something rise within him, something dark and secret. He smiled to himself. Alwyn and Magus could go and rot in the Otherworld. They might damage his body but they'd never touch his spirit. His body would heal and he'd survive, stronger and tougher because of their cruelty. They'd never, ever break him. Yul laughed out loud as the power prickled through him, his hunger and bruises forgotten.

Then he saw the log lying on the ground and remembered where the woodsmen had discovered the crop of Beechwood Sickener. Fungi had to be searched for carefully; it had a habit of disappearing into the background and becoming virtually invisible. In the failing light Yul hunted for the distinctive red caps, suddenly worried he wouldn't find them before it became dark. Mother Heggy had insisted they be harvested in the dusk of the Dark Moon.

He found them; a patch of mushrooms truly bright red in colour. How many to pick? He decided on five, being the sacred number of the pentangle, and pulled the bag from his waistband. He remembered tucking it there, and the ensuing encounter with Alwyn. As he harvested the five mushrooms carefully, so as not to bruise them, images from that morning's beating flashed before him – especially his father's sweating, excited face and the strange, merciless light in his eyes. White-hot, corrosive fury welled up inside Yul. His fingers shook as he picked the five mushrooms, shook with hatred for Alwyn and a searing desire for revenge.

As he made his way out of the woods with the light almost gone, he heard a strange high-pitched squeaking and smiled to himself. The bats! They'd sensed the deepening dusk and now poured out of several trees in a stream. Tiny black shapes flickered in the gathering darkness, the squeaking becoming louder and louder inside the hollow trunks. Yul stood absolutely still as they zigzagged around his head, never touching him, filling the beech grove with their dark movement. It was as if the bats' arrival heralded true night, and Yul welcomed them silently.

By the time he reached Mother Heggy's cottage the stars were glittering. There was no moon at all tonight, of course, and the deep blue velvet sky enveloped Yul like a cloak. He was light-headed with hunger. He held the flaxen bag carefully, tied up with a long string of ivy, and soundlessly approached the ancient cottage. A feeble light glimmered in the window and he smelled sweet wood smoke in the night air.

Just as he stooped to leave the bag on the step, the door creaked open. Mother Heggy stood at the threshold, a shrivelled little hump of a creature, her neck bent up so she could see ahead. She grimaced toothlessly at him and gestured him inside with a clawed hand. The strange smell of her cottage hit him and he felt queasy.

'Good boy, good boy,' she wheezed, as she shut the door. 'Come and sit awhile with Old Heggy and let me look at you. Eh, you've been on my mind since you last came. Give me your hand, boy. Let me feel what's about.'

Yul tried not to flinch as she grasped his hand between her claws. They sat as before, he on a hard chair and she in her rocking chair drawn up close to him. She stroked his hand and crooned harshly to herself, rocking all the time. After a while her eyes shot open, their milkiness quite shocking.

'So you want to kill the tanner, do you?'

He gasped. How could she have known that?

'I ... well yes, I did think that earlier on. The beatings are getting worse, harder and more painful. And I really can't take it much harder.'

'No, and you shouldn't have to. But you're already on the road. The Sickeners were picked with hatred in your heart. You've felt the power, I know. 'Tis all starting! Only a few weeks and then 'twill be *you* in the ascendancy. You have to hold on, my son of the solstice, and endure. 'Twon't be long now.'

He was silent, understanding little of what she said.

'That man Alwyn will suffer, just as he's made you suffer all these years. D'you want that, Yul?'

'Oh yes,' he whispered, his voice trembling. 'I really want him to suffer. I want that very, very much.'

''Tis said now and 'twill be done. But first you must bring me something of him. Skin, scab, hair or nail. Can you do that?'

'What? I don't understand.'

'Bring me some of his hair or a bit of finger-nail. I need that for the magic to work.'

'I suppose so. I'll try.'

'No, Yul, that's not enough. You *must* do it and it must be within the next day, before the waxing of the moon. And ... there's something else.'

She paused, still stroking his hand between her bony ones. He felt so light-headed – was he really here or just dreaming this?

'You must get out o' that cottage. Until the magic begins its work, you're in danger from him. I told you wrong before; 'twas not so clear. But now, at the Dark Moon, I see better. Aye, that Magus is the true danger. But Alwyn has become maddened and 'twill get worse before the magic starts. You must *not* sleep in that cottage until I say 'tis safe to return. Make a nest in the woods and live there. Your mother will provide for you. D'you heed me?'

He nodded, his eyes going in and out of focus as his head swam.

'And the girl, the newcomer. You must forge the bond stronger. She too is in danger. Someone is trying to trap her, to hunt her. She needs your protection.'

'I'd do anything for her.'

'Aye, my boy, you will need to. You and she are the darkness and the brightness and together you must be in harmony and balance. Seek her out and bind her to you. If you don't, this other one will harm her.'

Yul nodded again and swallowed, his throat like tree bark. Mother Heggy rose stiffly and shuffled over to the back of the room, returning with the stone mug.

'You'll feel better,' she muttered, pressing it into his hands. Grimacing, he raised the mug to his lips and drank. It was the refreshing liquid and it did revive him, hitting his empty stomach and acting fast. She shuffled off again and came back with a small dish of hazelnut kernels and a piece of honey comb. Ravenously he devoured her tiny supper and felt slightly better. Once more she hobbled back with a bowl, but this time told him to take his shirt off. Reluctantly he obeyed. She tutted at the sight of the heavy bruising and gently pasted an unguent onto his injuries. Then she turned him round to examine his back.

'These latest stripes are from the hawk who hunts the girl. He's marking his territory. He's displaying his strength. You must challenge him.'

192

Yul, his head clearer now that he'd eaten and drunk a little, jumped at this.

'You mean Buzz will hurt Sylvie?'

His heart raced at the thought of it.

'Aye, the one as did this to you. But never fear, Yul. You are a hundred fold more powerful than he, though he appears to hold all the power. But you must be aware of the danger, for the girl is defenceless.'

He nodded and realised that despite her grotesqueness and antiquity, he now trusted this old woman.

'And today you were at the Stone Circle?'

'Yes, this afternoon.'

'You felt the power today?'

How could she know this?

'Yes, I did.'

'Aye, well enough. Now you know how the magic of the Earth speaks when the Dark Goddess walks. You need to draw on that magic; you have need of much before you'll be strong enough. You must go to the Circle every day, twice if you can. 'Tis especially potent at sunrise and sunset. You've found the place where you feel the power strongest?'

'Yes, on the Altar Stone. I seem to be drawn to it.'

'Aye, the power will call you to itself. That spot is a gateway. The Earth Magic is strong there. Do you feel it anywhere else?'

He thought for a moment.

'Up at the Hare Stone, but it's better there for the Moon Fullness. I feel the quicksilver magic up there.'

'You are the one, Yul! I knew it!' she cackled triumphantly. 'Power calls to power. Magic calls to magic. It draws its own to itself.'

'And Sylvie, she loves it up at Hare Stone too.'

'Aye, because she shares it with you. She is the Maiden. The moongazy girl come at last to Stonewylde. You must bring her to me soon. I need to see her.'

'I will, I promise. As soon as I can.'

She stood and picked up the flaxen bag. Unravelling the ivy she peered inside.

'Good, 'tis enough. Five is just right. My Raven used to pick these for me.'

'Your raven?'

'My little girl. My dearest one.'

Then Yul remembered the story his mother had told him about Mother Heggy and Raven, the orphaned child she'd raised, the strange, wild girl she'd doted on.

'She was a bright blessed one,' crooned the old woman. 'Tiny and delicate like a faerie child. Even when she was grown to a woman, she were still a maiden. She had hair of pure silver, like gossamer silk it was. Her eyes were the colour of moonstones, ringed darker. She were moongazy and fey, 'tis true, but so kind and gentle. And such powerful moon magic in her. Nobody was more precious or magical than my little Raven.'

Mother Heggy then brought a silver knife with a white bone handle to the table. The great crow hopped over from its roost above the range and strutted along the edge of the battered wooden table-top, watching her movements intently. She placed the Sickeners on the surface and began to chop them finely. She muttered as she worked, seeming oblivious to Yul's presence. He wondered if he should go; he was so tired and still desperately hungry. He longed to lay his aching body down on a soft bed. Should he go home tonight to sleep, or take Mother Heggy's advice and stay away? She looked up from her chopping.

'Aye, boy, you must go now. I have work to do here while the skies are dark and the Goddess wears her black robes. You must return to your mother now for food, but sleep out tonight. Go to the hut in the woods if there's nowhere else. And return here tomorrow with something from Alwyn. Just a small piece o' him – something of his life-spiral. You *must* do this deed, Yul. If you don't, his cruelty will grow until he has beaten you to death. 'Tis his destiny, and yours, unless you act now.'

She looked deep into Yul's eyes as she spoke and he felt again the strange compulsion to do as she asked. He nodded and stood up shakily, flinching as the pain from the blows made its presence felt again. The tiny amount of food she'd given him had made his hunger worse, for his stomach growled and gurgled like a drain.

'I'll be back tomorrow,' he said, and stepped out into the dark, jewelled night.

13

Breakfast the next morning was an embarrassing experience for Sylvie. The talk amongst her contemporaries was mystifying at first, until she realised that the proposed mass exodus to the Great Barn after breakfast was a regular occurrence; a monthly one in fact.

'We all go down for at least the first couple of days,' explained Dawn. 'It's great – a time for craft-making and catching up on the gossip. All the Village women are there too and we spend the time relaxing and making things for the community.'

'I love sewing,' said Wren. 'I think this month, for the May Dark Moon, it's summer quilts. There's usually basket making and rush mats too, if you like that sort of stuff, and embroidery and knitting.'

'But I don't understand. Do you mean everyone has their period at the same time?'

'Of course,' said July. 'It's the Dark Moon.'

'But how come? In the Outside World everyone has theirs at different times.'

'Well not here,' said Dawn. 'Stonewylde's different. It's a special time for us women, the time of the Dark Goddess. So hasn't yours started today?'

Sylvie shook her head miserably.

'Don't worry. It'll probably come soon, now you're here with us. When's it due?'

This was the question Sylvie had dreaded. She stared down at her untouched toast, cheeks burning, and several faces turned to hear her answer.

'Have you lost track of it?' asked Dawn sympathetically.

'No. It's just . . . I haven't actually started my periods yet.'

Holly sniggered.

'Bit late aren't you? You're almost fifteen. I started mine when I was twelve.'

'Stop it, Holly,' warned Dawn. 'Never mind, Sylvie. It's bound to come soon. You were ill, after all.'

'I've started mine,' piped Rainbow, Fennel's younger sister, 'and I'm thirteen! Poor Sylvie – you must feel such a baby.'

Sylvie kept her head down.

'Rainbow!' said Dawn. 'There's no—'

'You'll be here alone with all the boys then,' said Holly crossly. 'Remember what I said to you, Sylvie. Keep your hands off Buzz. I'll find out if you've been up to anything.'

Sylvie looked up at her in consternation.

'I'm not after your boyfriend, Holly, honestly.'

July and Wren exchanged glances which Rainbow intercepted.

'So how come you were caught snogging him then?' she asked. She was precocious and loved mixing with the older girls, who found her outspokenness amusing. As Fennel's sister she also enjoyed a certain amount of status.

'I wasn't!'

'Rainbow, keep out of this,' said Dawn. 'July and Wren got the wrong idea when they saw Buzz with Sylvie. Holly knows that. Let's get ready to go.'

What made it worse for Sylvie was that Miranda was also going to the Barn. She'd started unexpectedly early, proving Dawn's theory.

'I'd better go,' she said to Sylvie as they stood outside the Dining Hall. 'It'll look strange if I don't. I'm sorry to leave you on your own, darling. But don't worry. You'll have a peaceful day here. You can get on with your English essay.'

'But I'll be the only girl here over the age of twelve or so,' said

Sylvie miserably. 'All the boys will know why. It's so embarrassing, Mum.'

'You'll start soon,' Miranda assured her. 'Look how fast you're developing. Really, Sylvie, it won't be long.'

When the women and girls of fertile age had left for the Village, Sylvie wandered aimlessly about the Edwardian wing, home of the Senior School. The exam students were due to leave Stonewylde soon and most of the teachers were involved in helping with their revision. There were no formal lessons and Sylvie's year group was expected to continue with course work. She saw a group of boys heading for one of the larger school rooms, and dodging into a doorway to avoid them, she bumped straight into someone coming out. Martin stopped dead and frowned down at her.

'Oh, I'm so sorry!' she said, finding his stony stare unnerving.

'It was my fault, miss,' he said quietly, standing back to let her into the room. 'Did you know the others have already left for the Village? If you hurry you'll catch them up.'

She looked down at the floor.

'I'm not joining them, Martin.'

'I beg your pardon, miss. I assumed . . . I'm sorry.'

She glanced up and caught his cold, grey gaze. She felt awkward with him, for he had the silvery blond Hallfolk hair and colouring and yet he was a servant. She wondered, as she'd done before, why Martin wasn't Hallfolk when he so clearly shared the same genes. Yet he seemed happy with his lot, if a little cold and stiff.

She had to go into the room as he now politely held the door open. Her heart sank when she saw Buzz and Fennel in there. They sat at a table covered in books and revision notes. This must be the most humiliating day of her life.

'Sylvie! What a nice surprise! Come and join us.'

'Sorry, I didn't mean to disturb you. I'll go.'

'No don't go. Come and talk to us. We could do with some light relief, couldn't we, Fen?'

The other youth laughed and stared at Sylvie, his eyes raking her up and down.

'We couldn't believe it when Holly said you weren't going to the Barn,' he said. 'Who'd have thought it?'

Sylvie felt her cheeks burning and tried desperately to think of some clever put-down.

'I don't see that it's anyone's business,' she said lamely.

'Of course not,' said Buzz. 'We're just pleased you're here. This physics revision is so dull. Come and cheer us up.'

'I can't. I've got some work to do myself.'

'Bring it in here then! Come on, Sylvie, we'd love your company. You must be feeling lonely with the other girls gone. We'll look after you.'

She shook her head and started to back out of the room.

'I'll come and find you,' laughed Buzz. 'You can't hide from me, Sylvie.'

'Buzz!' warned Fennel. 'Remember what Holly said.'

'Yeah, what about it? Holly doesn't own me. I don't know why she's getting so possessive. Magus doesn't stick to one woman so why should I?'

That was the final straw for Sylvie. She slipped out quickly, wanting only to escape.

When he arrived for work not long after dawn, Greenbough had been surprised to find Yul curled up on the floor of the woodsmen's hut. Yul had spent an uncomfortable night and ached all over, each blow that Alwyn had placed throbbing painfully and bruised deep purple. As his master stomped into the hut Yul scrambled to his feet, every muscle and sinew crying out at the sudden movement. He imagined Greenbough would be angry and rehearsed the excuse he'd come up with the night before.

'I'm pleased to see you here, boy,' said the old man gruffly. ''Tis about time you got out of harm's way. Did you run away or did he kick you out?'

Yul blinked through his tousled hair at Greenbough, who felt a rush of pity for the hollow-cheeked boy.

'I ran away,' mumbled Yul. 'Sorry about sleeping here.'

'No matter,' said Greenbough, putting a kettle of water onto the small stove and raking the embers into new heat. 'Best place for you, lad. Course, Alwyn'll come here first if he's trying to find you. Do you want a bed in my cottage? My goodwife would be happy to care for you.'

Yul's drawn face broke into a smile.

'That's very kind, sir. But I think he'd come looking there too. I was planning on building a shelter deeper in the woods somewhere. Mother Heggy said that would be best.'

'Did she now? I should've known she'd be mixed up in this somewhere. Well, you heed her advice, boy, for she's a wise old crone. And she has your interests at heart.'

Yul nodded and found the mugs to make their tea.

'I'm sorry, sir, but can I go home a little later on? I need to do something for Mother Heggy and I must get some food.'

'Course you can,' said Greenbough, remembering Magus' annoyance the previous day on discovering Yul had been given time off work. To his surprise, the old woodsman found his loyalty lay with this ill-treated boy and not the master. He'd cover for Yul if the situation arose. 'Just mind you keep out of your father's way. And let your mother know you're safe and I'm looking out for you.'

'Thank you, sir,' said Yul shyly. He'd never seen this side of Greenbough before. 'I'll be as quick as I can.'

'Aye well enough,' said Greenbough airily. 'If you're doing Mother Heggy's bidding, you take as long as you need.'

The Village was unusually deserted when Yul arrived later, and he'd counted on this. Most women were in the Great Barn for the Dark Moon gathering, the children in school and the Nursery, and the men at work. A few older women gathered at the pump gossiping, but Yul skirted the buildings unseen and slipped into the empty cottage. He took a deep breath and looked around. Maizie had left the place as clean and tidy as ever; Yul knew he had a difficult task ahead. But first he needed food. He spent the next ten minutes in the pantry wolfing down as much as possible.

Then he climbed the stairs and went into his parents' bedroom, his feet reluctant and heart thumping.

The room was spotlessly tidy and Yul hunted in vain for what he needed. He felt guilty rifling through their things. There were a few gingery hairs in Alwyn's brush, which he pocketed carefully, hoping it would be enough. He looked around, noting how impersonal and stark the room was. There was nothing that spoke of his mother, of her sweet ways or her love of animals, birds and flowers. She'd have liked a pretty bedroom. Yul felt a sadness creep into his heart at the way she had to live, everything locked inside her and safe from Alwyn's destructive rule. Surely she'd be better off without him? Whatever Mother Heggy had planned, it could only make Maizie's life better.

He remembered again yesterday's violence; the vicious expression on Alwyn's face as he pinned Yul against the wall by his throat, the awful pleasure the tanner took in beating him. With a growl of rage Yul kicked at the bedroom door – and then he saw it. Lying behind the door, right against the edge of the skirting board, was a great horny toenail clipping. A smile spread over his thin face and he laughed.

'Thank you, Dark Goddess,' he whispered.

Sylvie hurried around the side of the Junior School wing and across a small lawn leading into a grove of Scots pine trees. She didn't know this part of the grounds but had to get away before Buzz and Fennel came looking for her. She couldn't stand the thought of them hounding her all day. She was also worried about Holly's increasing hostility and its effect on the other girls. She must put Holly's mind at rest, and spending any time with Buzz today would only make matters worse.

She slowed down in the pine grove, sure the boys wouldn't look for her here. She wandered through the tall, straight trees, admiring the rough golden shingles of bark and drinking in the aromatic fragrance. Sunlight poured down in dusty shafts and Sylvie began to relax in the warm May morning. After a while the pine trees thinned and then she was in heath land. The gorse was brilliant with coconut-scented nuggets of yellow flower. Silver birches grew in clusters and the air was bright with dancing butterflies.

Enjoying her new strength and vitality, Sylvie steadily climbed the hill, noting how the soil had changed to silver-grey sand. The path followed a gully carved into the slope, laddered with tree roots exposed by past torrents of water. She spotted the startling chevrons of an adder basking by the side of the path, and froze. The snake was silver and black, kinked in a strange shape on the warm soil, its tongue flickering. Sylvie's heart jumped at the sight of it; she'd never seen an adder before. It was beautifully patterned but the sharp zigzags screamed of danger. She stepped past the snake very carefully and moved on swiftly, imagining fangs and venom.

The land flattened out, and walking on the higher ground she came across an expanse of water overhung with birch and willow. Sylvie stopped for a while, sitting on a fallen log and gazing across the huge pond, shielding her eyes from the brilliant, dancing sunlight. Massive neon-blue dragonflies darted over the sparkling water and young frogs swarmed around the shallow edges in the mud. It was an idyllic morning and she forgot her earlier humiliation as the natural beauty of Stonewylde engulfed her.

Continuing along the path, Sylvie left the heath and found herself in grassland. Sheep grazed rhythmically on the hillside, eyeing her with their strange vertical pupils and bleating as she passed by. Up ahead, built almost on the summit of the hill, was a strange stone structure looking like a giant π symbol. Two colossal upright stones formed an entrance, capped by a great horizontal stone creating a roof. Sylvie paused and stared. It looked prehistoric. Then she noticed a thin trickle of smoke above the stone shelter, and in the same moment a movement inside caught her eye. She saw a dark purple robe and a head of wispy blond hair, and recognised the familiar face of Clip. With a smile she climbed the hill until she reached the stone portal.

'Good morning!' she called cheerfully, peering into the dark interior. The structure went back further than she'd expected, becoming almost a cave at the back. Clip sat cross-legged by the small fire burning in the entrance. Instead of the friendly welcome she'd imagined, he turned towards her and stared blankly. His grey eyes were vacant, roaming her face but seemingly without recognition. It was an uncanny sensation and she wondered fearfully if he were ill or out of his mind.

'Clip? Are you alright? It's me, Sylvie.'

His eyes slid into focus and he looked at her intently.

'I've seen you, Sylvie, last night. I met with your guide.'

'What? What do you mean?'

He regarded her silently and a shiver chased down her arms.

'Clip, what's wrong with you? Are you ill?'

He smiled dreamily at this, his gaunt face creasing into furrows. He shook his head slowly and made an effort to concentrate.

'Blessings, Sylvie. Come in and sit with me for a while.'

A little reluctantly she stooped and entered the strange stone cave, settling herself down opposite him. She shook her hair back and tucked it behind her ears, feeling hot after the long walk up the hill in the heat.

'Do you have any water, Clip? I'm quite thirsty.'

Still smiling, he reached deeper into the cave and produced a large stone bottle. He poured some water into a small bowl and passed it to her. She drank gratefully and accepted a cake and an apple too. He seemed to be more aware now, the dreaminess in his eyes beginning to fade.

'I'm not ill,' he said softly. 'I've been journeying to other places. Last night was the Dark Moon and I felt a need to travel. I've been here all night.'

This apparent paradox was resolved as he continued.

'I'm a shaman, Sylvie. I journey in other realms and I try to understand the messages of my guide, the silver wolf. Last night I met you, or your spirit at least. And I spoke with your guide.'

'My guide?'

'Your spirit guide. The sacred one who looks over you, guards your soul. The one who takes you, when you're ready, out of this reality and into others.'

'I see. And who is my guide?'

She had visions of a long dead great-grandmother or some such nonsense.

'A great white barn owl.'

She swallowed.

'Your owl showed me that you've come to Stonewylde for a special reason. Stonewylde is your destiny and your fate, the threshold to a new world and yet also your final destination. You're here on a journey of your own, and you'll come across danger and unhappiness in the course of this journey. You're ruled by the Moon Goddess who loves your dance. But you have a link with the Dark Goddess, a connection. I don't see that so clearly. You're a saviour, Sylvie. You're brave and loyal and before the Solstice you will travel a long way.'

Sylvie stared at him in absolute confusion. She had no idea what his riddles meant. The situation wasn't helped by the strange sensations thrilling through her veins. Her body tingled and burned and she felt a sudden elation of the spirits. The world seemed vivid, every colour brighter and clearer, everything sharply defined. She smiled at Clip, imagining the white owl hovering over her and knowing instinctively that he was right. Her spirit guide was indeed a barn owl.

'That cake – it's the same as we had at Beltane, isn't it?'

He nodded happily.

'Do you want another one? I've a few left.'

He reached for a tin but Sylvie shook her head, colours streaming out like a comet's tail at the sudden movement.

'No, that's enough thanks. I didn't realise. I feel so strange.'

'There's nothing like Old Violet's special cakes. They open the mind and help you see the truth. I saw so much last night at the Dark Moon. It's going now, fading in this reality. Did I tell you that you're a saviour?'

'Yes. But I don't understand what that means.'

'I rarely understand. It doesn't matter whether we do or not.

Your owl told me you'll travel soon and your destination is a place of desolation and destruction, a place of death. I remember that much. But what it means is a mystery. Just be careful, Sylvie. The owl spoke of an evil that walks, and of a snake too, a serpent within an egg. That's an archetypal symbol, of course, and I've no idea how it relates to you.'

'But I don't want to travel, Clip,' she whispered, everything becoming a little jumbled in her head. 'I love Stonewylde. I never want to leave.'

He regarded her steadily.

'I don't think I said you'd leave Stonewylde, my dear. That's not what I meant at all.'

'You have it? Something of Alwyn?' Mother Heggy croaked in her reedy voice, opening the door to Yul.

'Yes,' he said, suddenly nervous. In the confines of his cottage, where so much violence had taken place, he'd been overjoyed to find the toenail and convinced he was doing the right thing. But now . . . he'd walked to Heggy's cottage through candy-pink thrift that grew abundantly in the cliff-side grass; he'd listened to the birds singing in the bright May morning and felt the warm sun on his skin. And now he wasn't so sure this was the right thing after all. This business was dark and sinister and seemed to have no place in the real, beautiful world. Poisonous mushrooms and pieces of toenail – what sort of wickedness was he contemplating? His mother had strong views about this crazy old woman and perhaps he should heed her advice and keep well away.

Mother Heggy gazed up at him with milky eyes, the deep lines on her face shockingly clear in the daylight.

'Eh, my boy – take heart! I spoke yesterday of what will come about if you do nothing. Touch the marks he's left all over your body. You feel it now? The bruising is deep, but 'tis as nothing compared to what he's working up to. Do you want to die, Yul?'

'No, of course I don't. It's just . . . what will happen if I give you what I found? I don't want my mother to suffer.'

'I cannot tell what will happen, for nought in life is set in

205

stone. But think on this – does Maizie suffer now? Aye, you know it. 'Tis all about putting a stop to that suffering. And remember, Yul – *I* do this, not you. *Your* soul is untainted.'

He nodded and felt in his pocket, his heart full of dread. First he produced the ginger hairs, only a few. Heggy frowned and took them carefully in her clawed hand, shaking her head.

''Tis hardly enough. Was this all?'

Silently he handed her the crescent of yellow toenail. Her face cracked into a toothless leer.

'Aye, that's it! That's what I need! 'Twill be strong now, strong and potent.'

She hobbled to the table where the crow pecked at morsels of bloodied meat, and placed the pieces of Alwyn in a small dish. An ugly old cat crouched, amber eyes maleficent and tail lashing, next to a great book that lay open on the table. Its pages were thick and yellowing, covered in spidery writing interspersed with drawings. A thick piece of glass, the bottom of a bottle, rested on the page. Heggy saw his glance.

'Old age has its many vexations,' she rasped. 'I can barely see the writing even with the glass. A pity you cannot read, my boy. When I were a child the magus wanted us all learnt proper. Didn't last, mind you. But no matter – I know the words in my heart, though my eyes can no longer make 'em out.'

Her gnarled hand stroked the book lovingly.

'My Book of Shadows, passed down from the Wise Woman afore me, though she could only draw. I've writ my knowledge in its pages, but there's no one to pass it on to when I go to the Otherworld. My Raven, she'd have been the one.'

She shook her head in its battered old hat and moved to the range, pouring Yul a mug of liquid.

'Can you stay awhile?' she asked, settling into her rocking chair and fishing out her pipe. ''Tis lonely for an old 'un up here, with only the crow and the cat.'

'No, Mother Heggy, I'm sorry but I must get back to work.'

'Did you sleep away from home last night?'

He nodded.

'Be careful, Yul. You are in great danger until I've done my work. Keep away from the tanner. Last night, at the Dark Moon, I scried with my black dish. 'Twas unclear. There's something looming but I cannot see what. I'll try once more tonight. I smell danger on you; it clings to you like mist around a stone. In the old days I'd have known, but not now. Not since I made the sacrifice that Red Moon all them years ago.'

She sucked on her clay pipe and a wreath of smoke snaked about her head. Then she reached forward and laid her wizened hand on his, patting it with something like affection. He met her eye and felt the strength of her feeling, incongruous though it seemed. She sighed and sat back in her chair.

'But still, you are here and 'tis what matters,' she mused. 'Look out for yourself, my dark boy. Else all will've been in vain.'

As Yul made his way back down the track he thought of what the crone had said. He was frightened. He knew the violence was getting worse, but surely Alwyn wouldn't dare go so far as to kill him? A couple of years before, a man had been banished from Stonewylde for killing his wife, but that was the first time in anyone's memory. Everyone knew the consequences of murder, and Alwyn wouldn't risk banishment.

But then Yul recalled the look he'd seen in Magus' dark eyes in the Stone Circle yesterday. Hatred and anger had glittered like frost, cold and crystal hard. Maybe Magus would look the other way if Alwyn lost control completely. Yul shivered in the sunshine and realised that Mother Heggy was right. He had to put a stop to it. Ancient though she was, there was strength and wisdom about her and he felt safer knowing she was on his side.

'I've spoken to Sylvie about moving up here,' said Miranda, 'but she's not keen at the moment.'

Magus smiled and twirled a strand of her hair around his finger.

'Give her time. She'll want the creature comforts of the Hall eventually. She's probably enjoying having a house to herself after spending her life cooped up in a hospital ward and a high-rise flat.'

'Yes, I hadn't thought of that. I tend to assume the worst with her at the moment. She's so difficult and argumentative! It's a pity though. Our cottage is lovely of course, but I really wanted to move into the Hall as soon as possible.'

She looked up at him through her lashes. He pulled her close; Miranda's head didn't even reach his chin.

'I hear you joined the women in the Great Barn last week,' he murmured into her hair.

'Yes, I did. What an experience that was! It's such a good idea.'

Her voice was muffled against his chest. She loved the feel of him, so solid and broad. There was nothing soft about Magus; everything was powerful and toned. She wished he'd kiss her. Since their night of passion up on the cliff-top there'd been no further intimacy between them and not even any time alone together. She thought of Magus constantly, practically every minute of the day, and wondered if he felt the same.

'Shall we go for a walk?' she asked casually. It was a lovely afternoon and she wasn't teaching again today. He'd come to find her in the empty school room and she hoped that maybe he planned to spend some time with her. But he held her at arm's length and gazed into her eyes.

'I can't, Miranda, much as I'd love to. I've just got too much to do this afternoon.'

She drooped in his arms and he squeezed her tightly.

'Oh come on, Miranda, none of that please! I know what you're thinking, but I promise you our love-making wasn't just a one-off. It meant a great deal to me.'

He bent down and kissed her coaxingly, and then after a while, deeply. She felt herself melt into him; his kiss was heaven on earth. She didn't want to stop but eventually he pulled away.

'You're a bewitching woman,' he said thickly, his eyes dark with passion. 'But I really must get back to work. You know I'm taking the seniors away to Exeter in the morning?'

She nodded and reached up to touch his face, students and exams the last thing on her mind.

'That's what I came to speak to you about. They'll all be away until the exams finish in the middle of June as it's too disruptive to come back and forth. And a spell in the Outside World does them good anyway. So I'll settle them in and then leave them there with the teachers who're going along too. After that I must spend some time in London on business. But I promise I'll come back to Stonewylde at the end of this month for a couple of nights, just to see you. We could have another picnic up on the cliff-top. Would you like that?'

'There's nothing – absolutely nothing – in this world I'd like better,' she whispered, still trembling from the kiss. He chuckled, stroking her hair.

'Your hair is so beautiful, the precise colour of glossy conkers. We've never had red hair like this at Stonewylde. A few of the Villagers are gingery but there's none of this deep red hair. Strange that Sylvie didn't inherit your colouring. I'd have thought that gene to be quite strong.'

'I know, I've often wondered too.'

'Was her father as blond as her? You've never told me anything about him.'

'I'm sorry, that's a closed subject. I don't discuss it.'

She turned aside and walked over to the window, looking out over the lawns. He followed her over and stood behind her. He nuzzled into her back, towering over her and holding her tight.

'Don't clam up on me, Miranda. It's okay if you don't want to tell me but there's no need to be so defensive. You must let go of the past.'

He felt her sigh deeply.

'You're right. It was a long time ago now and I should let it go. Maybe one day I'll be able to. Sylvie wasn't the only one in need of healing when you rode in on your white charger to whisk us away to this magical place.'

'And isn't she doing well?' he said, his lips brushing the top of her head and his hands stroking the contours of her waist and hips. 'Look, there she is now. Oh, and Buzz too.'

They watched as Sylvie ran across the daisied lawn, face upturned to the sun and silver hair swinging in a great halo about her, apparently unaware of the youth behind her. Then Buzz caught her up and grabbed her hand, spinning her around and around. They saw her mouth open in a shriek of laughter and then Buzz rather cruelly let her go. She flew off at a tangent and landed in a heap on the grass.

'What a difference!' said Magus, kissing the back of Miranda's neck through her silky hair as his hands continued their sure caresses. 'Hardly the same girl who came here only two months ago. She's so healthy and happy now.'

'And so stroppy and difficult,' said Miranda, trying to keep her mind on the conversation. 'But you're right – of course I'd rather have her like this. Her eczema's virtually gone, you know. There's barely a trace of it left. She's actually thrown away her inhalers, and she's put on weight and grown taller too. Now she's just moody and horrible.'

'That'll pass – it's only puberty. Girls can be very difficult, which is why we have the Rite of Adulthood when they reach sixteen. Once you've officially acknowledged them as women, in a public ceremony, they have to get over their silly tantrums and start acting like adults.'

'It's such a good idea,' said Miranda, then gasped as Magus cupped her breasts, pressing himself hard into her back. She shivered with longing, her breathing becoming heavier. 'Magus ... please ...'

'What, Miranda?' he murmured. 'Does that feel good? How I wish I had more time this afternoon.'

'Are you really sure you're too busy?'

He chuckled at this. 'Don't tempt me. No, I must get back to my office. Oh, look at your daughter now! So different to that frightened little child who could barely breathe. She's blossoming into a young woman, isn't she? '

Buzz had pinned Sylvie down on the grass and was tickling

her. She struggled but appeared to be laughing, though it was hard to tell from indoors.

'Is she alright?' asked Miranda, pulling slightly away from him to peer through the glass. 'I mean, should she be messing about with him like that? She's still only fourteen and he's not exactly a boy, is he? He's huge. '

'He's sixteen, and so will she be next year. Don't worry, he knows when to stop. The boys here know the rules, and Buzz better than any of them. All girls are strictly off limits until they've had their Rite. After that – well, it's up to each individual.'

'Oh, speaking of which, when I was in the Great Barn last week with the women, they were talking about pregnancies—'

'One of the favourite topics,' he laughed.

'I know! It's incredible how many babies are born here. The families are so huge! Anyway, apparently Rowan, that lovely girl who was the May Queen, wasn't in the Barn and everyone thought she may be pregnant. She obviously wasn't having a period this month.'

'Yes, I had heard.'

'But isn't it terrible? Poor girl – she's so young, only just sixteen.'

He swung her round to face him and looked down into her eyes.

'You're doing it again, Miranda – judging us by your Outside World standards. Having a baby at sixteen isn't terrible at Stone-wylde. Rowan is absolutely ecstatic about the possibility, I've been told. She'll get all the care and support she needs. And at sixteen, a girl's body is supple and strong and she has so much energy.'

'Yes, but—'

'Just imagine if you'd had Sylvie here. You'd have been happy and joyful instead of suffering the shame and worry I imagine you did. Sylvie would've fared much better too, growing up in such a close-knit community.'

'I hadn't thought of it like that.'

'There's so much you need to relearn, Miranda. You must

adjust to Stonewylde philosophy. Whilst I'm away, why not go down to the Village Nursery and spend some time there? You need to see just how well our system works. Who knows – maybe you'd like another baby? Sylvie's perfect, and it seems a shame to limit yourself to just one child when you're so good at it.'

Her heart leaped at this. Was that a proposition? She suddenly felt shy and unsure of herself. Have another baby – and with this man of her dreams? Magus chuckled again and ran a hand over her flat belly.

'See – you're not so averse to the idea, are you? You're ripe and beautiful and we can't let it go to waste. We'll talk more about it sometime. Now don't forget our picnic, will you? I want you ready and waiting for me when I get back at the end of the month.'

Miranda gazed up into his dark eyes and felt her free will dissolve to nothing. She was completely in his thrall. She longed to make some clever, enigmatic reply, something that would amuse and impress him. But she only managed a silly grin.

14

'Are they all here yet? And is all the luggage outside?'

Magus was becoming more exasperated by the second. Martin shook his head mournfully, eyeing the teachers with a look bordering on contempt.

'I'm sorry, sir – 'tis impossible to get anyone to give a straight answer. I'm trying to do a head count but none of 'em will keep still!'

Everyone milled about in the huge entrance hall, suitcases and bags piled up around them. Teachers tried in vain to keep the noise down, but the excitement grew as the senior students prepared to leave Stonewylde for Exeter. Those staying behind looked on with mixed emotions. People spilled onto the gravel circle outside the stone porch where Martin was finally organising the loading of bags onto a large trailer. The operation took some time.

Magus strode around impatiently, barking orders and becoming increasingly annoyed when people failed to move quickly enough for his liking. Holly clung to Buzz and made a great fuss about his imminent departure, for he wasn't coming back to Stonewylde immediately when the exams were over. She became quite tearful, but Sylvie, standing silently watching the whole busy scene, thought it was all for effect.

'I'll be back for Lammas,' laughed Buzz, extricating himself from Holly's grasp. 'Nothing could stop me coming home for the cricket match!'

Sylvie tried to shrink into the wisteria as he approached but couldn't avoid him. She saw Holly over his shoulder watching with narrowed eyes.

'Take care while I'm away, Sylvie,' he said cheerfully. 'Remember what I said about keeping away from that Villager. I'm sorry I won't be back for the Summer Solstice and your birthday, but this chance to visit South Africa with my mother is too good to miss. Have a lovely summer and think of me. I'll see you at Lammas!'

To her relief he only patted her arm; anything more would have enraged Holly, who was already looking daggers. Rainbow, taking a dramatic cue from Holly, hung on to her brother and presented him with a large good luck card she'd made. July and Wren flitted about showing off, hugging everyone and making a great deal of noise. Sylvie sympathised with Magus' growing impatience. He came over to where she stood quietly, and rolled his eyes in exasperation.

'What a load of drama queens!' he said, and Sylvie smiled in agreement. 'I hope you won't make as much fuss next summer.'

She hadn't thought of that; this time next year she'd be doing the same. She watched as Magus sought out her mother, which wasn't difficult as Miranda had positioned herself where he couldn't fail to notice her. Sylvie didn't hear what he said, but saw him whisper in her ear and noted the way her mother lit up at his words. He bent and brushed her lips with his. Sylvie noticed the discreet caress as his hand slipped over her buttocks, and looked away in embarrassment.

Finally they were ready to go. The tractor pulling the trailer of luggage set off first, and an assortment of cars and farm vehicles arrived to collect the people. They went in slow convoy up to the Gatehouse where a hired coach waited for them; Magus never allowed Outside vehicles in through the gates. When the party had left the Hall, amid much waving, blowing kisses and good luck wishes, the sleek silver Rolls Royce was brought round. With a final salute to everyone, Magus slid into the soft leather seat and purred away down the drive. He drove to Exeter alone.

Once they'd gone, the atmosphere at Stonewylde became very

relaxed. Clip roamed the estate, rarely making an appearance in the Hall. Occasionally he'd be seen leaving or entering his tower, and Sylvie saw him several times up on the roof gazing out over the crenellations. She was a little wary of him since the weird encounter up in the stone hut, which she'd since discovered was called a dolmen. She didn't like the idea of travelling, nor did she see herself as a saviour, and dismissed his ramblings as the consequence of eating too many special cakes.

Many of Sylvie's teachers had gone to Exeter and with more time on her hands, she decided to explore further afield. So far she'd only seen a fraction of the estate. Buzz's departure was a relief as he'd become a real nuisance lately, indulging in horseplay that was becoming increasingly rough. She wasn't sure whether she should say anything to anyone. Holly had noticed and wasn't speaking to her at all now.

In the absence of her usual friends, Holly had teamed up with Rainbow and they made a formidable pair. Rainbow was very pretty, with brilliant sea-blue eyes and thick wavy hair of a darker blond than most of the Hallfolk. Her outspokenness got her into trouble but she didn't care. She deferred to Holly alone, respecting the older girl's vicious tongue and status. Sylvie avoided them wherever possible, ignoring the snide comments and keeping to herself.

Yul had chosen an ancient holly tree whose spiky foliage formed a great dome, and had built his shelter where three thick branches grew horizontally, creating a natural platform. It was unnoticeable from the ground and Greenbough had supplied a blanket and thin mattress. He also brought food for Yul every day, and allowed him time in the mornings, after Alwyn had left for work, to go home for a while.

Maizie hated Yul living out in the woods. He saw the anguish in her eyes and regretted being the cause of it, but knew there was no alternative. He needed to be safe and hidden in case his father came looking for him at night while he slept. He was very frightened of this possibility and slept fitfully with his whittling knife to hand. Alwyn hadn't questioned the boy's absence, other than to remark that he'd never be allowed back again. Yul worried how his family were faring and hoped desperately that Alwyn wouldn't choose a new scapegoat. If that happened, he'd return home despite Mother Heggy's warnings.

One Saturday morning Yul sat in a patch of sunlight near his tree shelter eating breakfast and watching a pair of delicate Holly Blue butterflies dancing around. At the weekends Rosie brought food for him hidden in her basket while she went on errands for her mother. He'd had a bath and change of clothes the day before and was fairly clean. The bruises on his cheek and neck were beginning to fade and he relaxed in the warmth of the May morning, feeling happy for the first time in ages. The day stretched out ahead, long and inviting.

He saw Sylvie's silver hair gleaming in the speckled sunlight of the woodland and his breath caught with excitement. He hooted like an owl and watched her step delicately through the orchids and cuckoo pint towards him. She smiled radiantly, delighted to see him, but was shocked to learn that he was now living rough in the woods. She too was free for the day and they decided to go for a walk together. She ran back to Woodland Cottage and fetched some food and water. Then they walked through the blue-violet mist of late bluebells and the thick white carpet of wild garlic, with its pungent smell, up to Hare Stone.

They sat together with their backs against the great monolith, looking across the land towards the sea. Yul felt he would burst, being so close to her. A strand of her silver hair blew across onto his arm and he longed to feel its silkiness between his fingers. Unknown to him, Sylvie was feeling a similar yearning for him. Her nose twitched at his scent of herbs and sweet wood-smoke. His dark hair, now grown down to his shoulders, was glossy and curly. He looked happy and seemed taller than before, his legs stretching out way beyond hers, his body as lean and tough as a willow whip. His hands rested in his lap and she wanted very much to reach across and take one of them in hers. How did you start to hold hands with a boy? They sat together perfectly still, wrapped up in their dreaming, surrounded by the beauty of the May morning.

Down the hillside, amongst the boulders, they saw hares and tiny leverets loping about in the grass. The golden-furred creatures with huge velvet ears nibbled at young shoots of clover, whiskers twitching. Overhead circled a pair of buzzards, their great wings catching the thermals. Sylvie was amazed at the sight of the hawks and loved their strange cries and graceful, effortless flight.

To the south, the deep blue sea glittered in the sunshine; usually at dusk, when the moon was rising, it disappeared into a purple haze. It was glorious weather, everything green and fresh. The grass around them was bright with sky-blue speedwell and tiny white stars of eyebright – nature's confetti scattered around them in celebration. It felt good to be alive and good to be together.

'Do you have boats down on the beach?' Sylvie asked.

'Boats? No, we see them sail past out to sea but we don't have them at Stonewylde.'

'But don't you catch fish to eat, living so close to the sea?'

'Oh yes, we catch stripy fish that look like the September skies, called mackerel. We go down to the beach in the evening with fishing rods.'

She looked hard at him; his beautiful cheekbones, his strong profile.

'What?'

'Yul, have you ever left Stonewylde in your life?'

'No, of course not. Nobody has. Well, not the Villagers. Hallfolk come and go all the time, of course. But we stay here.'

'But don't you long to know what's going on in the world?'

'Well, I do know a bit. When I was at school the teachers told us all about the Outside World. And to be honest, I don't want to know any more. It sounds horrible. You weren't happy there, were you? You were ill and now you're well, which proves it's much better to stay at Stonewylde.'

'True,' she conceded.

After a while she looked at him again. His head was tipped back slightly against the warm stone, his eyes closed. She noticed the sharp strength of his jawbone, and how the bruise on his cheekbone had almost gone. She stared at his eyebrows, like dark winged sycamore seeds, and the way his long eyelashes brushed the delicate skin under his eyes. Yul was beautiful.

He opened his eyes and turned towards her. They were so clear, so very deep grey and slightly slanted. She felt a strange glow as their gaze met, and that peculiar somersault feeling again, down low in her stomach. Her mouth was dry.

'What? You keep staring at me, Sylvie.'

'Why did you fail the tests that decide if you stay in the Village or join the Hallfolk at their school?'

'*What*? Why do you want to know that?'

'Because you're so obviously intelligent. From what I've heard the whole point of the tests is to make sure that any bright person at Stonewylde gets a good education. How come you failed them?'

'I just did.'

'Were they very difficult?'

'Well they must've been if I failed them.'

'Can you actually read and write?'

'No. That's not what they teach at the Village School. We don't fill our heads with that stuff. We learn other things, important things about the world, and we're taught skills and crafts. I'm quite good at wood carving, and stone carving too.'

'But you don't realise what you're missing out on by not being able to read. Can you use the Internet?'

'The what?'

'I thought not. Have you ever even seen a computer?'

'Don't think so.'

'But that's terrible!'

'No it's not! What's a computer anyway? Why is it terrible that I haven't seen one? What use is it to me?' He scowled at her. 'Come on, it's time we moved on if you're going to get scratchy with me.'

He stood and reached down to help her up. She put her hand in his and as she rose to her feet they stopped. Their eyes locked into each other's. They moved slightly closer and his gaze dropped to her mouth. They both held their breath. She longed, with every single cell of her body, to kiss him. She saw his nostrils flare and his lips part slightly. She waited, completely still, hoping with all her heart. But he pulled away, picking up the lunch bag, and walked off from the stone.

'Wait!' she called. 'Just answer me this.'

'Now what?' he said, striding along the grass as she trotted to keep up.

'Why did you fail the tests?'

He grinned, but carried on walking.

'You don't give up, do you, Sylvie? Alright, I'll tell you. I've never told anyone this before, and you're not to talk of it to any of the Hallfolk, nor the Villagers for that matter. D'you promise?'

'Of course.'

'Well, Village children take the tests at five years old. If you pass, they earmark you for the Hall School later on. You get another chance when you're eight, if you failed the first time. If you pass at eight, you move up to the Hall immediately and just go home to the Village to visit. All the Hallfolk start at the Hall School when they're eight, without taking any tests. Did you know all this?'

'Yes, that's what I'd heard. And I know that a few Villagers do move up.'

'Ah, but you see, they're all Hall-children. You can tell by looking at them.'

'Hall-children? The Villagers?'

'Hall-children are different. They're half and half. Their mothers are Villagers but their fathers are Hallfolk. From the Rites of Adulthood and festivals, when Hallfolk and Villagers are allowed to mix.'

She blushed scarlet at this casual reference. How could Yul even mention it?

'So you see,' he continued, unaware of her embarrassment,

'it's really not very often that true Villagers pass the tests and move up to the Hall. When I was five and I took the test, I decided I'd never want to go to the Hall and leave the Village. I deliberately answered things wrongly, matched the wrong shapes and things. I was clumsy and didn't speak properly. So the Hallfolk teacher who was doing the testing failed me.'

'And you did that again at eight?'

'Yes, and even worse then. Actually, I was a bit stupid because I should've made sure I only just failed – that would've been more realistic. I'm surprised that nobody realised I'd done it on purpose. As it was, my teacher made a fuss about me having a chance to redo the test. But I refused, so that was that.'

'You still haven't told me why.'

'Because I'm not one of the Hallfolk! I don't want to become one of them. Look at Buzz and Fennel, and all the other useless gits. I don't want to turn out like that. And also . . . there was my family.'

'What? Didn't they want you to pass?'

'Oh yes, Mother was desperate for me to pass. She even broke the rules and took me up to Magus when I was only three. She begged him to take me in – I vaguely remember it. And I remember hating the smell of the place and the way Hallfolk looked at me and Mother as we stood waiting in the Galleried Hall. She'd told me that if I showed Magus what a clever boy I was, then he'd let me live there. So I was difficult and acted daft. Mother was furious with me, and even more so when I failed the proper tests later. I actually had three chances altogether and I ruined all of them.'

'But that's such a shame!'

'Why? Why is it a shame? I'll tell you, Sylvie, if you really want to know, why I failed their bloody stupid tests.' He glared at her, his face flushed with anger. 'I didn't want to leave my mother and Rosie and the other little ones with that bastard Alwyn. He's always picked on me and left them alone. So I couldn't leave knowing he may turn on them next, could I? And now can we please not talk about it anymore?'

Sylvie nodded and they continued along the ridgeway which snaked across the land, running parallel with the coastline. They were high up with the valleys dropping away on either side of them, the sea in the distance on one side and endless fields and woods on the other, as far as the eye could see. It was warm, slightly windy, and fresh. The sky was bright blue, pasted here and there with soft white clouds.

Sylvie tried to swallow her sadness. Stonewylde should be paradise and yet for some people it clearly wasn't. She reached across and took Yul's hand. He didn't look at her but squeezed her hand fiercely. They walked a couple of miles in silence, holding hands and feeling as close as anyone ever can to another.

It was late afternoon when they walked back along the Dragon's Back ridgeway, the sun and wind now behind them. They'd enjoyed a perfect day, Yul teaching Sylvie a great deal about the natural world. He knew every plant, bird and butterfly they'd encountered. He explained about the rock that formed the ridgeway and why the Dragon's Back held a serpent-line of earth energy. Sylvie realised that although Yul was poorly educated by her standards, he knew a great deal about his world. And he obviously felt a strong spiritual unity with Stonewylde. It was humbling for her, who earlier in the day had pitied him for his ignorance.

They were just a couple of miles from the Hare Stone when they heard a wild drumming and felt a vibration through their feet. Before they knew it, a great black horse was bearing straight down on them, a rider bent low over his neck. Yul immediately stepped in front of Sylvie and waved at the horse. It swerved, changing course sharply, and the rider came tumbling off and hit the ground hard. The horse continued past them, his eyes rolling, foam flecking his mouth. Then he wheeled around and trotted back, highly agitated. Yul had recognised Nightwing at once and called to him, while Sylvie ran over to the motionless body.

As she crouched to examine the rider, Yul spoke softly to Nightwing. The horse stood a few metres away rolling his eyes

221

and pawing at the ground. Yul held out his hand and moved his head in response to the horse's movements. The stallion reared and danced sideways but Yul persisted until, with a little whinny, Nightwing approached him. He lowered his head and gently butted Yul, who took the reins and stroked the horse's long nose, whispering softly.

'Yul, I think he's quite badly hurt. We must get help.'

Yul led the great horse over and looked down at the young Hallfolk man.

'His breathing's okay and his airway isn't blocked,' Sylvie continued. 'He's not bleeding anywhere, as far as I can see. I think he's just knocked out. But look at his arm. It's broken, isn't it?'

'Looks like it. We can't carry him and he certainly can't ride. Will you stay here with him while I go back to the Hall for help?'

'Yes,' she said, 'that's the best thing to do. But can you take the horse? I can't cope with him and this man.'

'Yes, of course. I'll ride him back. It'll be much quicker.'

'Good idea. You can ride?'

'Everyone can ride! I'll be back soon.'

What he hadn't said was that although he could ride the old horses that pulled the carts, and the ponies that grazed on the heath, he'd never ridden a thoroughbred like Nightwing. But Yul knew he had a special affinity with the horse and he was keen to impress Sylvie. So he grabbed the pommel of the saddle, managed to get a foot in the stirrup, and with a strong push, swung himself up.

Sitting astride such a huge beast so high up was an incredible sensation. Nightwing trembled between his thighs. He felt the massive power of the horse bunched in every muscle and sinew as he pranced on the spot, raring to go. Yul took up the reins very lightly and leant forward to stroke his neck and whisper in his ear. The horse tossed his head and turned around at the merest hint of guidance. Yul grinned down at Sylvie, his heart thumping in his chest, and gently squeezed his legs.

Nightwing launched off into a canter, his hooves drumming the hard chalk soil of the ridgeway in a tattoo of speed and energy. It was the closest Yul had ever come to flying. He could hardly breathe. The horse felt so good beneath him, fluid and powerful, almost part of himself. Galloping along Dragon's Back on Nightwing with the wind in his hair was pure heaven. And a dream finally come true.

At the stables, Tom the ostler was shocked to see Nightwing return with a slip of a boy on his back. He remembered then how Yul had forged an understanding with the great stallion, who was usually difficult and temperamental, if not downright dangerous. Tom took the reins as Yul leapt down, his legs shaking and heart pounding. He could barely speak with the exhilaration of it. He flung his arms around Nightwing's neck and to Tom's surprise, the horse nuzzled at the boy. Tom shook his head in wonder.

'Where's the young master who rode him out, then?'

Yul had almost forgotten why he was there, but explained quickly. Tom took over at once, sending a Land Rover with a driver and the doctor up onto the ridgeway. Yul enjoyed the experience as he'd never travelled in a Land Rover before. For Villagers, a ride in any vehicle other than horse and cart, or occasionally a tractor, was rare.

Sylvie was delighted to see them, for the man had started to regain consciousness. They travelled back together, the doctor in the back with the rider stretched out on the floor, and Sylvie and Yul squeezed together in the front.

'You were great on that horse,' she whispered.

He grinned, his legs still trembling from the hard gallop.

'It was the best thing I've ever done in my life,' he whispered back. 'I love Nightwing! I wish he were mine.'

'Weren't you scared? He's enormous.'

'I was terrified!'

They arranged to meet the following day at the same place. Sylvie dissuaded Miranda, keen to join her on a walk, by saying she was going out with her new friends. She was mindful of Buzz's warning and so kept her developing friendship with Yul secret, which made it even more exciting.

'So where are we going today?' she asked happily.

'There's somebody I must take you to meet,' he replied, equally happy. 'She's a little frightening and strange but she wants to meet you. She's the Wise Woman of Stonewylde, or she used to be. But let's walk up on the cliff-top first.'

'Do you think we'll bump into anyone? I'm worried. Buzz warned me about being friends with you. He said Magus would punish you, not me, for it.'

'I don't care what Buzz said! Of course Magus wouldn't like it but he's not here and neither's Buzz, so let's forget them. The only person I don't want to meet is my father. But on Sundays he's mostly down at the Barn playing skittles and drinking in the pub. I doubt he'll be up on the cliff-top. We'll be safe.'

They skirted the Village through the fields and joined the path leading to the cliffs further up. The hedgerows were thick with pink, freckled foxgloves and lacy white cow-parsley. They could see the Stone Circle across the hill and Sylvie felt a thrill at the sight of the ancient stones. Yul told her how he went up there most mornings and evenings at sunrise and sunset, sitting on the Altar Stone and watching the sun. He didn't tell her of the growing feeling of power; how he felt it seeping into him and charging his spirit with energy. He wasn't sure if she'd understand.

On the cliff-top the warm May breeze blew in their hair. The grass up here was tough and springy, cropped short by rabbits, pink with the thrift that grew everywhere and dotted with the velvet darkness of the dainty bee orchid. They walked for a while looking out at the sparkling sea, seagulls wheeling and screaming overhead. Sylvie began to feel a flying sensation, as if she could kick her feet off the ground and rise up in the air. She spread her arms wide, the breeze streaming her hair out behind her in a sheet of wispy silk. She closed her eyes and savoured the sensation of flight. Yul thought she was the most beautiful thing on earth.

'This is another special stone, Sylvie,' he said softly. They'd come to an enormous round stone, a great white flat disc that lay a little way back from the cliff edge with a panoramic view out over the sea. It glittered in the sunlight, sparkling like frost.

'The full moon usually rises over the water and Magus often celebrates the Moon Fullness here,' he explained.

Sylvie blanched, remembering her mother's revelation the morning after the full moon. They approached the huge stone and tentatively she reached out to touch it, feeling a little weird knowing that this was where Magus had made love to her mother. As her fingertips brushed the stone she felt a strange jolt like an electric shock, and her arm tingled sharply. She snatched her hand away and stepped back.

'Do you feel any magic up here?' asked Yul, watching the expressions pass over her face. 'Like at Hare Stone?'

She frowned, trying to dismiss the image of Magus on the sparkling stone in the moonlight. She thought of the jolt in her arm and the flying sensation on the edge of the cliff.

'Yes, I do feel something here. But it's stronger at Hare Stone, more powerful there and ... better somehow. I don't feel comfortable here. I wouldn't want to moon dance here.'

'That's what I've always thought too. It's a moon place but not like Hare Stone.'

'What are those iron rings in the ground over there?' asked Sylvie.

'If it's cold or wet, Magus puts up a tent, like a little castle. The rings are where the ropes are tied to hold it steady. You couldn't drive tent pegs into the ground up here, as there's solid rock just below the soil.'

'Imagine putting up a tent just to watch the moon rise,' said Sylvie. 'I'd hate that. I need to dance.'

'Well, Magus doesn't exactly dance.'

'No?'

'No. The rising of the full moon is the best time of all to make love and conceive a baby. Not that Magus goes around making babies, but they say sex is so much better then. And many babies are conceived ...'

'Yes, I get the idea,' she interrupted hastily.

'It's when Stonewylde women are most ripe and fertile, you

see. Some of the moon magic enters the baby at its moment of conception. My mother told me I was conceived during a full moon rising, but a very special one. A Blue Moon.'

'What on earth is that? I thought that was just an expression – once in a blue moon.'

He lay down on the stone, looking up at the sky above.

'Some years there are thirteen full moons, not twelve. One for every month and an extra one. It's the extra one that's the Blue Moon, the second full moon in a month.'

'I didn't know that.'

'More than that, I was born at a Red Moon.'

'A Red Moon? I've never heard of that either.'

'It was a blood-red eclipse. Sometimes during an eclipse the moon's just a little darker than usual, but other times it goes a deep, dark crimson. And that's how it was the night I was born, so Mother says.'

'Maybe that's why you're dark,' she said. 'You're different to most of the people here, Villagers and Hallfolk. You've a dark streak in you.'

He grinned at her.

'You make it sound exciting. It's probably why everyone has it in for me and why I'm always in trouble.' He sighed, gazing at the sky. 'Funnily enough, the next Moon Fullness is a Blue Moon. It's the last day of May, and the last Moon Fullness was at the very beginning of May – the Hare Moon.'

'Hare Moon! That's lovely. What's June's called?'

'The Mead Moon, and July's is the Hay Moon. The names are very old, handed down through the ages.'

'So you were conceived at a Blue Moon. How is it special? I mean, different to normal full moons?'

'They say it has extra powerful magic. I don't know. I'm not moongazy. I can feel the energy and I love the beauty of it, but nothing like you experience. I feel the magic up in the Stone Circle, which is a sun and earth energy place.'

'Shall we go up to Hare Stone for this Blue Moon?' she asked.

Stretched out on the stone, as long and lean as a snake in the sun, he looked over at her. She stood silhouetted against the sky and he longed to trace the delicate bones in her face with gentle fingertips. He felt a tugging need deep inside, where he knew he must keep it buried.

'Sylvie, I'll go with you to Hare Stone every Moon Fullness, if you want me. I've honoured the moon at that place for a long time. But now I know what's always been missing.'

'Me too,' she said quietly. 'The full moon's even more magical for me when you're around.'

15

'Ah, my Raven, my little one! Come back to me at last,' crooned Mother Heggy, her almost sightless eyes fixed on Sylvie's face. The crow in the corner flexed its wings wide and hopped onto the mantelpiece over the range, its beady eye also fixed on Sylvie.

'We can't stay long, Mother Heggy,' warned Yul.

The old crone raised her withered hand and stroked Sylvie's flaxen hair. She didn't flinch but stood silently, a slight smile on her face. Yul edged a little closer.

'My sweet girl,' whispered the woman. 'I knew you'd return to me one day. The silver has come and now the dance can begin again. Stonewylde will be redeemed. My little Raven ...'

She hobbled over to the back of the room and Yul cast an anxious glance at Sylvie, who was looking around the tiny one-roomed cottage with interest. The crow hopped onto the old woman's hunched shoulder as she stood mixing something at the range. She handed Sylvie the filthy mug and the girl drank down the contents without a murmur, surprisingly at ease in such strange surroundings.

'Now it can start,' muttered Mother Heggy, sinking painfully into her rocking chair. The crow stepped onto the chair back and surveyed the two young ones. Sylvie sat in the hard chair opposite with Yul standing by her side.

'The Summer Solstice draws near. But before it can start, there will be more suffering in the final days of the Oak King's rule. He will try to destroy you, Yul. I have warned you of this and you must be strong. Have faith in your destiny. You must never give up even when all seems lost. This silver girl will help you. Hold her in your heart.'

Yul nodded, although he had no idea what she meant.

'What can I do to help him?' asked Sylvie.

'Ah, that's the rub. You may protect him now, but you'll be a part of the suffering and torment as the wheel turns towards the darkness of the Holly King's hour. You will shine clear in the end, 'tis the truth. You'll be deceived and your light will be hidden like the moon shrouded in cloud, but in the end you'll shine clear. This dark one knows that, for you are part of his destiny. But before, before this, you must seek him and take him from the place of bones and death. When the time comes you'll know. You are his saviour.'

Sylvie nodded, alarmed at this further reference to being a saviour. Yul was mystified.

'So what must *I* do, Mother Heggy?' he asked. 'I don't understand.'

She rocked gently, the crow clutching on to the worn wooden chair top.

'You too will know, when the time comes. You've been to the Stone Circle every day?'

'Yes. I feel the power even stronger now.'

'Good, good. 'Tis all you can do for now, but remember this – Stonewylde is a place of ancient magic. You're a tiny piece of it, and so is the silver one. You're both a part of the moon dance, a part of the magic. Two threads in the robes of the Earth Goddess. It takes many threads to make the whole and you're both woven into the pattern.'

Yul frowned, wishing she'd stop talking in riddles.

'What about my father?' he asked.

'The tanner? If you can do it right, my boy, he'll be the first one to fall. Always listen to Mother Heggy. Heed me well and all will prevail as 'tis writ. You'll be left standing tall and powerful, with this bright one at your side.'

229

'Me and Sylvie together?' whispered Yul, his heart leaping with excitement.

'Aye, darkness and brightness, black and silver, 'tis as I foretold and the magus knows it. Solstice by name and solstice by destiny. Raven did right there. My girl always knew.'

'Please, Mother Heggy, talk straight,' said Yul with a note of exasperation. 'I want to heed you but I don't understand. What exactly will happen?'

'All I can tell you now is this – those who stand against you will fall, one by one.'

'But you say Magus is still the one who'll try to destroy me? I don't . . .'

'Hush, Yul,' whispered Sylvie. 'She can't tell us exactly. Nothing is definite. But don't worry, we have each other.'

'Aye, you have each other. Now you must go, for someone is about who may do you harm.'

She stood up creakily and ushered them towards the door.

'Remember, be strong and look to each other. You, my girl, be brave and remember why you've come here. Don't ignore your sight – take heed of it. This boy needs you. When his hour is darkest, you'll be the shining light to lead him to safety. Come to me again when you need my aid. 'Twill be soon, right enough.'

She sighed, clutching onto the doorframe for support, her little body hunched and twisted as a tree on a cliff-top.

'And you, son of the solstice, you have such a dark time ahead. When I see you next, you'll bear the marks of destruction. You'll be changed. The place of bones and death will call you for its own. The evil of the stones will hunger for your soul. You must hold the magic in your heart and walk with the Goddess. Blessings, my young ones.'

The crow hopped out of the door and flapped along their path ahead of them. They split up before they got to the Village, Sylvie walking up the main track towards Woodland Cottage, while Yul cut through the fields and made his way back to the woods. The crow perched on a rowan tree, watching them part and go their separate ways. He alone saw the tall, robed figure up on the hill, staff in hand, looking down on them and watching intently. The bird let out a mighty caw and returned to his mistress.

The day of the Blue Moon, the last day in May, dawned grey and damp. Yul had risen very early for the sunrise and sat on the Altar Stone in the drizzle. There was no sense of well-being, no bathing in the warmth of morning gold. The power, however, was as strong. He felt the familiar surge within, the mounting excitement and energy. He stood on the stone, legs apart and head flung back, raising his outstretched arms to the cloudy heavens. Every part of him throbbed with the energy. He remained at the Circle for some time, skin and clothes soaked through by the fine rain, until it was time to go to work.

Sylvie woke later and was disappointed to see the grey skies and rain. Magus was due back for a few days and her mother was meeting him for another evening picnic. Miranda had talked of nothing else since he'd left for Exeter the week before. Sylvie assumed it would now be postponed because of the weather, and was worried how she'd get to Hare Stone with Yul if her mother was at home fussing about.

Miranda was in a fever of anticipation all day. She bathed in the luxurious white marble bathroom at the Hall, carefully washing her auburn hair for Magus' admiration. She assumed that although their picnic would be cancelled she'd still be seeing him, either up at the Hall or in the cottage. She couldn't decide what to wear and, back home again, she tried on several different outfits. Sylvie was happy to escape to the Hall for an afternoon of French lessons. She found her mother's excitement both ridiculous and irritating, and was sorely tempted to put her straight on the matter of Magus and his history with women.

Yul put in a full day's work making hurdles in one of the hazel coppices. It was fairly strenuous, particularly as the older men

231

always got him to do the running around and fetching and carrying. By the end of the day he was tired and very hungry. He was also filthy and knew that he'd have to risk the bath house. He could never go moongazing with Sylvie like this. Eventually Old Greenbough came over to him.

'When you've tidied up here, Yul, you can go on. A good day's work, lad. Well done.'

'Thank you, sir.'

'Will you be alright in that miserable tree house of yours tonight? 'Tis the first proper rain we've had since you built it. Go back to our hut if your bed gets wet.'

'I will, thank you.'

'Aye well, you're no good to me if you catch a chill, boy.'

Yul smiled at Greenbough's apparent gruffness and trudged off towards the Village, ignoring the rain running down his face and soaking his clothes. It was too early; his father would still be at home eating supper like a pig at the trough. But Yul felt daring and decided to risk getting clean clothes before going to the bath house. He arrived in the Village and skulked along the main track. He was very dirty, his clothes non-descript brown and his long hair hanging in damp locks over his face. Nobody would notice him so camouflaged.

He reached the cottage where he'd lived all his life but now he felt like a stranger, rootless and not belonging. He could hear his family inside chattering noisily, their voices and laughter carrying out through the open window. Which meant that Alwyn couldn't be in there. Just in time, Yul pulled back as Alwyn left the privy at the end of the garden, buttoning his trousers. He'd gained even more weight recently and his great belly ballooned over his belt, straining the buttons of his shirt. As he entered the cottage by the back door, silence descended inside. Yul crouched under the window with a bitter heart.

Not long after, Rosie came out the back with some slops for the pig. She was shocked to see Yul, dirty from head to toe, but gave him a quick, fierce hug. She went upstairs and threw down some clean clothes from the open window. He ran off to the bath house and enjoyed a soak; for once there was plenty of hot water as most people were still eating supper.

Later, clean and scrubbed, he watched from the doorway for Alwyn to pass by so he could go home to eat. He was very hungry and the longer he waited, the more his resentment grew. Why should he have to live like an outcast because of that man? Yul leant in the shadows out of the rain, tall and lean, unaware of the sinister figure he made.

At last Alwyn came stomping along the track on his way to the pub. Yul's grey eyes smouldered hatred and his mouth twisted in contempt at the sight of the overweight, red-faced man. He remembered the beatings he'd taken over the years, the constant fear and humiliation he'd suffered since he was a small child. His fists clenched so hard his finger nails cut into his palms. But somehow he controlled his rage and waited for the object of his hatred to pass by.

Maizie was delighted to see Yul and dished him up a large plateful of food, secretly kept by for him in the oven. He was starving and sat down to devour it, his mother and sister fussing around and shooing the little ones away so he could eat in peace.

'Oh Yul, you'll get so wet tonight in that tree shelter. Please go to the hut, won't you? I don't want you ill on top of everything else.'

Yul grinned up at her through his drying hair, letting little Leveret climb onto his lap. The tiny girl kissed him and he held her tight. He missed his family so much but only dared creep home briefly when Alwyn was out drinking, and even then he couldn't relax. If his father came back unexpectedly and found his mother feeding him ...

'You're as bad as Old Greenbough, Mother. He said the same.'

'Well, the old boy's right. Listen to him if you won't listen to me. Rosie, take that child off poor Yul – she's clambering all over him. Now, my lad, do you want pudding? I've got some nice jam sponge and custard, so—'

'I can't, Mother. I must be off. It's the Moon Fullness tonight.'

'That's not for ages yet. And what do you need to do with the rising? You're not an adult yet. Oh Yul, you're not—'

'No I'm not! But I'm meeting someone.'

'Ooh, Yul's got a sweetheart!' laughed Rosie. 'Who is she? Tell us, Yul!'

'No! It's none of your business. And she's not a sweetheart. Well, not really.'

To his horror he felt himself blushing. Rosie shrieked with laughter and jigged Leveret in her arms in glee.

'Look, look, Mother, he's gone scarlet! So she is a sweetheart!'

'Leave the boy alone, Rosie. So what if he's found a girl he likes? He'll be sixteen at the Winter Solstice so there's no harm if he's walking with someone. I just hope she's worthy of you, Yul. You're a very special boy.'

'No, Mother. I'm not sure I'm worthy of *her*, believe me.'

Harold from the Hall arrived at the cottage with a note from Magus saying he'd be over at eight-thirty.

'There, you see? It'll be okay,' said Sylvie wearily, sick of her mother debating endlessly if he'd turn up or cancel the whole thing.

'But what does it mean?' wailed Miranda. 'Are we still going on the picnic, do you think? Or does he want to stay here? Because if . . .'

'MUM! I don't know! For goodness' sake, stop fussing and going on and on! You're driving me up the wall.'

'There's no need to be like that, Sylvie. It's just that if—'

'Please! I really have no idea.'

Sylvie was tense and strung up herself. The familiar sensation was building inside her and she had her own worries; how to get out into the woods to meet Yul with her mother and Magus about?

'Sylvie, what if he wants to spend the evening here?'

'What if he does?'

'But you're here. I mean ...'

She tailed off, looking uncomfortable, and Sylvie seized her chance.

'Oh Mum, don't worry about that! I'm going to the Hall tonight to watch a film with some friends. Sorry – I thought I'd told you.'

The relief on her mother's face was almost ludicrous.

'That's alright then. Will you be gone before eight-thirty? And darling, I don't want to sound like I'm chucking you out or anything, but don't come back too early, will you? It would be so embarrassing if—'

'Yes, alright, I can imagine. I'll stay out late I promise.'

She couldn't believe her luck. All that time with Yul! The only drawback was the rain splattering noisily outside.

In the shelter of the woods it wasn't quite as wet, although Yul was soaked to the skin by the time Sylvie hurried up the path towards him. She was still reasonably calm and in control as the moonrise wasn't for almost another hour, but she trembled with cold and excitement. In her eagerness to leave she hadn't thought about suitable clothing, and Miranda was far too distracted to notice what her daughter was wearing. They stood there, water dripping off the leaves in little torrents all over them, both wet through.

'It's ages till moonrise, Sylvie. We'll get so cold.'

'Can we go to your tree house?'

He laughed at this.

'It's not a house, it's a covered bed really. And it's soaking wet too.'

'Oh, I didn't realise.'

'We could go to the woodsmen's hut, if you like. It's rough and ready but we'll be dry and there's a fire.'

'Oh yes, let's go there!'

Once inside, Yul lit some candles and stirred the wood-burning stove to life. He put a kettle of water on to boil for some tea.

'One thing we've always got plenty of is wood,' he said.

'Yes,' she said, feeling shy now she was alone with him in such close proximity. He was very efficient, stoking up the fire and getting the tea things ready. She realised that other than the Great Barn, she'd never been inside a building with him before.

'That was a joke, Sylvie.'

'Sorry.'

Her teeth chattered with cold and nervousness.

'Here, this will help.'

He carefully wrapped an old blanket around her shoulders, leaning close to pull it together at the front. He smelt of herbs and his fingers brushed her hand as he pulled the blanket across her. The blanket, however, didn't smell so sweet and Sylvie wrinkled her nose. Yul laughed, pulling it tight around her.

'Don't be so fussy! If you could see where I sleep every night ...'

They sat companionably together, she on Greenbough's old armchair and he on the floor at her feet. The tea was hot and welcome. Gradually she relaxed and stopped shaking.

'Mum was driving me mad today,' she said, sipping her tea. 'She's meeting Magus tonight. She's been fretting about what to wear, whether or not their stupid picnic will still be on, and ...'

'Oh it'll be on alright,' said Yul dryly.

'How do you know?'

'Remember the iron rings? The tent I told you about? Magus won't let a bit of rain spoil his fun. And ... I think he may have something else planned for tonight too.'

'Something else? What do you mean?'

'I've been thinking about this, and I have a feeling he may try to make a baby tonight with your mother.'

'YUL!!' She gaped at him. 'A baby? Surely not!'

'Sylvie, I told you about the Moon Fullness and what happens here. Half the fertile women of Stonewylde will try to get pregnant tonight. It's the Blue Moon which is far more magical than normal and the very best time of all for conception. Remember I was conceived at such a time.'

'But my mum doesn't want a baby!'

'Well, I don't know about that, but I think Magus may try. I've heard he's very careful about how many children he fathers. Mother says there's lots of girls who boast they're carrying his child, but I can't say that it's common knowledge who his children are, other than that bastard Buzz of course. If everyone who said they've had his child really had, the place would be over-run with his babies. I don't think there are very many at all as he's been so careful. But Rowan's pregnant from Beltane, everyone says, and I reckon your mother's on his list too.'

'But not to make her pregnant, surely? I can't see that—'

'Just think about it – why did he choose to come back tonight of all nights? He could have had a woman in the Outside World if he just wanted sex, couldn't he? But he came back here specially, and I'm sure it's because he wants your mother to conceive. She's someone fresh, like getting in new stock for breeding the dairy herds and horses and suchlike.'

'I think the whole thing's disgusting! And why spoil the full moon with sex anyway?'

He laughed and stared down at his hands.

'Some people would say that the sex is magical too,' he said quietly, 'and all part of the celebration and joy of the Moon Fullness. You don't think very highly of it, do you?'

Now she looked embarrassed.

'It's just the thought of my mother and Magus ... it's horrible. Can we change the subject? In fact, can we go up to Hare Stone? I'm starting to feel strange.'

'Okay, let me damp down the fire a bit and blow out the candles.'

They left the snug cosiness of the hut, the relentless rain immediately stealing their warmth and dryness. Together they hurried along the path, climbing up through the woodland until they got to the place where it joined the field. They raced through the long, drenched grass past the boulders and rocky outcrops to the top of the hill.

237

Hare Stone stood grey and gloomy in the dark evening, the rain falling in silver needles. Sylvie's hair was plastered to her head and stuck to her back like long straight string. She lifted her arms to the heavy skies and started to sing, oblivious to the cold and wet. Yul wished he felt the same. His hair too was stuck to his skin, as were his clothes, and he was freezing cold. He sank down with his back against Hare Stone and hugged his knees. It may be the Blue Moon, but he didn't feel particularly magical. He wished he had a tent too.

Sylvie's dance lasted for ages and the wet hares ran for shelter long before she did. Although there was no sign whatsoever of the full moon, she seemed to know exactly when and where it rose, and tracked its progress in the sky. She danced and sang and then sank to her knees staring up at the dark clouds, the rain driving into her upturned face. Yul waited for a while but eventually could stand it no longer. She must be so cold. He certainly was, and he was used to being outdoors in all weathers. He stood up stiffly, his knees locked into a bent position, and went across to help her up. Her skin was unnaturally chilled.

'Sylvie, come on, you're freezing. We must get home.'

He pulled her upright and she swayed, stiff as a stone-carving.

'Sylvie! Wake up! Come on, wake up!'

He shook her gently but she was unresponsive. He was worried; she was so very cold. He chafed her arms, which hung limply by her sides, and took her hands in his.

'Sylvie! SYLVIE!!'

She blinked and shook her head but her movements were slow. He realised the urgency of her need for warmth and shelter. She was clearly chilled to the bone. Putting an arm around her shoulders, he guided her down the hill and into the woods. There he hesitated. What should he do now? Take her home and risk the house being empty and cold with no one to look after her? Or take her back to the hut and try to revive her by the fire? He chose the latter.

In the hut it was still warm. Yul quickly wrapped Sylvie in the smelly blanket and sat her in the chair. He built up the fire and made a hot drink, which he held to her lips and forced her to swallow. He chafed her hands to get the circulation going, and then her bare feet. She really was frozen. Slowly Sylvie responded, becoming aware of where she was. Then she began to shiver violently and nothing he did would stop it. She needed to get her wet clothes off but that was out of the question in the hut, and there was nothing dry for her to put on. He'd lost track of the time but thought that Magus must have finished up at Mooncliffe by now. Surely Miranda would be back in the cottage; the worry was if Magus was there or not. But Sylvie had to get home, so he put her shoes back on her feet, wrapped the old blanket around her shoulders, and spoke gently to her.

'Sylvie, it's still raining out there so we'll have to make a dash for it. Shall I carry you or can you walk?'

'I'll walk,' she mumbled, her teeth chattering so violently she could barely speak. 'I'm sorry to be such a nuisance, Yul.'

'No it's my fault and I'm really sorry. I shouldn't have let you stay up there for so long.'

The dash through the woods was a disaster. The rain was now torrential, making the path slippery and dangerous in the darkness. Sylvie's co-ordination had gone and she stumbled and tripped, barely able to stand, let alone run. She sobbed with frustration and cold; in the end Yul scooped her up in his arms and carried her, which wasn't easy in the dark and wet.

After an eternity they reached the cottage and Yul was relieved to see lights glowing. He pushed the gate open with a foot and staggered up the path, his arms aching. Miranda answered the kick on the door and was horrified to see her daughter lying unmoving against the boy's chest.

'Sorry, ma'am. I found her in the woods. I think she must've been on her way home from the Hall and got lost. She's very cold. She needs dry clothes, a fire and a hot drink.'

'I think I can see what she needs, thank you. It's Yul, isn't it?

239

Thank you for bringing her back. Just sit her down here, would you.'

As he bent to put her in the armchair his lips brushed her ear.

'You got lost on your way back, remember?' he whispered. 'I'll see you soon, Sylvie.'

Miranda watched him go and then turned to her bedraggled daughter. She sat pale and motionless in the chair where she'd been put, her eyes closed. Miranda felt a sharp flicker of annoyance at Sylvie for ruining her perfect evening. She thought of the snug, dry pavilion lit by many silver candles, the incense burning, the golden mead in goblets, the delicious delicacies to eat, and the soft, thick cover spread out on the great stone with silk cushions to lie back against. There'd even been a little brazier for warmth, and Magus had bundled her up in waterproofs with a large umbrella to protect her as they'd dashed back from the clifftop. She'd felt so pampered and cared for, so very special. What a man!

She smiled to herself as she removed the smelly blanket and stripped Sylvie of her wet clothes. She put her daughter to bed, not noticing just how very cold the silent girl was. It had been the most perfect evening of her whole life. She was in love for the very first time, and felt utterly fulfilled.

Yul plodded miserably up the muddy path back into the woods. Again he faced a dilemma: to sleep in his tree shelter or the woodsmen's hut. His mattress and blanket would be lying in a puddle of water by now as it was only a rough shelter, so he headed for the hut. It was risky but surely Alwyn wouldn't come looking for him on a night like this? His father would be snug at home eating a late night snack by the fire before lugging himself up to bed. Tomorrow Yul would have to dry out his bedding somehow, because he mustn't tempt fate twice. But tonight he needed somewhere warm and dry to sleep. Sylvie wasn't the only one chilled by the rain.

In the hut he stoked up the fire and stretched out in the old armchair, his long legs sprawled out damply before him. The blanket was gone, of course, and he thought of Sylvie in her cottage. Her mother would have warmed her thoroughly by now and ensured she was comfortable. He wished the Blue Moon had been more special for her. Outside he could hear the rain still lashing down in torrents, but it was cosy in the hut by the fire. Slowly his wet hair dried, springing into curls, and his clothes steamed dry. He dozed in the warmth and at some point crawled off the chair and onto the floor, where he curled up in front of the dying fire.

He was awoken by the door crashing open, and a loud shout.

'Here he is, sir, the little bastard! We got him now!'

It was the voice of the man Yul dreaded most in the world. He barged inside, followed by the next most dreaded man.

'Good. Wake him up then.'

Alwyn aimed a vicious kick but Yul was already scrambling to his feet, blinking in the blinding torchlight and shivering in the cold draught. The two men crowded the small hut, both watching him intently and looking very pleased with themselves.

'I told you he'd be here, sir.'

'So you did. Well, Yul, you didn't inform me you were leaving home.'

'No, sir,' Yul mumbled, his heart pounding. He considered making a run for it but the two large men were blocking the door.

'Don't even try,' laughed Magus. 'Alwyn, tie his hands and hobble him.'

Alwyn stepped forward and grabbed Yul's arm hard, yanking him almost off his feet.

'Pleasure, sir.'

Yul's arms were pulled behind his back and his wrists tied tightly. His ankles were each circled with rope, with a little slack between them.

'Right then. You've got your whip?'

'Oh yes, sir,' chuckled Alwyn, patting at his coat.

'Then it's off to the Hall.'

The flashlight did strange things to the wet woodland. The rain was a curtain of diagonal dashes; the tree trunks glistened and gleamed. Yul found it difficult to stay on his feet with his ankles hobbled, and Alwyn did his best to unbalance the boy, jabbing him in the back and cuffing him round the head as he stumbled along the path. Alwyn wore the great brown leather coat he saved for wet weather, the water running off the treated skin. He'd cured the hides himself. Magus wore more sophisticated extreme weather gear which shone wetly in the torch light. But Yul was soaked to the skin in his thin shirt and trousers, and shivering violently with fear.

At the Hall they turned off towards the stable block, then went round the back to some out-houses that lay beyond. Magus unlocked and unbolted a great wooden door and led the way into a stone building, a sort of byre. An electric light had been rigged up, its harsh white light illuminating the stark area inside. The stone floor was covered with dusty straw and there were several bales lying around. A polished chair of fine wood and old leather stood to one side.

Yul was sent sprawling onto the straw. Magus pulled off his dripping outer clothes and laid them over a bale. Alwyn followed suit. Magus then sat down in the chair and surveyed the boy cowering on the floor. Alwyn stood over him, gloating, his porky face creased in glee. At a nod from Magus he untied the ropes. Yul felt the hatred in both men's eyes; the desire to see him suffer. Their pleasure at his predicament was almost palpable in the musty air and his heart quaked with terror.

'Right then,' began Magus in his deep voice as Alwyn carefully rolled up his sleeves to expose bulging forearms. 'Let's get down to business. You really are a glutton for punishment, aren't you, Yul? I seem to recall talking to you at the Stone Circle and warning you of the consequences if you crossed me again. I distinctly remember telling you before then that if there was any more trouble you'd face a whipping. Yet here we are again. You've

242

brought this on yourself and you fully deserve the punishment that's coming.'

Yul remained silent. What was there to say? He wasn't even sure of his crime but was gripped by a deep, sick dread. His father had his whip, the thing Yul feared the most. The snake-whip was ferocious, and when wielded by his father, potentially lethal. Perhaps, tonight, he would die at his father's hand as Mother Heggy had predicted.

'Before we discuss how you've disobeyed me,' said Magus smoothly, 'we must first deal with family matters. You've angered your father, Yul, with your wild behaviour and constant lack of respect. You know that's not tolerated at Stonewylde under any circumstances. You're the eldest of seven children and almost a man now, yet you continually defy your father instead of making his life easier. We can't have that, can we, Alwyn?'

'No, sir! He's an insolent, disobedient little bastard and I—'

'So would you like to teach your son some respect? Would you like to show your son just how much he's displeased you?'

'Oh yes, sir. I'd like that very much!'

'Off you go, then.'

Alwyn kicked Yul to his feet and ripped the wet shirt off his back. He shoved the shivering boy up against one of the walls facing the cold stone. Yul's insides were liquid with fear, his bare arms and torso bumpy with goose-flesh. He put his hands out and braced himself against the wall.

'I returned home tonight after a pleasant evening, Yul, to discover you'd been up to mischief again. Mischief involving my thoroughbred horse. So I called at your home to deal with you.'

Alwyn stepped back and uncurled the whip, flexing his arms, lovingly stroking out the length of heavy leather braid. Magus spoke softly as the snake-tail cracked through the air and bit into Yul's back.

'But you weren't there! Your father told me you'd disappeared several days ago. Children don't run away from home at Stonewylde, Yul. Children honour and obey their parents. Isn't that right, Alwyn?'

'Certainly is, sir,' panted Alwyn, sweat already beading his face. 'All the other brats jump to obey me.'

He paused to peel off his shirt, revealing his monstrous, glistening body. Then he resumed the heavy, precise strokes, his great arm jerking back and slashing forward hard through the air, the whip uncoiling into a lethal line of pain as it lashed out and cut into the boy's soft skin. Once the tip had found its tender mark, the snake curled back at a flick of Alwyn's fist, ready to strike again.

'So you see,' said Magus, 'I was extremely annoyed to find you absent from your bed. And then to go on a wild-goose chase through the woods in the rain to hunt you down . . .'

He paused to watch for a while, the vicious snap of leather shockingly loud in the stone building. 'That's enough, Alwyn. For now.'

The man lowered the whip to the floor and sat down heavily on a straw bale. His chest heaved. Yul still leant on his hands against the wall, his head now hanging down. His back was a mess of criss-cross stripes. Magus sighed, crossing his legs comfortably.

'Turn around, boy, and look at me.'

Slowly Yul straightened up. He turned, shook the wet hair from his face, and looked Magus in the eye. His face was tight with iron control; he would not show his pain.

'I wished to speak to you tonight about the incident involving my horse. I was informed of it on my return to Stonewylde this evening. You know, of course, what I'm talking about?'

'Yes, sir.' His voice was small and shaky.

'Not only did you frighten Nightwing so badly that he threw his rider, you then had the effrontery to ride him yourself.'

'Yes, sir, but only because—'

'Silence!' barked Magus. 'I'm not interested in your excuses! *Nobody* rides that horse without my express permission. You were given no such permission and never would be. A Village lout like you would ruin a thoroughbred's mouth in just one ride. HOW DARE YOU!!'

He nodded at Alwyn to continue. Whilst the tanner resumed

his terrible handiwork with the snake-whip, Magus pulled a silver hip flask from his pocket and drank deeply. He watched the boy's horrific ordeal in a detached way. Unlike the public whippings, nobody was counting out a fixed number of strokes. The punishment went on and on until finally Yul crumpled to the ground, his back bloody and raw. Throughout the entire ordeal he'd remained silent. Alwyn, his breathing loud and laboured, gave one last slash at the boy on the floor and looked to Magus for instructions. He was scarlet with exertion, sweat dripping off his nose and jowls, his huge chest and belly gleaming wet.

'You've done an impressive job,' said Magus quietly. 'Go round to the kitchens and say I sent you. Someone will still be up. You deserve some sustenance after all that hard work and I want a word with Yul alone.'

'Thank you, sir,' Alwyn gasped, coiling up his whip and attaching it to the clip on his belt. He pulled on his shirt and leather coat and stomped out of the byre, shutting the door behind him.

'So,' purred Magus, standing up and walking over to where Yul lay, sprawled and trembling. 'Now it's just you and me.'

He prodded the boy with the tip of his boot and Yul groaned. He was beyond tears, his back on fire, the vivid lacerations raised and oozing blood.

'Your father certainly knows how to use a whip. I'll have to remember him if we ever have another public whipping. But strangely, there seems to be no call for such things nowadays. Can you remember the last time we had one? I barely can. Everyone at Stonewylde behaves themselves and keeps to the laws. Everyone, that is, except *you*!'

He knelt swiftly and grabbed a handful of Yul's hair, yanking him to his feet. The boy stood bent over, his hair held by Magus' grasping fist. Magus jerked Yul's head upright, let go of his hair and then slashed him full in the face with a vicious backhanded swipe. It sent Yul reeling against the wall like a spinning top. Magus walked over and sat down in the chair again, taking another draught from the hip flask.

'Come here and stand in front of me,' he commanded. Yul staggered across, trying to stand upright, his head ringing from the force of the blow. He saw strange coloured dots. The stone floor and walls shifted and tilted around him. Magus noted with satisfaction that his cheekbone and eye were swelling rapidly.

He felt again that surge of pleasure deep in his abdomen and recalled the time when he'd dealt with the boy up at the Hall. Here was a real challenge; here was a force to be subdued and then harnessed, ridden as he rode his spirited horse. He noticed how much Yul had grown in the past months, leaving childhood well behind. He reminded Magus of himself at the same age – lean, long-legged and strong. Magus would never have hit a child. But he was happy to hit a young man.

'And now we come to the final matter, brought to my attention tonight by a member of the Hallfolk. I was told about your repeated involvement with a young girl, a new member of the Hallfolk. You, a Villager.'

Yul swayed on his feet, barely able to stand. He stared at the straw on the ground, noticing how yellow and glossy it was. His heart was thumping hard.

'In the morning I'll speak to Sylvie and hear her version of events. Then I'll come back here and you'll tell me yours. The two had better be identical. I want the entire truth about what's been going on between the two of you in the past few weeks. If you appear in the least bit stubborn about talking, I'll bring your father in to persuade you. Maybe I'll bring him in anyway. See you in the morning, Yul. Sweet dreams.'

He snapped off the light and went out into the wet night, locking and bolting the door behind him. Yul took a ragged breath. His back was alive and crawling with raw, searing pain. His face hurt terribly, his head still ringing from the vicious blow. There was nowhere for him to lie and he couldn't stretch out on the straw bales because of their terrible scratchiness.

He fumbled on the floor in the darkness for his torn wet shirt, which he spread onto the stone and lay down upon. It was hard and very cold. He curled as small as he could, wrapping his arms around himself in a vain effort to control the dreadful shivering that overwhelmed him as shock and cold set in. There were rustlings and scuttlings in the straw over in the corner that spoke of large rats. Sleep did not come quickly for Yul on the night of the Blue Moon.

16

By the time Magus arrived at Woodland Cottage the following morning, Miranda was almost beside herself with anxiety. She longed to fling her arms around him but his grim expression as he crossed the threshold made her hold back and content herself with a brief kiss.

'I'm so pleased you've come – I've been so worried! There's something wrong with Sylvie – she's really ill.'

'What? What's the matter with her?'

'She's delirious, shouting in her sleep, burning up and having the most awful nightmares all night. She's been screaming that her back's on fire, and—'

'Let me see her,' he said curtly, following her up to Sylvie's room.

She lay with the covers pushed back, asleep but very flushed and with her hair in a wild tangle all over the pillow. Magus looked down at her for a moment, then felt her forehead and the glands in her neck.

'I've given her paracetamol and—'

'And what did you say she was shouting?'

'Well, last night it was that her back was being clawed to shreds and there was something biting into it. This morning she said she couldn't see anything in the dark, even though the daylight was streaming in her window. Oh yes, and that something was rustling in the straw.'

'Really? That is absolutely amazing,' he murmured.

248

'She's delirious with a very high temperature, isn't she?'

'Yes, she certainly is. May I see her back? I'm assuming she hasn't been bitten or clawed?'

'Not that I can see,' said Miranda, rolling her daughter over.

Magus looked carefully at Sylvie's slim, smooth back and brushed his fingertips over the satin skin. Miranda felt a twinge of desire at the sight of those long, square-tipped fingers that had touched her so expertly only a few hours earlier.

'There're no marks at all, nor any swelling. Not that there could be of course.'

Miranda turned Sylvie over again, smoothing the hair from her hot face.

'So what should I do? I've been sponging her down with tepid water.'

'I'm not sure there is much you can do other than keeping her fever down. She's obviously caught a chill or something. We'll get the doctor to take a look if she gets any worse of course.'

'Yes, I'm sure it is a chill. She got drenched in the rain last night coming back from the Hall. She's been so healthy lately I'd forgotten how delicate she can be. Poor Sylvie.'

When they'd made her comfortable they went downstairs for a cup of coffee. Miranda tried hard to recapture their intimacy but Magus remained aloof, acting as if their picnic on the stone at Mooncliffe had never happened.

'I'm sorry, Miranda,' he said. 'Since last night a great deal's happened and I'm afraid our love-making will have to go on the back burner for a while. I returned home to find all sorts of problems that must be dealt with. After I'd dropped you off here last night I bumped into Clip and he filled me in on what's been going on in my absence. I've been up half the night and I'm very tired.'

'Oh dear, anything I can do to help?'

Miranda was relieved that there was a good reason for his coolness this morning.

'Well yes, it does concern you, or at least, Sylvie, and it's why I came here this morning. Apparently over the last couple of weeks she's been seeing Yul, the Village boy whom I sent here to dig the garden.'

'Yul? But ... he's the one who brought her back here last night!'

'*What?* They were together last night as well? I didn't know that!'

'He arrived on the doorstep in the pouring rain carrying her in his arms. But what do you mean, "seeing"? Do you mean they're going out together, or what?'

'At the moment I'm not sure. It could be innocent, but knowing Yul it's probably not.'

She gasped, hand covering her mouth.

'But Sylvie's only fourteen! Surely you don't mean ... ?'

Magus shrugged. 'I warned you about him, didn't I? He's a nasty piece of work. I had him whipped by his father last night and—'

'*Whipped?* Magus, that's terrible!'

'No it's not! It's a punishment we use at Stonewylde in extreme cases. I thought a threat to your daughter's virginity to be an extreme case,' he said angrily.

'Well, yes, if you put it like that.'

'So I need to speak to her and find out what's been going on, and then I'll hear his version. Hopefully we'll arrive at the truth somewhere along the line.'

'And it was Clip who told you they'd been together?'

'That's right. Last night he told me that he's seen them together all over the place during the last couple of weeks. I'd heard about the young man coming off my horse as soon as I came home, but later I heard it was Sylvie and Yul who'd actually caused the accident. They were up on the ridgeway and startled Nightwing. And there's more. Clip told me they've been to visit an old woman who isn't suitable company at all. She's an evil, twisted old crone and she's been involved in some serious business over the years. She dabbles in witchcraft, and I mean the dark arts, not just a few herbal remedies.'

'And Sylvie's been to her house?'

'Yes. Clip saw her and Yul go into her cottage and spend some time in there.'

'Why on earth didn't he stop them if she's so dangerous?'

Magus sighed and rubbed his forehead. Miranda could see dark circles under his eyes and felt so sorry for him, kept up half the night with problems.

'Clip's a strange man. He lives on the periphery of life. He doesn't like to get involved or take responsibility in any shape or form. If he saw something going on, such as Yul leading Sylvie astray, he'd never intervene. It's just not his way. He'd observe and then maybe tell me, but maybe not. He might just forget about it altogether. He's a shaman. He lives in a different reality to the rest of us.'

'Are you sure he's not just imagining this about Yul and Sylvie?'

'Oh no, it's all true. The rider knew it was them, although he didn't tell me that initially. Tom, my head ostler, knew it was Sylvie and Yul too. He was the one who told me about that little bastard riding my horse home from the Dragon's Back.'

His eyes darkened and his lips tightened. Miranda watched in fascination. She wouldn't want to be on the receiving end of his anger, although this dark, rather cruel side made him all the more exciting. She shivered.

'Yul rode that enormous horse?'

'Yes, though Goddess knows how he managed it. Nightwing is a very expensive thoroughbred. Nobody rides him except me and a hand-picked chosen few; people who I know have a great deal of experience with such horses. He's a very intelligent and powerful stallion and he has a vicious streak, which is what makes him such a beautiful ride. It's a real challenge trying to control him. So how that Village lout rode him back to the Hall is a mystery. But he's been punished for it, believe me.'

Miranda shivered again at the expression on his face and felt a fleeting moment of pity for the dark-haired boy. She remembered how carefully he'd carried Sylvie in last night and laid her in the armchair.

'So what about last night?' asked Miranda. 'What do you think happened?'

He shrugged, his face tight with displeasure.

'I hadn't realised they'd been together last night as well. This makes it even more serious. I'll get his side of the story as soon as I've heard Sylvie's account. I have him up at the Hall under lock and key and he's staying there until I've found out the truth. There's more to this than meets the eye. There was something said once, long ago, about Yul. A prophecy of sorts, and I'm worried that ... well, never mind. It sounds ridiculous now.'

'Tell me! I'm sure it isn't ridiculous.'

He shook his head firmly.

'No, it's a load of nonsense. It's that mad old crone, Heggy, planting her evil seeds and trying to get revenge for something that happened before I was even born. But I've always had my doubts about Yul. I've always felt that there was something potentially dangerous there.'

'Really? I must say I thought he seemed very ... dark, secretive even, when he was digging our garden. And obviously full of pent-up aggression.'

'It wasn't a major issue before, but now he's become involved with Sylvie I'm really concerned. Apart from the fact that it's an abuse of newcomers who've been invited into our community, it's also against our laws if there's been any sexual activity between them. We're very strict about underage children controlling their emergent sexuality. Yul knows this even if Sylvie doesn't.'

'Oh no, Sylvie wouldn't willingly do anything like that. She's actually quite prudish. She doesn't approve of our ... trysts up at Mooncliffe.'

'You told her about that?'

He looked surprised.

'Well ... yes, I did. We're very close. We talk about everything.'

'Not everything. She didn't tell you about Yul, did she?'

'No, and that's what makes me think maybe there is something to hide.'

'I promise you, Miranda, if we find that anything has been going on, he'll pay for it. Really pay for it.'

They went back upstairs to where Sylvie was tossing and turning. Magus sat on the side of the bed and sponged her forehead gently. Eventually he managed to rouse her and she stared up at him glassy-eyed, her cheeks flushed.

'It's the magus,' she whispered, her voice unnaturally high. 'Solstice by name. And my birthday soon on the solstice. I'll be fifteen.'

He smiled at her, continuing to stroke the hair away from her face with the sponge.

'And my birthday too, Sylvie. We'll have a joint celebration, won't we?'

'A joint celebration. Up at the stones. I know what happens up there. I know what you do.'

'Ssh, ssh, that's enough. Listen, Sylvie, I want you to tell us what happened last night. We know you were with Yul. Nobody's cross with you but we need to know exactly what happened.'

Miranda stepped forward. 'Darling, did he hurt you? Did he—'

'Quiet, Miranda! Let me ask the questions,' he hissed.

'Yul would never hurt me. Yul doesn't hurt anyone. But *you* do. You scarred his cheek.'

Magus frowned but ignored the remark. Her eyes were all wrong.

'Sylvie, did Yul take you to the woodsmen's hut last night?'

'The hut. It was warm in there. Warm by the fire with the blanket.'

'Yes! He brought her back wrapped in a blanket!'

'Alright. So what happened in the hut, Sylvie? What happened by the fire with the blanket?'

'He looked after me. Before and after, he made me warm and he made me drink something hot.'

Magus turned to Miranda and whispered.

'Could have been something Heggy gave him. She's an expert on potions.' He turned back to Sylvie, taking her hand. 'Before

253

and after what? Do you remember what happened in the hut? What did you do? What did Yul do? Before and after what, Sylvie?'

But she was away now, her eyes even glassier, and she started to sing. Magus shook his head and stood up.

'I'll go and question the boy now.'

'But do you really think they've been up to something they shouldn't? What if she's pregnant? Oh my God, it—'

'I don't think so. I don't know . . . For all his wild ways, I don't think Yul would be that stupid. Sylvie's far too young and anyway, as you say, she isn't that sort of girl. I think it's more likely to be some kind of mischief that old Heggy's put him up to.'

'Really?

'Don't worry, Miranda, I'll get the facts out of him one way or another. And you must listen carefully if she says anything more, but don't put ideas into her head either. I need to know the truth about what's been going on over the past couple of weeks, and most importantly, what they were doing in the woodsmen's hut last night.'

He left with barely a backward glance and Miranda wanted to cry. How could someone be so caring and passionate one minute, and so cold and distant the next? Once again she felt a flicker of resentment towards her daughter for spoiling things.

When Magus returned to the stone byre, Yul was sitting on the hard floor in near darkness. Only a little light came in through the gaps around the wooden shutters and under the door. He didn't dare sit on the expensive chair. He was hungry, thirsty and cold. His ripped shirt was still damp but he'd put it on in the hope that his body heat would dry it. The mesh of slashes on his back was pure, raw agony. It was the most brutal whipping he'd ever had, but Yul was proud that he'd taken it well. He hadn't humiliated himself by begging for mercy or crying at the agony of it. He hadn't given Alwyn that satisfaction. He'd kept his self-respect intact and this now strengthened his purpose.

As he heard the bolt scraping on the door he vowed that he'd never betray Sylvie, whatever they might do to him. He wouldn't tell of her magical moongaziness, nor the strange things Mother Heggy had said. Magus would never know of those secrets. But despite his brave resolutions, Yul trembled at the sound of the key in the lock. Bright daylight blasted him, then died as the door closed again. Magus turned on the harsh light and sat on the chair, with Yul standing before him.

'You are now going to tell me everything that's gone on between you and Sylvie. I want every detail. I know about the walk on the ridgeway that led to my cousin's fall from the horse. I know about the visit to Mooncliffe and then to Mother Heggy. And I know that last night you took Sylvie to the woodsmen's hut and spent several hours with her before taking her home.'

Yul stiffened at this but kept his eyes to the floor. He must not betray Sylvie's secret. But what could he say to explain those hours away? How much did Magus already know?

'You will talk, Yul. Your father is sitting in the Hall kitchens right now, eating an amazingly hearty second breakfast. He's hoping very much that I'll call him in here to help elicit the truth from you. He asked me specially if he could whip you again. He'd love nothing better than to carry on where he left off last night and he doesn't think you've taken anywhere near enough punishment yet. But . . . that's up to you, Yul.'

Magus looked closely at the boy before him; he shook but was trying to hide it. He seemed smaller this morning, shrunk in on himself. He looked cold, hungry and frightened. His shirt was torn and bloody, his eye and cheekbone badly swollen and bruised. Magus smiled grimly. He was utterly determined to break this defiant boy.

'Well?'

'You know all there is to know, sir. There's no more.'

'I want to hear the details. When did you and Sylvie start to become friendly?'

Yul thought quickly.

'When I was digging their back garden, sir.'

'How did you move from that to going for walks together?'

'One day I found her wandering around in the woods. She

was lost. It was my day off, so I offered to show her some of Stonewylde.'

'Mmn. She had plenty of others to show her around, others far more suitable than you.'

Yul shrugged, and in that shrug, conveyed his absolute disdain for those others who could've shown her around. Magus rose swiftly and delivered a heavy backhander to the un-bruised side of the boy's face. Yul staggered from the brutal blow but managed to remain standing.

'And Mother Heggy? What's the story there?'

Yul found it harder to speak now and certainly harder to think.

'I ... we were ... we were just walking past,' he gasped. 'The old woman came out.'

'Did you go into the cottage?'

'N – no, sir.'

Another blow across the face, one which sent him crashing into the wall.

'Liar! You spent some time in the cottage. Sylvie told me everything this morning. She told me about the crow and the potions and all the things in the cottage. I know everything because Sylvie's blurted it all out to me already. And now I want you to tell me what the crone said to you. *Exactly* what she said.'

The boy raised his head slowly. He could barely speak.

'"Those who stand against you will fall, one by one",' he mumbled. Then he sank to his knees, groaning horribly as his head exploded with the pain of the two blows.

'Did she now?' mused Magus, smiling. He clearly thought Mother Heggy had been referring to those who stood against him. But the smile faded as he gazed at the boy huddled before him.

'Which brings me on to last night. What the hell were you doing out alone at night-time with Sylvie? At the Moon Fullness! I want the whole story, boy.'

Yul couldn't think. His head was teeming with violent colours. He couldn't work out what he must say in order to protect Sylvie. How much had she told Magus?

'I found her in the woods, lost in the darkness,' he mumbled again, his speech slurred. 'She was wet and cold so I took her to the hut.'

'Why didn't you just take her home?'

'She needed looking after and she said her mother was out. With you, sir.'

Magus frowned at him.

'What exactly happened in the hut?'

'I built up the fire and made her a cup of tea. I wrapped her in a blanket. Then I took her home.'

'You were with her for three hours or so. I know that for sure, because she didn't come to the Hall at all last night. Nobody saw her here. She was out from when she left Woodland Cottage an hour before moonrise to when she returned. So what else happened in all that time?'

'Nothing, sir. We were just talking.'

'What, for three hours? What were you talking about?'

'I don't know ... Stonewylde, my work in the woods, the Outside World, things like that ...'

'Did you touch her?'

'No!'

'Did you do anything to her? Kiss her, anything else?'

'No, sir, I'd never do anything like that!'

'Oh come, come, Yul. Don't play the innocent with me. I remember the incident with Holly. Don't pretend you're not interested in girls.'

'I wouldn't touch Sylvie.'

'I don't believe you. Nobody sits in a hut with a pretty girl in the pouring rain for three hours just talking. And I can't imagine your conversational skills are sufficiently developed to entertain someone intelligent like Sylvie for more than three minutes, let alone three hours. What else did you do in there? What else *is* there for you to do?'

'Nothing, sir, I swear!'

'I don't believe you. You have a taste for Hallfolk girls. You're not an adult yet, but you're already chasing after girls completely out of your league. I think you fancy yourself as a bit of a Romeo. Not that you'd know who Romeo is, would you? Do you really think a Hallfolk girl is going to look twice at an ignorant Village boy like you?'

'No, sir.'

'I'm still not convinced that nothing went on in the hut in all that time you were together. It just doesn't ring true. I can tell you're still hiding something and I'll drag it out of you, never fear.'

'No, sir, honestly—'

'Silence! And just remember, Yul, what the punishment is for a liaison with an underage girl, and particularly one who's Hallfolk. If I discover you've violated Sylvie in any way, I'll take great pleasure in banishing you from Stonewylde. After a thorough and public whipping.'

He stood up and stepped towards Yul, standing before him with his head bowed. The boy flinched, despite himself, and Magus smiled grimly. He grasped Yul's chin in one hand and twisted his face upwards for a better view of the damage he'd inflicted. He tutted and sighed at the sight.

'You're not looking so pretty today, Yul. I imagine your back's a little sore too. How much more can you really take? If you genuinely haven't touched Sylvie, you'd do well to tell me the truth. I *know* there's more to this than you're letting on, but is any secret worth so much suffering? Your father's disappointed he didn't break you last night. One word from me and he'll try again, and keep on trying until he succeeds. Ponder on that, Yul.'

Magus opened the door and brought in a water jar and an old bucket, which he placed just inside the byre. Then he snapped off the light, locked the door and went away, not returning until the following day. While he was gone, Yul sat in the cold darkness filled with terror at the thought of Alwyn returning with the whip. Would he die at his father's hand as Mother Heggy had warned, in this isolated stone byre, with only Magus as witness? They'd invent a story about an accident and everyone would believe them; everyone except Mother Heggy and Sylvie. But it would be too late for them to help him.

Sylvie was unaware of Yul's misery and torture in the byre. Magus called in regularly at Woodland Cottage over the next few days and questioned her repeatedly. As she recovered from the fever, Sylvie developed a chest infection which left her very weak, although perfectly coherent. She dreaded the visits from Magus.

Miranda had said Yul was being kept up at the Hall but would tell her no more. Magus interrogated her constantly about the time spent alone with Yul in the woodsmen's hut that night, refusing to accept her story that they were simply sheltering from the rain. She understood what he was implying and it made her angry. Yul would never do anything like that to her. She trusted him completely and always felt safe with him. Unlike Magus. She loathed him coming into to her bedroom alone, sitting on her bed and touching her forehead or taking her hand. His eyes were so dark and penetrating. She felt as if he were probing into her mind, violating her memory, and she didn't trust him at all.

Sylvie saw too how he treated her mother. It was as if there'd never been any liaison up at Mooncliffe and she hated to see Miranda looking so crestfallen. She thought of the man who'd rescued them from London and who'd healed her with Earth Magic, and then of the man whom Yul had described. Now she understood. Magus did have a dark side and slowly but surely it was being revealed. When she asked him if Yul was alright he just smiled that tight, cruel smile and told her to forget that Yul even existed. His expression and cold voice made her shiver with fear for the boy she'd befriended. She remembered the prophecies Mother Heggy had made on their visit. How could she save Yul if she didn't even know what had happened to him?

Whilst Sylvie gradually recovered from her chill in the comfort of the cottage, Yul little by little succumbed to the torture inflicted by Magus. Days and nights were a blur to him. He was given water and a tiny amount of bread, but that was all. His bucket was emptied once a day, but as time dragged on he had less need to use it. His stomach was hollow, he suffered agonies of cramp in his abdomen, and all he could think about was food.

The deep lacerations on his back had mostly scabbed over but hurt constantly, whether he moved or kept still. His face was a pulpy mess where Magus had repeatedly hit him, swollen so badly he could barely see from between the puffed eyelids. His head hurt so much he couldn't think straight. He was cold all night and for much of the day and had no bedding other than the mouldy straw. Although it was now June, the stone byre was always chilly and dark as no sunlight penetrated its thick walls and closed shutters.

Yul had no water for washing and smelled bad, but he was beyond caring. Magus interrogated him regularly and he'd begun to forget what he'd already said as his sense of reality slipped further away. But despite his weakening state, he was aware that Magus was still trying to catch him out. The master seemed to realise that he wasn't being told the whole truth and was determined to get it out of Yul one way or another.

Alwyn had been brought in again. The sight of the tanner's gloating face and ginger hair made Yul's heart race; the sight of the coiled snake-whip in his hand made Yul quake with absolute, abject terror. But to Alwyn's disappointment there were no further beatings. Yul was too weak to take any more and would be no use unconscious. Instead, Alwyn was given hot food that filled the byre with a delicious aroma, and Yul was made to sit close by and watch his father eat.

By the fifth day as the tanner sat down yet again at the makeshift table shovelling steak pie into his mouth, Yul was so far gone that he began to drool. Magus, watching the scene carefully, laughed out loud at the sight. The boy sat on the floor; he couldn't stand very well now. He hugged his knees, rocking back and forth, his torn shirt failing to hide the protruding ribcage that grew sharper with each day.

Yul's swollen eyes were fixed on the huge man as he devoured mouthful after mouthful, gorging himself on the rich meat and pastry and grunting with pleasure. He chewed noisily and with appreciation, wiping flecks of food and gravy from his lips and chin with the back of his hand. The steak pie was enormous but Alwyn was determined and worked through it steadily, washing it down with a pitcher of cider and belching every so often. At one point he loosened the belt of his trousers to make more room for his massive, distended belly. Magus kept it going, praising and encouraging Alwyn and urging him to further greed.

'Would you like some, Yul? You must be so hungry,' said Magus softly, cutting a sliver of pie. The starved boy was dribbling, all self-control finally gone, and nodded eagerly. He crawled unsteadily towards Magus who held the fork out to him, but just out of reach.

'Just tell me once more what Mother Heggy said, Yul. Tell me everything that happened between you and Sylvie. It's so easy, and you know there's no point trying to keep silly little secrets from me.'

'No no no I'll tell you . . .'

'That's right, Yul – just talk and this will all be finished. Tell me everything and then you can eat this delicious mouthful of pie and it will all be over.'

'She wanted the Beechwood Sickener but she gave me a potion and I couldn't move and she loved the toenail and the tanner will be the first to fall and it's solstice by destiny and her raven is back and she knows it's Sylvie because she's moongazy the moongaziest girl I ever saw and—'

'WHAT? What did you say? Sylvie's *moongazy*?'

Yul crept closer and feebly tried to take the fork from Magus' hand.

'Please,' he croaked through his split and puffy lips, 'please give me some food. Please, please, please . . .'

Magus had frozen where he stood, everything else forgotten in the light of this revelation.

'I *knew* there was more to this! I knew you were protecting some special secret. So our little Sylvie's moongazy! That's what you've been hiding from me! Who'd have thought it?'

Yul pawed at his leg and Magus shoved him off so hard he went sprawling across the floor. But the sliver of pie also fell on the floor. Before Magus could stop him, Yul had scooped it up out of the dirt and straw and crammed it desperately into his mouth.

'That's disgusting!' spluttered Alwyn through a mouthful. 'Filthy little bastard ain't no better than an animal.'

After five days Yul's ordeal came to an end. He was released blinking and squinting into the sunny yard outside the byre. He could barely stand. A bucket of cold water and piece of soap were provided and a change of rough clothes. He was given a meagre but welcome meal. Then he was put into the front seat of a Land Rover and Magus drove him out of the stable area and away from the Hall.

Tom shook his head as he watched them go. He'd been aware of some of the cruelty taking place in the byre and couldn't understand what the boy had done to warrant such treatment. He'd been tempted many times to slip some food to him, or just to comfort him. He'd heard the boy crying in the night and the pitiful sound had nearly broken his heart. But in the end his fear of Magus had stopped him from helping the boy. Tom had visited Maizie and let her know her son was still alive, although he'd spared her the details of what Magus and Alwyn were doing to him. Now, he hoped, the boy would be going home. Although with a father like Alwyn, that wasn't necessarily a comfort.

But Yul wasn't going home. As they drove past the turning to the Village Magus glanced across at him and laughed at the expression on his face.

'Did you think that was it? No, my lad, it's not over yet, not by a long way. That was just for starters, to make you talk. Now we're going to start the real punishment. You'll learn to serve me as everyone else at Stonewylde serves me. You still have some spark in you that dares to defy me. And that spark will be crushed out of you completely before I allow you back into the community.'

'Please, sir, I've learnt my lesson,' mumbled Yul. 'I'll never defy you again, I swear.'

'You've led me a merry dance over the last few days, Yul. Holding out on me, not telling the truth, daring to think you could take me for a fool. You should have understood that nobody gets the better of me.'

'No, sir, I—'

'I broke you in the end of course, and now you've betrayed Sylvie's little secret which you tried so hard to hide. How *dare* you? How dare you keep that sort of knowledge from me? Too damn right, you won't defy me again! You may not even survive what I have in store for you next.'

Yul swallowed painfully. He was very weak from the torture. His back and face hurt a great deal, a constant and relentless agony. Terrible pains gripped his starved stomach like pincers and his legs couldn't support him properly. He was dizzy and felt disorientated and confused. He wondered what more Magus could do to him.

But he sat silently; he'd learnt over the last few days to fear this man in a way he'd never feared his father. For Magus was not a brute like Alwyn whose cravings, whether for food, cider or inflicting pain, were easily assuaged. Magus was subtle and he was cruel. Like a cat with its prey, he enjoyed playing with his victim. Magus hadn't quite broken Yul, but he'd taught him to hide his defiance very deep.

'Would you like to know where I'm taking you?'

'Yes, sir.'

'We're going to Quarrycleave. You're to work there with the quarrymen.'

'Quarrymen? I don't understand, sir.'

Magus laughed again as he drove the Land Rover expertly up the bumpy track to the ridgeway. He was in high spirits now, his eyes gleaming darkly.

'I've reopened the old quarry, the big one up to the west behind the hills. There's still a great deal of very fine stone up there, even though the Hall and much of the Village are built with it.'

He glanced at Yul, who sat hunched and pale.

'I need more stone now for several new projects, and there's a gang of men working at the quarry right now under Jackdaw. Remember Jackdaw?'

Yul nodded. Jackdaw was the man who'd been banished for murder a couple of years ago, and he was still talked of in the Village. He'd killed his young wife one night in a jealous, drunken rage. His banishment had brought much relief to everyone, for the whole community had feared him.

'Yes, a man such as Jackdaw has his uses. Now he's back with a gang of workers surveying the site and clearing the debris at Quarrycleave, ready to start quarrying the stone next year. You'll spend the next two weeks working for him. If you survive it, you may return to your father's house in the Village and resume your training as a woodsman.'

'Thank you, sir,' Yul whispered and Magus chuckled cynically.

'I can assure you, Yul, that if you do return, you won't be the same person. Jackdaw is a hard master and a dangerous man; he'll break your spirit once and for all. And Quarrycleave is a treacherous place, especially for someone so young. Anything could happen to you there.'

Later in the day Magus called again at Woodland Cottage. There was a strange, triumphant light in his dark eyes. He flung himself into an armchair, stretched his long legs out before him and linked his hands behind his head, grinning at them both like a satisfied cat.

'What's happened?' asked Miranda.

'Problem solved,' he said smugly. 'Cracked him in the end, just as I knew I would. I'm surprised the boy lasted as long as he did, but he couldn't hold out for ever.'

Sylvie, lying on the sofa, sat up quickly.

'What have you done? Have you hurt Yul?'

Magus chuckled.

'That Village boy is no good, Sylvie, and you must forget him. There'll be no more contact between the two of you.'

'What have you done to him?'

'I've broken his silence and forced him into submission. And now he's gone away.'

'What? Where? Is he alright? When's he coming back?'

She jumped up and stood before Magus, her hair wild around her face. This was her first day out of bed and she was still weak. Magus laughed and held up a hand.

'Not so many questions! Yul finally told me everything. It all came tumbling out in the end, just as I knew it would. All the things Old Heggy said.'

'I don't believe you! You're trying to trick me.'

'No, really. "Those who stand against you will fall, one by one." Is that what she said?'

Sylvie nodded, feeling sick. What had Magus done to Yul to break him? He'd never have spoken willingly about that.

'Yul told me something else too, Sylvie. Something about you.'

Magus rose and stood in front of her and she took a step back, feeling suddenly dizzy.

'I know what you were doing on the night of the Blue Moon in the pouring rain. Yul's betrayed your little secret.'

Sylvie swallowed. Her mother's shocked face went in and out of focus. Magus loomed over her, his dark eyes glittering.

'Yul told me, Sylvie, that you're a moongazy girl.'

17

Quarrycleave was like nowhere on earth. A vast bleak place of tortured and blasted stone covering acres, it sprawled across the landscape like a white open wound. It bit into the land, shallow at the entrance but deep at the distant end where the rolling hills had been robbed of their stone hearts. Great craggy cliffs spilled out, boulders piled on boulders, faces of sheer white rock, stone protruding from the flesh of the earth like the very skeleton of the Earth Goddess.

She was laid bare and violate, spread open and looted, her body left desecrated and ugly when the men had taken their fill. No benign life force lingered here; no fertility or green earth energy remained in this place of desolation. Like an embittered woman whose beauty has been ravaged, the spirit here was malignant. It was an ancient place which screamed of suffering, moaned of torment, whimpered of death.

Despair hung like a foetid cloud over Quarrycleave, calling for sacrifice. It stalked the labyrinth between high walls of stone; lay in wait amongst the winding cuts cleaved into the very body of the land. Each jagged and vicious rock-face of the labyrinth represented untold aching sinews and groaning joints of the men who'd hewn and hammered here over thousands of years; men who'd given their youth, strength and lives to Quarrycleave in their quest for stone.

Stone – the one material representing permanence in a transient world where all else followed the natural cycle of growth and decay. The one material that marked man's dominion over nature and the landscape. Stone was power but, at Quarrycleave, too many lives had been claimed in its quest. Too many deaths had gone unmarked in the name of avarice; of haste and careless-ness in men's lust to rape the earth and plunder the pure white stone.

Quarrycleave sought human life to pay for all the centuries of pain and desecration. Greedy for blood to be spilt, the place soaked up lives to feed its hunger. The hunger was never satisfied, for nothing could atone for the obscene defilement of the land. Quarrycleave was the place of bones and death.

As the Land Rover had approached the shallow end of the quarry, Yul had felt a shroud of misery smother his spirit. Being so in tune with the Earth Magic from his daily visits to the Stone Circle, he sensed the negative, destructive energy of this place. He felt it snaking up out of the tortured landscape and curling around his soul. He began to shake and clasped his hands between his knees to still them.

Magus glanced at him, then swung the Land Rover away from the entrance. He pulled around the edge of the quarry, keeping safely away from the steep drop that marked the rim of the great horseshoe-shaped crater. He drove up the hill on the grass, by the side of the quarry, steadily bumping the vehicle over the rough ground towards the high summit on the skyline. It wasn't possible to drive right to the top, for rocky outcrops and boulders littered the land here and it was too steep. Magus stopped when he could drive no further, turning the Land Rover so it faced inwards to the quarry, and switched off the engine. Silence fell.

'Look, Yul,' he said softly. 'Isn't it beautiful? There's something about this place, a bleakness that touches me. I've always loved Quarrycleave. I rode up here as a boy, dragging Clip along. We used to play down there and he hated it.'

Yul sat silently, quaking inside and hoping his trembling wasn't visible. Magus sighed, gazing out over the vast scene below. Yul saw how the quarry, for all its starkness, had become overgrown over the years as soil had blown in from the land around. In places a few stunted hawthorns struggled for exist-ence, twisted into grotesque caricatures of trees. Ivy grew every-where inside the quarry, swarming up rock-faces in great sheets of glossy leaves, cascading down in torrents of dark green over the steep cliffs at the far end. Nature was attempting to reclaim the place, trying to clothe the stone's nakedness with green and cover her shame.

But man had once again intervened. There were modern yellow machines crawling all over her: dumper trucks, an enor-mous digger with claws, a great drilling rig. Yul saw men moving about below them and an ugly assortment of old caravans parked around the shallow end. His heart filled with despair at the thought of spending two weeks here. The place invoked crushing fear and misery. How would he ever survive?

Magus turned and Yul felt the power in the man beside him. The Earth energy coursed through him; he who'd always been the master. Magus' dark eyes glittered with authority and Yul could not meet his gaze.

'You will learn to obey me, Yul. You'll once and for all abandon any rebellious inclinations you may have felt in the past. Sylvie is Hallfolk and she's most definitely not for you. Your father must be respected and obeyed at all times. Buzz and any other young person from the Hall must be shown proper deference. You'll keep your eyes down and your head bowed when a member of the Hallfolk is present. Do you understand?'

'Yes, sir, I do,' croaked Yul, feeling close tears.

'And you'll never, ever challenge me in any way again. In six months' time you'll be sixteen and an adult. If I haven't seen evidence of your absolute subservience by then, I'll cast you out of the community.'

Yul nodded, his lips quivering. He wished with all his heart that he were at home now, in his cottage with his mother and the children, safe and loved.

'Never forget, my boy, that living at Stonewylde is a privilege, and one which I may choose to withdraw any time I see fit. Better people than you have been sent packing in the past, and I'd have no qualms about kicking out an unruly trouble-maker like you. Be assured, I'll tolerate no further trouble from you in any shape or form.'

Magus looked hard at the boy, now barely recognisable as the good-looking young Villager who'd been dragged from the woodsmen's hut five days ago. His face was so bruised and swollen, his body so hunched and shrunken that he could have been someone else altogether. Yul turned his battered face towards Magus.

'Please, sir,' he whispered, 'please don't make me stay here. I've learnt my lesson, I promise. I beg you, sir – don't make me go down into that place.'

Magus raised his eyebrows at this and shook his head.

'Oh no, young man! You wouldn't even dare ask me that if you'd really learnt your lesson – you'd just obey without question. You'll stay here for two weeks. If you've worked very hard and if Jackdaw is agreeable, you may come back to the Village after that. But not before.'

He switched on the engine and reversed, turning the Land Rover round and slowly heading back down the steep hill towards the entrance of the quarry mouth. Yul hung his head and began to cry silently, the sobs shaking his thin frame. He was too weak and confused to understand why he should feel so terrified of the quarry, but was unable to stop himself. Magus glanced at him as he drove carefully downwards along the quarry edge.

'I see that Quarrycleave has the same effect on you as it had on my brother. He was terrified too, but I can't see why. It's a place of incredibly strong power and magic. Though I'll grant you, the energy is strange here, unlike anywhere else at Stonewylde. I've considered celebrating a festival up here, just to see what sort of Earth Magic I'd receive. Interesting thought ...'

Yul shuddered and wiped his nose on his sleeve, having nothing else to use.

'And Yul – if I were you I'd stop the snivelling now. Jackdaw will have enough fun with you over the next fourteen days without branding you a cry-baby from the start. Pull yourself together, boy – you really won't survive this punishment otherwise.'

They parked by the shabby caravans. The area was a mess; rubbish and debris were scattered all around. An old minibus was parked next to a scruffy pick-up truck, and several dishevelled men hung about smoking and talking. As Magus pulled up, a large man emerged from one of the caravans, cigarette in mouth. Yul recognised him at once. The sight of Jackdaw filled Yul with further dread, for the man was infamous in the Village. He was enormous, heavily built with a huge barrel chest and exceptionally long legs. Unlike Alwyn his bulk was solid muscle. His large bald head was tanned nut-brown and both ears were pierced in several places. He was covered in tattoos and sported a few days' beard growth. But most menacing of all were his eyes. Brilliant blue and bulbous, they gleamed with a manic light that spoke of an unhinged personality.

He approached the Land Rover as Magus was getting out and gave a mock salute. He was even taller than Magus, which was unusual. He eyed Yul, huddled in the car, and spat on the ground.

'Afternoon, sir.'

'Good afternoon, Jack. Here's the boy as promised. He's yours for two weeks, although that takes us up to the Solstice and I doubt I'll be taking time out to come and collect him before the festival. Work him hard and don't spare him in any way. He's in a lot of trouble and I want him broken in, once and for all. You get my meaning?'

'Oh yes, guv. Work him to the ground and knock the spirit out of him. Easy enough to do here, I can tell you. These bloody immigrants are worse than useless. Still trying to lick them into shape but it ain't easy. Don't speak a word of bloody English. Look at the state of them! Slouch around doing bugger all. Don't trust none of 'em an inch.'

'Yes but you know why we've got them. They've come very cheap with no questions asked about health and safety, so make the best of it, Jack. Now watch this boy carefully. If he tries to run off you have my permission to punish him however you like.

If he never came back to Stonewylde it'd be no great loss to the community, miserable little runt. Do you understand?'

The man tapped the side of his nose and winked.

'Yeah, I got you. Disposable, if push comes to shove. Don't worry, I'll sort the little bugger out well and good. Just the sort o' job I enjoy most. He won't be no more trouble when I've done with him.'

'You'll need to feed him up or you'll get no work out of him. Normally he's pretty tough, but he's been starved the last few days and now he's very weak. But don't spoil him.'

'You know me better than that, guv! I don't do spoiling.'

'Everything else alright? Supplies getting in regularly?'

'Yeah, no problem. Food, drink, fags, laundry – all delivered regular to the Gatehouse and I go along every morning and pick 'em up. The small plant's all on site now, and we've started the core drilling. We're still looking for the working faces, and we're clearing some of the backfill too. We'll begin crushing it soon for aggregate.'

'Good – it all sounds in order. After the Solstice, you can give me a proper report. Right then, I'll be off. Any trouble, go to the Gatehouse and phone down to the Hall. Oh, and Jackdaw – get something done about this bloody mess.'

'Mess?'

'All this rubbish lying about. You should know better, even if those damn Outsiders don't. We don't desecrate Stonewylde with litter.'

'Right you are, boss. I'll have a word with 'em and the boy can get started on tidying it up now.'

Magus yanked Yul's door open and pulled him out roughly, marching him over to Jackdaw.

'He's all yours, Jack. Have fun.'

Yul very quickly got Jackdaw's measure. Jump when he said jump and keep out of range of his hands and feet. Jackdaw saw that Magus meant what he'd said about treating him hard, for the boy had been given a thorough going over. His face was so swollen it was a miracle he could see or talk. He stumbled and swayed and was of little use to anyone in his present state.

Jackdaw took him into his caravan, threw an old blanket onto the filthy floor by his bed, and told him to sit there. Yul was then given a large plateful of food which he had to eat sitting on the floor. It was horrible but he wolfed it down while Jackdaw sat on his unmade bed smoking. The caravan smelled disgusting.

'That's where you sleep, on the floor right next to me where I can see you. Any trouble and you won't live to tell the tale, boy. You think you'll be free to go in two weeks. But if you ain't satisfied me I'll keep you for longer. Magus won't care. He don't give a toss about you. Understand, boy?'

He shoved Yul hard with his boot and the boy nodded vigorously, keeping his head down.

'If you don't look out for yourself, you won't survive the two weeks anyway. Quarries are dangerous at the best o' times, and we don't do things by the book here. Magus wants the stone as cheap as he can get it, and so he shall have it. Corners are being cut, I can tell you. You and those miserable sodding foreigners out there are nothing to me or Magus. Your lives ain't worth shit. Just remember that, boy.'

And so, as Mother Heggy had predicted, began Yul's torment and suffering in the place of bones and death. Yul worked from sunrise until sunset; coming up to the Solstice this was a long time. He worked twice as hard as everyone else. Jackdaw was constantly on his back and kept him busy every second of the day. The other labourers had come from abroad and were working illegally. They soon realised that Yul had even less status than they did, and could be bullied into doing many of their jobs too.

The quarry work was hard and dangerous. The great digger lurched around moving stone, and the dumper trucks scooted all over the place clearing debris. Using picks and mallets, rock had to be prised away from the faces. Jackdaw and another man, a dour Portland quarryman who'd been drafted in for his expertise, were investigating the whole quarry and planning the future areas to work.

Despite the dumper trucks, much of the rock had to be shifted by hand and Yul moved far more than his fair share. He thought at times his back would break from the sheer effort of carrying or dragging the stone. There was no sympathy from anyone; nobody telling him to be careful or take a rest. His hair and skin were soon white from the stone dust and stayed that way. His fingers, sensitive and used to working with wood, were raw and bleeding from contact with the unyielding rock. He used to enjoy stone-carving but this was different. This was like smashing up the very bones of the earth; an act of destruction rather than creation.

Labouring in the quarry was only a part of Yul's work. He also had innumerable duties around the caravans doing all sorts of unpleasant jobs. He must empty the chemical toilets, clean the caravans after the men, wash up, help with food preparation, serve the men, bag up the dirty clothes and generally be everyone's dogsbody, at their constant beck and call. He was permanently exhausted. Sleeping on the floor by Jackdaw's bed wasn't such a hardship for he was asleep before he hit the ground.

But sleep held its own torture. Yul's initial dread of the quarry remained even when he became accustomed to the place; if anything it increased. He couldn't understand what it was that filled him with such terror. It was intangible and illogical. But he sensed evil all around them, not from Jackdaw or the men, but from the very quarry itself. He felt it stalking, always just around the corner. He tried never to be alone but to work within sight of others, even though it meant tolerating their abuse. On the occasions when he was by himself, the feeling of something malevolent creeping up on him was overwhelming.

At night he was tormented with terrible nightmares. In his dreams he felt the evil rising up from the ground and seeping through the floor of the caravan where he slept. It enveloped his body and began to drag him down, swallowing him into the maw of the quarry bed. He frequently awoke shaking and sweating in terror, and his shouts and screams earned him a good kicking from Jackdaw. As the endless days and nights rolled into each other, Yul began to give up and allow the bleak despair to engulf him.

Sylvie took a while to recover from her illness, and all the time she was cooped up in the house she pestered her mother about Yul's whereabouts. Miranda knew nothing, but Sylvie hoped that she in turn would bother Magus and find out where Yul had been taken. Her plan didn't work and Sylvie became increasingly worried. She knew he was suffering. She was haunted by flashes of despair and terror, snapshot images that disappeared as soon as they'd entered her mind. She felt his exhaustion and humiliation. The bright darkness that was Yul in her soul dimmed, becoming dusty and weak. She had to get to him, had to save him. The need was becoming desperate as she sensed his despair and his loss of the will to fight.

When Magus called at Woodland Cottage to check on her recovery, she confronted him. Her concern for Yul over-rode any natural caution or deference.

'Please, Magus, just tell me where he is.'

'No, Sylvie, you must let him go. You're making me very angry with this persistent interest in a Village boy. He's beneath you and you will not continue this liaison.'

'You're not my father! You can't tell me who I see and who I don't!' she retorted, to Miranda's dismay.

'I am the magus and what I say goes,' he said quietly.

'Why? Why should you dictate everything? That's what you are – a dictator! Like Hitler or Stalin.'

'SYLVIE! How dare you speak to Magus like that! You apologise now or—'

'It's alright,' he said, although Sylvie noticed a muscle in his cheek twitching tightly. 'She doesn't know what she's saying.'

'Yes I do! I want to know what you've done to Yul. Where is he? Why are you punishing him like this? You can't go around acting like God!'

'I can, actually,' he murmured.

'Mum! How can you even listen to this rubbish? What's

happened to you? You used to believe in equality and justice, yet you stand by while an innocent boy is punished just for being my friend! You're brainwashed!'

'I'm sorry, Magus, she's not herself,' gabbled Miranda, horribly embarrassed by her daughter's passionate outburst.

'I think she should go to her room,' said Magus coldly. 'We don't tolerate children speaking to adults like this at Stonewylde. If she doesn't like the order of things here, she's free to leave. If she wishes to stay, she'll do as she's told. And she's being told to forget the Village boy.'

With that he stalked out of the cottage, and Miranda had the most blazing row with her wilful daughter.

But Sylvie didn't forget the Village boy. She couldn't. She was haunted by visions and dreams which pursued her even in daylight. She began to have nightmares about a strange and terrifying place. It was made of stone, littered with boulders and the bones of ancient creatures. In this place of bones and rock lurked evil; a malevolence so monstrous it made her quake. It had been sleeping, lying dormant, but now it had awoken and was yawning and flexing. She knew that soon it would go in for the kill. Yul was in terrible danger. She must find him and help him escape.

As soon as she was well enough Sylvie began to go out walking again, determined to regain her health and vitality. It was different in the woods knowing Yul wasn't there; that he wouldn't materialise from behind a tree, grinning at her with twigs and leaves in his hair and a smudge of lichen on his cheek. One day she heard men's voices and came across Greenbough with a couple of the woodsmen. Sylvie thought that maybe he'd know what had happened to Yul, but he shook his head sadly.

'Sorry, miss. I know he were taken up to the Hall and that brute of a father gave him a terrible whipping. Every night down the pub he talks o' nothing else. Right proud of himself, he is. That man's the one who should be whipped, the bloody great porker! Yul's a good lad and we miss him in the woods. I hope 'tisn't too long afore he's back with us again.'

Sylvie's face crumpled at the thought of Yul's suffering and the old man patted her arm kindly.

'You could try Tom up at the stables, miss. He might've heard something.'

But Tom didn't know any more than Greenbough. He still felt guilty that he'd stood by and let the cruelty to Yul go unchallenged. He'd never forget the shocking and pitiful sight of the boy stumbling out of the byre after his five day ordeal and being made to wash in the yard. He too shook his head, trying to banish the awful image of that battered, almost unrecognisable figure from his mind.

'All I know is Magus took him off in the Land Rover and he weren't away for that long, so I don't reckon he's gone far. Somewhere on the estate I'm sure.'

'I do hope so,' she said. 'This punishment is for being my friend, and it's so wrong!'

'Aye, miss, I've always respected Magus but this ain't right. That boy didn't deserve what they done to him. If you find out anything of his whereabouts, do let me know. I want to help him, like I should've done when I had the chance. I'll not forgive myself for that.'

Sylvie's worry was that Magus had taken Yul to the main gates and handed him over to someone waiting there. But somehow she thought she'd have known if he'd left Stonewylde. She was sure her nightmares were a clue to his whereabouts. In the end it was gossip in the Dining Hall that led her to find him. She overheard some older Hallfolk talking one lunch time.

'Did you know? Magus has opened up Quarrycleave! He spoke about it this morning.'

'Opened Quarrycleave? Well I never! I thought the place was closed for good after what happened there – that terrible accident.'

'Magus said it's all perfectly safe now with the modern technology we have today.'

'Why's he opened it up?'

'He needs stone for his building projects. And the first phase, he said, is a new Village school to cope with all the children. But I heard other talk too. Apparently he's going to build some new accommodation for Hallfolk – holiday homes for the visitors.'

'Well, he's got to do something about the squash. There's barely room now with all the extra visitors for the Solstice, and there're more coming next week. We're too crowded.'

'I know – trust Magus to come up with such a good idea. Mind you, if he hasn't even got the stone out of the ground yet, we're in for a bit of a wait.'

Sylvie thought about it and realised that the place of her nightmares, with its massive boulders and cliffs, could well be a quarry. But how to find out if Yul was there? She would just have to ask Magus directly. She was scared of him, but she also felt a dangerous thrill of excitement in defying him. He was far too used to everyone jumping to obey him. And despite his implied threats, she didn't think he'd make her leave the community. She went straight to his office.

'For goodness sake, Sylvie,' he said irritably, annoyed when he realised the purpose of her intrusion. 'What is it you don't understand? He's a Villager, you're Hallfolk and you don't mix. It's very simple.'

'I just want to know where he is and if he's alright. Is he at the quarry? I can't stop worrying until I know.'

'But it's not your place to worry about him! He's nothing to you. He's just a Village boy who's got himself into trouble through his bad behaviour. He's being knocked back down to size and it's really none of your business.'

'It is my business. He's my friend.'

He groaned, shaking his head and glaring at her in exasperation, infuriated by her stubbornness.

'Listen, you stupid girl! He can never be your friend. He isn't good enough for you.'

'Yes he is!'

'No he isn't! You should be mixing with the Hallfolk. There are plenty of attractive boys up here.'

'It's not the fact that he's a boy.'

'Oh I think it is, Sylvie. Don't kid yourself that this is anything other than pure animal attraction. He's a good-looking boy, I'll give him that, but he's also an ignorant lout. You're far too well-educated for a yokel like him.'

'And whose fault is it if he's ignorant and un-educated? Who was it decided that Villagers should finish their education at thirteen? And even when they're in school, they're not taught to read and write. If I was in charge here, I'd make sure everyone had an equal, proper education.'

'Fortunately you're not in charge,' he replied coldly. 'And never will be. Anyway, he was given a chance of a better education, along with every other child at Stonewylde, but he proved unworthy.'

'Hah! That's just where you're wrong! He deliberately failed the tests, all of them.'

'He would say that, wouldn't he?'

'Not if he was really stupid. He could've passed the tests but he didn't want to leave his family.'

'Then he can't have wanted a proper education very much, can he?'

'That's not true! It was because of his father. Yul was scared of what Alwyn would do to them if he wasn't there to take the worst of it.'

'Pathos as well. He's very cunning.'

Sylvie glared at him, seething at his intractability. She refused to back down. Her chest rose and fell fast as her fury at the injustice mounted, her voice becoming shrill.

'Where is he, Magus? What have you done with him? I won't give up until you've told me the truth!'

And now he became angry too. His velvety black eyes glittered dangerously as he stared down at the defiant girl facing him.

'You *will* give up if you care for the boy like you say you do. I forbid any kind of liaison between you and him. Absolutely forbid it. You can rant and rave as much as you want but that's the bottom line. I am the law here whether you like it or not.

Accept my authority or leave the community – it's as simple as that.'

'Really? You'd throw me and my mother out?'

'If you won't accept my rules, yes! I'm warning you now so there's no misunderstanding. And if I find you've been consorting with Yul when he returns, I'll punish him all over again, but even harder.'

'You are the—'

'When he does come back and you see what he's been through and how he's changed, you'll understand just how unfair it would be to inflict that on him again. So stop being selfish and start mixing with Hallfolk who are your equals. *Is that clear?*'

If he'd hoped to intimidate her with his anger, he'd under-estimated Sylvie. Her light-grey eyes with their startling dark rims blazed at him. Her mouth was tight and quivering.

'That's very clear! But you still haven't told me where he is. Do I have to visit the quarry myself to find out if he's there? Because I will! I *know* he's in danger and I'm not letting this go until you've told me the truth!'

Magus moved so quickly that she jumped with fright, thinking he would strike her. Instead he grabbed her arm and marched her to the door. His wrath at her refusal to bend to his will seethed all around him. His face was white with it.

'You've asked for this, young lady. Come with me!'

'Come where? What are you doing?'

He hustled her down the corridor and through the busy entrance hall. People turned to stare at the sight of Magus, his face a mask of fury as he yanked Sylvie along beside him. He strode round the side of the Hall towards the stable block where all the vehicles were kept.

'Are you going to punish me as well? Let go of my arm! You're hurting me.'

He released her abruptly and continued towards the yard.

'I'm taking you to see him!'

'So is he at the quarry?'

'Yes he is at the bloody quarry! And when you've seen him

maybe you'll stop this whinging and whining and realise what a stupid mistake you're making.'

Sylvie gave a small smile of victory as he wrenched open the door of the Land Rover and bundled her inside. He drove from the Hall at an alarming speed and she hung onto the seat as the Land Rover bounced up the track. She glanced across at him and saw the rigid set of his jaw, the thin line of his mouth. He glared at her and she was blasted by the fire in his eyes.

'I'll show you just what's happened to Yul! That boy has really suffered, and largely because of you. I've never seen anyone take punishment of that magnitude with such courage, and all to protect *your* secret.'

'Poor Yul! How could you do this, Magus? How could you treat someone so cruelly?'

'Don't you try to blame *me*, missy! This is *your* fault! You've given him ideas above his station. He was perfectly happy until you came here, but now he's a broken wreck. Believe me, he won't want anything more to do with you when he gets back.'

As they drove further along the ridgeway, Magus started to calm down. Sylvie felt a lessening of tension in the air as he mastered his anger. Now it was over, she was amazed at her own boldness. If she hadn't been so angry herself she'd never have dared stand up to him like that. But now she began to dread what she'd find at the quarry. Was Yul really broken? Would he want nothing more to do with her?

'I heard you were opening up the quarry to build a new school,' she said tentatively.

He glanced at her and his lips twisted in an attempted smile.

'Yes, that's right. No point bringing in materials from the Outside when we have such abundance already here. The Hall and Great Barn and several other buildings are made of stone from this quarry. St Paul's Cathedral and great chunks of London are built of Portland stone, which is famous for its beauty and strength, and the stone from our quarry is almost identical. We're very fortunate to share the same geological strata and formation as Portland. Although not surprising really as we're on the Jurassic Coast too.'

'Why was the quarry closed in the first place? I heard some Hallfolk say something about an accident there. Was that the reason?'

Magus nodded.

'Quarrycleave has always had its dark history. Many people are terrified of the place, Yul included. You should have seen him when I brought him here last week. He actually cried with fear.'

His lips twitched at the memory and Sylvie felt a stab of pure hatred. How had she ever thought this man kind and gentle?

'I can't understand it myself,' he continued obliviously. 'I've always loved the place. At Quarrycleave there's a sense of ancient power, ancient magic. It's been quarried for centuries, possibly even thousands of years, if our professor's research is to be believed. Apparently there's evidence of Neolithic workings, and some macabre discoveries too: human sacrifice, battles, ceremonial rituals. All sort of things have been unearthed at Quarrycleave.'

'I think I've dreamed about this place.'

'But you haven't even been there! It does have a strange, dream-like atmosphere, I must say. And there're the fossils too. Dinosaur footprints, like those at Portland and Purbeck, and dinosaur bones like the ones found at Charmouth and Lyme Regis. Even fossilised trees. If those Jurassic Heritage people found out, the place would be crawling with bloody tourists and fossil hunters. Fortunately it's private land and I intend to keep it that way.'

'So what happened then to close the quarry?'

'There was a serious accident about a hundred and fifty years ago. They were blasting and apparently there was a terrible rock fall. Many quarrymen were trapped underneath and the lucky ones crushed to death. Most were buried alive.'

'That's horrific!'

'Yes, and there was more ... I can't remember all the details. But a lot of it's mere superstition. An evil spirit that walks the quarry taking lives, or some such nonsense. I remember talk of it when I was a boy, when I used to come up here for fun. The Villagers were always terrified of Quarrycleave and its predator – the beast that stalks, they called it. You know how gullible and ignorant these people can be. But I was conceived up there, I've been told.'

'Really? How weird.'

'My father loved the place too. He brought my mother there one Moon Fullness at the Autumn Equinox. There's a special stone, right at the head of the quarry, carved with serpents all writhing around it. That's where he took her to make love.'

Sylvie was silent, remembering the stone at Mooncliffe where Magus had taken her mother. He glanced at her and smiled.

'I gather you've heard about our custom here and how we celebrate the Moon Fullness? It's strange I know, but so is the magic of Stonewylde. It defies logic and reason. Remember how I healed you, Sylvie? You can't deny the power of the Earth Magic. It's all around us and it's strong at Quarrycleave too, if a little different. And here we are.'

Sylvie gasped at her first sight of the great white quarry. It was a desolate lunar landscape. As they pulled to a halt by the caravans, she too felt fear tiptoe down her spine. This definitely was the place of her nightmares. How had Yul endured a week here already?

'Follow me,' said Magus, striding off the litter-strewn grass and down into the mouth where the raw stone began. The air was thick with pale stone-dust as dumper trucks tipped their loads into a great heap.

'That's the waste, the backfill we're clearing,' shouted Magus over the din. 'It'll be crushed and used for the foundations of the buildings and for the road too. I'll need to rebuild the road properly to allow the lorries to get into the Village with their loads of stone. They used horse and cart in the old days but that'll take far too long.'

They picked their way through the white, chaotic graveyard, avoiding the trucks and the bedraggled men caked in chalky dust. There was a terrible noise pounding continuously and Sylvie felt the ground trembling beneath her feet.

'The core driller,' yelled Magus. 'We're taking samples all over the place to locate the best stone. It removes a plug of rock so we can analyse the depth and quality. They're establishing the working faces too. After the accident I told you about, all the records of the quarry work were destroyed so now we're starting again from scratch. Ah, here's Jackdaw.'

Sylvie shrank at the sight of the man approaching. His bright blue eyes with their tiny pinpoint pupils fixed on her and he leered, a gold tooth gleaming amongst a broken row of brown stained ones.

'Now there's a sight for sore eyes, guv!' he said. 'Keep her on a short lead with all these foreigners about. They ain't seen a woman in ages. And neither've I.'

Magus gave him a steely look and the man dropped his piercing gaze.

'We've come to see Yul. I want a word with him.'

'Right. You'll be pleased with the result so far. Knocked the cockiness out of him like I said I would. He can't obey me fast enough, and I ain't done yet. He'll be licking my boots when I've finished with him.'

He laughed harshly and Sylvie felt her anger rising again. What had they done to Yul?

'Bring him over then,' said Magus.

'I'll call him down. He's up there – see, up that rock face? We got to clear away the ivy so we can see the stone. Bloody stuff clings to the rock everywhere and it's a hard job getting it off. The only way is to climb up and hack it away by hand.'

Sylvie saw then a figure high up, swarming amongst the ivy and armed with a glinting blade. He was coated in white dust, hair and clothes caked with it. Was that Yul? She squinted through the haze of dust and bright light that bounced off the exposed stones. How could he bear to work here? It was a terrible place – noisy, violent and chokingly dusty. The core driller stopped its relentless hammering and Jackdaw put his fingers in his mouth and whistled. The figure up high stopped and turned its face towards them. Sylvie gulped. She'd never have recognised him.

Jackdaw laughed again.

'Trained him like a dog to the whistle. Go fetch. Sit up and beg. Come to heel. He knows all the tricks now.'

He whistled again and beckoned. The figure began to shin down the rock face rapidly, slithering through the glossy ivy. He jumped the last few feet of the drop and ran towards them, slowing as he approached. He bowed his head and kept it down, his steps faltering as he reached them, and stopped at a respectful distance. Sylvie was horrified at the sight of him. His thin body was cowed and stooping. Gone was the defiant tilt of his chin, the proud bearing. His thick dark hair was matted and stiff with white dust. She couldn't see his face at all, for he stared doggedly at the ground.

'Blessings, Yul,' said Magus softly, a smile on his lips. Sylvie swallowed hard. The boy raised his head slightly to look the master in the eye. She saw then the terrible aftermath of the beating. Although the swelling had gone down considerably, his face was still misshapen and covered with ugly bruising. His eyes were frightened. He ignored her completely.

'Sir,' he mumbled, bowing his head again as if unable to bear looking at them.

'I've brought you a visitor, Yul,' Magus continued. 'Someone who's been thinking of you and wanting to see you. Even though I've explained to her how inappropriate any form of friendship is between the two of you.'

There was a silence.

'Where's your manners, boy?' growled Jackdaw and raised his hand menacingly. Yul flinched instantly, cowering from the threatened blow. Sylvie couldn't bear it. She stepped forward slightly, stretching out her hand as one might to a frightened creature.

'I'm sorry, Yul. I just wanted to know if you were okay. I was worried what they'd done to you.'

He nodded but didn't raise his face or look her in the eye.

'So now you've seen,' said Magus smugly. 'And now you realise how Yul feels about the friendship. It's ended and he wants nothing more to do with you. Isn't that right, Yul?'

The boy nodded.

'I didn't hear you!'

Yul raised his head and his deep grey eyes looked full at the master's face, pleading silently for release.

'Yes, sir, that's right.'

Magus chuckled and turned away, saying something to Jackdaw. Sylvie looked at Yul still standing there, unsure whether he'd been dismissed or not. He darted a quick glance at her and she felt, in that moment, the full force of his misery. Her throat constricted and tears sprang to her eyes, spilling onto her cheeks. She turned away and stumbled back to the Land Rover. She shut herself inside, trying to stifle her sobs. She saw the two men turn back and notice Yul standing there with his head bowed. Jackdaw cuffed him hard, shouting belligerently in his face, and the boy went scurrying back to the ivy-clad rock face. Sylvie buried her face in her hands and cried.

She resisted all attempts at conversation on the return journey, sitting in hunched silence. Magus finally pulled up in front of the Hall, turned off the engine and faced her.

'Well? Satisfied now?'

'I hate you,' she said quietly.

He laughed.

'No you don't, Sylvie. You just don't like being beaten, but you'll get over it. Remember who brought you here and who healed you? You don't really hate me at all.'

She shook her head.

'When's his ordeal over? When'll the punishment end?'

'I said two weeks. That'll be the nineteenth. But it's just before the Summer Solstice and I'll be too busy to go around collecting waifs and strays. He can miss the Solstice holiday and I'll collect him afterwards.'

'That's not fair. Why can't Jackdaw bring him back?'

He chuckled at this.

'You don't know Jackdaw's history! He can't just appear in the Village – there'd be a riot. I'm going to reintegrate him, but it's got to be done gradually. So no, Sylvie, Jackdaw won't be bringing Yul back.'

'But why should he miss the festival? It's unfair.'

'Yes, life's like that. A shame you can't drive or you could go and collect him yourself. But never mind. A few more days at Quarrycleave won't do him any harm. He's shaping up nicely, isn't he? Jackdaw's done an excellent job where we left off. Between us all – me, Jackdaw and Alwyn – we've finally broken Yul.'

He chuckled again, and Sylvie opened the car door and stepped out onto the gravel. She turned back, and fixed Magus with her pale-grey gaze. Her hands trembled and heart thumped in her chest.

'Three men to break one boy? Wow, Magus, you must feel so proud of yourself.'

18

The visit from Magus and Sylvie upset Yul a great deal. He'd been trying to block everything from his mind, all thoughts and memories, and concentrate on getting through each day and night. Life was as bad as it could be. He couldn't imagine anything worse than this, and it took all his energy and willpower to survive.

He'd have died so many times by now, if his concentration had lapsed for even a moment. There was no safety equipment, and the men employed had little knowledge of what they were doing and no sense of responsibility. Yul was given many dangerous jobs and knew, each time he climbed up the ivy-smothered faces or crawled between crevices and boulders, that his life might be claimed. He felt death breathing down his neck, despair lurking around each rock, and it took every drop of willpower to keep himself safe and alive.

Seeing Sylvie brought it all back to him. She'd stood there clean and shining in her pretty summer dress, out of place in this filthy pit of death. Her moonstone eyes had blazed with love and pity and it had almost undone him. He couldn't afford any softness, any feeling, any relaxing of the iron control which was all that stood between his life and his death.

He'd already decided that if he survived this ordeal, Sylvie would have to be nothing more to him than a beautiful memory. They couldn't have any sort of friendship without antagonising Magus, and Yul had no intention of ever doing that again. He'd work hard in the woods with Greenbough and the men, keep out of any Hallfolk's way, and as for Alwyn . . . he was still hoping Mother Heggy would find a way to deal with him. Without his father at home, life would be peaceful and pleasant. Heart-breaking though it would be to lose her, Sylvie would play no part in it and he'd finally accepted that. Until today, when he was reminded of just what he'd be missing.

As he collected soiled clothes from the mucky caravan floors and stuffed them into black plastic bin liners, Yul thought of home and the approaching Summer Solstice. The great bonfire in the Stone Circle would be built, and they'd have found another boy light and agile enough to climb to the top with sticks and lichen to fill the gaps. Yul knew that this was the most special of all fires, to mark the day when the sun stood still briefly, before starting the journey back towards winter.

Yul had always felt glad when the effigies of wicker men were burnt at this festival, symbolising the moment when the Oak King was superseded by the Holly King. As a child of the Winter Solstice, he'd always identified with the Holly King. In the Village School right now, children would be soaking the withies, bending the pliable stalks and weaving their wicker men. Dances would be practised, the women would be baking and preparing food, the artists painting the stones in the Circle. Everyone would be happy and excited getting ready for the biggest festival of the year and the week-long Midsummer Holiday that followed.

Yul closed his eyes for a moment, ignoring the stink of the filthy caravan and the rank smell of unwashed men. He wished with all his heart that he were home now. He imagined himself standing on the Village Green surrounded by the great trees, the sound of wood pigeons calling softly, people he'd known all his life busy in the Great Barn or sitting on benches outside the Jack in the Green sipping cider. He hoped desperately that he'd be allowed home for the festival but had his doubts. He knew Jackdaw wouldn't want to lose him at the quarry, for he worked very hard and certainly made Jackdaw's life easier. Why would the man go out of his way to let Yul go?

Right now all the men lounged around on deck chairs outside the caravans, playing cards and enjoying their beer and cigarettes. Their day's work was done and now they relaxed and waited for their meal, which consisted mainly of heated-up catering tins of food. Yul's work however was far from done. Jackdaw had loaded him with enough duties to keep him occupied until everyone went to bed. Whilst everyone relaxed, Yul rushed around doing his jobs knowing that if he took too long, there'd be nothing left to eat but dry bread.

When he'd collected everyone's dirty clothes he must load the bags into Jackdaw's truck, before emptying the foul toilets and sweeping out the caravans. Stone-dust coated every surface and it was hard to keep it at bay. After he'd eaten, he'd wash all the dishes and clear the cooking mess away. Then he'd sort out the clean washing returned from an Outside laundry, making sure each man had clothes for the morning. When they'd all gone to bed, he'd clear up the beer cans and rubbish they'd left lying about outside and ensure the kitchen caravan was ready for breakfast in the morning.

If Yul forgot anything or didn't do something properly, he'd be beaten. Jackdaw needed little excuse to unbuckle his belt and lay into him. He was always careful to stop short of incapacitating Yul for work, but as the flayed mess on the boy's back started to heal, Jackdaw became less worried about it. Yul's jobs were never-ending and there was no one else who could do them all; Jackdaw wouldn't give him up easily. Yul dragged the heavy bin liners outside bitterly, knowing that the Summer Solstice was just a dream, and Sylvie a complete impossibility.

Sylvie couldn't face dinner in the Dining Hall. The place heaved with ever more Hallfolk who were arriving daily for the imminent festival. She hated the noise and chaos, people greeting each other and bursting with their news, catching up with each other's lives and acting as if they owned the place. Sylvie found she resented them, especially the way some of them looked at her as if she didn't belong. So she skipped dinner and made her way to the track leading to the tumbledown cottage. She knew where to find the help she needed.

Mother Heggy sat asleep in her rocking chair, her mouth hanging open to reveal her shrivelled gums. The crow perched on the chair back and surveyed Sylvie with jewelled eyes. She waited quietly in the corner by the hearth, not wishing to disturb the old woman, and looked around the cottage with interest. This was a place of magic and healing, with bunches of herbs and plants hung everywhere. On the ancient scrubbed table lay a sharp knife and chopping board, and a pestle and mortar. Mother Heggy might be very old but she still practised her craft.

'Ah, 'tis my little one! I knew you'd come today.'

Sylvie rose and kissed her withered cheek.

'So you also know why I've come, Mother Heggy?'

The crone nodded.

'He's at the place of bones and death, as I told you. You must get him out.'

'I saw him today. Magus took me up there to show me how he's suffering.'

Mother Heggy spat into the corner and the crow flapped its wings.

'And there's another there? He's returned?'

'You mean Jackdaw? Yes, he was there. Oh Mother Heggy, I can't bear it!'

She burst into tears. Heggy left her to cry for a while and eventually Sylvie sniffed and wiped her eyes.

'I'm sorry. That's not going to help him. What must I do?'

'You are the saviour. You must bring him back for the Solstice sunrise. The Holly King must take his rightful place in the dance or all will be lost.'

Sylvie nodded. She felt a sense of destiny unfolding, which gave her the courage to defy Magus.

'What exactly should I do?'

'You must go to him when the time is right. You'll know when. You'll lead him out of that stone graveyard and back to life and

290

safety. You'll be the bright light in his darkness. 'Tis a long way, my silver one, and you must travel far.'

A shiver chased down Sylvie's bare arms as understanding dawned; Clip had known all along.

'But I don't know if Yul will come with me. He's not the same as he was. If you could see what they've done to him ... he's lost his spirit.'

'Yul will never lose his spirit! Blue and red, he is the one. Conceived under a Blue Moon, born under a red moon. You are the brightness to his darkness. You must rekindle the fire in his soul. You will do it, my little one, and you're the only one who can. 'Tis why you're here and you know this in your heart.'

'Yes, I do know. I can feel this pull between us and it's so powerful. I don't have any choice in the matter – I *have* to help him. I just hope he'll be strong enough.'

'Aye, I'll make up something to revive him. Collect it from my doorstep before you go on your journey. And there's something else – a cake. 'Twill be wrapped in rhubarb leaves. Take it on the same day but hide it away and give it to Yul. 'Tis for Alwyn and only Alwyn, to be eaten on the day of the Solstice. Make sure Yul understands that.'

Sylvie sighed; she was scared about the journey and terrified of defying Magus. But now she'd seen Yul, in all his misery and fear, she'd somehow find the strength and courage to save him.

'Will everything be alright, Mother Heggy? Will it work out in the end? I know you can see these things.'

The old woman shook her head and sucked her gums.

'I see only glimpses. And nought is set in stone, despite our trying and our wanting. Sometimes I see what could happen, not what will happen. You are both up against powerful forces. That man, Solstice – eh, he is so strong. He has great power and he's clever with it. I tried once, long ago, and I couldn't stop him, only hold him at bay. I paid a forfeit for that, right enough. 'Twill not be easy, the path that lies ahead.'

Sylvie nodded, and then remembered the other issue that worried her.

'Mother Heggy, Magus knows I'm moongazy. Yul must've told him.'

''Twas to be expected he'd find out. Moongaziness cannot be hidden for long. But now you must beware of him for he will be after the magic you bring. He knew you were special – 'tis the reason he brought you here – and now he understands why. You have the moon energy and he has the power of the magus, the Earth Magic of Stonewylde. He will want them joined.'

'Joined? In what way?'

Mother Heggy rocked harder and the crow squawked and flapped frantically, before falling into her lap in a bundle of feathers. She stroked the bird lovingly and looked Sylvie in the eye.

'In the joining way, my bright one. Be very careful o' that man. 'Tis Yul who is the one, he who is the darkness to your brightness. Nobody else, however you may be tempted. Remember that.'

'I will, Mother Heggy. I know Magus is wicked and cruel, even though he healed me. I've seen his true colours now and he doesn't fool me. How on earth am I going to moondance at Hare Stone with Yul beside me now? I don't want Magus to see me moongazy.'

'We must hope the Triple Goddess will protect you when you're under her spell.'

'The Triple Goddess?'

'The Maiden, the Mother and the Crone – our Lady of the Moon. The Maiden is the silver bow of the huntress, the Mother is fertile and giving, the circle of life itself, and the Crone is wisdom and the darkness of death. For us women, 'tis the measure of our months and our lives.'

'I'm the Maiden and you're the Crone!'

'Aye, that's the truth. We're part of the same power, you and I, although I was ever drawn to the Dark Goddess, not the Bright one. But you are just starting your magic, and I am at the end of mine. Tomorrow is the Dark Moon and you'll start to bleed.'

'No!'

'Aye, you'll become a woman, a maiden huntress. Here, I made a little potion for you, if the cramps are painful.'

She put the crow on the table and shuffled off to a cupboard, producing a tiny bottle stoppered with a cork.

'Drink it when the bleeding starts properly. 'Twill ease the discomfort. Now you must go. Remember to collect the things from my step for Yul. And be brave, for you are the huntress and scared of no man. Magus knows your power and he will be careful.'

'Thank you, Mother Heggy.'

Sylvie kissed her leathery cheek again and the crow hopped up onto Sylvie's shoulder, gently pecking at her hair. Mother Heggy cackled at this.

'Take the crow with you. He's my messenger and 'tis good that he knows where you live. Blessings to you, child.'

Sylvie left the cottage with the crow on her shoulder, but once outside he flew off and flapped ahead of her all the way home, stopping and waiting on trees and posts for her to catch up. He seemed to already know where she lived, and at the cottage he flew up to her bedroom window and sat on the windowsill, preening himself.

Mother Heggy was right. The next morning Sylvie discovered she was indeed starting her first period. She rushed into her mother's room, very excited. Miranda hugged her.

'Hey, Mum, we can go down to the Great Barn together, can't we?'

'Well, I haven't actually started mine yet. But I'll walk down with you. I'm so proud of you, Sylvie! What a special day – my little girl becoming a woman!'

Although nothing could match the embarrassment of the previous month when she'd been left behind at the Hall, Sylvie felt shy going into the Great Barn. But she was warmly received by the many women already there.

'Do come over and sit with us, the pair of you,' called a Village

293

woman whom Miranda recognised from her recent visit to the Nursery.

'I haven't started yet,' said Miranda, having learned the protocol of the Dark Moon Gatherings. 'So I'm going home now, but I expect I'll be down later.'

There was some tongue clicking at this and Sylvie saw one woman wink across at another. She knew exactly what they were thinking, for it was what she'd thought herself. Had Yul been right? Had Magus succeeded in making Miranda pregnant up at Mooncliffe on the night of the Blue Moon?

By the time Sylvie's first period was over, the Summer Solstice had almost arrived. The women grumbled at the inconvenience of the Dark Moon coming just before a major festival when there was so much to do. During her time spent in the Great Barn, Sylvie had learned all about the Summer Solstice festival at Stonewylde, the biggest celebration of them all, falling at a time when the weather was usually fine and warm. Starting on Solstice Eve, the week-long festivities were given over to sports events, craft displays and competitions, swimming galas down at the beach, and daily picnics out in the open air. It was also Magus's birthday, which added to the holiday excitement.

Miranda hadn't joined the women in the Barn, but explained that her last period had been very early and she'd probably reverted to her old cycle. Sylvie knew better, but had other things on her mind to worry about – how to get to Quarrycleave and set Yul free. Every day more Hallfolk arrived for the festival, and on the nineteenth of June, the students and teachers would return from Exeter. Sylvie decided this would be a good day for the rescue, when everyone's attention was on the homecoming students. Yul must be back by Solstice Eve on the twentieth, ready for sunrise the following morning. She went to the library to look for a map of the estate.

She found some beautiful hand-drawn maps, meticulously coloured and labelled, and realised what a distance it was to Quarrycleave. She'd have to allow plenty of time and she hoped

Yul would be strong enough for the long walk home. She knew he was tough, but the thin, cowering boy she'd seen at the quarry was not the same person who'd won the tree-climbing competition at Beltane, ridden Nightwing along the ridgeway and carried her back through the woods on the night of the Blue Moon. He was weak and beaten now. The journey could be too much for him.

Poring over the map, Sylvie decided to follow the ridgeway westwards for several miles before cutting over the hills to the north and across the other side to Quarrycleave, tucked up in the far north-west corner of the estate. She couldn't follow the easier route the Land Rover had taken, nor the tarmac road route up to the Gatehouse and along the top of the hills in case someone was out driving that day. She'd never walked that far in her life and wondered if she'd make it there and back herself, never mind Yul.

Sylvie had just rolled up the maps and returned them to the shelf when Magus walked into the library, shutting the door behind him. He came over and looked down at her, gauging her mood. Then he smiled, but it didn't reach his dark eyes.

'I gather congratulations are in order.'

'What?'

'I hear you've started menstruating.'

She blushed at this.

'And just before your fifteenth birthday. You'll be an adult before you know it.'

'I'll never take part in that disgusting Rite of Adulthood ceremony, if that's what you're thinking,' she retorted sharply. 'And talking of menstruation, I'm sure you'll also have heard that my mother didn't. So your "picnic" at Mooncliffe was successful, it seems.'

He grimaced and took her arm, guiding her over to the deep window seat; the same place he'd sat with Miranda when he'd asked her to stay permanently at Stonewylde.

'It's time we talked, Sylvie. You're so hostile and negative towards me and I know who's the cause of that. Of course I'm delighted that your mother may be carrying my child, although it's very early days and we mustn't jump to conclusions. But there's no need to be nasty to me about it. Unless you're jealous?'

'Jealous? Don't be ridiculous – I'd love a little brother or sister! I just hate to see my mother being taken for a fool. She's mad about you, but you don't love her or even really care for her.'

'Of course I care for her!'

'Not in the way she needs. You just wanted to impregnate her. It's horrible – so cold-blooded.'

'There was nothing cold-blooded about it, I can assure you,' he said dryly.

'Maybe not the act itself, but the planning behind it, coming back specially for the Blue Moon like that. You're like a great spider sitting in its web, manipulating everything around you.'

He laughed at this and shook his head.

'I'm not going to win you over easily, am I? I don't like your rudeness and if you ever speak to me like that when other people are present, I shall have to cut you down to size. But between you and me, Sylvie, I do like your spirit. You're brave and loyal and those are qualities I admire.'

She shrugged, dismissing his compliments, and glared at him.

'I misjudged you when you first came here,' he continued. 'I knew you were special, but you seemed so timid and meek, such a little mouse. How wrong could I have been? There's a spark in you that I like very much, even though you infuriate me too.'

'When's Yul coming back?'

He groaned. 'Oh for Goddess' sake, you're not still going on about him? You've seen the state of him, and that was a week ago. He'll be much worse now after another week of hard labour in the quarry and Jackdaw's rough treatment. Can't you leave the boy alone? He said he wanted nothing more to do with you, remember?'

'Of course – I'll never forget it. Nor shall I ever forget your cruelty.'

'It's not cruelty, Sylvie, it's how Stonewylde society works. Yul broke our laws and had to be punished. His father gave him a very thorough whipping the night we found him in that hut in the woods, and was keen to whip Yul again. If I'd sent Yul home, he would've done. So I've actually done Yul a favour by taking him up to Quarrycleave for a fortnight.'

'Oh please!' Sylvie rolled her eyes. 'I'm not stupid, you know.'

'No, you're not, which is why I can't understand your persistence. If you feel any sort of sympathy for the boy, leave him alone.'

'All I want to know is this – are you intending to collect him before the Solstice, when his two weeks is up?'

'No, Sylvie,' he replied wearily. 'I've already explained this. I'll be too busy. I'll collect him after the midsummer holiday. That's my final word.'

'Thank you. That's all I wanted to know.'

On the morning of the nineteenth, Sylvie awoke early to the sound of querulous cawing outside her window. It was Mother Heggy's crow. He stayed a while, pecking at his wing feathers, and then flew away. But his message was clear and Sylvie understood that the things were ready to collect from the doorstep, so she dashed up to the cottage before breakfast. She spent a busy morning organising everything she needed for the journey and packed a bag carefully, conscious of the weight she must carry and noticing how fine and clear the day was. It would be hot and she must take enough water for both days.

Sylvie was very nervous, scared that something terrible would happen. She could get lost or sprain an ankle. Magus or Jackdaw could discover her. She might have no opportunity at the quarry to rescue Yul, with all the men about. But she had to trust to destiny. Hadn't two magical people both foretold she'd travel on a journey and was destined to be a saviour?

Miranda was distracted that morning, still waiting for her period, and barely noticed Sylvie. She certainly wasn't checking up on her, particularly as Yul was safely out of the way. Sylvie said she must practise a Solstice dance with the Hallfolk girls and would stay the night in the girls' wing at the Hall, and Miranda accepted the plausible story without question. Sylvie had earlier hidden the salves and potions from Mother Heggy in a cupboard at the Hall, and the cake wrapped in rhubarb leaves was concealed safely under her bed in Woodland Cottage.

Magus left Stonewylde at midday and would be home that evening with the students. If their return was anything like their departure, nobody would notice her absence in the chaos. Cherry's sister, Marigold the cook, had packed her a picnic and hadn't asked many questions; like everyone who worked at the Hall, she was so very busy. Cherry was up to her eyes organising bedrooms and laundry for the many guests, assisted by an army of extra servants drafted up daily from the Village. Marigold and her kitchen staff struggled to cater for the vast number of extra mouths to feed, particularly as for many of the visitors, the delicious organic food at Stonewylde was a highlight of their stay. Sylvie felt sorry for all the Villagers who had to work so hard during the holiday.

It was early afternoon when she finally left the Hall. The backpack was bulky and heavy and she worried it was too much to carry. But everything inside was needed; she'd packed no extras. She left by a side door, cutting over a lawn towards a path leading into the hills of the ridgeway. She'd only gone a little way across the lawn when she heard a familiar voice.

'Going somewhere, Sylvie?'

Holly and Rainbow sat under a tree by the lawn and Sylvie's heart sank.

'Just a walk. It's too crowded here.'

'Looks like a long walk with all that gear on your back. Where are you going?'

She stared at Holly's pretty little face, her brown eyes bright with curiosity. This was the first time Holly had spoken to her in ages. Maybe she was ready to make up.

'I'm not sure. Just wandering wherever my feet take me.'

'How poetic. You're not running away then?'

'No, of course not.'

'Don't you know they're all coming back today?' asked Rainbow, busy weaving a daisy chain into her long hair. 'Don't you want to be here when they arrive?'

'Well, yes. I mean . . . I'll see them later, I'm sure.'

'It's not very friendly though, is it, Sylvie?' said Rainbow. 'We'll be waiting for them by the porch and I've made a huge "Welcome Home" banner.'

'You haven't really integrated into our world at all, have you?' said Holly. 'You're not one of the Hallfolk, not one of us in any way. Several of the visitors have wondered what on earth you're doing here. I couldn't enlighten them because I have no idea myself.'

Sylvie frowned at her. So much for being ready to make up.

'Don't get nasty with me again, Holly,' she said. 'Just because Buzz isn't coming back there's no need to take it out on me.'

Holly's eyes glittered at this and her mouth became mean.

'And I bet if he was coming back today, you wouldn't be disappearing off like this!' she said. 'You'd be waiting at the door with your tongue hanging out, and—'

'I can't be bothered to listen to you,' said Sylvie firmly. 'See you later.'

'I hope you fall down a rabbit hole and break your ankle!' called Holly.

'Or sit on a viper and get your backside bitten!' yelled Rainbow.

'Why don't you both grow up?' retorted Sylvie, marching off to the sound of their mocking laughter.

She tried to put the unpleasant scene behind her as she slowly climbed up into the hills of the ridgeway. She really disliked them both, and with July, Wren and Fennel due back, it could only get worse. Thank goodness Buzz wasn't returning too. The only one she had any time for was Dawn, but she was older and had her own circle of friends. Sadly, Sylvie acknowledged that Holly was right; she hadn't integrated into their world at all and she wasn't one of them. But that wasn't such a bad thing, she thought angrily. They were horrible – arrogant and selfish. The only person whose company she really enjoyed was Yul's, and his friendship had been forbidden. She thought again how much happier she'd have been as a Villager.

Sylvie was walking steadily along Dragon's Back, hot and sticky in the blazing sun but trying not to drink too much of the precious water, when she saw a figure approaching in the distance. She groaned at the prospect of another encounter, though at least it couldn't be Magus who was safely in Exeter. She was a poor liar and worried she'd give herself away. As the figure drew closer she was dismayed to recognise Clip, in robes the colour of speedwell. He wore a piece of cloth, shot through with gold thread and decorated in an Indian pattern, loosely wrapped around his head. He raised his staff in greeting as he drew near, and she thought desperately what to say if he asked questions. It hadn't occurred to her that she'd bump into people on her journey.

'Blessings, Sylvie!' he called, his weather-beaten face breaking into a smile. 'I imagined I was alone in trying to escape the hordes.'

'Too crowded, isn't it?' she agreed. 'I had to get away.'

'You're carrying a heavy load!'

'Yes. I . . .'

She couldn't think of any reason why she should be. He stared down at her, his pale eyes twinkling.

'You wouldn't be planning on staying out overnight, would you?'

She glanced up at him in panic but he was grinning.

'Don't worry, I too feel the need to sleep under the stars. I take it nobody knows?'

'No, and please don't say anything. My mother fusses terribly.'

'Your secret's safe with me. You can't come to any harm,

although watch out for adders. There are so many at Stonewylde and I've seen several recently. Are you going far?'

'You said I was going to travel, remember?'

'So I did.'

His eyes took on their dreamy look and blinked into a different focus. He gazed right through her in silence, then laid a gentle hand on her shoulder.

'Your barn owl is with you, Sylvie. And another travels too, to offer extra protection. A raven!'

He blinked again and smiled down at her, patting her shoulder.

'Lucky girl having two spirit guides. You must be very special indeed. Here, let me give you something.'

He fished inside the small shoulder bag he always carried and produced two speckled cakes.

'When you're lying under the spangled veil of stars tonight, these will help you on your journey. If you see my wolf, greet him from me, won't you?'

He strode off humming softly and Sylvie continued along the Dragon's Back, remembering all that Yul had told her about the line of Earth Magic that snaked this ancient pathway. She tried to draw on it as she walked but realised it was no use. She was a moon person; Yul was the one who could tap into the earth energy. The sun moved lower in the sky, turning softly golden and stretching her shadow out long and thin behind her.

The larks were still rising around her, appearing out of nowhere from the ground and ascending rapidly into the wide open sky, singing joyously as they rose so high they almost disappeared from sight altogether. She'd never seen larks before coming to Stonewylde. The swallows were more familiar, but nevertheless a breathtaking sight as they swooped and dived in the bright blue skies above. She felt some of the spiritual unity that she realised was a constant factor in Yul's world. This was what mattered in life – the joy and freedom of the birds around her, the ancient path of the grassy ridgeway where people had walked for millennia, the blueness of the skies and the gold of the sun. Nothing on earth was more important than these simple things. This was the very essence of existence.

At last she reached the place on the ridgeway where she must turn off and follow a path leading north. She saw a small copse aligned with a distant pair of tumuli, like breasts, and knew this was the right spot; she'd noted this landmark from the maps in the library. It was early evening now and the sun had passed through the western sky and was heading towards its north-west summer bed. In two nights' time it would be at its furthest point of setting. She remembered Yul telling her about it during those wonderful couple of days they'd spent together, before Magus had snatched him at the Blue Moon.

As she walked down the slope of the ridgeway towards the wood, Sylvie thought of Yul. Not as she'd seen him last, broken and damaged, but how he'd been that weekend when they'd walked, talked and laughed together. Just the thought of him made her long for his company. He was so beautiful. She loved his smile, his smoky grey eyes, his hollow cheeks and sharp cheekbones. She thought of his mouth and felt a wriggle of embarrassment when she remembered how they'd almost kissed by the Hare Stone. She'd wanted to so much and yet she was scared too. Sylvie would be fifteen in two days' time and had never kissed a boy – had never even wanted to until now. She concentrated hard and tried to send a message of love and comfort to him.

I'm on my way Yul! I'm coming to save you from the place of bones and death.

As the sun sank lower in the sky, Yul collected up the dirty dishes lying scattered about on the grass. In this fine weather the men spent the evenings outside, pleased with the fresh air after breathing in stone-dust all day. Yul made several journeys to gather up the greasy plates and cutlery, almost tripping over as the men stuck their feet out whenever he passed. It had become a regular game; who could make Yul fall with his arms full.

He stacked the dirty things on the chipped table in the dilapi-
dated kitchen caravan and turned on the hot tap. The boiler
linked to a gas cylinder fired up and lukewarm water trickled into
the tiny sink. It always took several sink-fulls to wash everything.
Yul's back ached badly from loading broken stone onto the
dumper trucks all day and he felt queasy after the fatty, synthetic
food he'd just eaten. He was filthy, his hair a mat of thick white
dust, but there was no point washing. He'd get just as dirty the
next day and here everyone smelled horrible.

When he'd eventually finished, Yul went outside only to be
greeted by demands for more beer all round. He went back and
loaded up a crate with cans from the fridge, which he served to
the raucous group of men. The illegal workers sat together playing
an excited and noisy game of poker, a stack of coins in the
middle. Jackdaw sprawled in his luxurious recliner, a can in one
hand and cigarette in the other. The quarryman from Portland
sat with him listening to a portable radio.

'The reception here's bloody terrible,' he grumbled, trying to
tune the radio better.

'Yeah, I know. There's no mast for miles and the hills block
everything. That's why we can't use mobile phones here,' said
Jackdaw. 'I can't get used to having no mobile. 'Tis like losing
your right arm. No bloody signal at all on the whole estate.'

He noticed Yul heading towards the caravan where they
slept.

'Where are you going, boy?' he yelled. Yul stopped and
groaned; he'd hoped to lie down to ease his aching muscles.

'Just to the caravan, sir,' he said.

'No you ain't! Come 'ere!'

Yul trudged over to where the two men sat. Jackdaw glared
up at him, his brilliant blue eyes sparking like an overloaded
fuse.

'You don't leave till I say you can. You ain't finished work yet.
Sit!'

Yul sank to the dirty grass, full of ash, cigarette butts and globs
of phlegm. Now Jackdaw would keep him up half the night out

of spite. He hung his head, so weary he was almost asleep as he sat. Surely he must be getting to the end soon? He'd lost track of the days but could tell the Solstice was very close now from the size of his shadow at mid-day.

'Get me another beer, boy' said Jackdaw throwing the empty can at Yul's departing back and cheering when he hit his target. This resulted in all the men having a go, and Yul was pelted with a shower of cans, not all of them empty. He took no notice; any reaction just made it worse. Then they'd make him stand still and be a real target whilst they took turns to throw several cans each. It was one of the many humiliations they put him through daily and he'd learnt to accept it as normal. When he returned, Jackdaw again commanded him to sit, tossing the ring-pull in his face.

'Well, Yul, do you know what day it is tomorrow?'

'No, sir.'

'The twentieth.'

'Is it?'

'You'll have done your two weeks here.'

Yul's heart leapt with hope. Was he free to go? Would Jackdaw release him?

'Do you want to go back to the Village tomorrow?'

'Yes! Yes I do!'

'Yeah, I bet you do.'

They sat in silence. The Portlander was still trying to listen to the sports programme, fiddling with the tuner and cursing. Yul's heart hammered with hope but he didn't dare ask outright. Jackdaw pulled deeply at his beer and belched.

'Pity you're not going then!' he laughed.

Yul's spirit plummeted. He fought back the tears that threatened to spill. That would really make Jackdaw's evening; he'd have such fun if Yul cried.

'Why not?' he whispered.

''Cos I ain't had word from Magus!' shouted Jackdaw leaning down into his face. 'And don't you question me, you little bugger!'

'What's that?' asked the Portlander.

'I told him he ain't going home tomorrow 'cos I've had no message from Magus. Besides, I want to keep him here. He makes a good dogsbody, don't he? We got him half trained now and I don't want to lose him. When I see Magus next, I'll ask if you can stay on here, Yul. In a couple o' weeks' time we'll be doing a big blast and you'll be useful. Looking forward to that, ain't we?'

The other man nodded.

'Yeah, should be a good one. Clear all that backfill over on the west side. Looking forward to it myself.'

'So you ain't going nowhere tomorrow, Yul. And if I have my way, you won't be going nowhere for a long time. I like having a personal slave and you're shaping up at last. Now move your arse and get me another beer.'

The boy rose to his feet and was again hit by a flying can. He almost picked it up and hurled it back, but that would've been inviting death.

As the sun sank in a brilliant golden ball of light, Sylvie reached the quarry. She was exhausted, her legs aching and back stiff from carrying the heavy pack. She stopped on the slope leading down towards the shallow end of the quarry and took stock of the scene before her. There were lights on in a couple of the caravans and men sitting around outside. She could hear their voices but was too far away to identify Yul.

Sylvie wondered where to make her bed for the night. Nobody must see her, as the plan depended on her arriving in the morning as if she'd come straight from the Hall. She decided to skirt around the camp and go up the outside of the quarry towards the top of the hill. There were large boulders up there and she'd be well hidden, but able to watch what went on below.

Wearily she made a wide detour around the caravans and the lower end of the quarry. The sun had disappeared over the brow of the hill but it was still very light, being so close to the solstice. It was a beautiful sunset, the few clouds a glorious pink, bright against the pale-blue sky. For once Sylvie didn't notice in her aching effort to climb the hill before darkness fell. She must avoid the rocks littering the grass, as well as the precipice of the quarry edge.

At last she'd climbed high enough. She was nearly at the top and chose a great boulder to shelter her as she slept. She stopped with relief, shrugging off the heavy load from her back, and peered down into the quarry. She was only a few metres away from the sheer drop, very high up almost at the head of the great pit. She noticed an enormous stone there, rising like a pillar from amongst the boulders, too smooth and shaped to be in its natural state. Perhaps this was the stone Magus had told her about, the one on which he'd been conceived. In the morning she'd look for the snake carvings he'd mentioned. She mused at the strange Stonewylde custom of making love on rocks and vowed that when the time came, she'd never conceive her children in such a bizarre place.

Sylvie unpacked her bag and put on all the clothes she'd brought, wrapping herself in the blanket too. It was cosy enough, though she was sure she'd feel the cold later as the temperature dropped. She had a little food and drink but saved most of it for Yul the next day. The muscles in her legs twitched with fatigue now she'd finally stopped walking. She was looking forward to sleep after walking so far, with an equally long walk ahead tomorrow. It was quiet up here on the hillside, the generator down by the caravans just a distant throb, and the men's voices now quiet. It occurred to Sylvie that she'd never before spent a night out in the open, and here she was alone, at the place of bones and death. Magus had said he admired her bravery but she didn't feel very brave right now.

Gazing down into the quarry, she felt a sudden sharp prickle of fear. It was dark and shadowy down there but she thought she'd seen a movement amongst the deep canyons of stone. Daylight was fading fast, thickening into darkness, and her eyes strained in the gloom to see what crept in the quarry. Another movement over her shoulder, pale in the corner of her vision, made her jump. She swivelled in alarm, her heart thudding, ready to leap up and run. But then she smiled, exhaling in relief. A great white barn owl glided silently overhead, circling on soft wings. She felt safe now, as if her guardian had arrived to protect her. She closed her eyes, ignoring the yawning darkness of the quarry below, and hoped for sleep.

19

Sylvie found sleep impossible, despite her exhaustion. The night was alive with strange, inexplicable noises and the quarry, so very close by, frightened her. She lay tucked into the great boulder and knew she couldn't possibly roll over the edge in her sleep. Yet still she felt the terrible sensation that she was being sucked inexorably towards the quarry, dragged slowly along the grass till she reached the edge. And then something would suddenly rise up out of the darkness below and pull her in, swallowing her down into the black depths. She tried very hard to squash such terrifying, illogical thoughts.

Sylvie gazed upwards, watching the sky slowly darken and stars appear, one by one, thousand by thousand, until the whole sky was peppered with them. A crescent moon hung low over the hill, tilted and yellow as it set. Sylvie nodded to herself – the huntress' bow. She was the Maiden and must be brave and strong in her quest to save her friend. The barn owl soared above and gave her comfort. Inside the quarry the ivy rustled and shivered in the slight breeze.

Down by the caravans, Yul was dozing where he sat slumped on the hard ground by Jackdaw's feet. The men had been playing cards for hours and now slurred their speech, still demanding more beer every so often but slowing down as the effects of the long hard day took their toll. As they stumbled off to their caravans one by one, Yul rose painfully and fetched a bin liner to collect up the dozens of beer cans tossed all over the grass. So much rubbish – he'd never come across it before, as everything in the Village was made of natural materials and recycled or composted. He hated this Outside World junk defiling Stonewylde.

Finally Jackdaw heaved his bulk out of the recliner, breaking wind long and loud and rubbing his beer-filled belly. He was the last to go. Despite the copious amounts of beer he'd consumed, he was remarkably steady on his feet. He watched Yul stooping wearily to pick up the last of the cans. The boy was well trained and made life much easier for them all. Jackdaw certainly wouldn't let him go if he had any say in the matter. And he enjoyed having Yul around for a bit of sport too – the boy's pride and determination made him something of a challenge.

'Can I go to bed now, sir?' mumbled Yul, swaying on his feet.

'Yeah, if you've done all your work. I'm off myself now.'

'I'll check everything's done,' said Yul, not wanting to go into the caravan at the same time. If he wasted ten minutes or so now, Jackdaw would be snoring in bed by the time Yul crept in to lie on his blanket on the floor. He hated watching the man undress, nor did he like being watched himself. Jackdaw always made some crude comment and enjoyed humiliating him. It often ended in a kick or thump, sometimes a full thrashing, and Yul knew he couldn't take that tonight. His face was finally free from the swelling, although traces of the bruises lingered, yellow and shadowy. His back was still a terrible mess of long crusted scabs and fading bruises, but no longer hurt constantly. Magus and Alwyn had left their mark well and he tried very hard to avoid further injuries from Jackdaw.

He waited as the enormous man stooped and entered their caravan. He'd be trampling on Yul's bedding on the floor, not caring about his dirty boots. Yul sighed and without warning, misery rose up to overwhelm him. Exhaustion and despair pressed on him relentlessly and he felt his heart would break. He'd served his time, taken his punishment. He should be returning home tomorrow; back to his Village, to his mother and family, free to enjoy the Solstice festival. That was all that had kept him going. Instead ... he began to cry openly, free of an audience at last. He sank into one of the chairs and sobbed harshly into his hands, his whole body wracked with the violence of his weeping. Yul had suffered a great deal more than most in his fifteen years, but tonight he plumbed the depths of wretchedness. Tonight, hope had finally been snuffed out.

He simply couldn't go on. He couldn't take any more. He'd survived the fourteen days knowing that his punishment would come to an end if he could only hold on. And now ... it was to be extended. If this was to be his life – treated worse than a dog at Jackdaw's beck and call, mocked and humiliated by every half-witted man in the gang, worked harder than any slave without even the companionship of fellow sufferers, abused whenever Jackdaw had the inclination – he didn't want to live. What was the point? There was no hope, no prospect of release. If Jackdaw meant to keep him here indefinitely, he might as well die. He'd rather free his spirit from this miserable existence.

Yul rose slowly and took a few steps towards the mouth of the quarry. It would be so easy to climb one of the high faces, right up amongst the glossy ivy, and just let himself go. The falling boy, flying in slow motion through the air. Hitting the unyielding rocks below, the life trickling out of him slowly as his spirit slipped from his broken body and stepped in freedom to the open gate of the Otherworld.

He left the dirty grass and felt hard stone beneath his feet. Slowly he moved amongst the silent dumper trucks towards the dark labyrinth of stone that awaited him. As it had always waited, knowing that one day this would be his destiny, and his beautiful release from horrible suffering at Stonewylde. He felt Quarry-cleave calling and came willingly, wanting only to end his torment. Quarrycleave had come to his rescue and would give him joyful freedom from all pain.

Sylvie felt the spirit of Quarrycleave abroad in the darkness. The sensation had been growing now for some while; the stirring in the shadows below, the awakening of something that had been biding its time, waiting for the moment when its call would be heard and heeded. She felt terror prickle through her body and ripple down her arms. The evil was awake and walking; stalking its lair and summoning its victim. She knew with absolute certainty who the victim was and her eyes flew open in horror. He was in the labyrinth now, wandering its winding ways between walls of stone. He was heading for the heart of the maze where it waited for him in anticipation, greedy for blood to be spilled and its hunger to be satisfied.

Yul felt the protective stone walls around him, close and very high. He was deep in the maze now, the ivy bristling and brushing him as he walked the path towards his destiny. He knew what lay in wait for him and he longed to meet it. He wanted only to give his blood to feed the hunger, to add his life-force to the hundreds of others who'd given theirs too in this place of bones and death. He'd be one more of so many, no longer alone and isolated as he'd been all his life, but united in death with his triumphant dark-haired ancestors.

Yul smiled in the velvet blackness of the shadowy processional way. His thin face was eager and his damaged body ready for the sacrifice that must come. He heard it breathing up ahead, waiting patiently for him, welcoming him into its enfolding maw. His heart was glad and at peace, wanting nothing but to gloriously give himself to Quarrycleave and join everyone who'd done the same over the long centuries. Freedom from his wretched life was only a few steps away.

Sylvie sat bolt upright and looked about wildly. In the darkness she'd never get down there in time to stop him. The sparkling stars above her swung crazily as she turned her head, frantically trying to see some way to save him. She sensed rather than saw a dark shape above, blocking the white starlight in a huge winged silhouette. The raven had come.

Go! she screamed from her soul. *Go now – NOW – and save him!*

The black shape wheeled around in a whirring of powerful wings and dropped down into the quarry below. The white barn owl swooped low with its angel-feathered wings and disappeared too into the blackness. Sylvie knelt up, her heart pounding, and sent her spirit down to him.

Come back to the world of the living, Yul! We're the brightness and the darkness and we belong together. Don't leave me!

Yul paused. Something had joined him in the dark. There was a great flapping of wings and a mighty *KRUK!* A giant bird circled around before him in the dark passageway, hitting the ivy-clad stone in a flurry of noise and urgency. He stopped dead. Too big for a crow. Then he knew in his heart which bird had come to stop him, even though his eyes couldn't see it clearly. Mother Heggy had sent the Raven for him.

His heart pounded in a turmoil of conflict. He needed to continue, to answer the summoning of beautiful Quarrycleave. But the raven ... He swallowed, his hands trembling, indecision gnawing at his tired mind. He stepped forward tentatively as the great bird landed ahead of him on the path, blocking his way. Maybe he could edge round it, for he really must obey the summons.

Then he heard a sound that froze him rigid. The long low hoot of an owl echoed through the stone passageways of the labyrinth. Ahead in the darkness Yul saw the white shape gliding towards him, round moon-face heading straight for him. And he heard her desperate cry. His saviour, his brightness, the one he must never leave. The owl swooped at him, beak and claws aiming straight at his face. He turned, shielding his eyes from the vicious sharpness. He began to stumble back the way he'd come, retracing his steps in the labyrinth, away from the hunger and its lust for his blood, back towards life and safety.

The owl passed overhead several times, banking round on seraph wings to guide him, returning again and again to ensure he didn't falter. The raven launched itself into flight and flapped over him, leading him onwards until he reached the gateway of the labyrinth and was out in the open quarry, staggering between the dumper trucks, skirting the mountain of broken waste stone, leaving the stone floor and stepping once more onto the grass.

Yul lurched across to the caravan and crept inside, sinking onto the dirty blanket on the floor and shutting his eyes. He fell instantly into a deep, untroubled sleep, all threats vanquished, all harm averted. The barn owl landed on the flat caravan roof and closed its wings tidily. Its heart-shaped face swivelled and its bright black eyes blinked. The owl remained sentinel all night as the sun traced its short path towards the dawn.

Sylvie felt the raven return. It landed in a tumble on the boulder where she sheltered, flexing its massive wings and preening its glossy feathers with its sharp beak. The danger was passed. Quarrycleave would remain unsatisfied for now – Yul was safe. Shakily Sylvie lay down, pulling the blanket around her with trembling fingers. Lying on her back, she gazed up at the silvery arch of the Milky Way above, at the brilliant glitter of stars flung across the night cloak of the Goddess. She closed her eyes and slid into exhausted sleep. When her dreams came, the raven had vanished. Strangely, in its place on the boulder sat a tiny silvery creature. A wild girl with hair of gossamer silk and eyes that glowed like moonstones.

Sylvie awoke to the sound of engines and motors, a terrible cacophony from below. She sat up in confusion. Her blanket was damp with dew and she was alone amongst the boulders. She stretched her stiff limbs and spine, her hair a wild tangle around her face. Peeping over the edge of the boulder she surveyed the scene below. The sun was well risen and the day's work had started. The white, dusty landscape was alive with action – men moving around, the dumper trucks scurrying forward, the great digger lurching into motion. It was noisy and choking and she hated it all.

Keeping herself hidden from sight below, Sylvie rolled up her blanket and stowed it in the bag. She bathed her hands and face in cold dew, and relieved herself behind another rock. She ate and drank a little and then fastened the backpack securely. She watched for a while longer, locating the largest man in a hard hat who could be none other than the odious Jackdaw. She made out another figure that seemed to move twice as fast as everyone else. It must be Yul. Everyone had white hair and dusty clothes, but she was sure it was him. She smiled with anticipation. Not long now till his liberation from this terrible slavery.

Sylvie skirted down the hill, careful to keep out of sight. In daylight she saw the labyrinth of rock-faces clearly and shuddered at the thought of what had almost happened down there last night. One more sacrifice to swell the many. She glanced back at the great pillar of stone she'd noticed in the twilight at the head of the quarry. She paused for a moment, staring at its hewn shape and the strange way it rose up next to the cliff-face, its top forming a platform. Squinting in the brilliant sunlight that danced off the white stones, she made out a tangle of writhing serpents carved in relief that swarmed all the way up the huge stone. In the morning light it sparkled like snow crystals, and Sylvie was reminded of the disc of rock at Mooncliffe. Despite the warm sunshine, she shivered suddenly and turned away, heading down the hill towards the quarry mouth and caravans.

She waited a long time at a point about halfway down, hiding behind a boulder and a stunted tree. When the moment was right she'd know and would make her move. Eventually it came. She saw Jackdaw toss off his hard hat – only he and one other man wore them – and stride towards a battered pick-up truck that stood near by, full of bulging bin liners. He started the engine and swung the vehicle around, heading off down the track into the distance. When he'd been gone five minutes, Sylvie took a deep breath and stood up, stretching her stiff legs. She walked purposefully down to the quarry mouth and the settlement of caravans. She felt brave and strong again, sure in the knowledge that this was how it should be and that the Goddess was watching over her.

She reached the caravans, where several men hung about, and was disgusted at the mess and squalor. Soon somebody came over and she asked to speak to the boss. The man shrugged and pointed to a figure by a pile of rubble in the quarry. She picked her way across, stepping over chunks of stone, coughing in the dusty air.

'Are you the person in charge?' she asked the man in the yellow hard hat.

'No, you'd be wanting Jack, and he's gone on to get the supplies from the Gatehouse, m'dear.'

'So who's in charge when he's gone?'

'I suppose I am, seeing as how all these here are foreigners and don't know their arses from their elbows. I'm the quarryman from Portland.'

'Well I've been sent down by Magus, the owner of the estate, to collect Yul. He's the boy who's been working here for the past couple of weeks.'

'I know who Yul is. The only one here with a clout of sense. He's up the face over there. And you're taking him on, you say? Pity – he's a good worker.'

Sylvie followed the direction of his pointing finger and saw a figure clinging to a high rock face. He crawled into a crevasse, wedging himself with his legs braced while he hacked at the thick ivy.

'Can you call him down, please?' she asked. 'Magus wants him back immediately.'

'We wondered if he'd send word. Where's he to then?'

Sylvie jerked her head vaguely back in the direction of the hills behind her.

'He's with the horses,' she said. 'They don't like all this noise. We're in a hurry. Don't make Magus wait, will you?'

'Wouldn't want to do that! I'll get the lad down then. Jack won't be too happy losing him, but if Magus says so . . .'

Watching Yul slither down the rock face like a pale lizard was an amazing sight. He was caked in stone-dust, his long hair white and stiff, and he could have been anybody.

'Your time here is over,' said Sylvie simply. 'I've come to take you home.'

The dusty figure nodded, his chest rising and falling rapidly but his chalk-white face as impassive as a mask. Only the deep smoky-grey eyes that bored into hers with such intensity betrayed any emotion. He emptied his pockets of tools and unstrapped the heavy belt that held more tools, handing them to the Portlander.

'Be seeing you then, lad,' said the man.

Without a word Yul turned away and strode out of the quarry, Sylvie close behind. They walked very fast and she struggled to keep up. Yul noticed and stopped, taking the heavy backpack from her and slipping it over a shoulder.

'Can we slow down?' she gasped.

'Not yet.'

They continued the fast pace, remaining silent until they were a good couple of miles away from the quarry. Then Yul stopped, putting the backpack down at his feet. He turned to her and she read it all in his eyes, everything. Fighting down the tears, she opened her arms and held him tightly, ignoring the dirt and smell, just happy to have him safe and real in her embrace. She felt his thin body shudder with relief, the tautness and tension beginning to loosen a fraction. At last he pulled away, looking down at her.

'Why did Magus send you like this?' he asked croakily. 'Why didn't he come himself in the Land Rover? Have you walked all the way?'

She nodded and opened up the backpack, finding him one of the bottles of water. He drank deeply then offered her some.

'He didn't send me. I came on my own to take you back for the Solstice tomorrow morning.'

'What do you mean, he didn't send you? Does he know you've come for me?'

She shook her head.

'No, but I ...'

He was off, striding straight back the way they'd come.

'STOP!' she cried, running after him and trying to grab his arm. 'Stop, Yul!'

He shook her off and continued walking angrily, ignoring her. 'Yul, *stop*!'

She leapt in front of him and seized both his arms, pushing at him to stop the momentum of his movement. He halted and stared down at her.

'What are you doing?' she shrieked. 'You can't go back there! I've come to take you home!'

'I'm not going home unless Magus says I can,' he said. His mouth was bitter and tight. 'Do you really think I'm going to risk angering him again? He's won, Sylvie. I'll never cross him again and I won't leave Quarrycleave until he says so.'

'But he *did* say you could come back!'

'What? But you just said—'

'He said you could come back after two weeks. He said it several times and I checked again yesterday. The only reason he hasn't come to collect you personally today is because it's the Solstice and he's too busy. He said if I could drive I could fetch you myself. Well I can't drive but I can walk, so I came and got you. Honestly, Yul, you're not disobeying him. He said you could come home, I promise.'

He frowned down at her, wanting desperately to believe her but terrified he'd be crossing Magus in doing so. She smiled encouragingly at him, taking his dusty, torn hand in hers and gently tugging him around to face freedom again.

'Come, Yul,' she said softly. 'It's alright, really. Trust me.'

A while later they came to a stream. Yul stopped and removed the backpack, which he'd insisted on carrying despite Sylvie's protestations. He lay down amongst the emerald weed that floated in the water like green hair. The crystal clear water washed over him as he lay on the pebbly bed, his eyes staring up at the swallows in the skies. He lay there for ages, the thick white dust slowly loosening and washing away.

It wasn't until they were up on Dragon's Back ridgeway with

the sea in view and the woodlands around the Hall and Village in the approaching distance, that Yul stopped again. He flung himself down on the short grass and lay there, gazing up into the bright blue heavens. Sylvie unpacked the picnic and spread it out over the grass. After a while Yul sat up and started to eat ravenously. He ate for a long time and Sylvie held back, letting him take his fill.

Then he lay down again and within minutes was fast asleep. Sylvie was bemused; this wasn't the reunion she'd envisaged. He'd barely spoken so far. But she realised he was badly damaged and needed to heal; she must treat him very gently. She moved around as he slept so her shadow shielded his face from the hot sun. She had a good look at him whilst he lay sprawled on the purple vetch and butter-yellow bird's foot trefoil that grew so thickly on the dry grassland. It was hard not to cry at the pitiful sight of him. The stream had washed some of the dirt from his face and she saw the faded bruising all over his skin. The bones in his face were even sharper now and his mouth had changed; it seemed hard and bitter, even in sleep. He'd been robbed of the last traces of innocence.

Sylvie judged that it must now be late afternoon. Yul had slept peacefully for hours, oblivious to the vivid blue butterflies dancing about him. She picked up one of his hands, looking at the long, square-nailed fingers, now torn and sore. She ached with pity and love for him, longing to kiss his lips softly, stroke the bedraggled curls back from his forehead, smooth away the bruising. He awoke suddenly, his clear eyes focusing on her.

'Thank you, Sylvie, for saving me. Twice over.'

She shook her head and turned away, tears choking her throat. She stared out across the valley below towards the sea. He pulled himself up to join her, sitting close, his arm touching hers. She laid her head against his shoulder and a strand of her hair blew across his chest, as if trying to bind him to her. They sat for some time, feeling the joy of each other's company, needing no words to communicate. At last he turned to her, his grey eyes full of sadness.

'Sylvie, when we get back ... it can't be the same. I can't be your friend any more. We won't be able to see each other.'

She gulped at this, a wave of sorrow rising up inside her.

'But Yul, we can—'

'No.' He shook his head firmly. 'I've learnt my lesson. No more fighting back or standing up to them. The things that have happened to me ... I'm never going through that again. I must forget what Mother Heggy said. You're Hallfolk and I'm a Villager and we're not allowed to be together like this.'

'Then I'll become a Villager too!' she said fiercely, taking his hand in hers. He squeezed it but released her.

'No, Sylvie. You know he'd never allow that.'

'Yul, please, you're not thinking straight. You need to rest and heal before you make decisions like this. I've got something for you from Mother Heggy.'

She fished in the bag and pulled out a small glass bottle labelled 'Journey' in spidery writing. He drank it, then gazed out across the woodlands. She stared at his profile, struck again by the changes in him, saddened by the hardening of his boyish good looks.

'I can't wait to be home,' he said softly. 'I can't tell you how much I've yearned for this. I just want to get back to the woods, the Village, my cottage. See my family again ... except my father.'

'There's something else, Yul,' she said. 'I've got a cake hidden at home, a cake from Mother Heggy. It's for Alwyn. He must eat it tomorrow, the day of the Solstice. I think she must have put ... well, you can guess what'll happen. Those who stand against you will fall, one by one. Remember?'

He stared at her. She gazed steadily back at him, looking deep into his eyes, trying to fill him with strength and purpose.

'Oh Yul, you're much too far along the path to turn back now,' she said gently. 'Can you live under the same roof as Alwyn? Can you take more beatings and abuse? You know he won't stop now, despite what Magus has put you through. Or ... will you finish it, once and for all?'

He hung his head, remembering Mother Heggy's warning.

319

'You know what'll happen if you do nothing, if you try to be obedient and just do as they want,' she continued. 'You've gone too far and they'll never leave you in peace. You've got to see this through, Yul. I understand you don't want to suffer again as you have in the quarry, but . . .'

'And in the byre by the stables,' he whispered. 'I really thought they meant to kill me. You don't know what it was like in there.'

'No I don't. But I do know that you can't just give in. You've got to fight, Yul. You've got to face up to Magus and fight him. I've seen his dark side, and I'll help. You've got me and you've got Mother Heggy. We'll both help you.'

He laughed at this bitterly.

'What can you do, Sylvie? No disrespect to you or Mother Heggy, but what kind of match are the two of you against Magus? And if—'

'Hold on a minute before you dismiss us like that!' she cried angrily. 'What kind of match were we last night, Yul, in the quarry? You're here now, alive, because of us. We fought for you and we won! Is Magus more powerful than the beast we took on last night and overcame? Answer me that!'

He stared at her and she saw a tiny spark kindle in the grey depths of his eyes. He nodded slowly and stood up, stretching painfully, and gazed out at the sea in the distance. He stood like this for a long time, deep in reverie. Eventually he turned and smiled down at her, a new light in his eyes. And she saw then that Mother Heggy had been right. He may be battered and may appear broken, but Yul would never lose his spirit.

They left the ridgeway and passed the Hare Stone, touching it reverently like pilgrims at a holy shrine, before making their way downhill. Sylvie felt Yul start to unshrivel as they entered the woodland. He breathed deeply, brushing the bark of trees with his fingertips, gazing up at the bright green canopy above them. They stopped and listened to the sweet birdsong, watched a tiny wren flit around a bush in quick jerky movements and a songthrush perch on a twig singing its heart out. A pair of squirrels scampered up the trunk of a tree and leapt from branch to branch overhead, whilst in the dappled shade in the distance they saw a fallow deer and her faun standing frozen, watching them with velvety eyes and twitching their pretty snub noses.

'It's so good to be home,' he said softly, and Sylvie took his hand in hers and squeezed it gently.

'It's so good to have you home. The woods aren't as magical when you're not around.'

'Do you know, there were no birds or wildlife at all in the quarry?' he mused. 'Apart from the owl and the raven last night, of course. Creatures must know it's a place of evil and suffering. In the two weeks there I saw nothing except a viper basking on a rock. The biggest snake I've ever seen, black and silver and beautifully patterned.'

Sylvie thought of the great rock carved with serpents and shuddered. She wanted to put Quarrycleave to the very back of her mind. She guessed the place would haunt Yul for a long time.

Her plan from now onwards depended largely on luck, but luck seemed to be with them. Sylvie had counted on the fact that everyone would be up at the Stone Circle for the Solstice Eve ceremony. The community would be singing, dancing and drumming, waiting for the sun to go down. Everyone took part in the evening ceremony that heralded the week's festivities.

The Hall was deserted, as she'd hoped. They crept in a side door and using the servants' back stairs, went straight up to the white marble bathroom. Sylvie ran the bath whilst Yul gaped in amazement at the extravagant luxury of the place. He watched the scalding water gush from the polished silver tap, more ornate than he'd have dreamt possible for such a simple object. His fingers traced the flecked snowy-white marble of the enormous tub. He'd never seen anything like it.

He couldn't bear the sight of himself in the myriad of mirrors, for he was really filthy. Sylvie ushered him towards an adjoining shower room to wash off the worst of the dirt and stone-dust from his skin and hair. Then she fetched some of the things Mother Heggy had left for her in the wicker basket and read the labels carefully. She poured the contents of one bottle of potion into the steaming bath, and added a copious amount of fragrant bubble-bath for good measure.

Soon Yul lay soaking under a discreet blanket of thick bubbles, his eyes closed in contentment. Sylvie had a quick shower herself down the corridor, then sorted out clean clothes for him from one of the many linen cupboards, and picked up a couple of blankets. It felt strange being the only ones in the vast building. Then she hurried down to the kitchens and filled a large basket with food and drink for their own Solstice Eve celebration. Out of the bath, soaked and steamed clean at last, Yul began to apply the salve from Mother Heggy's basket as instructed.

'Are you ready for me to do your back yet?' Sylvie called from behind the door. 'Mother Heggy said you must put it on all over.'

'No! I don't want you to. Please don't come in, Sylvie.'

'Don't be silly,' she said firmly, opening the door. 'There's no need to be shy. Just keep that towel round your waist. Oh!!'

He'd turned away in shame and she saw the full horror of his livid back. In shocked silence, she took the jar from him and started to smooth the salve over his damaged skin, her fingertips as light as rose petals. Tears rolled down her cheeks as she understood a little more just how badly he'd suffered.

'Nobody will ever do this to you again, Yul,' she whispered with an aching throat. She sniffed and angrily brushed away the hot tears . 'This is sick, it's inhuman. Alwyn deserves everything that's coming to him.'

They took the baskets of potions, blankets and food and left the Hall.

'I must watch the sun go down,' said Yul. 'And I need to sleep outside tonight under the stars.'

'I understand. Where should we go?'

'The hill that overlooks the Stone Circle.'

They made their way there in the soft evening light, the violet shadows deepening as they walked. The air hummed with expectancy as the sun descended in the north-west. The sky was a pale lemon-yellow flecked with tiny grey-blue clouds. The golden orb glittered as it slowly sank into the enfolding hills. It was still warm and swallows arced all around, feeding on gnats.

Yul stood on the hill top, scrubbed clean and anointed with Mother Heggy's balm which made his skin tingle and glow. His hair fell in glossy curls to his shoulders, springing out to frame his face. He faced the setting sun and chanted softly, his arms stretched skywards, long fingers spread like rays. Sylvie stood just behind him. Across the shadowy fold of the land, she saw in the distance the Stone Circle and the community crowded within. She heard drumming, the heart beat of the Earth Goddess, of Stonewylde itself, and many voices singing in unison. The hair on her arms started to rise.

The sun sank below the horizon, a blaze of molten gold in a sky that was now tinged apricot. The earth seemed to hold its breath at such beauty. Gradually the sky lost its golden glow and the bow of the waxing moon shone silver against the palest of blue. Early stars freckled the heavens and the bats started to fly, flickering about their heads like soft leather gloves. Yul turned and took Sylvie in his arms. He held her close, their hearts beating against each other, his cheek caressed by her silky hair.

'Tomorrow his descension will begin. His reign is almost over,' he whispered.

20

Yul and Sylvie spread one of the blankets on the short grass of the hilltop and enjoyed their feast, savouring the delicious food from the Hall kitchens. Afterwards, as they sat close together gazing up at the velvet dome of glittering stars, they shared the cakes Clip had given Sylvie on her way to the quarry. The brilliant night took on a deeper dimension as the cakes worked their magic. The stars around them blazed in glory, shimmering in the sacred pattern of their dance.

Sylvie stared in wonder at the long twist of the Milky Way, the spiral helix of life. She thought of Yul's precious life, of how last night she'd cheated Quarrycleave of its victim, snatching him back from the brink of death. She thought too, on the eve of her fifteenth birthday, about her own life. It was only three months since she'd arrived here at the Spring Equinox, so very ill and weak. Sylvie knew that if she hadn't come to Stonewylde, she too would have been ready, as Yul had been last night, to abandon the struggle of living in total despair. But now ... she'd found her home and found her destiny. It seemed there'd always been an empty place in her heart waiting for Yul to fill it.

His shoulder touching hers, Yul too gazed up at the blaze of star-fire above. He knew with certainty that he'd never willingly give up on life again. Life was sacrosanct and beautiful and he rejoiced that Sylvie had saved him from the fatal lure of Quarrycleave. In the magic of the black satin night, he put his arm around her and held her close, wanting nothing more than this. And never anything less. He'd never give up this moongazy girl who had somehow been sent to him, a sparkling light in his darkness, and had turned his world around.

They heard the eerie call of owls hunting in the woods nearby, and both thought back to the previous night with a shudder. Sylvie found the potion labelled Midsummer's Eve in its little corked bottle and gave it to Yul.

'Where will you sleep tonight?' she asked. 'You can't go back to your cottage, can you? Not until ... not while Alwyn's around. Will you go to your shelter in the woods?'

'No,' he said. 'I won't skulk around like an outlaw any longer. I belong in the Village, back in the heart of Stonewylde.'

He felt the restorative power of the draught he'd swallowed, and with it bloomed a new sense of purpose.

'I'll sleep under the trees on the Village Green,' he said. 'I'll be out of sight there. You'd better go home, Sylvie. Your mother will wonder where you are.'

'She'll be too busy trying to get Magus' attention to worry about me. I'll walk down with you. I want to make sure you're alright first, and then I'll go home.'

By the time they reached the Village, the place was quiet. Everyone had returned from the ceremony at the Stone Circle, but with such an early start the following morning to herald the Solstice sunrise, people had gone straight to their beds. The Great Barn and Jack in the Green were both dark and quiet, and the lights in most cottages were out too. Sylvie and Yul walked in silence along the cobbled track, their hands entwined in a knot of partnership. They stepped onto the grass of the Village Green, the great trees encircling them in a ring of safe darkness. Above them the heavens sparkled and Yul breathed deeply.

'This is where I belong,' he said quietly. 'In the heart of Stonewylde. Thank you, Sylvie. I'll never forget what you've done for me. If it weren't for you, my saviour ...'

She squeezed his hand and leant against him. She was exhausted, the events of the last two days almost too much to contemplate now they were safely home.

'Whereabouts will you sleep?' she asked, looking around the huge circle of trees. 'Let's get the blankets out for your bed now, and then I really must go home. We have to be up so early tomorrow.'

Yul led the way towards the dark shape of the largest tree and Sylvie stumbled after him. They spread the blankets on the soft, dry floor of earth beneath the spreading branches. Under here it was much darker, all sounds muffled by the dense foliage that reached down to the ground, making a sheltered haven all around them. Sylvie checked he had the green tunic ready for the ceremony the next morning, and the little bottle Mother Heggy had prepared for him.

When all was done, they straightened and faced each other. Sylvie felt unexpectedly awkward. She shook with fatigue from the long walk there and back, and the excitement of the daring rescue. She trembled, too, from the sudden awareness of being alone in the moonlight with Yul, in the intimacy of the tree's sanctuary.

'Come here, Sylvie,' he said softly. She stepped forward shyly and he enfolded her in his arms. She smelt his herbal scent and laid her cheek against his chest, feeling his heart beating. He brushed the top of her head with his mouth and shuddered. He was as taut as a bow string, his body lean and hard against her as he held her. They stood like this for some time, enjoying being close to one another at last.

'I feel so happy when I'm with you,' whispered Sylvie, looking up at him in the darkness. She could just make out his face. 'You make me feel, for the first time, that I truly belong.'

'You're the most magical person I've ever met, Sylvie,' he murmured. 'When I'm with you I feel special, like I'm part of something greater.'

She snuggled her face into his soft shirt, wanting to be this close for ever. She felt his fingers, gentle but sure, running down the length of her hair. Then he touched her forehead and traced around her eyebrow and cheekbone. She knew his hands were damaged from the stone quarry but his touch was delicate. His fingertips whispered across her closed eyelids, her nose, and then found her lips.

With a gossamer touch he explored her mouth, the fine arch of her upper lip, the soft fullness of her lower one. Her lips tingled at his touch; his sheer gentleness set her on fire. Without thinking, she kissed his fingers as they caressed her mouth. He groaned and started to pull away from her. In a fluid and spontaneous movement, she reached up and pulled his head down to hers, her lips finding his like interlocking pieces of a puzzle.

As she felt his mouth on hers, the world spiralled dizzily around her. Everything else – the darkness, the moon through the branches, the silent Village across the Green – faded away as she dissolved into him. She clung to him and he crushed her in a fierce embrace. The kiss, soft and yet so desperate, seemed to last an eternity. Nothing else would ever matter quite so much again.

They pulled apart, breathless and trembling, and stood facing each other. Their lips were on fire, crushed and tingling for more. For the first time ever, Sylvie understood what all the fuss was about. In the moonlight filtering down through the tree, Yul saw her teeth gleam as she smiled. He smiled back, his heart hammering in his chest with elation.

'What tree is this?' she whispered. 'This place where we had our first kiss?'

'The yew,' he replied softly, running a reverent hand down her silky hair, feeling her delicate shoulder blades beneath, adoring every tiny piece of her. 'The tree of death and rebirth. The tree of the phoenix, of regeneration. I feel as if part of me has died tonight, Sylvie, gone forever. And something new has been born in its place. I'll never be the same person again.'

'Me neither. It's a Midsummer's Eve enchantment. Everything around us seems charged with magic.'

'Sylvie, we must be careful. We must keep this guarded and secret.'

He pulled her to him again, wrapping his arms around her.

She felt him shaking, and thrilled at his passion for her.

'You're so precious to me,' he whispered, clinging to her tightly as if he'd never willingly release her. But after a while she drew away from him, even though she wanted only to stay in his arms.

'I'd better go, Yul. It must be very late.'

He caught her hand and raised it to his cheek, pulling her back. She saw his eyes glint in the moonlight, burning like stars.

'Sylvie ... I want to kiss you again. Just once more. Please, Sylvie ...'

Under the ancient yew tree the old magic was strong. The silver moon peered through the branches at the boy and girl, locked together in their desire for each other. Neither could break away for the kiss was deep and sweet, the stuff that dreams are made of. Their passion crackled like phoenix flames around them as they kissed, entwined and forged them in a bond of bright new love. Finally they pulled apart. Yul raked a hand through his curls, his chest rising and falling fast.

'You must get back, Sylvie,' he said unsteadily.

'I know,' she whispered. 'It's just ... I can't bear to leave you. I want to be with you all the time, but it could be ages till we can see each other alone again.'

He gazed down at her, his eyes blazing. The moonlight was brighter now, pouring moonbeams through a gap in the branches. He could see her face clearly in the silver light, her eyes glowing with their own magical beauty.

'I love you, Sylvie,' he said softly. 'We belong together, you and I.'

She reached up and brushed her fingertips over his face, feeling the bones and hollows. Her heart filled with tenderness for him, a rush of emotion so deep she wanted to cry. She thought of the boy she'd watched digging the garden in the spring, angry and secretive, trying to hide his shameful injuries. She remembered the evening she'd found him sitting alone on the stone bridge, wrapped in his loneliness and misery. But now – his darkness had found her brightness. Something between them had ignited and he was transformed.

'I love you too, Yul,' she whispered. 'I'll always love you. We'll be together one day, I know it.'

He smiled in the shadows of the yew's branches, the moon silvering his glossy curls.

'It started today, on Summer Solstice Eve. Do you feel it, Sylvie? And tomorrow ... tomorrow's the day when the sun stands still in the sky and everything changes. I don't know how, but our lives are on the cusp of change. Our destiny has begun to unfold, just as Mother Heggy said it would. Tomorrow will be magical.'

Sylvie walked wearily up the track leading out from the Village. It was a fair distance to Woodland Cottage, and her legs were stiff and aching. Her heart still thrilled from the burning kisses under the yew tree, the passion and magic seared on her memory. She wondered what she'd done till she loved Yul, what had filled her life before this blazing certainty had taken hold. She knew he was right; tomorrow everything would change, but her worry was that it might be for the worse. When Magus discovered she'd brought Yul back from the quarry, what would he do? She couldn't face the thought of Yul suffering any more.

She jumped as a sharp scream rose from the trees beside the track. A fox barked and there was a flutter of wings as something flew up from its roost in fright at the brutal disturbance. The curved moon and brilliant starlight lit the way ahead dimly. Sylvie wished she were home in her bed. She, along with everyone else in the community, must be up again at first light and was now so exhausted she could barely drag her throbbing feet on.

She heard another sound behind her and turned fearfully, imagining some wild creature emerging from the woods. Her heart leapt in alarm as she recognised something infinitely more dangerous: the unmistakable form of Magus approaching. She considered hiding amongst the trees but realised he must have seen her on the moonlit track.

'Blessings, Sylvie!' he called as he drew closer. She turned and waited for him, her insides shrinking with dread. They fell into step together.

'What on earth are you doing out so late on Solstice Eve?' he asked. 'Everyone else is asleep in their beds.'

'But not you, Magus.'

'No ... I've just walked someone home to the Village. We stayed up at the Circle after the ceremony. I hope you enjoyed it there tonight, although it was nothing compared with what's to come tomorrow. The Summer Solstice is such a powerful festival! The Earth Magic is at its brightest and best. It must be something to do with the position of the earth in relation to the sun. I love the energy I get from the Solstice every year.'

He was silent for a while, clearly feeling contented and at ease. Sylvie prayed that he wouldn't ask further questions.

'So why are you up so late? Where's Miranda?'

'At home, I expect.'

'Is she?' Then his voice changed suddenly, taking on a hard note. 'Sylvie ...'

'Yes, I've been with Yul,' she said quietly. 'I brought him back from the quarry.'

He stopped dead and grabbed her arm, spinning her around to face him. In the dim light, she saw his eyes glitter.

'*You did what?*'

She gulped. His hand was like a vice on her arm, digging into the bones.

'You said he could come back for the Solstice! You said the only reason he wasn't coming home was because you were too busy to fetch him. You said if I could drive I could collect him myself! So I walked there and I brought him back. You said it was alright, Magus! He'd taken his punishment. He'd done his two weeks' labour.'

He relaxed his grip slightly and glared down at her. In the silence of the night she heard his breathing as he struggled to control his fury.

'I can't believe you did that! How dare you take matters into your hands! It wasn't your place to decide when he'd had enough.'

'But you said—'

330

'I know what I said. But you should *never* have done that. Where is he now?'

'In the Village. But Magus, it wasn't his fault! I told him you said it was alright. I had a hard job persuading him to come with me. He was so worried about disobeying you.'

'And so he bloody well should've been worried! How *dare* he come back without my permission?'

'He thought he did have your permission. Please don't be angry with him.' Her voice was thin with fear. 'It was all my doing. I had to fight to make him come back and it's me you should be angry with. If you're going to punish anyone, please punish me and not him.'

She felt the lessening of tension as he slowly calmed down. Then he sighed and released her arm. He began walking again and she tentatively fell into step beside him.

'You're brave; I'll give you that, Sylvie. You knew I'd be furious, didn't you?'

She nodded, glancing up at his strong profile.

'I'm sorry. I just couldn't stand him – or any Stonewylder – suffering alone up there and missing the festival. *Please* don't take it out on him. He said he never intended to disobey you again.'

He laughed at that.

'I should think not, after what he's been through. So it's you I should punish, is it? What a shame, when it's your birthday tomorrow and I've already bought you a lovely present.'

'Have you? I thought you didn't give presents at Stonewylde.'

'We don't. But this is something special – a dress for you to wear tomorrow at the evening celebration. A moongazy dress for a moongazy girl. You'll be fifteen tomorrow and you're turning into a beauty, Sylvie. You'll sparkle in the dress I've chosen for you.'

'It's very kind of you. Thank you, Magus. And I'm sorry for making you angry.'

They'd reached the small path that led to Woodland Cottage. Magus stopped, taking both her hands in his and gazing down at her.

'Don't ever defy me like that again, Sylvie. I'll forgive you this time but don't think you'll get away with it in future.'

'And you won't punish Yul for coming back?'

'Not if he keeps out of my way and doesn't cross me again. And not if you promise to have nothing more to do with him. No secret meetings, no clandestine assignations. You know it's against our principles here, relationships between Villagers and Hallfolk. Everyone else keeps to the rules and so must you. Is that a deal?'

'Alright,' she said quietly. 'But you must leave him alone.'

'Agreed. And now you'd better get to bed. See how light the sky is? I love the Solstice! You'll see how magical it is at the sunrise ceremony. Come here, Sylvie.'

He pulled her closer.

'What?'

'A goodnight kiss. A birthday kiss for your magus. Remember it's my birthday tomorrow too.'

Still holding her hands, he bent and brushed her lips with his, lingering for a second. She shuddered, and thought suddenly of the kisses she'd shared with Yul less than an hour ago.

'There's something different about you tonight, Sylvie,' said Magus, peering at her in the silvery darkness. 'Your energy's altered. You're changed somehow.'

'It must be the Solstice magic,' she replied quickly and extricated herself, backing away from him. 'Goodnight, Magus! See you in the morning.'

The sound of birdsong from the oak woods around the Circle was overwhelming, filling the air with a joyful dawn chorus. Many people were arriving; dozens of children came up the Long Walk with their parents, everyone whispering in hushed tones. Yul had no trouble mixing in with a group and arriving in the Circle amongst them. In the pearly-grey twilight everyone seemed cold and half asleep, for it was so very early. He made his way over to the enormous unlit bonfire; it was the woodsmen's job to light and supervise the fire and he knew he'd find them all there.

Old Greenbough's craggy face lit up when he saw Yul. The tough old man hugged him brusquely in a completely uncharacteristic gesture of affection.

'Eh, am I glad to see you back, young Yul!' he whispered hoarsely. 'I been worrying and worrying about you. Are you alright, lad?'

'I'm fine thank you, sir,' grinned Yul, delighted at the warm welcome. Many of the men greeted him quietly but with gladness, and he tried to avoid the painful back slapping. After the harsh indifference of Jackdaw and the men at the quarry it felt good to be amongst friends again.

'You turned up at just the right moment, Yul, because we got a problem on our hands. We must light the Solstice Fire soon but there's no one right to do it. We're all too heavy or too old, so 'tis your job this year, boy.'

Yul's heart leapt at this. 'But, sir, I—'

'I was going to ask you all along but then I thought you'd not be here. Thank the stars you're back! You must be the Herald of the Dawn, Yul, and I can't think of anyone better to do it. Here, put the sun robe on quick – there ain't much time.'

The heavy golden robe, embroidered with pure gold thread and countless shiny sun symbols, was pulled on over his tunic. The high stiff collar fanned up at the back and framed his dark head. The long robe fitted perfectly.

'See, here in this pocket is the lighter,' said Greenbough very softly, as the Circle was in near silence awaiting the sun rise. 'Climb up through the centre of the fire and wait on the platform with the lighter ready. Keep your eyes fixed on the horizon, lad. You'll be the first one to see the sun appear. That instant you must light the torch. You know the words to say? You know what you must do with the torch?'

Yul nodded, his heart beating fast at the thought of the task ahead. He'd be the key figure in opening the ceremony. He'd watched and taken part in this ritual for as long as he could remember and knew every stage of it inside out. But he'd never dared hope that he'd be chosen as Herald of the Dawn. It was the ultimate honour.

'Right, then. Just check the lighter ... good. Up you go, lad. Goddess be with you!'

Yul squeezed through the gap in the branches that formed the frame of the fire, and found the hollow centre. A roughly-made wooden ladder stood there, which would burn when the fire caught hold. It was strange inside the great bonfire; being enclosed in a wooden cage and knowing there were hundreds of people outside waiting in silence. Yul felt a stab of panic. What if he missed the sun rise?

He quickly began to climb the wooden rungs but his foot caught in the robe and he slipped. His heart pounded and his hands shook; he made himself calm down and started to climb steadily. He reached the top and stepped carefully through the narrow opening onto the small platform, just large enough for one person. He looked over the towering stones towards the north-east where the sky was salmon pink. No sun yet.

Yul breathed a sigh of relief and then checked; here was the torch, secure in its bracket. The brazier was stuffed full of bark and lichen that would catch quickly, and he could see the thin dry branches leading from the brazier into the main part of the fire. All was as it should be. He took the lighter from his pocket and gripped it firmly, ready for the moment.

He then glanced down and gulped at the sight below him. There were hundreds and hundreds of people packed into the Circle and spilling out beyond, and every face was upturned and looking at him. Every man, woman and child at Stonewylde came to this ceremony and there were many extra Hallfolk who'd returned especially for this, the most popular festival of the eight.

The horizontal Altar Stone lay right across the Circle and Magus stood behind it, wearing a grand gold robe similar to his own. His arms were upraised and he faced away from the bonfire. He was chanting softly and then the drums started, at first a gentle rhythm but slowly building in intensity. Yul looked again at the dawn horizon. It was even brighter, the sky blooming into a glorious mess of gold and coral pink against a backdrop of pure pale blue.

Down on the ground, Sylvie had gasped when she'd seen a dark, curly head emerge from the top of the fire. Surely it couldn't be Yul? It was hard to make him out clearly. Although the sky was increasingly light now, the Circle was still shadowy and he was high up and facing the horizon. But the straight, proud back and tilt of his head told her it must be him. This was the Yul of old, not the miserable, cowering figure she'd rescued from the quarry.

She saw him reach out; there was a tiny spark and then a flare of flame as the torch caught hold. The mass of people stood silently and expectantly, waiting for the Herald of the Dawn to make his announcement. At that moment there was a sudden flurry of black feathers above and a great crow landed on Yul's shoulder. The drums almost missed their beat. A collective gasp escaped from the crowd at the unexpected sight of the crow now perched on the golden figure so high up above them.

'The sun has risen! The sacred flame is lit! Folk of Stonewylde, rejoice!'

Yul's voice was resonant and strong, echoing around the space inside the Circle. He took the torch and brandished it aloft, his golden robe catching the glint of firelight. Then he plunged it into the brazier and there was a rush of light, a sizzling of blue and green fire. The crowd chanted in unison.

'The Solstice Fire is lit! The sun joins in sacred union with Mother Earth! Bright Blessings to all!'

The flames in the brazier burned voraciously as the drumming grew faster and louder. Then orange flames appeared, licking around the coloured ones and forming a crown of gold on the great pyramid of wood. Holding the torch upright, the golden figure started to descend through the centre of the fire. The crow flapped off and flew across to perch on one of the standing stones.

Inside the fire Yul was having trouble getting out. Under normal circumstances he'd have practised the tricky manoeuvre wearing the long robes. As it was he almost fell and dropped the torch before working out a way to balance it and hold on, while climbing down in the restricting robes. As the flames crackled above him he shook with excitement. The sensation as he'd stood there, so high up, and called across the Circle with all the folk of Stonewylde listening and watching, had been out of this world. He'd loved leading the ceremony, knowing everyone was focused on him. The unforeseen presence of the crow had made it even more spectacular.

Yul reached the ground and squeezed through the channel in the wood, trying to keep the flickering flames of the torch away from his robes and hair. The smell of burning wood surrounded him, as smoke penetrated down through the bonfire from the unseen flames high above. He could see Greenbough beckoning, showing him the way out of the huge structure, waiting to set fire to the base the minute he was out.

Suddenly Yul was free and safe in the open air. He lifted the flaming torch high and began to move towards the Altar Stone. There was a clear path before him. Magus had climbed onto the stone and now chanted with the throbbing drums, his arms upraised. He faced the beautifully painted Summer Stone, the one aligned to this special sunrise. The sun, although risen over the horizon, had yet to penetrate the Stone Circle and it was still shadowy inside. As Yul walked steadily across the diameter of the circle the crow flew down and settled once more on his shoulder. He smiled; Mother Heggy was here in spirit if not in body, and she'd found a way to ensure that all knew of her presence.

Sylvie held her breath as Yul crossed the circle. The sky was now rosy and bright and the Solstice Fire blazed fiercely. She could see Magus clearly as he stood on the Altar Stone. He was an impressive figure; tall and strong, his pale-blond hair gleaming in the pink light, his handsome face solemn as his deep voice wove in and out of the drums. His robe was beautiful, shot with gold thread and glimmering with hundreds of tiny golden beads and mirrors. Like Yul's, it had a high winged collar that framed his face.

Sylvie watched the great man as Yul passed her and headed for the stone. Magus turned and tilted his head down to watch the figure moving towards him. She saw his eyes widen as he realised who it was bearing the sacred flame of the Solstice Fire. He stared transfixed at the approaching Herald of the Dawn; the boy whom he'd intended to keep safely out of the way at Quarrycleave, the boy who must never cross him again. The boy he thought he'd broken.

Yul registered the shock in Magus' eyes too. The master's chanting faltered and stopped; the drumming increased to cover it. His mouth was a hard line clamped tight and he frowned, his face like thunder. Yul knew he should be worried but he felt a rush of power and lifted his chin. The arm holding the torch never wavered despite the strain. With the crow on his shoulder Yul unhurriedly approached the man standing so high and majestic above the crowd. He climbed the wooden steps onto the Altar Stone, turning so that he and Magus now faced each other.

Yul hadn't expected the surge of energy that shot up through his body, nearly knocking him off the stone. His eyes gleamed with exhilaration and he met Magus' gaze squarely and unfalteringly. The man's face was dangerously pale and his dark eyes smouldered. Yul didn't flinch, his gaze cool and grey. They made a stunning pair: the tall man with glittering robe and burnished blond hair, his granite face frozen, and the boy, smaller and slighter but somehow similar in build, his robe plainer but still beautiful, long dark hair framing his chiselled face. A king and a young prince.

Yul stood with one arm outstretched holding the flaming torch, the glossy black crow perched on his opposite shoulder. The first bright sunbeam cleared the top of the Summer Stone and blazed onto them in a piercing spear of light. Their robes shimmered and sparkled and their skin glowed gold. The wild drumming climaxed into an explosive crescendo as the shaft of sunlight penetrated the Circle, and then fell silent.

'The Solstice sun marks the rise of the Holly King and the fall of the Oak King!' cried Yul, his voice ringing out in the hush, the familiar words tripping off his tongue. 'I, Herald of the Dawn, pass on the sacred living flame to show the continuity of the never-ending cycle.'

Magus, glaring into Yul's eyes, held out his hand to receive the torch.

'I, Magus of Stonewylde, accept the sacred living flame,' he replied. 'May the sun's energy—'

The unthinkable happened. As Yul handed the torch to Magus, a bolt of power cracked up through the stone in a mighty green flash as if flying from the earth itself. Yul jolted as it shot violently through his frame, exploding into every fibre of his body with molten force. Taking the torch from Yul, Magus somehow fumbled as the energy leapt from the stone. His fingers loosened their grip and jerked in spasm. The torch fell, hitting the Altar Stone with a loud and distinctive thud, and rolled to the ground below. In the shocked silence there came a collective intake of breath from hundreds of throats as the torch lay quenched on the earth. The living flame was dead.

In the stillness the crow let out a massive *caw*, making everyone jump. It flew up onto the nearest standing stone where it perched, fixing Yul with a jewelled eye. Without thinking, he sprang off the stone to the ground below and seized the torch in one hand. The other hand flicked open at the smoking end of it and a green-blue flame shot from his fingers, reigniting it. He held up the torch exultantly and a great cheer echoed around the vast arena. Yul climbed the steps again and continued the words that had died on Magus' lips.

'May the sun's energy fill this hallowed circle of stone! May the folk of Stonewylde be blessed with life force and powerful magic! Bright Solstice Blessings to all!'

He turned to Magus, whose eyes glittered with dark hatred. Yul glowed with green energy, the Earth Magic pulsing around him in an aura of power. Magus had nothing. Yul smiled, his grey eyes dancing with light. Once again he held out the burning torch to Magus who snatched it from him.

'You've stolen my energy!' he hissed. 'You'll pay for this, boy!'

'The Oak King is dead,' Yul replied softly. 'Long live the Holly King.'

The throng of people cheered again as Yul stepped down from the Altar Stone. He caught Sylvie's eye and understanding flashed between them; Mother Heggy had spoken true. The crow flapped away out of the great Circle and back to his mistress. The children crowded excitedly around the bonfire to throw their wicker men into the blazing Solstice flames, symbolising the death of the old king.

Yul and Sylvie smiled at each other, their eyes blazing out happiness and their spirits singing with hope. This was the beginning and all would change from this moment! The Earth Goddess had chosen. The magic of Stonewylde had found its new heart.

Acknowledgements

My thanks and acknowledgements written for the original, self-published edition of this book still stand. So, continued and deepest thanks to:

Clare Pearson, my first agent, for your vision and attempts to teach me that less is more.

My three sons George, Oliver and William for your constant love and support over the years.

My friends and family, many of you in Dorset, for your kindness, enthusiasm and encouragement.

My father for lending me the money to start my publishing venture.

Rob Walster of Big Blu Design for the original covers.

Mr B – for everything.

Now that Stonewylde has been taken on by Gollancz and this new edition published, I must add some more sincere thanks to:

My readers – the thousands of you who bought and loved the original books. Deepest, most heartfelt thanks to each of you for your loyalty to me and enthusiasm for Stonewylde.

My family and friends again – for such constant love and support from you all. I'm so very lucky.

Piers Russell-Cobb, my literary agent, for being totally brilliant.

Gillian Redfearn, my editor, for your excellence.

My sister Claire of Helixtree and Rob Walster of Big Blu Design for the beautiful Stonewylde logo.

Mr B – once more, for making it happen for me.